Mr.

Darcy's

Journey

Abigail Reynolds

White Soup Press

Chapter One

Kitty Bennet shoved her sister Lydia to the edge of the carriage bench. "You are keeping the warm brick to yourself, and my toes are numb!"

Mrs. Bennet elbowed Kitty. "You are sitting in the middle, the warmest spot, and that should be enough for you. Why does your father not arrange to have the carriage window fixed? It lets in the cold so terribly. If I die from a chill, it shall be his fault."

Elizabeth Bennet shook her head with amusement. True, it was an unusually cold day, even for Twelfth Night, but nothing could interfere with her pleasure today, not even squabbling sisters. Soon she would be dancing with Mr. Wickham, and she had no doubt he would be as attentive to her as always. That thought was enough to keep her warm.

She had dressed with great care to look her best for the festivities – or more particularly, for him. Ten days since she had seen him last – not that she was counting – and she had felt the lack of his amiable company. Even when he called on her last, he had seemed more interested in speaking to her aunt about Derbyshire than in talking to Elizabeth. No doubt it was because he missed his home there. And whose fault was it Mr. Wickham could not go home? Proud, disagreeable Mr. Darcy, of course!

The carriage rolled to a stop in front of Lucas Lodge, the windows already ablaze with light even though it was barely dusk. How typical! Sir William liked everyone to know how rich he was, and wasting expensive candles was a way to show it. But what did she care about candles tonight? She planned to enjoy Mr. Wickham's company to the fullest, even if her aunt had reminded her at Christmas not to fall in love with him. Still, that was no reason she could not find pleasure in his company.

Lydia pushed her way out of the carriage first, followed by a fluttering Mrs. Bennet. Elizabeth waited until last, wanting to make a poised entry just in case a certain someone was watching for her. Unfortunately, she had no audience except the ostentatiously dressed footmen.

A crush of people filled the entry hall of Lucas Lodge. Charlotte had warned her most of the neighborhood was invited, since her father saw this also as a celebration of her upcoming wedding, his way of showing his delight at finally disposing of his eldest daughter. Of course, that meant her cousin Mr. Collins, the prospective bridegroom, would be there, but with luck Elizabeth could avoid dancing with him this time.

The humiliation of their last clumsy dance at the Netherfield Ball still stung.

Elizabeth stood on tiptoe and craned her neck to see over Lydia's shoulder. A year ago, she could have done it easily, but now her youngest sister was taller than she, and never missed a chance of pointing it out. As if height determined maturity! But none of the red-coated officers in the room had Wickham's golden curls. He must be further inside, or not yet arrived.

Disappointed, she shouldered her way past a variety of neighbors, but of course that meant stopping to converse with some of them, since she could hardly admit she was looking for a gentleman. She was able to excuse herself from several conversations, but then she was accosted by Miss Penelope Harrington and her sister, Harriet. They greeted her extravagantly, each taking one of her arms.

What mischief were they up to? Neither were particular friends of hers, and she had not forgiven them for mocking her sister Jane for failing to secure Mr. Bingley. "You both look lovely tonight," she said. That was inoffensive.

"As do you," giggled Penelope. "Is that not new lace you have sewn on your dress? It looks almost like this year's styles."

"And new shoe roses," added Harriet. "You do not usually go to such efforts for an occasion like this. Is there someone in particular you are trying to impress?"

As if they did not know she had been keeping company with Mr. Wickham! She had heard enough of their jealous whispers about what he could possibly see in her. "Just to give honor to Sir William and Lady Lucas for inviting us. Have you seen Charlotte? I must give her my best wishes on her engagement." And that might let her escape them.

"Oh, she is in the sitting room with all the dull people. You should go to the dining room where the dancing is. Have you seen Miss King tonight?" Harriet placed great weight on the name.

They were definitely up to mischief. Elizabeth said, "Not yet. I have only just arrived."

The two girls exchanged a smirk. Penelope said, "You must make a point to find her. She is in particularly good looks tonight."

Why in the world did they want her to see Mary King? She barely knew the shy, retiring girl. "I will tell her you said so. Now, if you will be so kind as to excuse me?"

"Oh, we could not possibly desert you in this crush! Do let us go into the dining room. Perhaps one of the officers will ask us to dance."

She saw no point in resisting their efforts, since she intended to go there anyway. The dining room was thronged with people. Most of the furniture had been moved out and the rugs rolled up to make room for dancing. Maria Lucas played a reel on the piano as half a dozen couples circled each other in a country dance.

There he was! Wickham's golden hair shone in the candlelight as he danced. He was facing away from her, but once he reached the top of the set, he would turn and walk past her. Then he would give her that wonderful warm look that made her insides turn upside down.

"Oh, look!" cried Harriet. "Mary King is dancing with Mr. Wickham!"

Did she suppose Elizabeth would be jealous because Wickham was dancing with another woman? He always sought out other partners after the two sets he could properly dance with her. He would ask her teasingly for a third, but he knew as well as she that it would cause gossip. "I imagine she is enjoying it. He is a good dancer."

"And you would know, wouldn't you?" said Penelope archly.

Elizabeth ignored her. Wickham and Mary King had reached the top of the set and turned to proceed down the outside of the set. Her heart beat faster as he approached, a welcoming smile suffusing her face.

He did not catch her eye. In fact, he looked straight through her as he passed, as if she were not even there, though he nodded to another acquaintance further down the line.

A heavy weight settled in Elizabeth's stomach. Why was he cutting her? Had she done something to upset him? She could not imagine what it might be, though he had been a bit cool when he called at Christmas. And why were Harriet and Penelope watching her with such avid expressions? They must have known what was coming, and attached themselves to her to gloat over her embarrassment.

Could it perhaps be a joke? Had Wickham set this up with them as a jest, or to see how she would respond? She would not give them the satisfaction of showing distress. "How much more pleasant dances are since the militia arrived in town! I think all the officers must be here," she said coolly.

Surely Wickham would come to her when the dance ended.

But he did not. Instead, he offered his arm to Mary King and took her to the far end of the room where a few chairs lined the wall. He sat down beside her, a little closer than was proper, and turned towards her. Elizabeth could not see his face, but Mary King was gazing up at him with adoring eyes. She felt sick.

A man in a red coat approached her and bowed. "Miss Elizabeth, might I have the honor of this dance?"

In her shock, it took her a moment to recognize Mr. Chamberlayne. She pasted a smile to her face. "I would be delighted, sir."

He led her to the head of the line, just a few feet away from Wickham and Mary King. She refused to look in their direction, but she could not avoid their voices. Wickham's familiar tones came first "...the next dance?"

"You know we cannot, Mr. Wickham! People would talk."

He gave a rumbly laugh. "I do not care if people know how I feel about you." Just as he had always said to her, down to the intonations.

The room was overheated, but Elizabeth felt suddenly cold. To her everlasting gratitude, the music started. Numbly, she took the hand Mr. Chamberlayne offered her.

He leaned towards her. "Smile," he said quietly. "People are watching. Do not give them the satisfaction."

So he knew. Everyone knew. Everyone but her.

At least Mr. Chamberlayne was being kind, rather than glorying in her distress. Fluttering her eyelashes, she gave him the most brilliant smile she could manage. "Mr. Chamberlayne, you do say the loveliest things!"

He patted her hand proprietarily. "It is easy to pay compliments to so charming a partner."

They took hands across with the couple beneath them, precluding any further discussion. Elizabeth kept the smile fixed to her face as they cast down the line, most especially when she had to pass Wickham and Mary King.

So Wickham had thrown her over without a word, and Mary King was her replacement. But why? They had not quarreled, and she would not have thought Mary would hold any particular attraction for him. She was far from a beauty, and could certainly not be called clever. Wickham and Mary King. The image of the two of them together seemed burned on the inside of her eyelids. It was too painful to contemplate, at least while people were watching her.

Somehow she made it through the first dance of the set. During the pause before the music began again, Mr. Chamberlayne said, "Well done. You have nothing to be ashamed of."

His sympathy threatened her composure. Lightly she said, "Mr. Wickham does not owe me anything. If he prefers the company of Miss King, it is nothing to me."

He smiled as if he understood and said in her ear, "I believe it is not so much her company he prefers as her fortune."

"Her fortune? You must be mistaken. She has no particular prospects."

"Have you not heard? She recently inherited ten thousand pounds. He is not the only officer to have suddenly noticed her appeal, but he got there first. Wickham has many debts of honor."

Suddenly it was less painful to swallow. To be thrown over for money was more tolerable than if he had done it out of preference for Mary King; still painful but not as personal. "No, I had not heard. Thank you for enlightening me. It explains a great many things." But she still had no desire to watch him pay court to another woman while he ignored her.

It was going to be a very long evening.

Lydia rushed into the sitting room. "Lord, I cannot stand one more minute in this house! The rain has finally stopped, and I am going to Meryton. Who is with me?" She swung her gaze to encompass Kitty, Mary, and Elizabeth.

"Oh, yes," cried Kitty. "I hope there will be officers. It has been so long since I had the chance to flirt with them. And the milliners should have received the new shoe roses from London by now."

Mary did not even look up from her book. "Such frivolity has little interest for me. Lizzy can go with you."

Elizabeth straightened. "I will do nothing of the sort," she snapped. Lydia was right about one thing: they had all been cooped up in the house too long.

Lydia smirked. "Afraid of what people will say? Perhaps you should have tried harder to snare Mr. Wickham."

Mary snapped her book closed and rose to her feet. "Have you nothing better to do than to harp on that? I am sick of hearing about it. First Bingley, now Wickham! There are more valuable accomplishments for a lady then her ability to attract gentlemen." She stomped out of the room.

Lydia called after her. "You only say that because it is beyond your powers!"

Kitty giggled. "Mary is so silly. But it is such a novelty to be able to tease you, Lizzy! Usually it is the other way about."

"I am glad to provide you with such a fine source of entertainment," Elizabeth said evenly. Allowing Lydia to see she had hit a nerve would only encourage her. "I imagine you will be even better entertained by the officers and Meryton. I daresay they will all be out and about now that the weather has improved."

"Do you think so?" asked Kitty. "I must wear my new bonnet!"

"I was planning to wear that! You know it goes better with my dress than yours!" cried Lydia.

"No, it is mine!"

Perhaps Mary had the right idea. Elizabeth dropped her sewing into her basket. "Enjoy your walk," she said.

"Shall we give your regards to Mr. Wickham?" Lydia taunted.

Elizabeth ignored her as she left the room. Where could she go that they would not follow? The still room, perhaps? The dried flowers there made Lydia sneeze, so she avoided it whenever possible.

The tiny room was empty and cold, of course. The lavender stems Jane had been drying before her departure were still scattered across the worktable. Taking a deep breath of the fragrant air, Elizabeth slowly began to gather the stalks of lavender into a bundle.

Lucky Jane, to have escaped to London! Lydia and Kitty had taunted her as well over losing Mr. Bingley, and even worse, their mother had not been able to stop mourning the loss of his five thousand pounds a year. Now Elizabeth understood why Jane had become so quiet when in company. Little jabs made by their acquaintances hurt Jane the most, but for Elizabeth, it was the pitying looks and the false sympathies offered her until she wanted to rage and strike out. Jane had just grown more withdrawn and out of spirits until Mrs. Gardiner had taken note of it and offered to take her back to London where no one would know of her disappointment.

She cut a piece of twine and tied together several stems of lavender, then hung the bundle from one of the hooks in the low ceiling. At least her mother did not keep reminding her about Wickham; after all, he had never been a particularly good marital prospect, unlike Bingley. But now, like Jane, Elizabeth disliked going into company where so many people seemed to glory in the knowledge that the two most admired Bennet sisters had been jilted. Why did so many people take pleasure in their pain?

The door squeaked open and Mr. Bennet peered in. "So this is where you have been hiding! I have received a letter from your aunt which concerns you."

Odd - why would Mrs. Gardiner write to her father about her? "What does she say?"

"Such impatience, Lizzy! Will you not even guess? Or are you still nursing your broken heart? I thought all

13

young ladies delighted in such things. After all, Wickham jilted you quite credibly, much better than that runaway Bingley."

She gave a hollow laugh, since he clearly expected one. "The letter?" she asked pointedly.

Mr. Bennet sighed. "Well, if you must be a spoilsport, she wishes for you to travel to London as soon as possible. Apparently Jane is ill with some trifling cold and Mrs. Gardiner could use your assistance in nursing her. Just think, you and Jane may enjoy your heartbreak together!"

"To the Gardiners? May I go?" The idea of leaving Meryton and her annoying younger sisters sounded like heaven. "My aunt would not ask for my help unless she truly needed it."

Mr. Bennet fiddled with his spectacles, drawing out the tension. "I suppose so, especially as she enclosed fare for the stage."

"She did? May I go tomorrow, then?"

"So eager to flee your poor Papa and leave him with no one who can speak a word of sense! Such cruelty! But I suppose you could leave tomorrow if one of the maids can be spared to travel with you. You must speak to Hill about that."

"I shall do that straight away." Elizabeth quickly tied up the last bit of lavender, her spirits suddenly bright. Bless Mrs. Gardiner!

It did not occur to her until later that it was unlike her aunt to ask for help because someone had a trifling cold.

Darcy sat back in his chair once Lady Matlock signaled the footmen to begin the first remove of dinner dishes. At least he assumed she had signaled them. He and Richard had tried for years to determine what signal she used, but it remained a mystery. In that, like so many things, Lady Matlock had proven too subtle for them. Tonight he could not even be bothered to try.

"Darcy, my dear," her ladyship said, "are you quite well? You seem out of sorts tonight."

He straightened. "Quite well, I thank you." Relatively speaking, it was true. His fortnightly dinner with the Matlocks was actually distracting him from thoughts of Elizabeth Bennet. He had dreamt of her the previous night, and resultantly had been half-watching all day for her to miraculously appear somewhere. "Has there been any word yet from Richard regarding his leave?"

"He should be here in February," she said. "In other words, in plenty of time to accompany you to Rosings Park to face the dragon."

Lord Matlock harrumphed. "Do not tease the poor boy, my dear. All of us, with the exception of you, prefer to keep our distance from Catherine."

The young man across from Darcy speared a piece of beef from a new dish before the footman had even placed it on the table. "I would not go to Rosings for love nor money," said Jasper, the youngest and most outrageous of the Fitzwilliam sons. "Well, not for love, in any case."

Darcy heard an odd choking sound to his left. Turning to his cousin Frederica, he said in an undertone, "Is something the matter?"

She shook her head, but did not look at him or respond. That was enough of an answer from Frederica, who, like the rest of her family, rarely lacked for words. Still, she would not appreciate an expression of concern from him. Frederica preferred to take care of her own problems, and she already had three overbearing brothers to deal with.

But apparently there were undercurrents he was unaware of, since at the end of the evening, Lady Matlock pointedly informed him she would be at home the following day. That was as good as a royal command, and he knew it. She did not sound as if she were upset with him; but then again, she never did.

Sometimes Darcy wondered which of his aunts was more troublesome to deal with. Lady Catherine de Bourgh was annoying and demanding, but he could ignore her easily enough. Lady Matlock was the exact opposite: gentle, pleasant and thoughtful. But no matter what Darcy desired or believed, somehow he ended up doing exactly what she wished, asking himself all the while why in heaven's name he had agreed to her latest scheme. So it was with substantial apprehension that he approached Matlock House the next day.

She appeared to be delighted to see him, even though it had not been a full day since he left her presence. Taking his hands in hers, she turned her cheek for his kiss. "Darcy, how lovely to see you! Nothing could have made this day complete for me so much as a visit from my favorite nephew."

He laid his lips lightly on her rouged cheek. "Madam, I am your only nephew."

"Had I three dozen nephews, you would still be my favorite!" she said warmly. "Come, may I pour you some tea?"

"Thank you." Darcy dropped into a chair and extended his legs in front of him.

Naturally, she knew precisely how he took his tea without having to ask. Did she memorize the preferences of all her hundreds of acquaintances, or was it simply for family?

It was too much to hope that she would come directly to the point, so he responded to her questions about Georgiana's well-being and made the appropriate inquiries into the health of her family. Lord Matlock and her three sons all received glowing reports, which was something of a surprise. Usually her requests for his presence were in response to some mischief into which her youngest son had fallen, since Jasper had been known on occasion to actually listen to Darcy. So he settled back to wait for her to reveal the real cause of his visit.

After half an hour of pleasantries in which his aunt said nothing of import, he decided to drop a hint. "I have not heard of Jasper being in any difficulties of late."

"In fact," said Lady Matlock, "I am relatively satisfied with Jasper's recent behavior. As for Frederica..." She gave a delicate sigh.

"No," said Darcy instantly.

She blinked at him in ladylike confusion. "Whatever do you mean?"

"No, I cannot help you with Frederica. The minds of young ladies are a complete mystery to me, as has been more than evident in the last few years. Nothing I say or do could possibly influence her. And if she needs someone to defend her honor, you already have three sons who would only be too delighted to attend to the matter – that is, if they all survived the fight over which one of them most deserved the pleasure." He crossed his arms with finality.

She leaned towards him in a confidential manner. "And that, my dear boy, is precisely my problem. I do not dare to speak to any of them about this. That would simply make matters worse."

"How could defending her honor make things worse? And why does her honor need defending in the first place?"

"It does not need defending, my dear boy, at least not according to Frederica or to me. Her brothers would likely feel differently, but as you know, they are exceedingly quick to see slights to the family honor."

He could not argue the point, given that most of the slights his cousins saw did not exist in the first place. "As I am unaware of the difficulty, I cannot say how they might react." Had someone behaved inappropriately? He could not imagine any gentlemen taking liberties with Frederica, not when everyone knew that to do so was to risk facing one or all of the Fitzwilliam brothers.

Lady Matlock cleared her throat delicately. "There was a man who was most attentive to Freddie. A very suitable gentleman who did not make any effort to disguise his interest, but never formally asked to court her. Freddie became quite fond of him and believed they had an understanding. She was expecting him to approach her father for permission, but he did not do so as planned. When she saw him several days later and confronted him about it, he told her his circumstances had changed and marriage was no longer a possibility. However, he refused to explain what those changes were, and the only difference we can ascertain is that he immediately leaves any room she enters."

Caddish, but it could be much worse. "How has Frederica handled his defection?"

"She says nothing, but the true problem is too many people were aware of his attentions to her, and thus know she has been jilted. Her female friends avoid her and spread gossip, and the gentlemen will not ask her to dance."

"I am sorry to hear it, but I do not see how I can be of assistance. The fashionable set will not listen to me."

"Perhaps not, but marriage-minded young ladies will do almost anything for the opportunity to dance with you. If you were to go to Almack's with Frederica a few times, and make a point of only dancing with young ladies Freddie presents to you, they will forget all this nonsense about excluding her. And if you are seen to be attentive to her, that may incite the interest of other gentlemen."

Darcy's face tightened. "Must it be Almack's?" He tried valiantly to keep a plaintive note from his voice.

"I have always wondered why it is men would rather risk their lives in battle than put on a pair of knee breeches and go to Almack's. Yes, it must be Almack's, because that is where those who decide on social fashions are found. I do recognize how much you detest attending these marriage mart affairs and having to dance with mercenary girls whose eyes are set on Pemberley. I would not ask it of you were it not so important to re-establish Frederica in society."

Sometimes he hated his duty to his family. It did not matter how unpleasant it would be. He could see her difficulty, and it was his duty to help his cousin. And if he had to go to Almack's, at least Frederica would provide good company. If only he could keep himself from comparing all those husband-hunters to Elizabeth Bennet! But *that* was even less likely than enjoying himself at Almack's.

Chapter Two

Mr. Bennet made a show of giving Elizabeth the use of the carriage to travel to the posting inn where she would board the stage. It was not a true concession, since she could hardly walk there while carrying her trunk, but Elizabeth carefully thanked him anyway. She did not want to give him any excuse to change his mind, especially after lying awake half the night worrying about just how sick Jane might actually be.

Nelly, the young scullery maid who was to accompany Elizabeth, seemed awed by the grandeur of riding in a carriage, not to mention the prospect of traveling to London. "I've been in a donkey cart once or twice, but nothing like this, miss!" But her excitement did not last. As they proceeded towards the posting inn, Nelly grew quiet and lines of strain began to appear on her face.

"Nelly, is something troubling you?"

"Oh, no, miss!" Nelly swallowed hard, clutching her stomach. Apparently carriage travel did not agree with her.

Elizabeth swallowed an unladylike curse. If Nelly could not tolerate slow travel in an empty carriage, the crowded, smelly stage was certain to be too much for her. Would Elizabeth have to return to Longbourn and try again another day with a different maid, a delay when Jane was ill and her aunt needed her? If only she could travel alone!

Or could she? Who would stop her?

"Nelly, taking the stage is bound to make you ill, and I cannot allow that. I will see if any acquaintance of mine might be traveling to London. If so, they can escort me, and you may return to Longbourn."

"But I am supposed to go with you," she said miserably. "Mrs. Hill will be so angry."

"Hill will blame me, not you."

When they pulled up at the inn, Nelly was close on Elizabeth's heels as she descended from the carriage. Holding her hand over her mouth, the maid ran behind the building.

Elizabeth gritted her teeth. No. She felt for Nelly's distress, but she would *not* go back to Longbourn. If there was no one suitable to accompany her on this stage, she would wait for the next. She entered the inn and purchased a ticket, something she had never done herself before; her uncle or her father had always taken care of the task.

She found Nelly kneeling on the ground and shivering. Attempting to sound unconcerned, she said, "I have found a fellow traveler, so there is no need for you to come. You must stay here until your stomach settles, and then the groom will drive you home."

"Yes, miss. If you are sure." Nelly huddled in her shawl.

Elizabeth reassured her several times and gave her half a shilling to buy something to drink when she was ready. By that time the stagecoach was rumbling up to the front of the inn, so she hurried towards it, tightening her pelisse against the icy chill.

No familiar faces were waiting for the stage. Bother! Still, it was broad daylight, and what could go wrong in the few hours it would take to reach London?

She hung back until the stage door opened and she could peer inside. Good — there were two women already on board. That should be safe enough. She signaled the groom to move her trunk onto the stage and pretended not to see as he gave a disapproving shake of the head. Well, if he chose to spread the tale, at least the Meryton gossips would talk about her foolish behavior instead of Wickham's abandonment of her for Mary King!

Would she always feel this pain inside her when she thought of him? She had not been in love with him — at least she assumed a broken heart would be worse than this — but it still hurt her pride.

Determinedly she stepped into the stage and took the seat between a freckled woman of middle years and a portly man wearing a clerical collar. Trying to appear inconspicuous, she folded her hands in her lap, imitating Jane's most proper expression.

Fortunately the stage was not as crowded as it might be, but still the facing bench was full. A florid country gentleman and his wife sat together. Elizabeth smiled at the young child of two or three years bouncing on his mother's lap, but his only response was to place his thumb firmly in his mouth. A serious young man beside the couple met Elizabeth eyes momentarily, gave a polite nod and returned to his book.

The driver slammed the stage door closed and clambered up to his seat. He called to the horses and the carriage began to roll, picking up speed as they turned onto the turnpike road. As if in response to a cue, the child removed his thumb and began to scream.

From the pained expressions of her fellow passengers, apparently this was not the first time this had occurred. None of them looked at the boy, though the woman beside Elizabeth muttered under her breath and wrapped her scarf over her ears.

His shrieks grew more piercing, despite his mother's attempts to calm him. This was going to be a long journey. Elizabeth envied the young man who simply buried his face in his book. If only she could read on a coach! But she knew from sad experience she would only end up as ill as poor Nelly should she try.

Was that new, barely audible rhythm the pattering of raindrops on the coach? It was hard to tell over the child's crying, but drops began to speckle the glass panes of the coach. Elizabeth tried to count her blessings; even if she was being deafened, at least she was not outside, cold and wet.

How long could one child scream? It seemed like hours before they reached Hoddesdon, where the woman beside Elizabeth disembarked with a look of profound relief. Since no other passenger came aboard, Elizabeth slid over into the newly vacated space.

The child's cries gradually subsided to hiccoughs on the next leg, and finally he fell asleep on his mother's shoulder. Relieved, Elizabeth closed her eyes and rested her head back against the bench.

Even though the child continued to sleep, she was glad when the couple with him left the stage at Cheshunt. Apparently this new motion must have woken the child, and he shrieked anew, but blissfully his cries faded as they retreated. The young man, now sitting across from her, heaved a sigh, then exchanged a quick smile with Elizabeth.

Oh, dear. Now she was alone with two men, neither of whom she was acquainted with. Her heart sped up. This could be very damaging to her reputation if anyone discovered it, even if nothing untoward occurred. The glass had fogged over as the temperature outside dropped, so they were quite alone and unobserved. Her hands clutched tightly to her reticule. No one must ever find out.

Her heart sank as the portly cleric began to edge towards her, near enough that she could hear his heavy breathing. Should she confront him? Would the young gentleman assist her or turn a blind eye? Perhaps she should scream and hope the coachman would hear.

The cleric snaked out a hand towards her leg. A sharp rap sounded, and then he grunted in sudden pain, clutching his knee. The young gentleman's cane was quickly disappearing beside him. His eyes appeared not to have left his book. With a huff, the cleric moved away from her.

Apparently she had a protector, one who did not wish for thanks, but in her head, she expressed her fervent gratitude to him. Elizabeth's tight shoulders gradually began to relax. This was absolutely the last time she would attempt to travel without a chaperone, that much was certain! And they were still only halfway to London. Usually this trip went so quickly. She hoped the young gentleman would stay aboard until they reached Town. If he did not, she would have to disembark as well, and then what would she do?

Outside Enfield, the coach slid sideways as they rounded a curve, then corrected itself and continued, albeit at a slower pace. Elizabeth rubbed her glove against the glass pane, making a small opening in the fog, and peered out without success. Apparently the glass was now coated with ice, and it was growing dark outside. No wonder the coach had skidded; the road must be even more icy.

The stage continued to slow until it was barely crawling. Would they be able to reach London in this weather? Perhaps the road would clear when they made it to the more traveled London outskirts.

But the coach skidded again, and this time Elizabeth had to grab the strap to keep her seat. Fortunately, they remained on the road, but she was relieved when at last they pulled up to the next inn. Perhaps they could wait there until the road improved.

The door handle rattled but did not move. Was it frozen shut?

The young man put aside his book and tried the door handle with a frown. Having no success, he wrapped one hand around the other and brought them down hard on the handle. With a cracking sound, it finally moved. Unfortunately the door itself was still stuck and required a strong shove from his shoulder to open.

Cold air rushed into the compartment. The driver stood just outside, rain dripping from the brim of his hat. "Inside, all of ye. I'll not go farther until daylight."

The young man spoke up. "But we were to reach London, and it is no more than an hour away!"

The driver shook his shaggy head. "No chance of that now, not with these roads, not in the dark. Covered with ice, they are. Better to rest here, young sir, than be run off the road."

"Oh, dear!" Elizabeth did not realize she had spoken aloud until she noticed an odd look from the young gentleman. Weakly, she added, "I had not realized how late it was."

"Damned nuisance," muttered the cleric.

The young man descended first and offered his hand to Elizabeth. She had little choice but to take it, as the coachman seemed to have no intention of assisting her; and after all, the young man had done her a great service.

But now she was in a truly difficult situation. She was alone, and there was no guarantee the inn had rooms available for the night, nor that she possessed funds sufficient to pay for one if it did. It had been risky enough for her to ride the stagecoach alone, but to stay the night alone without a female companion was beyond the pale.

She trudged into the smoky interior of the inn, her cold feet as heavy as lead bricks. How did one take a room for the night? Her father or her uncle had always arranged such matters. Perhaps she could learn by observing the others.

She trailed after the young man as he made his way to the bar and asked for the host. A hefty fellow wearing a large apron turned to him. "Aye, that'll be myself."

"Very good," said the young man. "I require a room for the night, and —" He turned around and smiled at Elizabeth. "And one for my sister."

The host rubbed his hands on his apron. "Too late. Only one room left."

The young man replied, "Very well; it will have to be for my sister, in that case. She will need a woman to stay in the room with her, of course."

"That will cost extra." The host sounded pleased by the prospect.

"Naturally. I assume there is dinner to be had as well."

"Of course. And your name?"

The young man drew out a card and handed it to the host. "Anthony Hopewell, and my sister, Miss Hopewell."

The host scrutinized the card. "Mary! Show Miss Hopewell to t' upstairs back room."

A young girl in a surprisingly clean dress came forward and bobbed a curtsey. "Right this way, Miss Hopewell. Careful, these steps are narrow. Have you any luggage?"

"It is on the coach. A small brown trunk with brass bindings." Elizabeth cast a glance over her shoulder at her new-found brother. Why had he decided to help her? Did he have an ulterior motive? He could not have seduction on his mind since he had arranged for a maid to stay with her.

"I'll make certain it finds its way up here." Mary ushered her into a dark, narrow room dominated by a wide bed. "I'm sorry it's so small, miss; but it's the only room left."

"It will do nicely." How was she to repay Mr. Hopewell? She suspected he would not take her money.

"Very good, miss. I'll just bring some water, then. It's almost dinnertime, so you might want to come downstairs for that."

Elizabeth followed her down to the main room where Mr. Hopewell waited by the end of a long table. She could hardly ignore him when he had so graciously offered his assistance and protection at the expense of his own private room. He raised an amused eyebrow at her approach. "I hope your room is satisfactory, my dear sister."

"Quite satisfactory, Mr. Hopewell, and I thank you for your kind assistance."

He waved a hand. "It is nothing. I have two sisters, and I hope some gentleman would do likewise for them should they find themselves in similar straits."

"I am sorry you will not have a room for the night."

"There is always a common room where an extra man can sleep, but not a lady. I shall be quite comfortable, I am certain."

Feeling all the discomfort of their present situation, Elizabeth said, "Under the circumstances, I hope you will forgive me for introducing myself. I am —"

"Pray, do not tell me your name! Having said you are my sister, I cannot be referring to you as Miss Smith or whoever you might be. And if I do not know your name, I cannot repeat it to anyone."

Elizabeth laughed. "I suppose not. But you must call me something, and while I could not permit you to call me by *my* Christian name, I have no objection to being called by your sister's name."

Amusement danced in his dark eyes. "Then you shall be my dearest sister Anne. Would you care to sit down to dinner, my dear?"

"I thank you." She seated herself next to Mr. Hopewell, a few feet from an elderly widow dressed all in black. "I greatly appreciate all you have done on my behalf." She hoped he would understand that included the protection he had given her in the coach.

"What brother would do less?" he teased.

"I cannot say, as it is a unique experience for me to have a brother. It is a pity my father does not know of your existence; our estate is entailed away from the family, and he would no doubt be greatly relieved to learn I had a brother."

"Alas that I shall never make his acquaintance!"

Elizabeth cast a glance at the window. "Do you suppose the rain will continue long? Or perhaps I should say the snow, as it seems to be changing to that."

"I expect it will pass by morning, and we shall be on our way."

"I hope so," said Elizabeth with a shiver.

"Has there been much snow here? Despite the cold, there was but an inch or two of snow in Sheffield."

"Mostly it has been just flurries, but too often and altogether too cold! It has been the bitterest winter I recall. Tell me, brother, does our family live in Sheffield? I find I am singularly forgetful of these details."

"No, we are not Northerners, you and I. I travel to Sheffield to attend meetings." He leaned towards her and said in a voice just above a whisper, "I am a Radical. I hope you will not disown me for it."

Elizabeth tipped her head to the side. "Like Mr. Paine?"

"My sister is well educated! I would be honored to be grouped with Thomas Paine. His *Rights of Man* is an excellent statement of my principles."

"My uncle suggested I read it. Everyone is born equal, votes and education for all?"

His face lit in a smile. "Yes, I support votes for working people, not just for the wealthy and landowners. But the rich fight to continue their current privileges."

"Do you think reform is possible? It seems so... unthinkable."

He laughed. "It will not happen this year, or this decade, and perhaps not even in my lifetime, but the recognition of the natural rights of the common man is coming. The French overthrew their king for it. The American colonists threw off the yoke of England for it.

Our government lives in terror that our citizens will do the same, so they repress them and keep them in utter poverty, which only makes them angrier." He lowered his voice as the widow glanced in his direction. "I must curb my enthusiasm. According to our present government, I am preaching sedition and treason."

Her uncle had spoken to her of Radical principles, but as far as she knew, he never did more than talk about it. Mr. Hopewell was risking his life for the cause. She looked at him with new consideration. "Is it so dangerous, then, speaking out as you do?"

"Parliament has decreed it is treason to say we want the working class to have representation in Parliament, so the danger is quite real. But so are the risks of doing nothing. The Luddites are starving and close to open revolt."

It was hard to imagine. The North was so far away, and no one in Meryton seemed to be starving, but she believed him. "I wish you every success in convincing them to employ peaceful means instead."

"I thank you. But what of you? I hope you will indulge my curiosity – and my concern. How do you come to be traveling all alone, my dear new sister?"

Elizabeth glanced heavenwards. "I am not supposed to be doing so," she admitted. "I had planned to travel with a maid, but she took ill at the posting inn. I did not wish to go home again, so when I saw there were two ladies already aboard, I decided to take the risk. Unwise of me, as I have discovered, though I am very grateful for your intervention with our clerical friend on the stage."

"It was nothing." His brows creased. "Is something the matter at home that you do not wish to be there?"

"I am not running off, if that is what you are thinking! I am going to visit my sister in London who is ill, and the society closer to home is not conducive to my pleasure at the moment." She caught herself a little too late. She had no reason to tell him of her difficulties in Meryton, but he was easy to confide in.

"A man?"

His inquisitiveness surprised her, but his concern for her was clear and he had told her so much about himself already. "In a way, yes, but it is nothing of significance. An admirer proved fickle, tempted by a girl who had just inherited a fortune. I could bear his desertion well enough, but the pitying looks from everyone, the way they would stop talking when they saw me and watch to see my reaction when Miss King or my former friend came into the room – that was nigh unbearable. So you see, it is nothing more than wounded pride on my part."

He seemed to relax. "I am sorry for it, though glad it is nothing worse. I am well aware of some of the ways men can make life unbearable for the women in their power, and when I see a young gentlewoman traveling alone, I worry about what she might be fleeing."

She smiled. "It must be tiring to spend so much of your time thinking about who might need your help next! If it is not a starving Luddite, it is a damsel in distress."

He looked down at his hands. "I have been extraordinarily fortunate in my life. I have never gone hungry, nor been without money or a roof over my head, and I have never been as powerless and without rights as a woman is in our society. In some ways, that makes it harder to accept that others are not so privileged as I." He raised his eyes to her. "Many people believe I am foolish to even think of these things."

"*I* do not," said Elizabeth warmly.

A serving maid set a platter of meat in front of them with a clatter. "Soup's coming," she said.

The rest of the evening passed quickly with lighthearted conversation. Mr. Hopewell proved to be well-read and witty. He did not reveal much about his origins, but from his clothing and speech, Elizabeth suspected he was from a background not dissimilar to her own. A wistful feeling pervaded her. If only she might meet a gentleman like Mr. Hopewell – one without treasonous leanings, preferably. He was charming and had shown a quick mind in protecting her good name, without any attempt to impose himself on her. She could easily see introducing him to her family as an equal. But there was no one like him in Meryton, and her only offer had come from ridiculous Mr. Collins.

"Is something the matter?" Mr. Hopewell's concerned voice broke into her reverie.

"I am a little tired, nothing more, but I thank you for your concern." She had told him too much already. He did not need to know of her loneliness in Meryton, much less her worry for Jane and her suspicion that her illness might be more severe than Mrs. Gardiner had suggested in the letter. She could do nothing about it until morning in any case.

Her arrival at Gracechurch Street was greeted with evident relief. "Thank heavens you are safe!" cried Mrs. Gardiner. "We have been fearing the worst since hearing the stage did not arrive last night. Was there an accident?"

"No," said Elizabeth, hugging her youngest nephew. "The driver insisted on stopping for the night owing to the slippery roads."

"Do not tell me you were alone at a coaching inn! How terrible for you!"

"I was very fortunate. A kind gentleman told everyone I was his sister, so no one troubled me." She had decided earlier it would be wiser not to mention that her rescuer had been young, handsome, and inclined towards treason.

"Come, Thomas, let your cousin Lizzy alone! She needs hot tea and something to eat."

"It would be very welcome," admitted Elizabeth. "But I would rather see Jane first. How is she?"

Mrs. Gardiner's earlier expression of relief disappeared as if it had never been. "No better, but at least no worse, which the doctor says is a hopeful sign."

"So it is more than a trifling cold. I suspected as much."

"I did not wish to say it was serious, since that would have brought your mother here as well. That would not have helped either Jane or me!"

"No, it most certainly would not! But what is the matter with Jane?"

Mrs. Gardiner did not meet her eyes. "An inflammation of the lungs. Come, I will take you to her."

"Poor, dearest Jane!" She followed her aunt up the stairs, her heart thudding.

"She is in my own bedchamber. We moved her there because it is warmer and has no drafts."

Elizabeth tried to smile. "How good you are!"

Her aunt opened the door and peeked in, then turned back to Elizabeth. "She is asleep, so you must be very quiet. The doctor says sleep is the best medicine for her."

The maid sitting by the bedside looked up from her mending at their entrance. Elizabeth covered her mouth to stifle a gasp. Jane's face was pallid, her cheeks sunken, and her rasping breath was apparent even from several steps away. Elizabeth tiptoed closer, but halted at the sight of Jane's fingers plucking at the counterpane. At least she had not awoken. This was far, far worse than her illness at Netherfield.

Elizabeth jumped when a hand descended on her arm, but it was only her aunt drawing her out of the room.

"How long has she been like this?" Elizabeth had not meant it to sound accusing, but it did.

"This is the fourth day. I sent for you as soon as she took a turn for the worse. At first we thought it was just a bad cold..."

"What does the doctor say?"

Mrs. Gardiner did not meet her eyes. "He hopes she will have the strength to fight it off. But there is more we must discuss after you have had a chance to rest and refresh yourself."

Elizabeth bit her lip. "If there is more, I would rather know it now."

Her aunt glanced down the passageway, then led Elizabeth to the small sitting room and closed the door behind them.

"What is it, Aunt? You are frightening me."

"There is nothing to be frightened of. I was not quite honest with your father in my letter. It will come as a shock to you, but this began when our dear Jane drank a bottle of laudanum in an attempt to end her life."

Elizabeth's jaw dropped. "I cannot believe it! Jane has had her bouts of low spirits, but never has she said anything which would indicate…"

"I cannot say for certain, but I believe it was but an impulse of the moment, not something she planned. The apothecary had given her the laudanum for a cough she had developed, so it would not waken her when she slept. Foolishly, I did not even think of locking it up. I could not conceive of Jane misusing it, so I let her keep it by her bedside. But then, after those awful women called on her, she was so dreadfully out of spirits."

Elizabeth shook her head, not in disagreement but in an attempt to make sense of it. "What awful women?"

"That Miss Bingley and Mrs. Hurst. Oh, I wish I had given them a piece of my mind!"

The Bingley sisters? "Could it not have been an accident that she took too much?"

"No. She admitted as much when she first woke up. Beforehand, she had been barely eating and seemed disinterested in everything. Then one morning she did not rise at her usual time." Tears brimmed in Mrs. Gardiner's eyes.

"It does sound like one of her episodes. But she has not had one in years."

"If I had any idea she was so distraught…" Mrs. Gardiner's voice trailed off. "I feel as if we failed her somehow."

Elizabeth embraced her. "Of course not, dear aunt! If Jane had been willing to speak to anyone, it would have been you. But why is she not better? Surely the laudanum must have worn off long since!"

Her aunt dropped into a wooden chair, her face drawn. "It has, but her long sleep caused the cough to settle into her lungs and she developed a fever. The doctor says she should be able to fight it off. But I am not certain she *wishes* to get better. I did not know what to do, so I sent for you in hopes you could raise her spirits."

It was hard to imagine being able to raise anyone's spirits with this new knowledge weighing on her so heavily, but she would try.

Jane awoke shortly after dinner, her eyelids fluttering open as she turned her head to the side. "Lizzy, is that truly you?" Her voice was hoarse and weak, but Elizabeth was relieved to hear it.

"Yes, I am truly here, and I will remain here until you are fully well again."

"I am sorry to be such trouble," whispered Jane.

Elizabeth laid her hand on her sister's forehead. Still burning hot. "It is no trouble. I was glad of the chance to come."

"It is all..." Jane coughed violently, her body curling up with the effort. She coughed longer than Elizabeth

41

would have believed possible. Helpless to do anything but hold out a handkerchief, Elizabeth bit her lip.

Finally the paroxysm subsided. Jane wiped her mouth with the square of linen, then dropped it on the pillow beside her. "It hurts so much."

"I am sorry. Do not try to speak; just rest. Shall I read to you?" Elizabeth retrieved the handkerchief. Jane's cloudy sputum was tinged with blood.

"That would be pleasant." Jane's eyelids drifted down.

"Excellent. I have borrowed a novel from our aunt." She opened the first page. " 'On the pleasant banks of the Garonne, in the province of Gascony...' "

The next few days seemed to last an eternity. Elizabeth coaxed Jane to take a few sips of broth, and wiped her forehead after her spasms of coughing, but she did not begrudge a minute of it when she saw her beloved sister slowly improving. Each day she was a bit more alert. Finally, on the third day, her fever broke and the doctor proclaimed her to be on the mend. Elizabeth, bleary-eyed, could think of no better way to celebrate than to crawl into bed beside Jane and promptly fall asleep.

As Jane's strength began to return and she could sit up in bed and speak more easily, she steadfastly steered conversations away from any topic of sensitivity, saying her spirits were good and there was nothing to worry about. Elizabeth, seeing her forced smile and the droop of the corners of her eyes that betokened Jane's dark moods, was less convinced.

There was nothing to be done for it but to demand answers. Elizabeth waited for a propitious moment when Jane seemed at least in tolerable spirits, and then she said, "Our aunt tells me Miss Bingley and Mrs. Hurst came to call before you fell ill."

Jane looked down, her fingers picking at the counterpane. "Yes, they did."

"What did they say? Did they give any excuse for waiting so long to call on you?"

Her sister shook her head. "They did not need to. Caroline's countenance told it all, how little she wished to be there and to see me. You were right; she has no interest in continuing friendship with me, and I wonder why she singled me out so in Meryton."

"That must have hurt, to discover she was not the friend you thought she was."

Jane said nothing but blinked her eyes rapidly.

"What is the matter, Jane dearest?"

"It was not so much that as the deliberately cruel things she said to me. She was like a cat toying with the mouse, telling me every detail of the lady her brother now hopes to marry, how he said she was the loveliest woman he had ever seen, and how different his sentiments were now from what he had ever felt about another woman.

Apparently he goes about the house whistling all the time with his head in the clouds." The words poured out of Jane as if each one had been branded on her brain. "And she watched me, Lizzy, with a little superior smile, and I could tell she was delighting in my pain." She paused. "I was much deceived about Caroline, but perhaps her behavior was only because she was so angry."

"Angry at you? How could anyone be angry at you? You are the sweetest, kindest person who ever lived!"

"No, not at me. I made the mistake of asking after Mr. Darcy, you see, and that set her off on a tirade. It seems he has dropped their acquaintance and is instead spending all his time with his cousin, Lady Frederica Fitzwilliam. I will never forget her name because of the way Caroline kept repeating it, and with such venom! She believes an announcement is imminent. You must know Caroline had hoped to marry him herself, so it is a terrible disappointment to her. Perhaps that is why she behaved so badly to me." Jane's voice had grown steadier as she spoke. Apparently it was easier for her to talk about Mr. Darcy and Caroline Bingley's disappointed hopes than Mr. Bingley.

"What about Miss Darcy? I thought Caroline hoped her brother would marry her."

"No longer, not since this other paragon appeared on the scene. But I should not speak so about her. If she makes Mr. Bingley happy, then I am pleased for his sake."

"If she even exists. I have no reason to think the paragon is anything but a figment of Miss Bingley's unkind imagination." Elizabeth stopped speaking. This was not the moment to express her anger towards that horrid woman who had hurt Jane so badly. She could not forgive Mr. Bingley, either. All of this, Jane's attempt to harm herself and her subsequent illness was their fault — his sister for no doubt pressing him to abandon Jane, and Mr. Bingley for being weak-willed enough to allow himself to be persuaded to leave Jane. How much pain they had cost with their selfishness! If Miss Bingley was suffering from Mr. Darcy's defection, it was no more than she deserved. And she heartily hoped that Lady Frederica Fitzwilliam would make Mr. Darcy miserable for years to come.

A tear slid down Jane's cheek. "Perhaps, but this is the last time I will regret him. From now on I will think of him only as an amiable man whom I once knew."

Elizabeth said nothing. She did not imagine it would be so simple.

Chapter Three

Georgiana Darcy turned pleading eyes on her brother. "May we go in? I will not be long, I promise."

It was a promise he had heard made and broken many times before, but Darcy understood perfectly how she could lose herself with hundreds of choices of books. She always needed more; she had become a rampant reader of three-volume novels. Sometimes he wondered if Georgiana preferred reading books to the company of people. Then again, he often felt the same way himself.

"Very well, if you wish." It was not as if he was likely to find anything else enjoyable to do. He held the door to the circulating library for her.

He found a seat while Georgiana hurried to join the line at the counter. Taking a piece of paper from her reticule, she ran her finger down her list as she waited for the clerk to serve the ladies ahead of her.

An achingly familiar voice said, "Are you certain this is an exciting tale?"

Darcy's head whipped around. It could not be her. Why would Elizabeth Bennet be in a fashionable London circulating library? No, it was only his damned imagination again – just someone who sounded like her, with an air of laughter around every word. If only he could stop thinking of her! But at every one of those cursed balls he attended with Frederica, he found himself comparing every lady he partnered to Elizabeth, reliving in memory the touch of her hand on his when they danced at Netherfield. None of the London ladies could match her. Now he was starting to imagine he was hearing her voice.

Georgiana said, "Oh, I have read that one! It is most thrilling. I could hardly bear to put it down."

"That is just what I want, then – the perfect thing to capture the interest of an invalid. I thank you for the recommendation."

There, it could not be Elizabeth. Georgiana never dared to speak to strangers. He could not hear his sister's murmured reply. Then for a moment he could not hear anything at all, for the woman who haunted his dreams turned so her profile was visible to him.

He gripped the arms of the chair so tightly his fingers ached. It *was* Elizabeth, accompanied by a fashionably dressed woman some years her senior. What was she doing here?

His breath caught in his throat, but even as he debated the wisdom of allowing himself to speak to her, he was on his feet and advancing in her direction.

"Miss Elizabeth?" he said tentatively.

Startled, she turned towards him. "Mr. Darcy!" There were dark circles under her fine eyes.

"I had not realized you were in London." What a foolish thing for him to say – of course he had not realized it. How could he have known? Why did his ability to make sensible conversation always vanish when he was in her company?

"It was an unexpected trip, and I have only been here a few days. My sister, who has been visiting my aunt and uncle, is ill, and I came to help care for her. Oh – do allow me to introduce Mrs. Gardiner. Aunt, this is Mr. Darcy." She stole a sly glance at him.

The fashionably dressed woman murmured a polite greeting. This was one of the relations in trade? At least at first glance, her manners were much superior to Mrs. Bennet's.

Georgiana looked at him questioningly. Had he truly forgotten to introduce her? What was wrong with him? Quickly he made the introductions.

Georgiana said, "Miss Elizabeth Bennet from Hertfordshire? My brother told me about you in his letters."

Elizabeth's eyebrows shot up and she gave him an arch look. "Oh, dear. I imagine he was not particularly complimentary."

"Oh, no! He told me how much he enjoyed hearing you sing and play."

"I am all astonishment! I assure you, I have no great talent for either." Elizabeth's eyes might be shadowed by dark circles, but they still sparkled with laughter.

Darcy recovered from the last of his shock at this familiar challenging look. "It is fortunate for me, Miss Elizabeth, that I am aware you take delight in expressing opinions not your own, or I might have to succumb to the temptation to argue with a lady in public."

"That would never do," declared Elizabeth. "How fortunate for me, since that means I can express any opinion I like without provoking retaliation! I must think of some truly objectionable opinions merely for the sake of forcing you to agree with them!"

How he had missed crossing verbal swords with her! Such a delightful change from those insipid, flattering young ladies he was forced to dance with. If only Elizabeth were at those balls, he might even enjoy himself rather than finding them slow torture. "I await your worst, Miss Elizabeth," he said with a bow.

Elizabeth leaned towards Georgiana, saying in a voice both confiding and easily audible, "Do not fret, Miss Darcy; your brother and I quarreled quite regularly during his stay in Hertfordshire. One might almost say it was our favorite diversion. But of course it cannot compare to novel-reading, of which I can see you are also a devotee." She gestured towards the small pile of books the clerk had brought.

Georgiana smiled shyly. How neatly Elizabeth had spotted her incipient dismay and turned it around! "I hope your sister enjoys that book as much as I did. It is very exciting."

"As long as it keeps her diverted and interested in hearing more, I will be happy." A shadow seemed to pass over her face.

Suddenly it struck him – the circles under her eyes, the lines of fatigue, a book to entertain her sister. "I hope Miss Bennet's illness is not serious."

She looked away suddenly, biting her lip, but said nothing.

Mrs. Gardiner placed a reassuring hand on Elizabeth's arm. "It is very kind of you to think of Jane, Mr. Darcy. Lizzy has been exceedingly worried for her. This is the first time she has been out of her presence since arriving, and she only came at my insistence that it did her no good to stay inside all the time."

Shaken by Elizabeth's distress, he said, "That is sensible advice, Mrs. Gardiner. Everyone needs a change of pace now and then. And I am sorry to hear Miss Bennet is so ill. Pray give her my best regards and hopes for her rapid recovery." He spoke directly to Mrs.

Gardiner, half-afraid to even look at Elizabeth. If she had tears in her eyes, he did not know what he would do.

There was nothing he could do to relieve her pain. Should he offer to send his own physician? No, that would suggest they were not caring for her well enough. Surely there must be something within his power to do!

Who was he trying to fool? What he wanted to do was to take her in his arms and tell her all would be well, and that was the one thing he could never, ever do.

So he did the only thing he could, which was to bid her farewell, even though she still would not look up at him. He tried not to watch as she placed her book in her basket and tucked a cloth over it, but he could not stop himself from resting his eyes on her retreating back as she disappeared from his life forever.

"Brother?" Georgiana asked tentatively.

Had he really been staring at the closed door? He gave his head a shake to clear it. "Yes, dearest? Did you find all the books you wanted?"

"Yes." But it sounded as if she wished she could say more.

Darcy gestured to the footman waiting by the door to collect Georgiana's stack of books, and then offered his sister his arm.

He forced himself to concentrate on Georgiana as they left the library. He would *not* crane his head to look up and down the street like a lovesick fool hoping for one last glimpse of his beloved. He would *not*. No matter how much he wanted to.

Georgiana said abruptly, "I hope I did not say something I should not have."

"What? To whom?"

"To Miss Elizabeth Bennet, of course."

What had Georgiana said to her? Darcy could barely remember. Nothing had registered but Elizabeth. Automatically he said, "Of course not. You were perfectly polite, and I was pleased to see you conversing with her." It had been a shock. Georgiana always became tongue-tied faced with strangers.

But Elizabeth was gone.

"I am glad. I liked her."

Now his sister had his full attention. "Why?" It must have sounded abrupt, but it was a question he had asked himself so many times it was practically a litany. He had never found the answer. Now he was asking his sister, a bare slip of a girl with no experience of the world, to answer the question he could not. What was wrong with him?

Georgiana chewed on her lower lip. "I do not know. I just felt...comfortable with her. As if it would not matter to her if I made a mistake."

"As if you would make a mistake serious enough to offend someone! But I understand what you mean. I cannot imagine her being deliberately unkind."

"But then she did seem upset at the end, so I thought I must have said something wrong."

"It was not you, but my mention of her sister. She is clearly distraught over her illness. They are very close, and, if I am not mistaken, she must be exhausted. She would not have wished to distress you in any way."

"If only that were more common among the *ton*! They always seem to be looking for something to criticize." Although she did not say more, he could hear her unsaid words, that they were very successful at it.

"Yes." If the *ton* had not turned on Frederica like bloodthirsty vultures as soon as she showed a weakness, he would not have been forced into escort duty on her behalf.

"I suppose you must be acquainted with Miss Elizabeth's sister, the one who is so ill?"

"I am." The last thing Darcy needed was for Georgiana to become interested in the Bennet family.

"We must have flowers delivered to her, then," said Georgiana.

Darcy's heart skipped a beat. "To Miss Elizabeth? I think not."

"No, to her sister, of course. They taught us that at school. One must always take some action when a lady is seriously ill, either a note or flowers."

Why had his father insisted on sending Georgiana to a ladies seminary where they taught her inconvenient rules of society but not how to avoid predators like

George Wickham? "It is not that sort of acquaintance. It would look odd." Especially if Bingley ever caught wind of it.

"Oh." Georgiana sounded subdued again. How could a disagreement so small set her off? Women! Sometimes they were simply incomprehensible. "It is a kind thought, though. I will consider it." But he knew he would not do it. Any contact with Elizabeth Bennet was too dangerous.

Darcy's resolve lasted through dinner, but afterwards, as he sat listening to Georgiana play a Mozart sonata, the first cracks in the wall began to appear. Would it not ease Georgiana's mind to make some token acknowledgement of Miss Bennet's illness? And what would Elizabeth think of him if he did nothing at all after being told of her sister's condition? Would she believe he did not care enough to make the gesture? Or might it ease some of the pain he had seen in her eyes?

It was not as if Elizabeth had to be involved in the gift at all. He could direct the flowers to Mrs. Gardiner with a request that she give them to Jane Bennet. Or should he send fruit? Elizabeth had appeared worn and fatigued. Perhaps she was not eating well, and fresh fruit might tempt her to eat.

It was not how he had planned to spend his rare evening at home, writing and rewriting a note to Mrs. Gardiner. Elizabeth would no doubt read it, so it had to strike the correct balance, kind, but without the sort of warmth that might indicate an ongoing interest in the family.

He crumpled up his first attempt and tossed it in the fireplace. He never had to rewrite letters; it was something he prided himself upon. But Elizabeth would hold this note, her elegant fingers touching the same paper he touched now, and she would think of him. It must be perfect. Would she save it as a keepsake?

Another sheet of notepaper fed the fire when he realized he had written Elizabeth's name on the outside instead of Mrs. Gardiner's. What was wrong with him tonight? This task should have taken a quarter hour at most.

But it was the last contact he would ever have with Elizabeth. He could not expect to cross paths with her by chance again simply because it happened once. He paused, and then carefully set his pen in the inkwell before he ended up blotting the paper like Bingley. His fingers clutched into a fist. The last contact.

How had this weakness crept back upon him? It had been a wrench to leave her behind in Hertfordshire, and he had nourished some pangs for a few fortnights, but he had returned to his senses. He might still mentally compare the silly young ladies he danced with to

Elizabeth, and she might cross his mind every time he saw a light and pleasing figure of a woman, or when he wished for more challenging conversation than the *ton* provided, but the helpless, aching pain which dogged his every step had faded. Or at least mostly faded.

And now, after a mere few words of conversation, here he was again, fully entangled in a web of Elizabeth Bennet. He should not have approached her today; he should have kept his distance and she most likely would never have noticed his presence. But no, all it had taken was one glimpse of her, and he could not stay away. What a fool he was! How long would it take him to put her behind him this time? Would he ever manage it, or would she haunt him for the rest of his life?

He poured a glass of brandy, his hand unsteady on the crystal stopper of the decanter. Rolling a sip around in his mouth, he leaned back in his chair. Why was this so difficult? Even leaving Hertfordshire had not been so devastating.

Of course, when he left Netherfield, there had been the possibility Bingley might insist on returning there, in which case he would see Elizabeth again. It had not felt as final, at least not initially. This time it would be the end, and he was the one making that decision.

The brandy burned down the back of his throat. Perhaps that was the answer — to leave the possibility open. He would end things with Elizabeth now, at least in his own mind, and try to put her from his thoughts.

But if he failed, and still felt this way in a year's time, he would attempt to see her again. If all went well, by that time she might seem to him no more than another pretty woman with fine eyes, and he would go away satisfied. Or perhaps she might have married someone else by then, and he would have no choice in the matter.

No. No. Better not to think of that possibility. No. Besides, who would offer for her given that outrageous family of hers? No, he was safe from that fate at least.

The tight knots wrapped around his stomach eased a little. Yes, that would help. This was not final, because if he still wished to see her next February, he would do so. Though a year was a very long time, and it was always difficult to leave town then because of the Season. Perhaps Christmas would be a better time, when everyone was still in the country. Or perhaps the anniversary of the night he danced with her at Netherfield, the twenty-sixth of November.

He set down the brandy with a snort. If he kept thinking this way, he would conclude that waiting a fortnight would be adequate! But no, Christmas it would be. A possibility to keep him going without her.

Now he would be able to send her flowers, but not be left with the sensation his world had come to an end.

Not until Christmas, at least.

If only he could sleep through the night, unhaunted by dreams of a pair of fine eyes! Perhaps he simply needed to tire himself out more. A few good bouts of fencing might distract him from memories of the highly unsuitable Elizabeth Bennet.

A familiar face caught his eye at Angelo's, the exclusive fencing club he favored. "Duxbury! It has been too long!" said Darcy, shaking the hand of the slight gentleman his own age.

"Well met, Darcy. Care for a match?" Duxbury smiled, but without his usual liveliness.

"It would be my pleasure." It was the truth. Sir Anthony Duxbury was one of the few gentlemen of the *ton* who could give Darcy a contest of swords worthy of the name. It would demand every bit of his attention.

They saluted one another with their epees and began. Darcy found his footing quickly, pressing forward to test Duxbury's defense. He was quickly forced to parry and launch a riposte. Odd; he did not recollect Duxbury as so aggressive a fencer, but it suited his mood. Back and forth they went, evenly matched. Darcy's world narrowed to the point of Duxbury's blade as all the restlessness of the last weeks fueled him and turned his old friend into an enemy. Darcy managed to land one hit to Duxbury's two, but they continued to engage each other long after the match would usually have been called.

It was Angelo himself who finally halted the match. "Enough, gentlemen! I do not wish to see one of you injured through the carelessness of fatigue. A good fencer must know when to stop."

Darcy saluted Duxbury once more, then fished out his handkerchief to mop his sweating brow. The room gradually came into focus around him, and he became aware that everyone was watching them. Had it been that fierce a bout? From the aching in his muscles and his dry mouth, it must have been. Someone handed him a glass of wine and he tossed it back a little too quickly, making him cough.

Duxbury hung up his epee and flexed his arms, his mouth curled as if he were disappointed they had to stop. "Well fought, Darcy. You fenced like a madman. A very skilled madman."

"You are hardly in a position to criticize. You were just as mad as I." How had he come to allow his distress to be noted in public?

"True. But I needed a good fight, and I daresay you did as well."

Darcy took a second glass of wine, downing this one a little more slowly, but far faster than good wine deserved. "True."

Duxbury glanced over his shoulder at the crowd of men still watching them. "Come, let us sit downstairs. It has been too long since we talked."

A very long time, now that Darcy thought about it. They had been close friends at Cambridge, where Duxbury had been the best debater in their year. But then

Duxbury had spent two years on the continent, and on his return he did not often stop at White's. And until he was required to escort Frederica, Darcy had avoided the ballrooms and soirees where he would most likely have been found. Why had he never thought to invite Duxbury to dinner? "A fine idea."

They found a quiet corner of the room. Naturally, a decanter of brandy appeared, and they toasted each other's health. They fell into the habits of their old friendship easily, exchanging stories of mutual friends.

Darcy said, "And what of you? The last time I saw you, your father was trying to force you into a match with a squint-eyed young lady. I take it he did not succeed?"

Duxbury barked a laugh. "No, more's the pity. Had I been safely married, I would not have had to fence like a demon today."

Darcy poured more brandy in both glasses. "Marriage would keep you from fencing?"

"No, but it would have kept me from falling in love with a woman I cannot have, and thus having to work off my anger on your innocent epee. I used to think it would be so simple – find a woman I liked and marry her. So that is why I fenced like a lunatic. What is your reason?"

Darcy hesitated. Duxbury moved in different circles than he did, and unless he had changed drastically, he was not a gossip. "The same. A woman I cannot marry."

"Beneath you?"

Darcy nodded. "Damned duty to my family."

"Duty before love. Who would have guessed it would be so painful? Not I."

"Nor I." A sigh escaped him. It was a blessed relief just to admit it to someone.

Duxbury merely nodded, and they sat in silence sipping their brandy.

Elizabeth looked up from the novel to see Mrs. Gardiner entering the bedroom carrying a large bouquet. "Oh, Jane, look at these lovely flowers!" she exclaimed. "They are the perfect thing to brighten the room. Wherever did you find them at this season, Aunt?" Hothouse flowers were ridiculously expensive. Then she saw the basket of grapes in her aunt's other hand. Hothouse fruit was even dearer.

Jane went so far as to push herself up on her elbows to smell the flowers Mrs. Gardiner held out.

"*I* did not find them," said Mrs. Gardiner. "A messenger brought them to me with a note. Shall I read it to you?"

"Yes, please do."

Mrs. Gardiner glanced pointedly at Elizabeth as she unfolded a sheet of fine notepaper. "Mrs. Gardiner, I hope you will not think it too presumptuous of me on such short acquaintance to beg of you the favor of giving these flowers to Miss Bennet in the hope they may brighten her sickroom and remind her spring is coming. My sister asks me to convey her sorrow over hearing of Miss Bennet's illness and that she will add her to her prayers. Most respectfully yours..." Mrs. Gardiner paused and again looked at Elizabeth. "Fitzwilliam Darcy."

Elizabeth's jaw dropped, but, conscious of her aunt's inquisitive gaze, she quickly turned the motion into a cough. Mr. Darcy had sent flowers and fruit to Jane?

Jane's brows drew together. "Mr. Darcy? But how did he know I was ill?"

Elizabeth exchanged a look with her aunt. "I must have forgotten to tell you. We ran into him at the circulating library, or rather I ran into a girl who turned out to be his sister, and Mr. Darcy came over and introduced us. We only exchanged a few words."

"But you told him I was ill?"

"Only to explain why I was in London." And in the hope he might find a scrap of decency in his prideful soul to pass the news along to Mr. Bingley.

Her sister's face fell. "If he knows, Mr. Bingley must know as well." She closed her eyes and lay back on her pillow.

With a touch of reproach in her voice, Mrs. Gardiner said, "It was very kind of Mr. Darcy to think of you."

"Yes, of course. Will you thank him for me?" Jane sounded somehow distant.

Mrs. Gardiner set the vase of flowers on the bedside table. "Of course I will."

Jane raised herself on an elbow. "Lizzy, you must go. You promised Charlotte you would visit her, and there is no reason for you to remain here."

Elizabeth looked at her sister's pale face and gaunt cheeks. "You are still far from well, and I would be more content remaining here with you."

"That is silly. The doctor says I am recovering steadily and simply need to regain my strength."

That was precisely what worried Elizabeth. "How can you regain your strength when you barely eat a thing, and only take that much at my insistence?"

"My appetite is certain to return soon, and then I shall eat more," said Jane stoutly.

"I will believe it when I see it!"

Jane's shoulders drooped. "I pray you, Lizzy, go to Kent. I do not need to be treated as an invalid and watched over every moment. In any case, our aunt will take care of any needs I might have."

"*If* you will but tell her what you need!"

"Oh, Lizzy. If I promise I will be careful, and that I will eat every meal, will you go to Kent?"

"Why is it so important to you that I go? And do not tell me it is because Charlotte needs me."

Jane sighed and looked down at her hands. "You have taken such good care of me and I cannot thank you enough for it. But I need some time to myself, without your presence to remind me how foolish I have been."

Elizabeth sucked in a breath. Jane wanted her to leave? "Very well, then. If you wish it, I shall go. I will be glad to see some of Kent." She forced herself to smile so Jane would not worry about her.

"I thank you for the dance." Darcy bowed to the irritatingly talkative Miss Pewsey.

"Oh, it was such a pleasure!" simpered Miss Pewsey.

He bowed again, feeling like a cornered stag. "Pardon me; Lady Frederica is beckoning me." She was not, but it would allow him to escape Miss Pewsey before he blurted out exactly what he thought of her.

Shouldering his way through the crowd, he found Frederica chatting with one of her friends, a stiff smile on her lips and her shoulders high and tight. What was her so-called friend saying to her? So much for escaping to the card room for a set!

Darcy almost thrust himself between the two. "Lady Frederica, dare I be so bold as to hope you might have the next set free?"

She looked up at him, fluttered her lashes, and smiled a smile which must have looked like great pleasure to anyone else, but he knew her better. "Oh, Mr. Darcy, I can think of nothing in the world I should like better!"

That was not how Frederica spoke. Something was extremely wrong. He offered her his hand and made a perfunctory bow to her friend before leading Frederica away.

As they took their place in the line of dancers, he said quietly, "I hope I was not wrong to interrupt you."

Her breath hissed out between her teeth. "Not at all. But if you could manage to appear utterly enthralled with my presence, I would appreciate it."

He gazed deeply into her eyes, pretending she was Elizabeth Bennet. But Frederica's eyes were green, and they did not make his soul dance with pleasure. "What is the matter?"

"*He* is here, and everyone is watching me to see how I respond." She smiled beatifically up at him.

"Where?"

"Do not look now, but he is dancing with Eleanor Lyndsey, much joy may she bring him!"

Darcy could not stop himself from glancing up the set. He had been wondering what man had mistreated her, but his aunt had forbidden him to ask. No doubt she was worried he might take it on himself to settle matters. She was, after all, the mother of three men who would be delighted to do so.

He frowned. "Is not Miss Lyndsey the one in the pale green dress? Duxbury is dancing with her."

"Do not say his name!"

The music began, preventing him from asking the question he wanted to blurt out. It was several minutes before the dance brought him near enough to Frederica to speak. "He is the one?"

"Shh. And smile."

He obeyed mechanically, his mind awhirl. He would have sworn Duxbury was not the sort to toy with a woman's sensibilities. Could he have changed that much in the last few years? Then he remembered their conversation after fencing. Duxbury had said he had fallen in love with a woman he could not marry. Could he have been courting Frederica as a good match, then fallen in love with another woman, one who was beneath him? Perhaps he felt he could not go through with marrying Frederica when he was so violently in love with another. That would make sense, but still, he would have expected Duxbury to treat Frederica with more kindness when ending matters between them, or at least had the courtesy to allow her to jilt him.

But then why was Duxbury glaring at him when they passed in the dance? He was the one with the right to anger in defense of Frederica.

Chapter Four

Darcy presented himself at the door of Matlock House precisely at the hour his uncle had commanded. The butler looked surprised to see him and hesitated noticeably before admitting him, but he took him to the drawing room and announced him to Lady Matlock and Frederica.

His aunt offered him her cheek. "Darcy, what a pleasant surprise!"

A bad sign. Lady Matlock did not like surprises. "His lordship invited me to dinner," he said cautiously.

She sighed theatrically. "And never said a word of it to me, naturally! Well, sit down. It is only a simple family dinner, so I hope you will not be disappointed. Though I do not see why you would be, since you have always preferred that. Frye, there will be one more for dinner."

"Yes, your ladyship." The butler bowed and disappeared.

Something was odd. Why had Lord Matlock insisted on his presence? "I hope he knows better than to bring up the question of my running for Parliament again." It had been a bone of contention between them for years, but he had thought it finally settled.

"He has not mentioned it to me recently. I cannot blame him for hoping you might follow in his footsteps. He has worked so hard to influence the government and wishes for someone to carry on his legacy, but none of his own sons are suited for politics."

"Just because *I* can manage to disagree with someone without resorting to fists or swords does not make me a good prospect for Parliament! You know how often I manage to offend people without any intention of doing so. How could I possibly sway anyone's opinion?"

"I agree, my dear, and I believe he has accepted that. This may be something else completely."

True to form, nothing was said until the first remove of dinner was served. Then Lord Matlock cleared his throat, always a signal, and everyone turned their faces to him.

"Darcy," said Lord Matlock. "My wife and Frederica will accompany you and Richard to Rosings next week."

Lady Matlock's eyebrows rose slightly, but that was the only evidence she had been unaware of this. "To Rosings?"

The Earl glowered at her. "Did you have difficulty hearing me?"

"Of course not, my dear."

Frederica looked as if she might burst. "Not Rosings, I pray you! I cannot bear Lady Catherine and Anne."

Sometimes Lord Matlock had a soft spot for his daughter, but this was apparently not one of those moments. He did speak more gently, though. "I am not offering you a choice."

"But why?"

Her father ignored her completely. Darcy exchanged a concerned glance with Richard. Lord Matlock rarely gave his family commands, but on the occasions he did, he was immovable.

Frederica slumped in her chair, all animation gone from her face.

"Lovely!" said Richard brightly. "It will be cheering to have your companionship. There will be plenty of room for all of us in Darcy's coach, will there not?"

"Of course." As if he were likely to have a traveling coach which could not seat four people! "It will be my honor to escort your wife and daughter, your lordship." Even if he did not particularly appreciate the way Lord Matlock had forced his family's hand in the matter.

"You will take my coach and coachmen." It was not a question.

Frederica, without even asking to be excused, bolted from the room, leaving silence behind her.

Finally, as if nothing out of the usual had occurred, Lady Matlock said, "How delightful the salmon is tonight. Do try some, Darcy."

On Elizabeth's first night at Hunsford, Charlotte came to her room after everyone else had retired. The presence of Charlotte's father and younger sister had kept them from any personal exchange earlier, but now they were finally alone.

"I am so glad you came, Lizzy! I feared you might need to stay in London with Jane, and I was selfish enough to desire your company anyway. Is her health much improved now?"

Elizabeth unpinned her hair before she spoke. "Her health is improved, but she is still weak, and in one of her periods of low spirits. She hardly touches her food, and tosses and turns half the night. As glad as I am to see you, I wish I could have stayed to help her."

"Oh, dear. I hope you did not feel obligated to come here for my sake. Despite all my teasing about being desperate to see you, I would have understood had you stayed with Jane."

Elizabeth shook her hair loose. Running her fingers through it to loosen the snarls, she said, "In truth, I was planning to remain with Jane and send you my apologies, but..."

"But what?"

Elizabeth drew a deep breath. "But Jane did not wish me to stay." It was a relief to finally say it.

"Oh, my poor Lizzy! That must have been painful, especially after you have been so devoted to her, but I am not surprised."

Abruptly Elizabeth swiveled to stare at her friend. "Why is that?" She attempted to ask it lightly, but Charlotte knew her well enough not to be fooled.

"Jane does not like to be taken care of. I think she feels guilty when anyone pays too much attention to any difficulty she may have. She would much rather be self-effacing, and she never allows anyone to catch a glimpse of her pain. It is not about you, Lizzy. My guess is she wished to be alone so she could allow herself to be miserable rather than to put on a brave face."

"Perhaps so," said Elizabeth. She wished she could share with Charlotte exactly why she was so worried about Jane's low spirits, but Jane would not want anyone to know what she had done. With new resolve, she added, "But I am here now, and I plan to put that behind me and enjoy myself."

Charlotte smiled. "I am glad."

A fortnight later, Mr. Collins made an announcement at breakfast. "We are invited to dine at Rosings Park tonight."

"How lovely," said Elizabeth without enthusiasm. She would have to remember to eat something before they left. In addition to the dreary company, the food at Rosings Park, which Lady Catherine claimed to be a most healthful diet, tended to be tasteless at best and indigestible at worst.

"I am glad you are aware of your great good fortune in coming to Lady Catherine's attention, Cousin Elizabeth. It is indeed an honor. But I must caution you, for in a few days Lady Catherine's nephews will arrive. You must not be distressed if our invitations to Rosings cease during that time. As obliging as Lady Catherine is, our consequence is not sufficient to mingle with Mr. Darcy and his cousin, Colonel Fitzwilliam." He continued to ramble on about Lady Catherine's great condescension towards them, and was showing no sign of coming to a conclusion when, to Elizabeth's relief, a boy arrived with the news that Lady Catherine desired Mr. Collins to attend upon her immediately. Naturally, that gentleman could not depart quickly enough.

This was such a common occurrence that no one at the parsonage gave the matter much thought until a second messenger came, this time from Mr. Collins. "He says to tell you the plans for dinner have been changed, and you are to remain here," the boy said.

Charlotte handed him a coin. "Is Lady Catherine angered with Mr. Collins?"

"Not what as I can tell, Mrs. Collins. There was a letter this morning, and she's in a frightful rage. None of us dare go near her."

"Perhaps Mr. Collins will be able to soothe her," said Charlotte.

The boy snorted. "That would take a miracle."

Mr. Collins did not return until late, fairly bursting with agitation. "Mrs. Collins, we have much work to do tomorrow! We must make certain everything about the parsonage is perfect. The hedges must be perfectly trimmed, the gravel walk perfectly raked, not a speck of dirt to show anywhere!"

"Apart from the garden," said Elizabeth. "I hope you will tolerate a little dirt there so the plants may continue to grow."

"Yes, yes, of course, but that dirt must be well-banked and neat!" He rubbed his hands together. "Perhaps we should wash the palings and the gate. Yes, I believe so."

Charlotte seemed to be having difficulty in repressing a smile. "What, pray tell, is the occasion for all this perfection?"

Mr. Collins straightened his shoulders, like a peacock preparing to spread its tail. "Have you not heard?" His voice became reverential. "The Countess of Matlock is coming to Rosings Park."

"In hopes of inspecting the parsonage?" asked Elizabeth, her eyes dancing.

"Of course not, my foolish cousin! She will be accompanying Mr. Darcy and the rest of his party."

"The *rest* of his party?"

"Yes. The Countess's son, Colonel Fitzwilliam, was already due to accompany Mr. Darcy, but Rosings will also be honored by the presence of her daughter, Lady Frederica. And..." Mr. Collins paused dramatically. "Lady Catherine has told me she wishes me to be in attendance there as much as possible! Such gracious condescension on her part! What a privilege it is to serve such a lady! But with all due humility, I must say it is a most wise precaution on her part to arrange for a clergyman such as myself to be present."

Charlotte exchanged a glance with Elizabeth. "Has she a particular reason?"

Mr. Collins looked pointedly to each side, as if worried about being overheard, and said in a dramatic whisper, "Her ladyship anticipates receiving some dreadful news."

Elizabeth wondered how much longer he would draw out his tale. "Some dreadful news?"

"Dreadful, indeed! As you know, Mr. Darcy has been engaged to our dear Miss de Bourgh since they were both in their cradles, but now Lady Catherine fears Mr. Darcy intends to break off their engagement in order to marry his other cousin, Lady Frederica. Although how he could live with himself after such disloyalty I do not know, but no doubt he believes an earl's daughter will bring him more than Miss de Bourgh, who is but the granddaughter of an earl."

Charlotte cocked her head to one side. "I cannot see it. If that is the case, why would Mr. Darcy bring Lady Frederica here? Would it not be wiser of him to inform Lady Catherine in a letter?"

"It is not for us to understand the ways of our betters, my dear. Lady Catherine is distraught, and it is my duty and my honor to offer her comfort in this trying time. But she wishes everything about Rosings to be in perfect condition so the Countess will not find anything amiss in her management of the estate, and we must do our part!"

It was almost dusk when Darcy reached Rosings. He had given the clear weather as his excuse to beg off riding in the carriage with Richard, Frederica, and the Countess, but the very idea of spending several hours listening to his voluble cousins filling every moment with chatter gave him a headache. It was enough that he had to accompany Frederica to crowded balls and soirees when he would rather stay at home in the quiet of his study.

Apparently he had timed his journey well, since the servants were still unloading the luggage from the Matlock carriage in front of Rosings. The others must have just arrived. He dismounted quickly and tossed the reins to a waiting groom, with instructions to see he was rubbed down well.

He found the family gathered in the large sitting room where Lady Catherine was holding court. "Darcy, you are late. It is very inconsiderate of you," she snapped.

Lady Matlock said, "Surely it makes no difference, since we have only been here ten minutes."

"You might have come earlier as well. You know perfectly well a late dinner troubles Anne's digestion, but I suppose you slept till noon after Lady Macomber's ball last night. I understand it was quite a crush." She made it sound like the worst of insults, rather than a compliment to the hostess.

"Indeed, there was quite a crowd," said Frederica. "It was one of the highlights of the season."

"And who did you dance with, young lady?"

Frederica glanced at her mother, then said, "I did not realize I should have brought my dance card, but if it matters, Darcy partnered me for the first set, then Mr. Grove and Lieutenant Carville, then I sat out for a set, then Darcy again, Sir Robert Elliotson for the dinner dance and Lord Elton after him, and then we left early to prepare for today."

"I am surprised you had so many partners. You have let your skin grow too brown. I do not allow Anne out of doors without a parasol, and her complexion is nicely pale. Darcy, do you not think Frederica's face is quite brown?"

"I had not noticed anything of the sort," said Darcy coldly. Lady Catherine was rarely easy company, but he had never seen this level of rudeness from her, and certainly not on first arrival. So much for the idea she would be pleased to have Lady Matlock and Frederica added to their party!

Richard gave him a warning look, then said, "I am so looking forward to seeing Cousin Anne at dinner. She was in such good looks last year that it was a pleasure to be in her company."

Darcy winced at the blatant flattery, but Lady Catherine looked slightly mollified by it. "Well, then, I hope an hour will be enough time for you to ready yourself for dinner. Some of you –" She turned her glare on Frederica. "*Some* of you may require all that time and more to look presentable. I will have you shown to your rooms."

Dinner was punctuated by long periods of silence, a blessed relief from Lady Catherine's continual corrections of Frederica's manners and everything else about her. Lady Matlock's expression made it appear as if she had not noticed anything was amiss. The set of her jaw, however, told a different tale.

Darcy mechanically helped himself to several bland dishes. Beside him, Anne spoke only to her companion. How her mother could possibly think they were suited to each other was beyond Darcy's comprehension.

Lady Catherine turned her gimlet eye on him. "Darcy, my parson's new wife tells me she became acquainted with you in Hertfordshire. I cannot imagine what you were thinking. Although she is a good enough girl, she is far beneath your notice."

Jolted awake at the mention of Hertfordshire, Darcy said, "I met your parson – Mr. Collins, is it not? He was impudent enough to introduce himself to me, but I cannot recall his wife." How could he forget Collins after having been forced to watch him embarrass Elizabeth by dancing with her?

"He did not marry her until January. You would have known her as Miss Lucas."

"Yes, I recall Miss Lucas. A sensible young lady, from what I could tell."

"She has been sensible enough to recognize good advice when she receives it, which is more than I can say for that friend of hers who is visiting."

A friend visiting? Could it be? "Is this friend from Hertfordshire as well?"

"Yes, a Miss Bennet. She seemed to know you as well."

His pulse began to pound in his ears. "Miss Elizabeth Bennet? We met on several occasions, I believe. I met a great many people in Hertfordshire."

"I hope some of them were of decent birth, but if you were visiting your tradesman friend, I suppose that would be too much to expect."

There was no point to attempting to defend the absent Bingley to his aunt when he could not even keep her from insulting Frederica, who was sitting at the same table with them. And he had more important things to think about. Elizabeth was only a short distance away. Could he trust himself in her presence? But even as he thought it, he knew he would not be able to stay away.

Frederica paced in front of the dark bookcases in the library. "But why is Aunt Catherine so angry at me? I have done nothing. She replied to my letter at Christmastime with pages of advice, but perfectly civilly. I sent Anne a netted purse for her birthday, and it was one of the best I have ever made, not that I received a word of thanks in reply. And I could not have done anything to upset her on this visit since she was furious with me as soon as I stepped in the door!"

Richard lounged in a deep leather chair. "If you ask us that a dozen more times, Freddie, perhaps we will magically discover an answer for you. For now, I am as much in the dark as you."

"And I am in almost as great disfavor as you," said Darcy. "Normally she fusses over me."

Richard snorted. "Only because she wants you to marry Anne. Of course, the worst part of marrying Anne would be turning your aunt into your mother-in-law."

79

"Have no fear. I have no intention of marrying Anne, or any other woman for that matter." But the image of a pair of fine eyes danced before him. He would see Elizabeth soon.

"The young ladies of London will be bereft," Frederica teased. "You have raised their hopes by asking them to dance."

It seemed foolish to point out he had done it for her sake, rather than out of any desire to dance with a series of dull young ladies, each one more witless than the last. How much longer would the Countess expect him to put on this performance? If Frederica's popularity was not ensured by now, there was no hope he could fix it. "I have never danced with anyone but you more than once. They should know what that means."

"They can still hope. And *I* hope there will be refreshments for tea, as I could hardly eat a bite of breakfast with Aunt Catherine glowering at me the entire time."

"It disappeared from your plate magically, then," Richard said with a grin. His sister's healthy appetite was famous.

"How can *I* manage to stay out of her sight? It is too cold for a long ride, and there is nowhere to go."

"Darcy, what of your friends from Hertfordshire?" asked Richard. "We could call on them, even if Aunt Catherine does think them beneath your notice. As long as they have a warm fire and no one scolding us, I for one will like them very well indeed. Especially if either of them is pretty. I could use a pretty girl to look at."

"If you wish." Darcy endeavored to show no reaction, either the pleasure coursing through his veins at the excuse to see Elizabeth sooner than he had expected, or the instant fury at Richard for even daring to consider admiring her.

"Oh, do let us go, then!" Frederica tugged at his sleeve as if she intended to drag him all the way to the parsonage. "Or Aunt Catherine might discover our plan and lock us all in the dungeons."

"There are no dungeons at Rosings Park," Darcy said.

"I beg to differ," said Frederica feelingly. "The entire place is a dungeon."

Elizabeth looked out the back window in the direction of Rosings Park. Mr. Darcy was there now. But why should that matter to her? She heartily disliked the man. "I wonder if Lady Catherine is keeping her anger in check," she said to Charlotte.

Her friend laughed. "I think it quite unlikely. Our Lady Catherine is one who speaks her mind. I would not be surprised if they all turn around and go straight back to London." She stopped to peer out the opposite window. "But apparently they have not. I believe we are about to receive callers."

Elizabeth said, "Is Mr. Darcy among them?"

Her friend nodded, then hurriedly gathered her work into a basket and tucked it in a corner of the room. "Come, you have a stray curl here. Allow me to tuck it back in." She was still leaning over Elizabeth when they heard the front door open.

Elizabeth rose to her feet as the maid showed their guests in. Mr. Darcy looked as ill-tempered as always.

Fortunately, Charlotte had no difficulty in playing the role of the hostess. "Mr. Darcy, it is indeed a pleasure to see you again. Please do come in."

"I thank you." He turned to the finely dressed young woman with striking green eyes who accompanied him. "Lady Frederica, may I have the honor of presenting to your acquaintance Mrs. Collins and Miss Elizabeth Bennet? Mrs. Collins, pray allow me to introduce my cousins, Lady Frederica Fitzwilliam and Colonel Fitzwilliam."

Lady Frederica was not a beauty, but she could be called handsome, and did not portray the bored languor so fashionable among the *ton*. Instead, she looked about her in a lively manner. Lady Frederica would be a better wife for Mr. Darcy than Anne de Bourgh. Elizabeth felt a strange pang at the thought.

With an odd hesitancy, Darcy said. "Miss Elizabeth, may I hope your family is in good health?"

His true meaning was obvious, especially since he seemed to disdain most of her family. "They are, and my sister is much improved from when I saw you last. It was very kind of you to send her flowers and fruit."

"It was my pleasure. My sister will be glad to hear Miss Bennet's illness has passed." He lapsed into an uncomfortable silence.

Charlotte stepped in to offer the best seat by the fire to Lady Frederica. "We are honored Mr. Darcy would bring you to visit us the day after your arrival in Kent. I had assumed Lady Catherine would have plans for you, so it is a delightful surprise. We are always eager for new faces here."

Lady Frederica said in a confidential tone, "I am glad to make your acquaintance, but I had an ulterior motive. Lady Catherine is furious with me for some mysterious reason, and I decided I would be more comfortable elsewhere, among pleasant people. My mother is attempting to calm her and discover what is amiss. I hope she succeeds, since this will be an unpleasant visit indeed if I am constantly in my aunt's black books and I have no idea why."

"I hope her displeasure will pass soon," said Charlotte diplomatically, exchanging a glance with Elizabeth. "Perhaps it is just a mood of hers."

Lady Frederica narrowed her eyes. "Wait. You know something of this; I can tell."

"She has said nothing to me," said Charlotte.

"Yet this was not news to you. I pray you to do me the very great service of explaining what I have done to anger her. I would be happy to make amends if I knew what my fault was."

"Lady Catherine is a very generous benefactress, but I cannot claim to know her mind." Charlotte's warm smile diffused the coolness of her refusal to answer.

"Darcy!" Lady Frederica beckoned him to join them. "Your friends know why Aunt Catherine is upset with me, but they will not tell me. Perhaps they will be more open with you."

Darcy's countenance showed some annoyance at this rudeness. "The ladies no doubt wish to be tactful. But if there is any hint you could give us, it would be of great assistance."

Charlotte looked down at the floor. "I owe a great deal to Lady Catherine's generosity. Perhaps Lizzy might be able to assist you."

Elizabeth's cheeks burned. Of all the situations to be put in! She addressed herself to Lady Frederica, choosing her words with care. "Lady Catherine has always hoped Mr. Darcy would marry Miss de Bourgh."

"Yes, of course," said Lady Frederica impatiently. "We all know that."

She glanced at Charlotte, but there was no help coming from that quarter. "I am under the impression she believes you may be a threat to that plan."

"I? What have I to do with it?"

Elizabeth cast a swift glance at Darcy, but he looked as puzzled as his cousin. "She believes... she has heard rumors he plans to make a match with you instead."

Lady Frederica laughed. "With me? She thinks Darcy and I...why, that is simply ridiculous! No one could believe such nonsense."

Elizabeth replied, "I heard the same rumor in London as well. Miss Bingley told my sister it was a near certainty."

"This is the last thing I need!" exclaimed Lady Frederica. "How anyone could think it is beyond my comprehension! Darcy is practically my brother."

Elizabeth lifted her shoulders in a shrug. "I live in the country and know little of the concerns of the *ton*."

"Naturally, it has nothing to do with you," said Lady Frederica, in a mercurial shift to affability. "I do not blame *you* at all. Poor Aunt Catherine! She must have been restraining herself mightily. I am certain she wishes to strangle me."

Darcy frowned. "Did you discuss this idea with my aunt, Miss Elizabeth?"

His distrust stung more than she would have expected. "Not at all. The only discussion I have had with Lady Catherine about you was to acknowledge we had met in Hertfordshire. I imagine she deduced it herself from how frequently the two of you were mentioned together in the newspaper." Bother it! She had not wished to admit she herself had checked those. She added in a lighter tone, "Even if I were inclined to repeat unsubstantiated gossip, that would be the last thing I would tell her. I value my life too highly to risk her wrath on that subject!"

Lady Frederica smiled. "I can well imagine that! I do hope my mother manages to set this to rights, since I am half-afraid to return to Rosings myself. I would sooner go up against Bonaparte himself than disturb Aunt Catherine's sacred plans for Darcy and Cousin Anne to wed!"

"There are no such plans," Darcy said, looking straight at Elizabeth. "I never agreed to marry Anne, and I never will."

"You know that and I know that, but Aunt Catherine does not," said Lady Frederica.

Elizabeth wondered if Rosings Park would be left standing when Lady Catherine finally realized the truth.

Chapter Five

Lady Frederica and Mr. Darcy called at the parsonage again the following day and each day thereafter. Elizabeth wondered how much of this could be attributed to enjoyment of their company, to escaping Lady Catherine, or to the desire for food more edible than that served at Rosings Park. Lady Frederica, who appeared to have taken a liking to Elizabeth, always displayed a surprisingly hearty appetite when Charlotte served refreshments.

So it was not a surprise when some days later, Elizabeth received a note from Lady Frederica. She opened it and scanned it quickly. "How odd!"

"What does she say?" asked Charlotte.

"I do not understand it. 'My dear friend, if you are not so compassionate as to visit me and provide the balm of feminine understanding, I cannot answer for what desperate circumstances may occur. I am held prisoner in my bedroom with a foolish complaint, and the aforementioned feminine understanding is sorely lacking in Rosings Park! Yours etc., Frederica Fitzwilliam.' Whatever could she mean?" exclaimed Elizabeth, handing the note to Charlotte.

Her friend read it, covering her mouth with her hand. Although Charlotte could hide her smile, Elizabeth could recognize the laughter in her eyes.

"What is it?"

Charlotte folded the note and returned it to her. "Lady Catherine's view is that anyone who is ill is simply playing for sympathy; unless, of course, she is speaking of her daughter or herself. And Miss de Bourgh will deign to visit an invalid only to impress upon them how much worse her ailments are than theirs. As a result, no one at Rosings will admit to any illness, and then Lady Catherine takes credit for the good health of all who surround her."

Elizabeth chuckled. "No wonder Lady Frederica wishes for other company! Well, I shall obey my summons immediately."

She found Lady Frederica sitting up in bed with her knees pulled up to her chest. Albeit slightly pale, she did not appear ill. Was she perhaps simply avoiding her aunt?

"Miss Bennet! Thank you so much for taking pity upon me. You bring a breath of fresh air."

"I am sorry to hear you are unwell."

Lady Frederica waved a hand. "Just female trouble. It is vexing and bothersome, nothing more."

"If it keeps you in bed, I imagine it must be quite painful. I have been fairly fortunate myself, but two of my sisters suffer a great deal."

"But *none* of us suffer as much as my cousin, nor do we do it as well as she!"

Elizabeth produced a small sack from the basket she had brought. "Indeed! In case you are well enough to enjoy them, Charlotte packed some supplies for you. Biscuits and cake, and a jar of her own applesauce in case your stomach troubled you."

Lady Frederica reached for the bag. "Bless her! Mrs. Collins has preserved me from starvation during this visit. The food is one reason I dislike coming to Rosings Park so much. I would have refused to come this year, had my father not insisted. You have no idea how grateful I am to have a woman my own age here. Darcy is a good friend, but he is a man." Lady Frederica took a shortbread and offered one to Elizabeth. "I have never heard how you came to be acquainted with Darcy. He visited your neighborhood, I believe?"

"I cannot recall when I actually met him, but I saw him first at an assembly. After that we were in company on several occasions."

"Did anything unusual happen while he was there? Did he quarrel with anyone?"

Elizabeth blinked. "Not that I am aware of, but ours was no more than a trifling acquaintance. I would be unlikely to know if anything did occur."

Lady Frederica frowned. "Pity. He has been out of spirits since his return to town but will not discuss it. I hoped you might know something."

Elizabeth shook her head. "He did not show any interest in becoming better acquainted with any of the local people, preferring to stay with his own party as much as possible."

"Oh, how like him! Giving offense wherever he goes. Poor Darcy. He is truly one of the kindest and most generous people of my acquaintance, but you would never know it to see him among a group of strangers."

Elizabeth wondered what Lady Frederica would think if she told her how Darcy had insulted her at the assembly, but she had no desire to malign him to his cousin. Surely there must be something positive she could report of his behavior in Meryton! "He did condescend to ask me to dance once, which was kind of him." Even if she wished he had done nothing of the sort.

Lady Frederica sat up straighter. "Truly? He asked you to dance? But he detests dancing with anyone he does not know well." She giggled. "But of late the poor man has been forced to do so quite frequently for my sake and has done so with good grace."

"But *you* are not a stranger to him."

"Oh, but it was much worse than just dancing with me. The poor man has had to escort me to every ball, dance with me twice, and then dance with any young lady

I introduced to him. Believe me, it is his personal idea of hell, but he has done it anyway."

Mr. Darcy doing something he did not wish to? Elizabeth could not believe it. "Then why does he do it?"

Lady Frederica beckoned her closer and said confidentially, "He does it for my sake. I was jilted recently, but the *ton* cannot make a pariah of me when Darcy is by my side. He is very much in demand as a potential husband. I wish I could have fallen in love with him instead; he is one of the few trustworthy men I know. Unlike my previous admirer." Her tone was sharp and she blinked rapidly.

"You have my sympathy. Recently a gentleman who was quite attentive to me changed his allegiance to a girl with a larger portion than I. Although my heart was not touched, it was still most unpleasant to have everyone pitying me and talking of nothing else. I was glad to leave for London."

"At least you know why he left you. Mine is a mystery. It was a perfectly good match for him, and he went as far as telling me he intended to speak to my father – and then nothing. It was days before I could corner him and ask what had happened. His response? 'Things have changed.' And then he apologized for the inconvenience to me. The *inconvenience*?" Lady Frederica's lip curled. "And I still have to watch him ignore me at balls and soirées, except for those blessed times when he is out of town. Unfortunately, he always returns."

"Do you suppose gentlemen have any idea of how much ladies suffer when they do these things? My dear sister fell in love with the most amiable young man who seemed quite enchanted with her, but then... then his friends talked him out of the match, and she never saw him again. That was months ago, but she is still sadly out of spirits. I had judged the gentleman trustworthy, too, but I was mistaken." Elizabeth could not keep the bitterness from her voice; it was enough of a struggle not to tell Lady Frederica that her beloved cousin might have played a role in Jane's heartbreak.

"Sometimes I wish they would all just disappear!" Lady Frederica's hands tightened over her stomach. "And I pray you, say nothing of this to my brother. He would become quite violent if he discovered I have been jilted."

"Colonel Fitzwilliam? I shall certainly say nothing, but I cannot imagine him being angry or violent. He seems so very amiable."

Lady Frederica made a sound that might have been a laugh had she been in less discomfort. "That is because you are a lady. All my brothers are like that — totally charming with ladies, but should a gentleman cross them in any way, they transform into belligerent idiots."

"I do not doubt your word; I simply cannot picture it."

"Fortunately you are unlikely to be forced to witness it, since the only other gentleman here is Darcy and he is exempt from Richard's wrath. Besides, Richard is taken with you. Not as much as Darcy, of course, but he still admires you."

Now unaccountably annoyed, Elizabeth said, "I assure you, Mr. Darcy does not admire me. He even said to my face that I was not handsome enough to tempt him!" So much for her attempts to keep that information to herself! Why could she not learn to control her tongue?

Lady Frederica's brows drew together. "Darcy said that? I cannot believe it. Unless... unless he thought you were pursuing him. That is the only time he is ever so rude, when he thinks a mercenary young lady has set her sights on him. He thinks it will discourage them, foolish man. But how could he have thought that of *you*?"

A cold finger seemed to move down Elizabeth's spine. At the Meryton assembly, her mother had made it quite clear that she hoped her daughters would catch one of the wealthy newcomers, so it would not have been an unreasonable assumption on his part. And Mr. Darcy had not seemed unwilling at first to consider Bingley's suggestion that he dance with her, looking around to see her. He had not delivered his set-down until he caught her eye. Could he have read her interest in a dance partner as husband–hunting behavior that needed to be nipped in the bud? It was not true, but still, if half the other women at the dance had smiled at him, it would have been in hopes of winning his affection and fortune.

Her throat grew tight. It was even more humiliating to be seen as a fortune-hunter than as not handsome enough to tempt him. What an ill-mannered man he was!

Since Lady Frederica was watching her with evident curiosity, Elizabeth said crisply, "I can safely promise you that I would never set my cap at your cousin or anyone else in that predatory manner. I would prefer to be a spinster than to marry a man for whom I do not feel respect and affection."

"Oh, well said!" said Lady Frederica faintly. "Perhaps we shall be spinsters together. Though my mother says the only cure for my pains is to bear a child, and at the moment that seems as good a reason for marriage as any!"

Regretting her former sharpness, Elizabeth said, "I do not know if it would help, but Charlotte— Mrs. Collins—has a talent for herbal remedies and she makes a tea which she says relieves her monthly pains. I am sure she would be happy to send you some."

"Pray tell her I would be very grateful. Although nothing I have attempted so far has helped, I am willing to try anything that might!"

At the parsonage door, Darcy barely remembered to ask for Mrs. Collins. His official errand was with her, but he had jumped at the chance to do it himself rather than send a servant in the hope of spending a few minutes in Elizabeth's company.

But when the maid showed him into the sitting room, only Mrs. Collins was present. The spirit which had infused him on the way to the parsonage abruptly vanished, leaving him an empty shell.

He bowed mechanically and exchanged the requisite greetings. Still no sign of Elizabeth. He might as well finish his business. "Mrs. Collins, I come at the behest of Lady Frederica. She would be very much in your debt if you would send her the receipt for your special tea. She said you would know which one."

Mrs. Collins smiled. "Of course I will be happy to send it, along with more of the tea. It was good of you to come yourself when you might have had a servant do it."

He could not tell her the truth of why he had done so. "I, ah, felt the need for some fresh air and a little exercise, so this was a convenient excuse."

"You and Lizzy have more in common than one might think! She said much the same thing earlier." She seemed to be scrutinizing him.

"Indeed, I understand Miss Elizabeth is a great walker. It is a fine day for a walk." Good God, he sounded like a callow youth.

Amusement flashed in Mrs. Collins's eyes. "I believe she planned to walk in the grove today. Perhaps you might encounter her on your way to Rosings."

He shifted from one foot to the other. "Perhaps."
Now he was certain Mrs. Collins knew his secret. Had
Elizabeth confided her hopes in her friend? He would
have to be more circumspect; it would not do to raise
Elizabeth's expectations yet further. She was without
question the most bewitching woman he had ever met,
but that did not make her a suitable mistress of
Pemberley. Still, there was no harm in enjoying her
company, was there?

"It will take me some time to copy the receipt and to
package the tea. Perhaps I had best start that, and will
send it to Rosings with my maid as soon as it is ready."

How long could it take to write a receipt? Usually he
despised women who used their wiles to charm him or, as
in this case, to allow their friends to charm him. In
ordinary circumstances, he would have responded with a
set-down, but this time he was too eager to see Elizabeth.
Besides, Mrs. Collins would learn soon enough that the
master of Pemberley could not choose his wife based
solely on love.

Love? The thought jarred him. When had he moved
from mere fascination to love? What magic had Elizabeth
worked to thaw his heart? No, he could not be in love.
Not now, not with Elizabeth Bennet, not ever.

He bowed stiffly to Mrs. Collins. "I thank you." The
words were dust in his mouth.

When Lady Frederica called next at the parsonage, accompanied as usual by Mr. Darcy, she had no sooner greeted Charlotte and thanked her for the tea than she took Elizabeth's arm and said, "I pray you, Miss Bennet, would you do me the great kindness of walking through the parsonage garden with me? I find I am quite curious about it."

Elizabeth blinked at the blatant maneuver to speak to her alone. No doubt an earl's daughter could bend the rules of polite behavior without consequence. "Of course, if you wish." She was sorely tempted to point out Charlotte could tell her far more about the gardens, but that would only draw more attention to Lady Frederica's odd behavior.

Instead she put on her bonnet and followed Lady Frederica outside and through the garden gate. "Is there anything in particular you would like to see, or did you simply wish a private word?"

"A private word, of course." Lady Frederica's expression was unwontedly somber and her brows were drawn together. "You told me there was a gentleman who showed great interest in you and then abruptly turned his attention to a wealthier woman. I must know; was it Darcy?"

She burst out laughing. "Mr. Darcy? Heavens, no! He barely noticed I existed."

"But he danced with you."

"No doubt it was only to be polite." Was there any way to convince Lady Frederica she was beating the wrong horse?

She frowned. "Were there any other women whom he seemed to like?"

"Not that I am aware of, apart from the ladies of his own party. He seemed cordial enough to them."

"How annoying! I was so certain I had solved the mystery." Lady Frederica picked a leaf from a rosebush and began to shred it. "But there must be something. Some woman."

"I beg your pardon?"

"Darcy and Richard had a terrible quarrel last night, all about love and marriage, and they *never* fight. Darcy has always prided himself on his untouched heart, but the bitterness with which he kept insisting that love has no place in marriage made me think…" She trailed off, dropping bits of leaf on the graveled garden path.

"It made you think he must be in love to rail against it so?"

The ghost of a smile touched Lady Frederica's lips. "Put that way, it does sound a bit silly, but I assure you, Darcy would never be so agitated about something which did not trouble him deeply. And then Richard, of all people, started defending love and praising it — my brother, who would marry any woman of sufficient fortune willing to take him! Richard was so angry that, had it been anyone but Darcy, they would have been meeting at dawn."

"I cannot imagine it would go so far."

"Not with Darcy, but Richard *likes* duels. All my brothers do. Madness, is it not?"

"Without a doubt! Well, I am sorry I could not shed any light on your mystery."

"I will solve it, I promise! My mother says I am like a terrier worrying at a bone."

Elizabeth laughed. "But a very well-bred terrier!"

It was far too lovely a day to spend indoors, easily the mildest day of the spring so far, so Elizabeth decided to walk with Charlotte as far as Rosings Park. Charlotte had been summoned by Lady Catherine on some sort of business, no doubt manufactured, but Elizabeth planned to take advantage of the fine weather by wandering through the gardens at Rosings.

To her delight, she found the formal gardens empty of all but two gardeners. She left them pruning the already immaculate topiaries and hurried through the over-formal Italian garden to the rose arbor. The buds were already beginning to set. How impressive the show must be in midsummer! She followed the path along a small lake, and then bypassed the Temple of Artemis folly to find herself a shady spot in the grotto. This was her favorite part of the gardens since it was the least ostentatious, and she could sit here for hours in peace listening to the birds and the rustling leaves, imagining travels in faraway lands.

Her enjoyment of the bird songs was interrupted by the sound of voices approaching. Annoyed, Elizabeth shrank back into the grotto. Perhaps they would not see her if they passed this way. Who would wish to spend a beautiful day like this making stilted social conversation?

Even worse, one of the voices sounded like Mr. Darcy. Elizabeth willed herself to become invisible.

"None that I have heard of," said Mr. Darcy.

Lady Frederica's voice responded. "That is a surprise. I would have expected her to attract many suitors."

"If all else were equal I imagine that would be true, but I fear no one wishes to attach themselves to her family."

Elizabeth sighed. Gossip of the *ton*, no doubt.

"Trade? I would not have thought it would matter so much in a country town."

"Her mother's side, but that is not the largest problem. It is their behavior."

"Truly? Her behavior seems perfectly proper to me."

"I do not speak of her. She and her elder sister are generally praised and well-liked, but her mother and younger sisters betray a total want of propriety, not just occasionally, but almost uniformly. The youngest ones are a scandal waiting to happen."

"Does her father not intervene?"

"Her father, while clever and generally pleasant, seems unconcerned. Instead he mocks them all, even in public, and he does not exclude Miss Elizabeth from his mockery."

Elizabeth's throat closed. It was *her* family he was insulting! How dare he! He had made his scorn of her mother clear enough in Hertfordshire, but to say so, and to Lady Frederica who was acquainted with her! Shame burned her cheeks.

"Did you hear something?" Lady Frederica asked.

Elizabeth stopped breathing.

"Most likely just an animal."

"No, it seemed to come from the grotto." A moment later Lady Frederica's form darkened the grotto entrance. "Miss Bennet! I did not expect to see you here."

"Apparently not!" Elizabeth's anger was consuming her. "I am certain if you knew of my presence, you would have stopped Mr. Darcy from disparaging my family — at least until I was out of earshot."

"But it was not like that!"

Now Mr. Darcy's shadow had joined Lady Frederica's.

"A total want of propriety? Mr. Darcy is fortunate since *I* would return the compliment by giving my opinion of *his* family, but *you* do not deserve that, so he is spared." Elizabeth's voice shook. "I hope you will excuse me for taking my leave of you, and in return I shall not blame you if you avoid further visits to the parsonage." She turned her back on them, grateful for the relative darkness of the grotto which hid her tears, and ran out the other entrance.

She had never felt so humiliated in her life.

Frederica shaded her eyes, watching after Elizabeth's retreating figure. "You had best go apologize."

Darcy felt frozen inside. Elizabeth was distressed, and it was his fault. "I spoke nothing but the truth."

"What does that have to do with anything? The poor girl must be mortified beyond belief."

"You were the one who was asking me about it. I would have said nothing otherwise."

"Darcy, it does not matter whose fault it is. If you do not care what Miss Elizabeth thinks of you, then you need do nothing. I intend to apologize to her myself, even though she seems disinclined to blame *me*."

Darcy scowled. He hated apologizing, but he knew all too well how it felt to be humiliated. "Very well." He strode off after Elizabeth.

She had disappeared around the curve. That path led to the shrubbery, where it should be easy enough to find her. But when he reached the walk with high hedges on both sides, he could not see her ahead.

Had he missed another path? He looked back over his shoulder, but did not see another option. Perhaps she had walked faster than he expected. He set off again down the path, his long legs eating up the distance.

He almost missed her. Had it not been for that odd prickling sensation he felt whenever she was near, he would have rushed past the small alcove in the hedge where she stood. Her head was tipped back and her eyes closed, almost as if she were expecting a kiss. He took an involuntary step forward.

She must have heard the gravel scraping under his boots, for she opened her eyes. Her shoulders slumped at the sight of him.

"Miss Elizabeth, may I speak with you for a moment?"

She heaved a sigh. "If you wish," she said flatly.

"It is regarding what you overheard. I am not in the habit of discussing such matters with others, and I should not have done so in this case. More than my own error, it pains me to have offended you. But amidst your displeasure at my representation of your family, I hope it will give you consolation to consider that it is generally believed you and your eldest sister have conducted yourselves so as to avoid any share of the censure."

She cast her eyes heavenward, then stared over his shoulder so fiercely that he turned his head to see if someone was there. No one was in sight. "Nothing you said was a surprise. It merely confirmed suspicions I have held for some time."

Her odd tone confused him, but he plunged ahead. "Then you understand I meant no harm to you?"

Her eyes widened. "No, I do not understand why you thought it your place to deride my family to an acquaintance of mine!"

He took half a step backwards. "I did not mean to do that. My cousin had asked me if I knew why you had no suitors, and I endeavored to explain it is because of your family, not you."

"You believe my family is why I lack suitors?" Her voice was dangerously even.

Here he was on solid ground. "Yes. At first I wondered why your sister had no gentlemen dangling after her, given her extraordinary beauty. I thought perhaps there had been a scandal, but when I inquired, I was told that while many wished to court her, they would not ally themselves to your family. Having seen your youngest sisters chasing after the officers and observing your family at the ball at Netherfield, it became clear to me why that was."

Elizabeth just stared at him for a moment, her lips in a tight line. "You are making quite an assumption, sir!"

He held his hands out in front of him, as if to ward off her anger. "Do you never wonder why your sister has no suitors? Even with a limited dowry, gentlemen should be beating down the doors."

"You will forgive me if I do not tell her of your kind concern for her." Her voice shook. "Pray pardon me, Mr. Darcy." She brushed past him and half ran down the path.

Everything he said seemed to have made matters worse. This time he did not follow her.

Dashing tears from her eyes, Elizabeth picked up her skirt and ran, not towards the parsonage, but into the open fields beyond the gardens. She clambered over a stile into a field of sheep who looked up from their placid grazing as she passed, and then into a copse. She had never been on this footpath before and did not know in which direction she was heading, but she did not care. The only thing that mattered was that no one see her tear-stained face.

She was paying little attention as she crossed the next stile and did not notice when her skirt caught on the top cross-piece. It was enough to knock her off balance as she stepped down. She heard a ripping sound as she plunged onto her hands and knees.

It was too much. Now, on top of her humiliation by Mr. Darcy, her skirt was torn, her hands and petticoats were covered with mud, and her right knee felt as if she had scraped the skin off. She could no longer control her sobs as she sat heavily back on the bottom step of the stile to survey the damage. Her handkerchief was as muddy as the rest of her, so she wiped her eyes on her sleeve.

Yes, a little blood was seeping through her petticoat as well. How many more ways could she destroy her favorite day dress?

A young woman's voice with a light French accent floated past her. "*Eh bien*, what has happened to you? You poor thing! My cottage is just beyond that tree. Do come there and we will clean off all that mud, no?"

Elizabeth sniffled. "You are very kind, but I do not wish to make any trouble for you."

"It is no trouble. I am happy to have a guest, yes?" She was a slight woman who was heavily pregnant. Her day dress and bonnet suggested gentle birth.

Elizabeth's knee stung as she pushed herself to her feet, but it seemed to hold her weight. "I thank you."

"Do you need assistance to walk?" She patted her swollen abdomen. "I may be clumsy with this little one, but I am strong."

"I believe I am the clumsy one today," said Elizabeth ruefully. "But I can walk, thank you."

"This way, then." The woman led her to a pleasant cottage Elizabeth had not seen before. "I think we will go into the kitchen."

Elizabeth removed her muddy half boots at the door and walked in. A boy turned a roast on a spit in the well-equipped kitchen, and a cook was stirring something. The room smelled of herbs.

"How fortunate you managed to keep your skirt out of the mud!" the woman said.

"Only by dint of ripping it!"

"*Alors*, that we can sew with no trouble."

Elizabeth stepped into a small room her hostess showed her and unfastened the petticoat. As the woman took the muddy garment and left the room, Elizabeth assessed the damage to her dress. It could be mended, yes, but it would never be the same. Still, it did not reveal anything beyond her ankles, so she returned to the kitchen where the maid was preparing a tea tray.

The Frenchwoman came in from outside without the petticoat. Was there a laundry maid as well?

"Come into the sitting room," she said, taking the tray in herself.

How curious! She seemed to have plenty of servants, but did not hesitate to do the work herself. Elizabeth trailed her into a comfortable room and took the seat indicated. "I thank you for your kindness, madame."

"Oh, do call me Sylvie!" She lifted the lid of the teapot and sniffed the tea inside. "Perfect. It is a tisane of chamomile, lavender and lemon balm, very good for the nerves." She poured Elizabeth a cup without asking if she wanted one.

"I am Elizabeth Bennet," said Elizabeth somewhat stiffly.

Sylvie glanced up at her. "Oh, I am always forgetting! You English and your formal introductions! Do forgive me."

"It is nothing. There are many different customs, and it is less surprising than finding a Frenchwoman here of all places!"

Sylvie looked down at her hands. "I do not live here. I am just here for a holiday. I keep my presence quiet, except when young ladies fall in the mud, because some of the people here would see me as one of the enemy. You are the first neighbor I have met."

"I am a visitor, too, staying with Mrs. Collins at the Hunsford parsonage."

"My husband has mentioned the parsonage to me. It is near Rosings Park, is it not?"

"Quite near. Mr. and Mrs. Collins often wait upon Lady Catherine de Bourgh."

Sylvie nodded. "I have a request of you. It would make matters difficult for my husband and me if anyone at Rosings Park knew of my presence. Lady Catherine does not approve of the French."

"One more among the many things Lady Catherine does not approve of! Never fear, I shall not say a word."

Sylvie beamed. "You are so very good! Pray have a lemon cake."

Elizabeth was growing weary of staring at the ceiling of her room at the parsonage. The next time she decided to hide, she should remember to take a book or her sewing basket. Of course, it was all Mr. Darcy's fault, as usual. She had made it perfectly clear she did not wish to see him, so what did he decide to do? Why, pay a call on her, what else?

A knock at the door made her jump, but it was only Charlotte with the tea tray. Mr. Darcy must be gone, then. Good riddance!

Charlotte set the tray on a small writing table, poured a cup and brought it to Elizabeth. "My sovereign headache remedy. Not that I believe you truly have a headache, but I had to tell the servants something."

Elizabeth accepted the cup with a wry expression. "I am sorry, Charlotte; I did not mean to place you in a difficult position."

"In that case, pray do not ask my servants again to tell Mr. Darcy you are not at home! If word of it reached Lady Catherine, I shudder to think of what might happen. If you truly must avoid him at all costs, I would suggest a series of sudden headaches or fainting spells."

Elizabeth's cheeks grew warm. "Of course. I did not think of anyone's reaction to it, and I ought to have."

"There is no need to worry. I was able to cover it up this time by telling him you were ill." Charlotte stared at the teacup for a long moment. "But Lizzy, you must tell me if he has tried to harm you in any way or to take advantage of you. I will find some way of stopping it, I promise."

Elizabeth gave a harsh laugh. "Why would Mr. Darcy try to take advantage of me? I am not worthy of his notice."

Charlotte raised her eyebrows. "Given how often he notices you, I doubt that. But he must have done *something* to you, and I am frightened of what it might be."

"You may put your mind at ease. He did not touch me, threaten me, harm me or attempt to take advantage of me. Does that cover all the possibilities? No, the oh-so-proud Mr. Darcy simply humiliated me, a skill at which he excels. I suppose he called here only to be certain he had thoroughly put me in my place."

"I find that difficult to believe, but even if it were true, you usually manage to laugh off that kind of nonsense. What was it this time? Did he mean to be hurtful, or was he simply oblivious as he so often is?"

Elizabeth set down the teacup before her shaking fingers betrayed her. "I hardly know. He seemed surprised I was offended."

"What did he say?"

She pulled her knees up to her chest and wrapped her arms around them. "He told Lady Frederica that Jane and I have no suitors because no man would ally himself with our family."

Charlotte watched her with concern, and then prompted, "And what else?"

"Is that not enough?" Elizabeth's voice shook with rage.

Her friend looked perplexed again. She folded her hands, studied them, unfolded them and then folded them once more. "Lizzy," she said with great care. "It was very wrong of him to say as much, but surely you already knew that."

"Not you, too? Does everyone think my family so intolerable then?"

"Oh, Lizzy, of course not! Your mother may be silly at times, and your younger sisters as well, but the same could be said for my own mother. There is a difference, though. I have brothers. A man could offer for me without any fear of having to someday provide my mother a home. But a man who offered for Jane or for you — and there are men who wish they could — knows he will have no choice but to invite your mother and sisters to live in his home once your father dies. Four extra mouths to feed, four more women to provide clothes and servants for the rest of their lives, and he would carry the burden of their irritating behavior. No matter how much a man may admire Jane, it is unlikely to outweigh the fact that he would essentially be marrying your mother and sisters as well. Can you not see why that would make them reluctant?"

Bile rose in Elizabeth's throat, and she pressed her forehead against her knees to hide her tears. It was true, then. She had been able to deny it when Mr. Darcy said it, but Charlotte would not lie to her and had no reason to hurt her. And it made sense; even Jane, beautiful, sweet tempered Jane, never had an admirer apart from a gentleman in London who wrote her poems when she was sixteen. Elizabeth could only claim two admirers herself: Mr. Collins, who knew little of her situation, and Mr. Wickham, also a stranger to Meryton, who had dropped her acquaintance after only two months. Had it been solely Mary King's dowry which had attracted him, or had he decided Elizabeth Bennet came at too high a price?

Did Jane know? Had she seen Mr. Bingley as her one and only chance, a man who was unfamiliar with her family and who could afford to provide a separate household for Mrs. Bennet? No wonder she had been so devastated to lose him!

Elizabeth swallowed hard. "Charlotte, I thank you for your concern, but I would prefer to be alone at present."

Charlotte stood. "Of course. I am sorry. I wish things were different – for both of us."

Chapter Six

The next day Lady Frederica called at the parsonage earlier than her usual wont. Stifling a yawn, she said, "I am throwing myself on your mercy. Lady Catherine has announced she will not tolerate slug-a-beds who do not rise before noon, so she sent a servant in to wake me. Unfortunately, she was more frightened of Lady Catherine than of me."

"You are accustomed to keeping town hours, then?" asked Elizabeth sympathetically.

"That is the excuse I use, but the truth is I simply detest mornings. They put me in a perfectly foul temper. I thought it safer for me to be grumpy here, since there are far too many things I am tempted to say to my aunt as it is. On top of it, my mother is being icy to everyone today, and although I know it has nothing to do with me, I still feel as if I must tiptoe around her."

"I hope Lady Matlock is not unwell."

Lady Frederica waved her hand as if to brush the question away. "She is perfectly well, simply unhappy about news she received from my eldest brother. His wife has had another stillbirth, her third. And since my mother would never allow her distress to show, she turns into an icicle instead. But she gave herself away by suggesting to Richard that he should consider selling his commission, and then he grew all stiff and rode off to wherever it is he goes, and I wanted to hide under the table."

Unable to make any sense of this, Elizabeth said, "I see."

"Oh, your expression is priceless! Am I being mysterious?"

Elizabeth laughed. "Only a little, but I am sorry to hear of your eldest brother's loss."

"Charles has all the bad luck in our family. He is living in Ireland until the fuss over his last duel dies down, and also to keep him from losing the family fortune at cards. He has been married ten years but none of his children have lived, and now Richard will be angry with him because it means he may have to leave the army to protect the succession, even though it is unlikely he would ever inherit."

"What about your other brother? Is he not enough to protect the succession?"

"Jasper? Oh, no. He is too frivolous and impulsive to handle such a responsibility, so poor Richard is stuck with it."

"I begin to see there are advantages to being the child of a country gentleman instead of an earl!" Elizabeth teased.

"There are certainly advantages to visiting a country parsonage instead of Rosings Park! Everyone there is always in a tizzy about something or another, and I am always too tempted to say things I should not."

"Sometimes it is a challenge to bite one's tongue."

"Sometimes? It is always a challenge for me, and an indefinite stay at Rosings is not helping! Did I tell you I heard back from my father? He says I may not leave Rosings until he gives his express approval, and I should settle myself for a protracted stay. What does he think I will accomplish by being marooned on the edge of nowhere?" Lady Frederica took a biscuit from the tea tray before the maid had even set it down.

"Your father gives no reason for you to stay at Rosings?"

"No, or rather his secretary does not, since he was the one who wrote the letter. But my father cannot think any of us are happy about it. Both my mother and I wrote him about how much Lady Catherine resents my presence. It is better than it was at the beginning, but she still loses no opportunity to compare me unfavorably with Cousin Anne."

Elizabeth clasped her hand to her heart teasingly. "How can there be any comparison? Miss de Bourgh's superior taste, of which there has never been any evidence, and the superior accomplishments she would have had, had she been permitted to learn, her superior appearance and noble condescension — why, you are quite correct. You are inferior to Miss de Bourgh in every way!"

Lady Frederica grinned. "But I am an earl's daughter and she is but a granddaughter without even a courtesy title, for which I must be forever punished. Only Darcy and my brothers are acceptable to Lady Catherine. And Georgiana Darcy, of course — she does approve of Georgiana, since she has the good sense not to outrank her daughter."

"And Miss Darcy is not a threat to her plans to wed Mr. Darcy to Miss de Bourgh."

Lady Frederica held out her hands as if to stop an oncoming enemy. "Do not even dare to mention that! You would not believe the row she and Darcy had last night about it. Lady Catherine looked on the verge of apoplexy. What a pity she did not succumb to it! That would have solved so many difficulties. But Darcy was angrier than I have ever seen him, and told her if she ever mentioned the subject to him again, he would leave Rosings and never return. But he had been out of sorts all day yesterday, so I suppose it was not surprising."

Elizabeth picked up her mending to avoid Lady Frederica's sharp eyes. "I hope they manage to resolve their quarrel." Surely that was neutral enough. She was happy Lady Frederica apparently wished to continue their acquaintance after the quarrel in the gardens, but Mr. Darcy was another question.

"And I hope *you* will resolve your quarrel with him as well. He asked me to deliver his apologies to you, and..."

"I pray you, no more! I do not wish to discuss Mr. Darcy."

Apparently Lady Frederica was prepared to ignore even the boldest of hints. "He truly is repentant. He was most disturbed yesterday when you would not see him."

Elizabeth stabbed the needle into the fabric. "So I ought to take pity on poor, sensitive Mr. Darcy?"

Lady Frederica's mouth twisted. "You will not forgive him, no matter how repentant he is?"

"He does not repent anything except being overheard."

"That is not true. He has a great deal of sympathy for your situation."

Her hands now trembling with anger, Elizabeth said, "How very kind of him to have such concern for my lack of prospects. Should I find myself starving on the street someday, I will be certain to call on him to beg a crust of bread!"

"Oh, he does not think you lack prospects, not at all. He was speaking only of the past."

Elizabeth's eyebrows shot up. Could this be a hint that Colonel Fitzwilliam's occasional attentions to her were more serious than she had believed? But the colonel was more often riding out somewhere than calling at the parsonage, and Darcy would never permit his cousin to lower himself so far, especially if he had the least hope of inheriting. In any case, the conversation was pointless. "If you wish, you may tell Mr. Darcy that he is quite forgiven, and that I will look forward with great anticipation to hearing what other insulting opinions he may have about my family. Besides, I cannot imagine the slight matter of my feelings on the subject will trouble him for long."

Lady Frederica shook her head. "Can you not simply accept that your good opinion matters to him?"

Elizabeth considered it briefly, more to rein in her temper than out of indecision. A vision of Jane's pale, gaunt face lying on her sickbed rose before her, and she could hear Mrs. Gardiner telling her about the bottle of laudanum. But Jane would not wish her to be harsh. "If it will ease your mind, I promise to behave in a perfectly civil manner to your cousin. Now pray let us speak of something else! I do not wish to quarrel with *you*."

"Very well." Lady Frederica glanced at the clock on the mantelpiece. "And look, it is nearly noon. Soon I will become less of a bothersome wretch and more like a reasonable human being."

This was as much of an olive branch as she was likely to receive. "Perhaps some further refreshments might aid your transformation. Shall I ask for some?" Lady Frederica always seem to be hungry.

"Oh, yes, please. My digestion was too wretched at that unreasonable hour of morning for me to touch a bite of breakfast. Especially a Rosings breakfast. Where do you suppose Lady Catherine found her cook? In a prison? Or cooking for a poorhouse?"

Elizabeth's anger began to retreat. "I suspect she came from Bedlam myself."

"If I must tolerate her cooking and Lady Catherine's behavior for much longer, Bedlam is where you will have to send me!" exclaimed Lady Frederica.

Chapter Seven

Gregory, Lady Catherine's favorite footman, held out a silver platter to Darcy with a card on it. "A caller, sir."

Who would be calling on him at Rosings? He read the card, then glanced at Frederica and back at the card. "Frederica," he said carefully. "Are you perchance expecting a visit from Sir Anthony Duxbury?"

"Of course not. He cannot even bear to be in the same room with me. Why?"

"Because he is here, and I do not know why." Darcy turned to the footman. "I will see him in the library."

"No, Gregory; bring him here," said Frederica, her voice level.

The footman glanced at Darcy, who nodded. After he left, Darcy said to Frederica, "Are you certain you wish to see him?"

She stuck her chin in the air, every inch an earl's daughter. "I have nothing to hide. If my presence causes him discomfort, that is his problem, not mine."

At the door, Gregory announced, "Sir Anthony Duxbury to see Mr. Darcy."

Duxbury usually exuded energy, but today he looked exhausted. "Darcy, I am glad to have finally run you to ground. I – " He stopped short and grew pale. "Lady Frederica! I did not expect to see you here."

"Obviously, Sir Anthony," she said smoothly. "You would not be here otherwise. Do sit down. Gregory, be so kind as to bring some refreshments for our guest."

"It is not... I needed to speak to Darcy, and he was here."

She gestured towards Darcy with one hand. "There he is, and you may speak to him as much as you wish. Pray do not allow my presence to disturb you." Frederica ostentatiously picked up her book and began to turn the pages.

Without asking whether he desired any, Darcy went to the sideboard and poured a glass of wine for Duxbury. He appeared to need it.

Duxbury gave him a grateful glance when he held it out to him. "My thanks." Frederica's presence seemed to have flustered him more than Darcy would have expected. Duxbury had been the one to break off their understanding, after all. He was not the injured party.

"So, you have gone to some effort to find me," Darcy prompted.

His eyes flickered towards Frederica. "Yes. I hoped to speak to you... of the situation in the North – the Luddites and the unrest."

Darcy blinked in surprise. "You came all this way to discuss politics?"

"This is a cause which is very dear to my heart, and I stand in dire need of assistance because of it."

What sort of help could he need? It could not be a matter of money. Duxbury had plenty of his own.

The footman announced, "Mrs. Collins and Miss Bennet to see Lady Frederica."

Elizabeth! All thoughts of Duxbury's mysterious mission fled his mind at the sight of her light and pleasing form. He had not seen her since that painful day in the gardens, and her anger had gnawed at him ever since. Had she finally forgiven him? He must know.

Belatedly remembering his manners, he said, "Ladies, will you permit me the honor of introducing..."

Elizabeth stepped past him before he had even finished. "Mr. Hopewell! It is an unexpected pleasure to see you again."

Darcy looked over his shoulder to see to whom she was speaking, but Duxbury was bowing over her hand.

"Why, if it is not my dear sister Anne!" said Duxbury with a hollow laugh. "Well met, madam."

Duxbury's *sister*?

Elizabeth must have noted his confusion, for she laughed and said, "I was only a temporary sister. Mr.

Hopewell and I were fellow stagecoach passengers, and when our coach was unexpectedly forced to stop for the night, Mr. Hopewell was gallant enough to arrange a room at the inn for me and to tell everyone I was his sister. I am greatly in his debt." Her smile faded at Darcy's grim look. "He was a perfect gentleman."

Darcy looked at Duxbury, who was even paler than before. "A perfect gentleman? Except for one little matter of the truth. His name is Sir Anthony Duxbury, not Hopewell."

Elizabeth glanced back and forth between the two men. "I do not understand."

"Nor do I," said Darcy pointedly.

Duxbury tugged at his cravat. "It is a long and complicated story, though not unrelated to the one I came to tell you."

From the doorway Richard said, "Then you had best get started in telling it, Duxbury."

"So you are here as well, Fitzwilliam? The question is where to begin." Duxbury rubbed his forehead. "These are not the circumstances I would have chosen for this discussion."

Frederica said sharply, "The beginning is usually considered a good place to start."

Duxbury looked at her for a long minute, then turned to Darcy. "You are well acquainted with Sir Anthony Duxbury, gentleman about town, a moderate Whig who occasionally flirts with philosophical radicalism. That is nothing but a façade. My true beliefs are different, and have been since I returned from the Continent – views too dangerous for Sir Anthony Duxbury to espouse, much less act upon. That is where Mr. Hopewell comes in. He is a Radical who travels among the Luddites, writing pamphlets in favor of giving them the vote and the same rights you and I possess, speaking at their meetings, and helping to garner support for their cause. Sedition, resisting arrest, hiding fugitives – you name it, Hopewell has done it, and then come back to London as Duxbury and played the role of a dilettante."

Darcy frowned. "Why the double life? I would think you could do more good as a baronet than by disguising yourself as a humbler man."

"Perhaps, but I am also selfish. Hopewell has one important quality Sir Anthony lacks. He has no family to disgrace and no family estate to forfeit to the crown. When Hopewell is arrested and sent to Newgate – and truly, it is more of a 'when' than an 'if' – Sir Anthony Duxbury will vanish, his whereabouts unknown. I will be presumed dead and my brother will inherit, our family name unsullied with charges of treason and sedition. And that is also..." He paused to take a deep breath and looked at Frederica. "That is also why I am not able to take a wife."

In the deep silence following this astonishing pronouncement, Darcy hardly knew where to look – at the boyhood friend who had kept such a secret from him or at the cousin whose heart he had broken. Then, with a brisk swishing of slippers on the tile floor, Frederica crossed in front of her former lover. The crack of her palm striking his face resounded throughout the room.

With an oath, Richard started forward, but Darcy grabbed his arm and he subsided.

Duxbury's hand rose to touch his cheek. He turned back to face Frederica but said nothing, just watched her.

"Why, then, did you court me all those months?" Frederica's voice throbbed with fury. "Was it simply to amuse yourself?"

"The truth?" he said steadily. "At first it was because of your father. He is powerful in the House of Lords, and I hoped to be in a better position to influence him as a son-in-law."

She slapped him again, this time forcing him to take a step backwards. "Try again," she spat. "You cannot have it both ways. You cannot marry, yet you deliberately courted me with a plan to marry. Which is it?"

"Both. I was prepared to marry you for my cause, but then things changed." The scarlet where she had slapped him stood out dramatically from his pallor. A trail of blood trickled down his face where her ring had caught his skin.

"What changed?" Her voice snapped like a whip.

He raised his chin. "My feelings changed. I started out pretending to be in love with you, and one day realized the pretense had somehow turned into reality. Your father no longer mattered, and instead I was waiting every moment until I could see you next. But then the rebellion in the North began, and I had a dangerous part to play. The stakes were suddenly much higher. I could not expose you to that risk."

Richard shook off Darcy's arm and strode forward, his fists clenched. "That is the first thing you have said which has made sense, and you have said quite enough. Outside, Duxbury – now."

Duxbury gave a resigned nod, and Darcy would have sworn he looked relieved at the prospect of being thrashed by Richard rather than continuing to face Frederica's wrath. Darcy would have to follow them. When Richard was this angry, there was a real risk he could inflict permanent harm, especially since it appeared Duxbury had no intention of defending himself.

"Stay out of this, Richard," Frederica said icily. "This is none of your affair."

"Defending your honor *is* my affair. Now out of my way."

Frederica balled her hands into fists, showing an extraordinary resemblance to her brother. "Richard, so help me, if you..."

Duxbury held out a hand to silence them both. "Let her have her say, Fitzwilliam, then I will come with you. She deserves the opportunity to tell me what she thinks of me."

"Fine," Richard snapped. "It will give me time to decide which of your arms to break."

Frederica moved abruptly, her foot coming down hard on Richard's boot. With an involuntary grunt of pain, he glared at her. Her expression reminded Darcy of the little girl who had put leeches in her brother's bed in revenge for some long-forgotten slight.

She turned back to Duxbury. "Did it *ever*, even once, occur to you to *tell* me this – to use all that vaunted eloquence of yours to explain yourself rather than simply jilting me, leaving all the world to wonder what *I* had done to *you*?"

He licked his lips. "I wish... I never intended... but no. It did not." He sounded utterly defeated.

"Or to ask me about *my* beliefs in the matter?"

"I know you are a Whig and sympathetic to the sufferings of the poor, but that is something very different from advocating for a change in government."

Frederica stared at him disbelievingly for a moment, then turned away. Taking the small volume she had been reading, she slapped it against Duxbury's chest hard enough that he flinched back. "Go ahead. You think you know all about my beliefs."

Duxbury ducked his head as he examined the spine of the book, then his eyebrows shot up. "*The Rights of Man*?" he asked disbelievingly. "You have read this?"

"No, I simply carry it for the exercise!"

Richard grabbed the book from Duxbury. "Freddie, who allowed you to read this rubbish?"

"I chose it myself, at my sewing circle. You know, the weekly one I never miss, which is surprising as I detest sewing and never bring home any embroidery I have done there. That is because we are too busy reading Radical books and writing pamphlets. Which I would have told you, oh-so-knowledgeable Sir Anthony, had you thought to ask me! But no, you had to walk away like a tragic hero." Her voice dripped scorn.

"I...I had no idea," Duxbury stammered.

Her lip curled. "Obviously! You men are hopeless idiots, the lot of you! I cannot believe I ever saw anything to admire in you." She turned away and flounced back to her chair. "Well, you might as well tell Darcy whatever your urgent business is. Richard, you may break his arms later."

Duxbury stared after her as Elizabeth and Mrs. Collins approached her and spoke in low voices.

Frederica said to the ladies in a flat voice, "No. Please stay." Silently Darcy seconded her wish. This might not be a scene he wished Elizabeth to witness, but he did not want her to leave, not before he had a chance to speak with her.

Duxbury helped himself to another glass of wine and drank half of it before he had even sunk down in his chair. Who could blame him? "Darcy, how long has it been since you were in the North?"

"I was at Pemberley in August, but not since then."

"You have not seen, then, the toll this terrible winter has taken on the people of the North. Oh, not at Pemberley; I know you are a generous landlord, and none of your people would be allowed to suffer. But in the cities and towns it is a different story, with destitution and starvation among the fabric workers who can find no employment. Parliament has ignored their pleas for relief. With another bad harvest last autumn, and then the long winter, their situation is truly dire. In their desperation, they turned to breaking the machines which put them out of work. Many have been arrested. Since February, when Parliament in its wisdom made loom-breaking a capital crime, many have hung."

"I did not agree with Parliament's decision to hang the loom-breakers, and have said so publicly," said Darcy. What was Duxbury's point in all this?

"I know, and that is why I dared come to you. Also, you are not uninvolved. I am not your only old school-fellow involved in this. Thomas Beaumont and Edward Latimer are in gaol in Sheffield. Unless something changes, they will go to the gallows within the fortnight."

"What?" Darcy sat forward, his fists balled on his knees. "Beaumont and Latimer? Are you certain? Can they not simply tell the authorities who they are?"

"They could, but they will not, for the same reason I would accept a sentence at Newgate rather than claim the

129

privilege of my rank. We knew what could happen when we started this work."

Richard's foot tapped rapidly on the floor. "I cannot believe this. Beaumont is a friend of mine, and he is no fool. Why would he break looms? It accomplishes nothing. They just build another."

"Beaumont had nothing to do with the looms. Latimer was trying to stop some local workers from breaking into a mill, but was arrested with the others when they were betrayed. Beaumont tried to rescue Latimer from the constables and was captured himself. None of us support loom-breaking. Our goal is reform of the electoral system and recognition of the rights of all Englishmen." He cast a sidelong glance at Frederica, who was studiously admiring something on the floor.

Darcy frowned. "Can you not prove they were not involved?"

"We have tried. The other prisoners testified neither Latimer nor Beaumont had been near a loom, but the magistrate refused to believe them. And I have yet to tell you the worst of it, which is that this will not end with the deaths of two good men. They are well-known and respected by the common people there, even loved. They have been the only hope these desperate men have, the only men of stature who have been willing to stand up for them in a country where only the educated and well-to-do have rights. They have helped the unemployed workers write petitions to make their voices heard, hired tutors to teach them to read and write, and given them food when their children were starving. If Latimer and Beaumont are hung, there will be rioting in the streets at the very least. At worst..." He paused to take a deep breath. "They are already on the verge of armed insurrection and have banded together with men from the other Northern cities. This could be the spark which will set off a full-fledged rebellion of the common people against our government."

"This is England, not France," said Richard disdainfully. "There will be no revolution."

"I hope you are correct." Duxbury pulled out a folded paper and handed it to Darcy. "This was posted in Chesterfield last week."

Darcy opened the printed broadside and began to read, with Richard standing over his shoulder. "'There is six thousand men coming to you in April and we will go and blow Parliament House up for us laboring people can't stand it no longer. All Manchester, Derby, York, Chesterfield, Sheffield, Nottingham, and Mansfield local is going. The nation will never settle till these great heads are cut off. We will knock down the prisons and the judge we will murder.'"

As Richard pursed his mouth in a silent whistle, Frederica said, "It must be true. That would explain why Father would not allow Mother and me to go North with him and suddenly wanted us to leave London for Rosings instead."

Horrified, Darcy looked up at Duxbury. "Will they actually do this?"

"We – Latimer, Beaumont and I – have been doing everything we can to prevent it. But when they see the men who argued for peaceful reform rather than revolution hanging from the gibbet..." He shook his head silently.

Darcy turned the paper over in his hands. Two friends hung and armed revolt! It was a terrifying prospect. "You seem to believe I can do something to prevent this. What do you have in mind?"

"The Earl of Matlock is coming to Sheffield to meet with the Master Cutler regarding the East India Company monopoly. The magistrates would not dare refuse a request to release the prisoners if it came from him. I came today to beg you to intercede with your uncle on their behalf." He paused and looked towards Richard and Frederica with a wan smile. "I did not expect to find his children here."

Darcy rubbed his forehead. "I am willing to try, of course, but I do not know how much influence I have. Richard, is there a chance he would listen?"

Richard said, "Why should I even believe this fellow is telling us the truth? He has already admitted he lied to Frederica."

A sudden fire blazed in Duxbury's eyes as he rounded on Richard. "Because, you fool, I have said enough in the last quarter hour to hang for treason. My very *life* is in your hands. Why in God's name would I make up a story like that?"

Frederica said idly, "Regardless of his past behavior, he has a point."

Richard crossed his arms. "I say there will be no revolt. The militia will stop it."

"Perhaps, and many good Englishmen will die in a massacre that will stain Britain's name for generations!"

Frederica rose to her feet. "If you gentlemen will be so kind as to excuse me, I must be going. I have some important matters to take care of." She took a step towards the door.

Suspicion tugged at Darcy. He did not trust Frederica when she wore that defiant expression. "Where are you going?"

She turned to give him an artificially bright smile. "Why, to Sheffield, of course, to speak to my father. Where else?"

Duxbury was beside her in a second, his hand gripping her wrist. "No. It is too dangerous. I will not permit it."

"You have no power over me. I will go wherever I please."

"Not while I live and breathe!"

Her smile did not falter. "That can be arranged. Richard, you may kill him now."

Richard marched towards Frederica, stopping only when his face was mere inches from his sister's. "And who will kill *me*?" he growled.

"I imagine I can find dozens of candidates. At least you and Sir Anthony have found something upon which you agree. That is a minor miracle in itself!"

Then Elizabeth stepped into the fray. In the heat of the moment, Darcy had almost forgotten she was there, something he would not have thought possible. She laid a gentle hand on each man's arm. "I admire your sentiments, gentlemen, but I imagine there may be a better way to help your friends than by fighting with each other."

Trust Elizabeth to know what to say! Duxbury released Frederica's arm, and even Richard took a step back.

The least Darcy could do was to second her efforts. "I will go to Sheffield myself," he announced. "Frederica can remain here in the safety of Rosings.

Duxbury's face regained some of its color. "Thank you, Darcy. I cannot tell you how much I appreciate it."

Darcy nodded. "I hope you will accompany me there, as I have never been to Sheffield and hardly know where to begin."

"Of course."

Frederica smiled coldly at her brother. "There, Richard, you see? All will be well, and you need not worry. Darcy and Sir Anthony will ride into danger while you and I remain here in safety."

Richard's cheeks mottled with fury. "You will remain here. I will go with them."

Darcy glared at Frederica. "Richard, she is trying to provoke you. Pay no attention. Duxbury and I can manage this."

"Hah! Has either of you ever seen battle before?"

Duxbury said mildly, "As a matter of fact, yes. Just not the sort where Napoleon is the enemy."

Richard snorted. "You may think it the same thing, but I assure you, it is not."

Frederica said, "All three of you will go then. How lovely. I will accompany you as far as London."

"Are you sure you wish to do that?" asked Richard. "We will be leaving early, well before you are usually awake."

"I will make the sacrifice," she said. "I hope you will not object if we make a stop at Doctors' Commons."

Her brother gave her a puzzled look. "Why? What kind of business could you have with ecclesiastical lawyers?"

"A marriage license," she announced airily. "Sir Anthony will marry me before he rides off to his death or disgrace, whichever comes first. I do not care."

Duxbury's jaw dropped. "Lady Frederica, I am beyond honored that you would consider forgiving me, but —"

"I said nothing about forgiving you. This is about repairing the damage to my reputation you caused by jilting me. After we are wed, I do not care if I ever see you again." Red flags were flying in Frederica's cheeks.

Darcy stepped between them. "Perhaps this is something you and Duxbury should discuss privately." Preferably before either Richard or Frederica exploded.

Frederica met his eyes directly. "Sir Anthony has no choice. I was compromised by him."

"No, you were not," said Duxbury in a surprisingly reasonable voice. "Though I am willing to marry you if that is what you wish."

Richard jumped up from his chair. "No. Absolutely not. You are not marrying that man. Not now, not ever. I will not have it. Do you hear me?"

Frederica showed her dimples. "I hear you very well, but I am afraid you have no choice. You see, Sir Anthony and I lay together, so there is no remedy but marriage."

Richard hauled Duxbury out of his chair by his cravat before the last words had left her mouth. He held the smaller man up so Duxbury's feet barely touched the ground. "Choose your weapon," he snarled.

Rather astonishingly, his victim seemed unperturbed by the prospect of a duel. Sounding half strangled, he said, "I will meet you if you insist, but it is not true. She is making it up in order to force you to allow her to do as she wishes. Surely you must know your sister well enough to understand that."

Richard glared, first at Duxbury, then at Frederica, whose smile was unwavering, and then Duxbury staggered as Richard abruptly released his cravat. Rubbing his throat gingerly, Duxbury said, "I take it accusing your sister of lying is not a dueling offense."

"She does not have enough brothers to fight that many duels," growled Richard. "Well, Freddie, it seems you are out of luck this time."

"By no means. If I say we lay together, my reputation is ruined, regardless of whether it is true or not. And I do say so." She smiled beatifically. "Shall I go tell Lady Catherine about it?"

Richard narrowed his eyes. "It is a highly unattractive habit in a young lady to insist on her own way. But I know what to do when you are being impossible." He strode towards the door.

"And what is that?" Darcy asked.

"Fetch my mother, of course!"

As he departed, Gregory returned with a tray of refreshments. No doubt he was taking the place of a maid in order to be sure he overheard any important news he could report to Lady Catherine. Fortunately, Elizabeth had taken Frederica to sit with her at the opposite end of the room, where her dark hair contrasted nicely with Frederica's fairness as they whispered together. Darcy somehow tore his eyes away from her and turned back to Duxbury, who looked exhausted.

Mrs. Collins took it upon herself to serve the tea, although it should have fallen to Frederica. It was probably wise, since Darcy would not trust his cousin not to pour the hot liquid into Duxbury's lap. Once the tea was served, she placed the plate of pastries and fruit at Duxbury's elbow, which seemed an odd choice until Darcy saw how his friend wolfed down the food. When had he last eaten, and how had Mrs. Collins realized he was hungry? Anyone who would eat the food at Rosings with such alacrity must be half-starved.

It was just as well, as it kept conversation to a minimum until Lady Matlock swept into the room, stopping short at the sight of Duxbury. She gave him the barest of nods, and then turned to Darcy. "Richard, who appears to have smoke pouring out of his ears, informs me the world is coming to an end and that my presence is required to remedy the situation. I dearly hope you will be able to provide me with a few more details than that."

Darcy sighed. "I shall do my best, madam."

But before Darcy could begin, Frederica took her mother's arm and led her to the sofa. Placing her hand on Lady Matlock's, she said, "It is all very simple, really. Tomorrow morning we are going to London where I will marry Sir Anthony as soon as a special license can be obtained – whether he likes it or not. Then Darcy and Sir Anthony plan to go to Sheffield to meet with my father and convince him to prevent a rebellion and rescue their friends from prison, during which course Sir Anthony may well be hanged, but my reputation will be preserved."

Lady Matlock's expression did not change in the slightest. Darcy found himself holding his breath, waiting for her to produce her usual miracle. Half a minute passed before she said calmly, "You will need the large carriage for the journey north. I will send instructions to have a team of horses ready in London."

Duxbury stepped forward, looking as stunned as Darcy felt. "Your ladyship, Lady Frederica will be returning here from London, not going on to Sheffield with Darcy and me. The situation in the North is not safe at present."

"I am well aware of that, Sir Anthony. I would not venture to guess at your intentions, but the expression on my daughter's face tells me she intends to go to Sheffield as well, even if it entails stealing away in the middle of the night and following you there. As she will apparently be traveling there one way or another, would you not prefer she did so under your protection rather than completely alone?"

Duxbury looked incredulously at Frederica, waiting for a protest that did not come. "Of course, Lady Matlock, but I cannot emphasize enough that the situation in Sheffield is highly unstable, and while I would give my life to protect Lady Frederica, it would be of little use if we were facing a dangerous mob. I could never forgive myself if anything befell her. The danger is grave, and I could not be with her at every single moment."

"That, Sir Anthony, is why I will be traveling with you. It will also add credence to my explanation that we are all traveling to Matlock owing to Frederica's childhood dream to marry in the chapel there, which will prevent the unfortunate gossip which would otherwise follow such a hasty wedding."

Richard stood in the doorway. "Mother, did you know Freddie has been attending Radical meetings?" he asked accusingly.

Lady Matlock looked at him calmly. "Of course I knew."

Frederica sat up straight. "You did?"

With a delicate sigh, her mother said, "Do you suppose I would believe you were regularly attending a *sewing* circle? You have never voluntarily held a needle in your life. Naturally I had it investigated."

Richard stepped forward, his fists clenched. "And you are willing to permit this?" he asked darkly.

"My dear boy, Frederica is every bit as apt to get herself into mischief as you and your brothers. Meeting with other ladies and discussing politics is a much safer form of mischief than many other things she could choose. Why should I object?"

Frederica dropped her face into her hands.

On the other side of the room, Elizabeth nudged Charlotte with her elbow and whispered, "This seems like a good time to escape." It had been a most uncomfortable half an hour, having to pretend that confessions of treason, slapping, confrontations, challenges, betrothal demands and family crises were typical drawing room conversation. Thank heaven Lady Matlock had arrived to keep the peace!

Charlotte nodded and approached Lady Frederica, who was now actively engaged in planning their journey. "Lady Frederica, we seem to have chosen a singularly inappropriate moment to call on you, so I hope you will excuse us. If you are leaving in the morning, I imagine we will not meet again until your next trip to Rosings Park. Pray permit me to tell you how honored I have been by your attentions to us."

"Do not be silly," said Lady Frederica. "Your company was the only thing which has kept me from running mad during my stay here. Not to mention saving me from starvation! I owe you my thanks. In fact..." She pursed her lips thoughtfully.

Charlotte glanced at Elizabeth. "Is there anything we can do for you before we leave?"

"Why, yes." Lady Frederica gave Elizabeth a winning smile. "I have a favor to ask of Miss Bennet, a very great favor. Could you possibly see your way clear to altering your plans and joining me on this journey? I would very much like to have companionship more pleasant than I am otherwise likely to have." She glared at her brother and Sir Anthony. "And while my mother can serve as my chaperone, it is unlikely I would travel with her in only the company of three young men unless there was a powerful reason. It would help appearances greatly if you would consider it."

Elizabeth stiffened. Where had this come from? She was certainly not that close a friend. "I am honored, your ladyship, by your offer, but as you know, I am expected to remain with Mrs. Collins for some weeks yet."

Lady Matlock came to stand beside her and placed a gentle hand on her arm. Why did the light touch feel so much like a steely grip? "I will add my voice to my daughter's, Miss Bennet. We would be most pleased to have your company and this foolish matter in Sheffield will not take long to resolve. We will be traveling through lovely countryside and will make stops to see the sights, and you would be welcome to join us at our home in Matlock afterwards."

Elizabeth cast a helpless look at Charlotte, but found no ally there. Her friend said, "While I would be sorry to lose your company, Lizzy, Lady Frederica is right about keeping up appearances. And you do love to travel and see new places."

"But I am supposed to travel to the Lakes with my aunt and uncle in June!"

Lady Matlock beamed. "All the better! They can collect you at Matlock Park. It is just off the North Road, and we would be delighted if they would break their journey with us."

This was beginning to feel like a kidnapping. She had no choice but to play her last card. Taking a deep breath, she said, "Mr. Darcy, may I impose on you to bear witness that my aunt and uncle are perhaps not suitable guests for Matlock Park?"

Instead of the scowl she had anticipated, he merely raised one eyebrow. "I cannot see why not. It would not be the first time a tradesman crossed the doorstep and been made welcome."

Heat burned in her cheeks. Why was he not helping her? He could not wish to spend long days traveling in her company any more than she did. There had to be a way out for her. "Your ladyship, perhaps you could give me a short time to consider your generous, but quite unexpected, offer?"

Lady Matlock patted her arm, again somehow leaving the sense of a tight grip. "Of course, my dear. Perhaps you would like to discuss it with Mrs. Collins, whom we would be so cruelly robbing of your company."

Elizabeth smiled weakly. "I thank you."

Charlotte took her arm and half-dragged her out into the hall. "Lizzy, are you out of your mind? You ought to be leaping at this opportunity. Just think of the connections you will make!"

"Just think of having to sit in a carriage all day with Mr. Darcy glaring at me in disapproval, while Colonel Fitzwilliam and Sir Anthony nearly come to blows at every moment!"

"Now listen to me, Elizabeth Bennet! I do not understand where you developed this idea Mr. Darcy disapproves of you. You were the only local woman he danced with in Meryton. He came to visit us within hours of his arrival at Rosings, and has been back almost every day since. He cannot take his eyes off you. When are you going to open *your* eyes?"

Elizabeth shook her head. "I must be having a bad dream. Nothing anyone is saying makes any sense. Mr. Darcy does not like me!"

"Oh, I could just shake you! Just because that is your opinion does not make it true, but I know there is no moving you."

"And you wish me to go traveling into what everyone agrees is great danger?"

"You will be traveling with the Countess, and unless I miss my guess, enough armed footmen to stop an army. You will be in no danger. However, if you return to Longbourn and your mother discovers you refused an invitation to Matlock Park, you will be in very great danger indeed!"

"Now *that* is true," said Elizabeth feelingly. "She is still furious with me over refusing Mr. Collins. Perhaps this might restore me to her good graces." Clearly she had no choice but to give in graciously when Charlotte, Lady Matlock, Lady Frederica, and Mr. Darcy had all made up their minds. And it would save her reams of lectures from Mr. Collins about her duty to attend to the whims of her betters. Suddenly the journey sounded like the lesser of two evils.

Charlotte could apparently read her expression. "It is a pity you must leave so quickly. I will miss you, but I hope you will write me with word of all your adventures."

Elizabeth made a face. "I suppose I must. When Colonel Fitzwilliam kills Sir Anthony, you will be the first I shall tell."

Charlotte laughed. "Unless I miss my guess, that is why the Countess wants you to join them, in the hope the gentlemen will show more restraint in the presence of a lady they are unrelated to."

"That would take a miracle, I believe!"

That evening, Lady Matlock requested her daughter's presence in her private sitting room and gestured Frederica to a chair. "So, you are determined to marry Sir Anthony, yet seem disinclined to be his wife."

Frederica squirmed. "I do not wish to live the rest of my life as the lady he jilted, especially when his reasoning was so foolish. He even claims he was in love with me, as if I were likely to believe that!"

"But let us suppose he somehow survives this expedition. What will you do then?"

Her daughter shrugged. "I will address that if it comes to pass. But I am delighted Miss Bennet will be joining us. Darcy will be very happy."

"Darcy? Why should he care? And do not suppose for a moment that changing the subject will make me forget it, young lady."

Frederica rolled her eyes. "Have you not noticed? Darcy is fascinated by her. I believe he is in love, but she thinks he dislikes her. This way they will have an opportunity for further acquaintance."

Lady Matlock tapped her fingers on the chair arm. "Miss Bennet and Darcy? I cannot see him condescending to marry so far beneath him. No, I wish to know Miss Bennet better for my own reasons. She may be just what your brother Jasper needs."

"Jasper? He has not even met her!"

With a serene smile, her mother said, "Jasper needs a very special wife, one who can not only stand up to him, but manage him with wit and humor so he does not realize he is being managed. Miss Bennet seems to possess a rare talent for that."

Frederica wound her finger in one of her ringlets. "Hmm. I suppose that is true."

Chapter Eight

Early the following morning, Elizabeth seated herself between Lady Matlock and a yawning Lady Frederica in the elegant Matlock carriage. Unfortunately, that also meant she faced Mr. Darcy, who seemed to have decided it would be preferable to give Colonel Fitzwilliam the window seat rather than to allow him to sit beside Sir Anthony. It was going to be a long trip indeed.

"I am sorry it is such a squeeze, Miss Bennet," said Lady Matlock.

There was easily a hand of space between each of the ladies, far more than any carriage she had ridden in. "I assure you, I am perfectly comfortable, your ladyship." Apart from enduring the stares of Mr. Darcy, Colonel Fitzwilliam's glowering visage, and Lady Frederica's scowls. At least Sir Anthony seemed resigned to his position, but he was seated as far from Lady Frederica as possible, no doubt Lady Matlock's doing.

Darcy knocked on the roof of the carriage and it swayed into motion. At least the ride would be comfortable. Even Nelly, who had become ill after a short time in a carriage, could have been able to tolerate this. Elizabeth blessed the fate which had given her a good stomach for travel.

Once they reached the turnpike road, Lady Matlock asked after the health of Sir Anthony's family, and a tediously polite conversation persisted for some time. Sir Anthony, while participating actively, kept stealing glances towards Lady Frederica's disdainfully averted face.

Taking pity upon him, Elizabeth said, "Is it not an amazing coincidence, Sir Anthony, that we should find ourselves sharing a carriage once more? I never thought to see you again after we reached London that day."

He seized on the subject gratefully. "Nor I! It was quite a shock, although a pleasant one, to discover you at Rosings."

"And to think that day we had no idea we had a mutual acquaintance in Mr. Darcy!"

"Even then?" asked Sir Anthony. "I assumed you had met him for the first time at Rosings."

"No, although I had not previously met Lady Frederica or Colonel Fitzwilliam, Mr. Darcy was already an acquaintance. We met last autumn when he was visiting his friend Mr. Bingley, who had taken a house in the county where I live."

To her shock, Sir Anthony seemed to recoil. "Bingley? Darcy, is Charles Bingley a friend of yours?" he asked disbelievingly.

Darcy frowned. "Indeed he is, and I wonder that you question it. His background is in trade, it is true, but I do not hold it against him. He is an amiable fellow."

"Bingley!" snorted Sir Anthony. "He may be the most amiable man in the world to his friends, but if you set foot in one of his mills, you would change your mind about his value. They are some of the worst in Yorkshire. Do you have any idea how many children have died because Bingley will not invest in safe machinery?"

Darcy's head snapped to face him. "Bingley? Are you sure you do not have the wrong man?"

"I barely know the man, but I am well acquainted with the mills that provide his income!"

Elizabeth held her breath. Was another quarrel about to break out? It was hard to believe Mr. Bingley of all people could be an unkind employer, but it seemed equally unlikely Sir Anthony would make a false accusation. And why was Darcy now looking at her?

Darcy said slowly, "I do not intend to question your word, but it is incongruous. It is possible Bingley knows nothing of the conditions. His father built the mills and took care to keep Bingley far from them to avoid the soil of trade. I cannot recall him mentioning seeing the mills, and he knows nothing of where the money comes from. I have cautioned him about relying solely on his managers, as it would be easy for them to cheat him, but he says they worked for his father before him and he trusts them to know their jobs."

"If it comforts you to believe him innocent, pray do so, but his money is blood-stained and he has the power to stop it."

If Darcy frowned any harder, his chin might shatter. "I shall speak to him and encourage him to investigate the conditions."

Sir Anthony narrowed his eyes. "It cannot hurt." His tone showed he did not think it likely to help, either.

Colonel Fitzwilliam leaned forward. "You need not worry. He will listen to Darcy. He always does, and he owes Darcy a great deal."

"Oh! yes," said Elizabeth drily. "Mr. Darcy is uncommonly kind to Mr. Bingley, and takes a prodigious deal of care of him."

"Care of him! Yes, I really believe Darcy does take care of him in those points where he most wants care," said the colonel. "I have reason to think Bingley very much indebted to him. Darcy lately saved him from the inconveniences of a most disadvantageous marriage, so I am certain he will take his advice seriously."

Elizabeth stiffened. She did not dare to look at Darcy. "I suppose Mr. Darcy must have had good reasons for his interference, or at least ones he thought to be good."

The colonel glanced at Darcy. "I understood that there were some very strong objections against the lady."

Darcy said icily, "I also told you it was a circumstance I would not wish to be generally known, because if it were to get round to the lady's family, it would be an unpleasant thing."

Colonel Fitzwilliam made him as much of a bow as sitting in a carriage could permit. "My apologies. You are, of course, right. I spoke in the heat of the moment, and knowing we were among family."

"Not all family," said Elizabeth sharply. "And I do not see what right Mr. Darcy had to decide on the propriety of his friend's inclination, or why, upon his own judgment alone, he was to determine and direct in what manner that friend was to be happy."

The colonel looked surprised. "Would it be the act of a friend to allow him to make a mistake of such proportions by saying nothing?"

Elizabeth struggled to calm herself, and managed a light shrugging of her shoulders. "Perhaps not, but my sympathies would lie with the lady, who may now be dealing with a broken heart, and also with the scorn and pity of all her friends and neighbors for failing to secure the gentleman's affections." Too late she noticed Lady Frederica's hands folding into white-knuckled fists.

Sir Anthony had not missed it either. "You are quite correct, Miss Bennet. I have only lately learned it is a fault of selfish gentlemen to underestimate the consequences to a lady, especially when she has fewer resources to avoid the situation. I deeply regret my own mistakes in that regard, and I can only hope the lady whom Bingley left behind will be more fortunate."

Biting her lip, Elizabeth said, "My apologies, Sir Anthony. My tongue ran ahead of my thoughts, and I assure you I was referring to no other situation than that of Mr. Bingley." But why was she apologizing? It was true enough of his situation.

Lady Frederica, her face pale, ostentatiously turned to gaze out the window.

Unable to take refuge in the same action from the middle of the seat, Elizabeth could only turn her furious glare on Mr. Darcy. Surprisingly, he did not avoid her eyes, though she could easily perceive a blush even in the poor light of the carriage. "In this particular case, I observed no symptom of peculiar regard in the lady's expression when she was with Bingley, and therefore judged her to be indifferent to anything but the pecuniary advantages of the match. If she truly cared for him as he did for her, then perhaps I made an error."

Lady Matlock said firmly, "Does anyone else find the dust of the road to be affecting their eyes? Fortunately, we are almost to London. I believe we would all benefit from the chance to escape the carriage."

Hearing the implied rebuke, Elizabeth bit back the reply she would have liked to make, and instead nodded politely.

By the time they reached Matlock House, Elizabeth was nearly shaking with repressed fury. As soon as she could, she took refuge in the retiring room, the one place she could be sure Mr. Darcy would not follow her. Lady

Frederica joined her several minutes later. "Are you quite well, Elizabeth?"

Elizabeth tried to smile. If only she could have some time alone! She had not had a moment to herself since leaving Kent, and no matter how spacious and comfortable the Matlock coach might be, she was still trapped in it with five other people, one of whom she detested.

To think she had begun to believe better of Mr. Darcy after hearing his family's praise of him! She should have listened to her first instinct. Proud, disagreeable man! How dare he separate Mr. Bingley from Jane, the dearest woman who ever lived? By what right did he interfere in Mr. Bingley's choice? But the great Mr. Darcy must always know best! And then to boast of the success of his efforts to his cousin! How he must have congratulated himself on creating Jane's misery.

Elizabeth forced a smile. "Quite well, just in search of a little quiet."

"Is something the matter?"

Elizabeth tried to unclench her hands. There was little point in attempting to deny something was troubling her. "I was wondering why Mr. Darcy thinks it is his place to interfere in Mr. Bingley's private affairs."

"He was only attempting to prevent him from making a mistake he would regret, as any friend would do." Lady Frederica suddenly frowned. "But you were in the right as well. I would have thought nothing of his

153

story, had you not mentioned the effects on the lady. I know full well what a painful position it is, yet initially I disregarded the fact that another woman was being injured as I was. Why is that?"

"You saw it from Darcy's point of view and accepted his assumptions. It is natural enough." Had she herself not known Jane, would she have thought there was nothing amiss with Darcy's actions? No, that was ridiculous! Lady Frederica was swayed by her fondness for her cousin, nothing more.

"I suppose so," Lady Frederica sounded discontented.

But perhaps this was a moment when she might find a chink in Lady Frederica's armor. "Do you suppose Sir Anthony also felt he was doing the proper thing?"

Lady Frederica's mouth twisted. "How can you say that? How could he have failed to realize I would be hurt by his defection? Did he think I had no feelings, like a china doll?"

"I agree; he was quite wrong not to consider the effect on you. But at least he has admitted to his failing. Darcy sees nothing wrong with what he did." She practically spat out the last words.

"Sir Anthony says the proper words, it is true, but does he mean it? He has already shown himself to be an accomplished liar who tells everyone what he thinks they wish to hear."

Elizabeth winced at the unfair description. "Do you intend never to forgive him, then? I do not think you can depend on his being hanged, especially now that he will have even more powerful connections."

Lady Frederica bit her lip. "Someday, I suppose. When I have learned not to care so much." Her voice cracked a little.

"You do not believe he cares about you? He seems happy to marry you."

"If he cared about me, would he not have considered my position when he jilted me? Why did he not tell me the truth about himself? No, he did not care, nor did he trust me."

Elizabeth chose her words carefully. "Your points are well taken, but you did not tell him about your radical activities either."

She sniffed. "I did not tell him about my weekly sewing society meeting. He did not tell me about his most abiding passion, the true love of his life, the cause he risks everything for. They are both omissions, but not the same." Her eyes were suspiciously shiny.

"True," said Elizabeth soothingly. It would not do to have Lady Frederica burst into tears just because she herself wanted to avoid the subject of Mr. Darcy. "Sometimes it is easy to believe men think of nothing but themselves and their own pleasures." And Mr. Darcy was the worst of them.

Naturally, as soon as Elizabeth left the retiring room, she found Mr. Darcy lying in wait for her in the entry hall. Since there was obviously no way to escape speaking to him, she paused when he spoke her name. "Yes?" she said.

Mr. Darcy said quietly, "Regarding the earlier discussion, I am sorry the discovery of my actions was so painful for you."

Just when she thought she could get no angrier! She straightened slowly, cold fury filling her. "For me? You are sorry for hurting me?" she said icily.

"Yes, more sorry than I can tell you. I would never wish for you to be hurt."

"But not sorry for what you did?"

"What I did was done with the best intentions. If you are correct about your sister's sentiments..."

"If I am correct? If my hours of conversation with Jane, the nights of hearing her cry herself to sleep, give me a more accurate impression than your few minutes of observation of her at a public event? How highly you must rate your perceptive powers, sir!" She knew she should stop, that she was saying things she would later regret, but a demon of anger had taken possession of her.

"I defer to your greater knowledge of your sister, but it is true my perceptions rarely fail me. "

His perceptions? If he had the slightest bit of perceptiveness, why was he trying to speak to her, when it

156

should be obvious she was utterly furious with him? "Your insight astonishes me." Her voice dripped sarcasm.

He stiffened. "You wish me to say something I do not believe to be true? Disguise of every sort is my abhorrence."

"What I wish is for you to stop thinking of how this reflects on yourself and on me, and instead think of what you did to poor Jane. She was devastated when Bingley abandoned her without a word. She is still..." Elizabeth broke off, tears filling her eyes. Jane had come so close to paying the ultimate price for the heartbreak he had caused.

"I am sorry for her pain. I truly did believe her to be indifferent to him."

"And that it would be a disgrace for your friend to ally himself to my family – is that not the defense you made? Well, he is free of that burden now, and what does it matter that my dearest sister, the kindest, loveliest person in the world, tried to take her own life when she heard he was in love with another woman?" Her voice trembled.

Darcy's face paled. "I did not know. And why does she think he is in love? There have been no women in Bingley's life since we left Netherfield."

"Then that was another fiction, this time portrayed by Miss Bingley who told her all the details of the purported love affair. How I wish none of you had ever come to Hertfordshire!"

His brows drew together, and if she had not known better, she might have thought he was hurt. He reached out a hand towards her.

Why did she suddenly have an urge to take it? Was it to comfort him – or herself?

A maid approached her. "Miss Bennet, shall I show you to your room?"

Elizabeth wrenched her eyes away from Mr. Darcy. "Yes, if you please." As she followed the maid to the curved staircase, a hollow feeling seemed to grow inside her. What had she done?

Elizabeth paced the generous dimensions of Lady Frederica's room. "I was dubious about the wisdom of this trip from the beginning, and now I am certain of it. It was very gracious of you to invite me, but I simply cannot continue."

"Why not?"

No one else would have asked her so direct a question. Why could Lady Frederica not simply accept her decision? "The situation is too uncomfortable. You are aware Mr. Darcy and I do not get on together, and it seems to be worsening rather than improving. With all the other stresses of this journey, you do not need our quarreling on top of everything else, and I assure you, should I continue, a quarrel is inevitable. I do not wish to lose my temper with him, for I say the most abominable things when I do. I came very close to that a few minutes ago."

"That I should like to see! Much as I love Darcy, it would do him good to have someone read him the Riot Act. No one ever crosses him, you know, and it is not good for him."

"Perhaps, but he will have to take his medicine from another hand. I have no wish to be the first to give it to him."

Lady Frederica swung her legs onto the bed and propped a bolster behind her. "I suppose I can understand that, and it is true my family is not pleasant company at the moment, but selfishly I wish so much you would reconsider. I cannot tell you how much easier your presence makes me. I fear what might happen if your restraining presence is absent."

Elizabeth laughed. "Somehow I have perfect faith in your mother's ability to restrain even the most disruptive gentlemen."

"Oh, Mama," she said dismissively. "Richard will not attend to her and neither will Darcy if Richard does not."

"You are shattering my illusions about aristocratic families!"

Suddenly serious, Lady Frederica grabbed her hand. "For my sake, then. I do not wish to be alone with Sir Anthony without an ally."

"Perhaps, then, insisting on marrying him is not your wisest course! Or perhaps *you* should remain in London rather than journey with him to Sheffield."

"And have them think me afraid? Never! But I beg you to reconsider. At least stay with me through tomorrow to stand up with me, and perhaps things will look different in the morning."

Elizabeth thought it highly unlikely. "If you wish. I will pay a call to my aunt and uncle tonight and take counsel with them." Not that she intended to allow them to change her mind, but if she could tell Lady Frederica her family opposed the journey, perhaps she would accept her decision.

Lady Frederica was too clever for her, though, or perhaps too stubborn. When the footman informed Elizabeth the hackney to take her to Gracechurch Street had arrived, she found Lady Frederica waiting by the door, bonnet and gloves already on.

"I hope you will not mind if I join you. I would so like to meet your family."

Elizabeth bit back the hasty words which longed to escape her mouth. "You are welcome, of course, though I cannot guarantee our reception. It is late in the day for social calling, and it is not the sort of society you are accustomed to."

"Oh, but you are family, and I am your friend. Besides, your uncle should have the opportunity to meet at least one of your proposed travel companions."

Lady Frederica chattered all the way to Gracechurch Street. To her credit, she did not seem at all troubled by the less than fashionable neighborhood. At least in this she was quite different from her cousin. No doubt Mr. Darcy would never deign to dirty his boots on the pavement of Cheapside!

At the Gardiner house, Elizabeth handed her bonnet to the surprised looking manservant who opened the door. He asked, "Are you here to stay, miss?"

"No, just calling this time, Wilson. A very late call, but I assume my aunt will forgive me."

"Of course, Miss Lizzy. She already has a caller and is in the sitting room." He squinted at the card Lady Frederica proffered to him, and then gestured down the passageway.

Odd. Who else would call so late in the day?

Wilson opened the sitting room door. "Miss Elizabeth Bennet and Lady Frederica Fitzwilliam."

Before Elizabeth was halfway through the door, Jane was embracing her. "Lizzy! What a lovely surprise!"

Jane was oddly flushed as Elizabeth presented her to Lady Frederica. "A pleasure indeed, Lady Frederica. May I introduce you to my aunt, Mrs. Gardiner, and our friend Mr. Bingley?"

Frozen in place, Elizabeth could only stare. What in heaven's name was Bingley doing there? Had he somehow learned of Jane's presence in London and gone behind Darcy's back to see her?

Lady Frederica said, "It is a pleasure to make your acquaintance, Miss Bennet, Mrs. Gardiner. Mr. Bingley, it is lovely to see you again."

Mrs. Gardiner clapped her hands together. "So you are already friends! How lovely. Wilson, tea for two more, if you please."

Elizabeth said pointedly, "It is quite a surprise to see you here, Mr. Bingley, but a pleasure, of course."

Jane rested her hand on Elizabeth's arm. "Is it not delightful? Did you know, Lizzy, that Mr. Bingley had no notion of my presence in London until today?"

Bingley laughed. "Indeed, I knew nothing of it until Darcy told me! My sisters will be in for a lecture when I return home. No doubt the matter simply slipped their minds, but I do wish they had told me of your call. How much time I have wasted!" He smiled fondly at Jane.

Jane lowered her eyes. "I was ill for much of the time."

"Then I missed the opportunity to offer whatever assistance I might."

Mrs. Gardiner said kindly, "You could be of great use right now, Mr. Bingley, by convincing my niece to return to her chair. She should not tire herself by standing so long."

"Of course!" Mr. Bingley jumped to his feet with alacrity and offered his arm to Jane. He led her to a loveseat, then fussed over arranging her shawl before sitting beside her. Yes, he certainly was still enamored of her.

Mrs. Gardiner patted the arm of the chair beside her. "Come, Lizzy, and tell me how you come to be in London. We thought you still in Kent."

"It is something of a long story and one I do not completely understand myself! But I am traveling with Lady Frederica and her family."

Lady Frederica stepped in to explain their acquaintance at Rosings and how she had begged Elizabeth to join her on their journey, somehow managing to avoid any reference to the reason for their trip. It was unfortunate; the Gardiners would be much more likely to object to her plans if they realized the danger involved. Perhaps she would be able to speak to her aunt alone later.

It was not to be. Mrs. Gardiner, having discovered Lady Frederica was from her beloved Derbyshire, was soon fully engaged in discussions of her favorite places in that county. "Lizzy, you will have a chance to see some of these sights on our trip to the lakes this summer. We will be stopping in Lambton to visit some of my old friends."

"In fact," said Lady Frederica before Elizabeth could speak, "she may see them somewhat sooner than that. We have not yet had the opportunity to tell you that our journey is to Matlock via Sheffield. We hoped Elizabeth might stay with us until your journey, and we would like to invite you and your husband to be our guests on your travels."

Mrs. Gardiner seemed lost for words for a moment. "How very kind of you, your ladyship! I must speak to my husband, of course, but I am beyond honored!"

Mr. Gardiner's voice boomed from the doorway. "What must you consult me about, my dear?" His eyes darted around the crowded drawing room. "Lizzy, I thought you were in Kent!" He did not sound particularly pleased.

Elizabeth gave him a look of appeal. Although her uncle was fond of company, it was well known he preferred to come home to a quiet house. Would his innate good manners prevail?

Mrs. Gardiner fluttered over to him and took his arm, gracefully performing the introductions and explaining Lady Frederica's invitation. If Mr. Gardiner was taken aback to find the long-awaited Mr. Bingley *and* an Earl's daughter in his sitting room at an unfashionable hour, he covered it well.

Mr. Gardiner eyed Mr. Bingley, seated close to Jane, then turned to Lady Frederica. "I thank you for your generous offer. If our travel dates do not prove inconvenient for you, we would be honored to accept."

Elizabeth opened her mouth to protest, but was silenced by the sharp pressure of her aunt's slipper upon her toes.

"Excellent!" cried Lady Frederica, ignoring the disgruntled look Elizabeth sent in her direction. How neatly Lady Frederica had trapped her! She could hardly refuse to continue the journey now. Colonel Fitzwilliam had been correct when he said his sister liked to have her own way.

Mrs. Gardiner said, "Would you care to dine with us this evening? We would be delighted to have you join us."

Lady Frederica shook her head. "I wish we could, but my mother expects us at Matlock House, and we will be starting north early tomorrow."

"You are leaving London so soon?" Jane asked.

Elizabeth said carefully, "Lady Matlock set the plans."

"That is unfortunate," said Mrs. Gardiner. "What about you, Mr. Bingley? Would *you* care to dine with us?"

Mr. Bingley beamed at Jane. "I would be delighted!"

Mrs. Gardiner looked thoughtful. "Lizzy, if you must leave soon, perhaps you would like to say hello to the children?"

Elizabeth assented, although she would much rather have spent the time with Jane. But interrupting Mr. Bingley's monopolization of her sister would not be helpful, so she followed her aunt out of the sitting room. She was unsurprised when Mrs. Gardiner led her to the study rather than the nursery. "No children?" she asked.

Her aunt closed the door behind her. "It was but an excuse to speak to you privately. You did not look best pleased when your uncle accepted that invitation."

Elizabeth's frustration bubbled over. "It does not appear my opinion mattered in the least! He did not even look at me before accepting. I did not wish to go on this journey in the first place, and have been searching for an excuse to avoid it!"

Mrs. Gardiner winced. "I am so sorry, my dear. I hope they have not been behaving inappropriately to you."

"No more than I have been! Mr. Darcy has been traveling with us and I am tired of his insults to my family, and everyone else is quarreling with one another as well. It is far from pleasant company. But none of the gentlemen have attempted to take liberties, if that is what you are asking."

"None of them? How many gentlemen are there?" Mrs. Gardiner sounded slightly scandalized.

Elizabeth curled her lip. "Three. Mr. Darcy, Lady Frederica's brother, and her... suitor, Sir Anthony Duxbury. Lady Matlock and I try to keep the peace between them.

Mrs. Gardiner frowned. "That does not sound pleasant." She looked down at the rug, and then seemed to come to a decision. "Lizzy, may I be frank with you?"

"Of course!"

"Your uncle's business is not doing well. Not well at all. Last year he visited the mills where the cloth he sells is made. The working conditions in one mill he toured were so bad that he refused to buy from them again unless improvements were made. The owner had him thrown out and told other mill owners he was interfering, so they refused to sell to him as well. Your uncle has been getting by with his imports and products of the one mill which will still work with him, but he no longer has the range of fabrics buyers want, and now one of the ships he invested in has been taken by the French. An opportunity for him to connect with Lord Matlock is a gift straight from heaven. With just a word Lord Matlock could open the Indian markets to him, and his opinion carries great weight in the manufactories of the North. They would not dare to refuse to sell to Lord Matlock's friend."

Her uncle had certainly not been his usual jolly self during her earlier visit, but she had attributed it to worry over Jane's illness. "I had no idea it was so bad."

"We have tried to keep it quiet. If word got out, other merchants would stop giving us credit. We cannot afford that."

Elizabeth chewed her lip. "We are supposed to meet Lord Matlock in Sheffield. I will do whatever I can to make a good impression on him." She smiled suddenly. "I will even endeavor not to quarrel with Mr. Darcy!"

"I thank you from the bottom of my heart. I am sorry it will be distasteful for you, and I would not ask it of you if the stakes were not so high."

Elizabeth embraced her aunt. "I am certain I will enjoy it perfectly well now knowing that I am doing something helpful to you, no matter how small. Thank you for trusting me with this."

As she said her farewells, Elizabeth longed for silence to consider her aunt's revelations, but Lady Frederica, with her typical forthrightness, did not allow a moment to pass once the carriage started towards Matlock House before embarking on her own questions. "So, I take it your sister was the one Darcy detached Bingley from? How foolish of him! Anyone can see she is perfect for Bingley. I do not know what Darcy could have been thinking."

Elizabeth leaned her head back against the seat. If only the carriage would hurry so she might escape to her room! "Perhaps he had other plans for Mr. Bingley."

"Yet he must have gone straight to him today and told him of her presence, so he had to have changed his mind after our discussion."

Elizabeth gave her an odd look, then recalled Lady Frederica was unaware of the further words she had exchanged with Darcy on the subject. "Perhaps."

"At least that need not stand in the way of your traveling with us now," pronounced Lady Frederica, as if her opinion settled the matter.

"As if I could have changed my mind once you invited my aunt and uncle to Matlock!"

"Oh, I am sorry! Did you still object, then?"

Of course Lady Frederica would not have thought of whether Elizabeth's wishes should come first, just like her cousin Mr. Darcy. "I am still not looking forward to traveling in close company with Mr. Darcy. He irritates me excessively, even if he did attempt to repair this one piece of damage he caused."

Lady Frederica shifted on the bench to face Elizabeth. "He irritates you excessively? What about Jasper?"

Jasper? The precious stone? How could she possibly be irritated by that? Sometimes Lady Frederica was utterly baffling. "I am not in the habit of being irritated by precious stones, and I find jasperware quite attractive."

Lady Frederica gave a peal of laughter. "Oh, you are so droll! I refer to my brother Jasper, of course!"

"Your brother? Oh, pardon me! How could I be irritated by him? We have only just met." She could barely call his face to mind apart from a ready smile, but she had been so angry with Darcy at the time of their introduction that she had hardly noticed Mr. Jasper Fitzwilliam. "Why? Should I be irritated by him?"

"No, I was just wondering." Lady Frederica subsided.

To Elizabeth's great relief, Mr. Darcy did not make an appearance at dinner at Matlock House. Not wishing to press her luck, she pleaded fatigue as soon as the ladies withdrew and went to the chamber prepared for her.

She rid herself of the maid as soon as she could and sank back into the luxuriously soft bed with its silk damask counterpane. What a contrast to her simple bed at Longbourn! Not even her mother's bed approached this degree of luxury, and this was but a guest room. What would it be like to grow up expecting every comfort in the world and liveried servants ready to jump to her bidding? If the result was being proud and disagreeable like Mr. Darcy, it was not worth the price, but Lady Matlock and Sir Anthony were perfectly amiable and never made her feel deficient in any way.

How was she to face Mr. Darcy again? She had been so abominably rude to him, and if his previous actions had deserved her antipathy, it did not excuse her poor manners. And now he had gone out of his way to right the wrong he had committed. Would he expect her to be overflowing with gratitude for his generosity and condescension? She gritted her teeth.

But when Mr. Darcy returned to Matlock House the following morning, he said nothing to her about the previous day and behaved in his usual manner. Could it be he did not plan to claim credit for what he had done?

Chapter Nine

Darcy arrived at Matlock House after breakfast, just in time for the impromptu wedding. The sitting room had been lavishly decorated with flowers to mark the occasion. "Lovely!" cried Lady Matlock, as if this were an ordinary wedding.

Frederica said tersely, "Let us get on with it."

"Very well," said her mother. "Come, Miss Bennet, pray stand next to my daughter, and Darcy, you may stand up with Duxbury."

Richard snorted but said nothing. Only Duxbury looked comfortable with the situation. Darcy wondered what he was thinking. He had said nothing to Darcy at Rosings except that if Frederica wished him to marry her, he was content to do so. Of course, Richard's glares might have had something to do with that willingness, but Darcy rather thought Duxbury to be sincere. But he could not be sure; clearly Duxbury was a skilled actor to have hidden so much from the world.

Darcy could not keep his eyes from Elizabeth standing across from him. Even after their quarrel the previous day, her liveliness shone through, and the passage of expressions over her face enchanted him. She seemed amused by the proceedings. Perhaps she would cast that warm look on him when she discovered he had confessed her sister's whereabouts to Bingley.

He barely heard the familiar words of the wedding ceremony rolling past him. Watching Elizabeth was much more interesting. Then the curate droned, "Wilt thou love her, comfort her, honor and keep her, in sickness and in health?" The words shot through Darcy like a lance, echoing in his ears. Yes! That was what he wanted. Not just to have the pleasure of resting his eyes on Elizabeth or to imagine running his hands along her lithe body, but to love her, comfort her, honor and keep her. As long as they both did live.

The realization shook him down to his boots. Silently loving Elizabeth Bennet was one thing, but to *marry* her? He could not do it. Her station was too far beneath his, her portion almost non-existent. It would be betraying his duty to his family. It was impossible.

Duxbury slid the ring onto Frederica's finger. It was done. His little cousin was married to his old friend, no matter how estranged they might be.

Elizabeth's fine eyes met his, and in that moment he knew the truth. He would marry Elizabeth Bennet.

After the ceremony, Lady Matlock informed them the coach would leave in half an hour, giving them just enough time for refreshments.

"Would it not be simpler to pass the night here and start tomorrow?" Elizabeth asked Colonel Fitzwilliam quietly.

He glanced towards his mother with narrowed eyes. "No doubt she has her reasons. She always does. At a guess, she does not want whatever scene occurs tonight between Freddie and her new husband to be played out in front of the servants."

Elizabeth glanced at Lady Frederica, who was speaking to Mr. Darcy and pointedly ignoring Sir Anthony. "Perhaps it will not be difficult. I had hoped..."

He shook his head. "She does not forgive easily, particularly when someone has embarrassed her."

Presumably he knew his sister better than she did, but Lady Frederica had not struck her as unforgiving. She wondered if the presence of so much of her family was feeding the new bride's anger. "It will make for an interesting journey."

The colonel threw back his head and laughed. "That is one way to describe it! I am glad you are with us; it is probably the only reason any of us is showing any restraint!"

Elizabeth could not help herself. "This is restraint?" she said archly.

"Oh, yes. You have seen nothing of the infamous Fitzwilliam frankness yet. We are all on good behavior at present."

She peeked up at him through her eyelashes. "Tell me, will it be necessary to call out the militia to ensure my safety when you *are* frank?"

"No, but some might think it a good idea!"

When they were ready to leave and Elizabeth approached the coach, Mr. Darcy hurried forward to offer her his hand. Startled, she glanced up at him and found herself captivated by the unexpectedly intense look in his dark eyes. Handing her in was supposed to be a mere courtesy, but this was something more. Was he attempting to tell her something? Her skin tingled as if a light breeze was running down her arms. Did he know she had discovered what he had done?

As she somehow managed to break his gaze and stepped into the carriage, her senses were assailed by the scent of roses. Her foot slipped on something, causing her to drop onto the bench between Lady Frederica and Lady Matlock with a graceless thump.

Lady Frederica chuckled. "You need to be more careful when you walk on rose petals."

"Rose petals?" Her eyes adjusting to the dimness inside the coach, Elizabeth noticed rose petals everywhere — sprinkled over the opposite bench and covering the floor. No doubt she was sitting on them as well.

Lady Frederica shrugged. "Apparently the servants thought it only suitable for a newlywed couple."

Lady Matlock said, "Rightly so. It is their duty to think of such things."

Elizabeth shook her head at the extravagance. "Roses in April? Where did they find so many?"

"Hothouses." Lady Frederica sounded annoyed.

Sir Anthony entered the coach next, his hat in his hand. Quickly Elizabeth said, "Beware of slippery rose petals."

He cocked an eyebrow at her. "Thank *you* for warning me, Miss Elizabeth."

Lady Frederica huffed and turned her face away.

Sir Anthony sat across from Lady Matlock. "Richard has decided to ride with Jasper, and they will meet us at the inn."

"Lucky Jasper," muttered Lady Frederica, earning a cool look from her mother.

The carriage darkened as Darcy's form filled the doorway. His legs brushed against her knees as he took his seat, and suddenly Elizabeth's pulses began to race. What was wrong with her? Suddenly the spacious coach seemed far too small.

The hours of the journey dragged on slowly. The heavy scent of roses gradually receded, or perhaps she had merely become accustomed to it. Her neck ached from being turned to the side; appearing to gaze out the window was her only way to avoid Mr. Darcy's eyes, which seemed constantly fixed on her. She had given up the attempt to guess what he was thinking.

Elizabeth was relieved when the carriage pulled up to a coaching inn just before dusk. Although there had been no conflicts since leaving London, there had also been little conversation to distract her from Mr. Darcy's constant gaze on her. She felt as if she had spent the entire afternoon blushing.

She could hardly wait to dress for dinner, simply because it would give her a few minutes alone. But before she even had an opportunity to be shown to her room, Lady Frederica announced to Sir Anthony, "I will be sharing Miss Bennet's room tonight."

"As you wish," he said calmly. He pulled out the book he had been reading in the coach and sat down with it.

Lady Matlock was not as unperturbed. "Nonsense. A few hours ago you made vows before God, and you will honor them. I will tolerate no obstinance on this point."

As Lady Frederica looked ready to explode, Elizabeth said quickly, "I have such a desire for a walk after sitting so long and I have never been to Peterborough before. Mr. Darcy, might I impose upon you to accompany me on a brief stroll around the square?" He might be annoyed by her presumptuous behavior, but it would be worth it for the chance to escape the impending quarrel.

"I would be honored to escort you, Miss Elizabeth." He did not even sound ironic; perhaps he wished to escape as well.

"I will join you," announced Lady Frederica.

Lady Matlock said placidly, "Not today. I require your company, Frederica."

Sir Anthony did not look up from his book.

Elizabeth retied the bonnet she had only just removed and joined Mr. Darcy, who held the door open for her. She took a deep breath of air as she stepped outside. Peterborough was not a large city such as London, but still soot hung heavily in the air. "Thank you for accompanying me. I thought it best to absent myself from the discussion, but I am sorry for having imposed upon you in order to do so."

He offered her his arm. "It is my distinct pleasure, Miss Elizabeth, as you well know."

She cast a skeptical glance at him as they began to walk, but forbore from saying she knew nothing of the sort. Gathering her courage, she said, "I must apologize for my harsh words to you yesterday. Although we disagreed, my behavior was quite inappropriate."

"You did nothing but speak your mind, and your loyalty to your sister is admirable. I was impressed by it when she was ill at Netherfield, and again yesterday."

Was he not going to claim credit for bringing Bingley back to Jane? "I visited Jane last night at my uncle's house, and was surprised to discover Mr. Bingley there. I imagine I have you to thank for that."

He seemed suddenly interested in something across the square. "I also saw Bingley yesterday, but you owe me no thanks for doing my duty to my friend. When you told me I had been mistaken about your sister's sentiments, I felt an obligation to inform him about my error at once."

Why could the foolish man not simply accept her thanks? Was it beneath his pride to do so? Well, she would thank him anyway. "Nonetheless, many men would not have done so, and certainly not with such promptness at a time when you were preparing for a long journey. A letter would have sufficed."

"Some things are best said face to face. I had meant to speak to him about your sister earlier, after we met at the circulating library that day, but he was out of town and I did not want to put it in a letter. By the time he returned, I was already at Rosings." His voice turned low and intimate. "And waiting any longer was not an option. I could not bear to know you were in pain and I was the cause."

A hollow seemed to form in the pit of her stomach. Could he really care what she thought of him? It was beyond belief. Could he be mocking her? It was too much at the end of a long, tiring day. She could not even think how to respond.

He took advantage of her silence to continue. "I have struggled against my own inclination for so long, but no more. I can no longer deny how ardently I admire and love you. Your low connections, the improper behavior of your family, the degradation to my family name — none of it matters. I must have you by my side. I beg of you to do me the honor of accepting my hand in marriage."

Elizabeth's mouth dropped open. Was she hearing correctly? She snatched her hand from his arm. "Mr. Darcy, my behavior has been far from admirable, but that is no reason to mock me with pretended admiration."

Darcy appeared stunned. "Pretended admiration? I assure you, Elizabeth, I have never been more in earnest!" The intensity had returned to his eyes.

She swallowed hard. Surely he could not mean it! But he must, since no matter how proud and disagreeable he might be, it was not his way to toy with people. Struggling for words, she said, "In such circumstances, it is appropriate for me to express my gratitude for your sentiments. I am grateful, but I am convinced we would not suit, and that I should make you at least as unhappy as you would make me. I am sorry for any pain this may cause you, and I hope averting the degradation such a match would bring you will offer you quick consolation." She sounded like a babbling idiot.

He blanched. "Am I permitted to ask why, with such little attempt at civility, I am refused? Is it because of your sister?"

How dare he question her after insulting her family? Her temper made her reckless. "In part, though I now understand you meant no harm. Even so, by your own admission, your temper is resentful and you are proud and disdainful. You insulted me at our first meeting. You disapprove of everything about me. My family is a disgrace in your eyes, not that the behavior of your aunt, Lady Catherine, is any better. But most of all, I have no desire to be a degradation to you or anyone else. Pray tell me, then, why do you think I should accept you?"

He stared at her, his expression unreadable. He began to speak, but his words were drowned out by hoofbeats on the cobblestones.

"Ho, is that you, Darcy?" Colonel Fitzwilliam's rumbling voice was accompanied by a laugh as he neatly dismounted. "Miss Elizabeth." Behind him his brother Jasper remained astride. "We have just arrived. I assume that is the inn yonder?" He gestured across the square.

"The very one." Darcy's voice was hollow.

Elizabeth said quickly, "We are just returning there, and will walk with you." Anything to avoid being alone with Mr. Darcy!

How dare she? How *dare* she? First Elizabeth went out of her way to arrange to be alone with him, then broached personal matters by bringing up his visit to Bingley. Then when he responded to these overtures by declaring himself, she pretended shock and insulted him beyond measure. Proud? Of course he was proud, and for good reason. Disdainful? Only when circumstances merited. He could concede her point about Lady Catherine's manners, but the rest of his family was presentable, unlike hers!

She disliked him. Detested him, perhaps.

A knife, stabbed into his gut and twisted, would not have caused such agony, and would have had the benefit of ending his life. Instead he had to continue on, taking one step after another as if he were not in an agonizing hell of pain.

And such familiar pain. How often had it happened, that he had unwittingly given offense when he wanted most to earn someone's liking? At school, he had thought the other boys were his friends, and the next moment they would turn on him. He never understood why. He had made a few good friends at Cambridge, it was true, but he had made many more enemies. By the time he had entered the *ton*, he had almost stopped hoping to be accepted. Young women would always fawn over him like a pig to be slaughtered, but it was never because they liked him. And so many men laughed behind their hands at him because he did not take part in their ostentatious debauchery or frequent their gaming hells. None of them liked him, so instead he spent his time with Bingley, who never took offense at anything anyone said. But Bingley was not his social equal.

And now it was Elizabeth.

Elizabeth, whom he had thought to be different from all the others. Elizabeth, who had laughed at the odd things he had said rather than taking offense, but in such a sweet manner that he always wanted more. But apparently she had taken offense. He had thought she was his lifeline, and now he was cast adrift.

He slammed his fist into the heavy oaken bed frame which groaned ominously in response, but he did not care. The shooting pain in his hand and the stinging of his knuckles provided a temporary distraction from the bottomless hole deep within him.

And now he had to dine with her, pretending nothing had happened, that he did not have an aching wound deep inside him, that he did not want to take her by the shoulders and demand that she marry him.

What would she be thinking when she saw him? Would she be gloating over her success in bringing the proud Mr. Darcy low? Would she relish his pain, since her sister had suffered the same because of him?

His shoulders slumped. No, of course she would not. Elizabeth's fundamental kindness would not allow such a vengeful attitude. It was one of the things he loved about her.

Oh, Elizabeth!

After spending an unjustifiable amount of time fiddling with his perfectly tied cravat, he finally went down to the inn's private parlor. Was this how the French aristocrats felt on their way to the guillotine?

From the parlor doorway he could hardly see Elizabeth, half hidden behind the bulk of his cousin Jasper, who was on his feet leaning menacingly across the table at Duxbury.

"I mean it," growled Jasper.

Duxbury unfolded his napkin and placed it on his lap. "I have no doubt of it. Good evening, Darcy."

Jasper did not even glance in Darcy's direction. "Husband or no, if you so much as touch my sister against her will, you will answer to me."

A familiar, lovable gurgle of laughter came from behind him. Jasper swung towards Elizabeth with a mighty scowl. "You find this amusing?"

She nodded, with that familiar arch smile. "I admire your willingness to defend your sister, but I cannot think of anyone less in need of defense. Should Sir Anthony attempt any unwanted advances, she will tongue-lash him into submission; and if that should fail, I have great faith she will have a knife secreted somewhere on her person to, shall we say, make her argument. She is, after all, your sister, and would likely hate to be deprived of the opportunity to exact her own vengeance."

Duxbury lifted his glass of wine in her direction. "Truer words have never been spoken. Fitzwilliam, I would far rather face you at dawn than your sister in a rage. At least I might have a slight chance of surviving unscathed — though only if your pistol misfired, I venture."

Jasper looked back and forth between Elizabeth and Duxbury, and then a reluctant grin split his face. "Under the cat's paw already, Duxbury? I wonder why you were such a fool as to offer for her."

"It was my honor to marry her," said Duxbury calmly. "I like a woman with spirit."

Deeming it safe to fully enter the room now, Darcy took a step forward and bowed, acutely conscious of Elizabeth's presence and determined not to look at her. He succeeded for perhaps half a minute, until his eyes almost involuntarily flickered in her direction. A surge of combined pain and pleasure stabbed him. She did not meet his gaze. Elizabeth, who never backed down from any challenge, was keeping her eyes on the floor.

Lady Matlock's skirts rustled as she stood. "As Richard and Frederica apparently cannot trouble themselves to arrive in a timely manner, we will begin without them." She moved to the head of the table and gestured Duxbury to the foot. "Jasper, please take the seat next to Miss Bennet. Darcy, you are on the other side, in the middle. Ah, Richard, you finally deign to join us! You will be next to me."

184

Arranging seats? Lady Matlock would not ordinarily impose such a thing at an informal family supper. Was it to force Frederica to sit beside her new husband?

Darcy shuffled mechanically to his assigned place. At least he would be across from Elizabeth, not next to her. He did not trust himself to make conversation with her, and failure to speak to her would be far too obvious if he were beside her. No, it was better to sit opposite her. So why did he suddenly want to murder Jasper for pulling out her chair for her?

Frederica waltzed in just as the first covers were laid. Her mother said, "How kind of you to join us."

Frederica's brows drew together and she glanced at the mantelpiece clock. "You said we would dine at half past eight."

"At eight, my dear. You must have misheard. But now you are here, so pray join us."

The narrowing of Frederica's eyes showed her disbelief, but she quietly took the remaining seat between Darcy and Duxbury.

Elizabeth appreciated the distraction of Mr. Jasper's outburst. She had dreaded seeing Darcy again after her churlish refusal of his proposal. What had she been thinking? His offer had taken her completely by surprise, but that was no excuse for losing her temper. Why could she not have calmly said she was honored by his offer, but did not wish to accept? And why, oh why, had he persisted in asking the reason for her refusal, giving her the opportunity to say even worse things? The pained look on his face after she gave her reasons haunted her.

But her self-castigation went beyond that. Her quick temper might have ruined her uncle's chance to restore his business. Lord Matlock would not be likely to offer assistance to her family when his nephew held her in contempt. As well as hurting Darcy, she had failed the Gardiners.

Thankfully, she was seated next to Mr. Jasper at dinner. It would have been intolerable to be beside Mr. Darcy. Mr. Jasper was easy to talk to and told amusing stories, even teasing her about her earlier defense of his sister. Why could it not have been someone like him who chose to propose to her? She could not imagine marrying him, but at least he would have asked politely and accepted her equally polite demurral. But no, Mr. Darcy must be the one.

The hardest part was that in many ways Darcy was exactly the sort of man she would like to marry. Intelligent, well-educated, loyal to his family and friends, and with a strong sense of responsibility. She could even live with his pride, if only he did not look down on her and her family. But she could never marry a man who saw her as his inferior. His affection would only last as long as his desire for her, and then he would hate her almost as much as she would hate herself. It could never work.

And tomorrow she would have to ride in the coach all day with him again, without Mr. Jasper to divert her attention and make her laugh, just an angry, ominous cloud filling the small space. If only Darcy would ride outside as his cousins did! Perhaps he might choose to do so, but she must be prepared for seeing him in any case.

She had to find a way to apologize, for her uncle's sake if not her own. Jane would want her to as well. Mr. Darcy had sent Mr. Bingley to her sister, and she had repaid him with rudeness. But at the same time, she must not make him think she wished for a renewal of his attentions. She doubted he would consider it, but how humiliating it would be to have him think she wished him to!

With sudden resolution, she said to Mr. Jasper, "I hope your long ride today was not too tiring."

"Not at all. It was much faster than riding in the carriage, and the day was pleasant. My only complaint is that I lost a bet with Richard, and now he will never let me forget it."

"A bet? Were you racing?"

From the head of the table, Lady Matlock said, "Of course he was racing. My sons are constitutionally unable to travel together without racing."

Mr. Jasper laughed. "How right you are! But you must admit we did well in only having one short race, rather than racing the entire distance."

Colonel Fitzwilliam drawled, "I seem to recall three races, since you refused to acknowledge my horse was a better one."

With a wide smile that showed flashing white teeth, Mr. Jasper retorted, "I admit your horse may be the better over short distances, but my horse's rider is the better one, as I demonstrated when we exchanged mounts!"

"Pure luck. Your horse would not obey my commands."

Seeing tempers beginning to flare, Elizabeth said quickly, "I can tell both of you found the ride most invigorating! Alas, I cannot claim to be as good a traveler. Long journeys always leave me fatigued and in an abominable humor. It is all I can do to maintain civility, lest I should be most distasteful company!" She looked across the table at Darcy for the first time, experiencing a shock as her eyes met his. He must have been watching her.

Mr. Jasper raised his glass to her. "Miss Elizabeth, I am forced to disagree with you. I cannot imagine ever finding you to be disagreeable."

"Hear, hear," said the colonel. "Occasionally even Jasper is correct."

Elizabeth took a deep breath and forced a teasing smile. "That is only because you have not known me long enough. Mr. Darcy can claim a longer acquaintance with me, and I am sure he can testify that I can be disagreeable at times! I always regret it afterwards, and chastise myself for my quick temper."

If it were possible, Mr. Darcy's gaze grew more intense. A shiver went down her back, and she looked quickly away towards Lady Matlock.

Astonishingly, her ladyship wore a satisfied smile. With a gentle dip of her head, she said, "Miss Bennet, it is a wise person who knows her own failings. I know many who could learn from you. But I venture to guess that by the standards of the Fitzwilliam family, your temper would be considered extraordinarily mild."

Mr. Jasper scowled in a fine display of the Fitzwilliam temper. "Mother, it is difficult to make a good impression on a young lady when you insist on pointing out our faults!"

Elizabeth could not help laughing. "You need not worry, sir. I would have to be the world's greatest fool not to have noticed that you, the colonel, and even your sister possess quick tempers. It is part of your charm."

With another mercurial change, Mr. Jasper beamed at her. "I hope I will always be able to charm you in more traditional ways as well."

Elizabeth heard the scuffle of boots under the table. "I have no doubt of it, sir."

At least that was done. She had expressed her regrets to Mr. Darcy.

Once in her nightclothes, Elizabeth sank down on the bed. What a blessing it was to be alone at last! Even at Longbourn she could manage to escape the clamor at home by taking long walks alone, but today she had not had a moment to herself. Putting on public manners starting in the early morning, cooped up all day in the coach, followed by the nightmarish walk with Mr. Darcy and the long tense dinner was simply too much. She was not even going to think about tomorrow yet, she would revel in the present quiet. Well, the quiet inside her room, at least. She could ignore the boisterous voices rising from the taproom and the clattering of hoofbeats outside.

A rap at the door made her groan. "I am not in need of anything," she called, hoping the maid would leave.

Instead the knocking came again. Heaving a sigh, Elizabeth got out of bed and padded to the door. "Who is it?"

"It is I." Frederica's voice was barely above a whisper, but it was recognizable nonetheless.

So the wedding night had not gone according to plan. Elizabeth unlocked the door to find Frederica in her nightshirt and gown. Silently she held the door open for her friend.

"Thank you for letting me in. He was watching for my safety, or so he said." Frederica's voice shook, but whether from annoyance or fear was not clear.

Elizabeth prudently decided not to point out it was wise and thoughtful of Sir Anthony to do so. "Is there anything I can do to help?"

"Just let me stay here tonight. I cannot sleep in the same room as him."

"Was he...insistent?"

Frederica curled her lip. "Not in the least, which was almost worse. He said he did not wish to force me to do anything I did not want to do, and offered to sleep on the floor. He did not even try to kiss me!"

Elizabeth fought back a smile. "What would you have done if he had?"

"Slapped him, of course! But he was not even interested, despite his words of love." She practically spat the last word. "I should have known better than to believe him."

"Perhaps he did wish to kiss you, but not to be slapped. He is not like your brothers, you know."

"What do you mean?" Frederica demanded.

"Only that you and your brothers resolve your differences by quarreling. That does not seem to be your husband's way." Elizabeth bit her tongue to hold back further words of unwanted advice. "But of course you are welcome to stay here." As if she had any other choice, given that Matlock money was paying for her room.

So much for her chance to be alone.

Despite Elizabeth's trepidation, the next morning proceeded smoothly enough. Mr. Darcy was civil to her, if distant. As she had hoped, he elected to ride rather than travel in the carriage. No one else seemed to notice the change, but that might have been because Frederica and Sir Anthony kept up a heated debate in the coach about a certain passage in *The Rights of Man*. She should have been happy, but instead her eyes were drawn again and again to the empty space that had been his, wondering if he was thinking of her.

In the afternoon, the party met again at Belton House where Lady Matlock had planned a visit to the gardens, providing an opportunity, as she said, both for exercise and the chance to see the pleasure grounds there. The riders had arrived before the carriage, so Darcy and the Fitzwilliam brothers were waiting for them.

Lady Matlock expressed her desire to see the formal gardens and requested Jasper's arm to support her. Frederica had of course immediately vacated the vicinity of her husband and instead stood talking to Darcy and Colonel Fitzwilliam, so Sir Anthony turned to Elizabeth with a rueful smile. "What is your pleasure, Miss Bennet? The formal gardens or the pleasure grounds?"

"The pleasure grounds, if the choice is mine. I feel the need to walk among trees." It would also give her more distance from Mr. Darcy. She had been avoiding looking in his direction since they had arrived.

They set off in the direction the gardener had indicated, walking between a row of trees towards the first folly, a Palladian temple, and then proceeding down towards the river where a gothic ruin rose over a formal cascade.

Elizabeth exclaimed at the beauty of the cascade and stepped closer to admire it while Sir Anthony leaned back against a stone wall, resting his elbows on the top of it. When she turned back to him, he said, "So, if I might take the privilege of an imaginary brother and inquire into matters that are none of my concern, may I ask you what Darcy has done to offend you so?"

Elizabeth did not meet his eyes. "He has not offended me."

"Now that is a bouncer if I have ever heard one! I saw how you looked away from him earlier, and last night you were avoiding looking at him for most of dinner."

Elizabeth flushed. She would have to learn to guard her expressions better, especially with someone as perceptive as Sir Anthony nearby. She could not possibly tell him about Darcy's proposal. "I admit he is not my favorite person, but I assure you, his opinion of me is not high, either." It was true enough. After all, he had said she would be a degradation to his family name.

He cocked his head to the side. "You believe that? That is odd, since I would say his opinion of you is quite the opposite."

"Sir Anthony, I am aware he is your friend, but how he treats his equals is quite different from how he behaves towards those he believes to be beneath him." Darcy's disdainful words had been echoing in her head much of the day.

"He can be proud, and looks down on foolishness, but at the same time he, more than most in the *ton*, is willing to befriend tradesmen."

She could grant him that much, since she had seen it firsthand with Mr. Bingley. Searching her memory for an example of Darcy's scornful behavior towards someone both amiable and sensible, she said, "In his dealings with his inferiors, his behavior has not always been honorable." Why was she having so much trouble recalling the reasons she had disliked him so much?

"Now that I simply do not believe!"

"It is true. A friend of mine was promised something in Darcy's father's will, and Darcy refused to give it to him." Let him explain that!

He had no chance to explain, for Colonel Fitzwilliam abruptly appeared between them, his expression choleric. "You know where George Wickham is?" he demanded.

The sound of the cascade must have covered his approach, but this was hardly something she wished to discuss with Darcy's family. She should not have allowed Sir Anthony to have drawn her out so far. "Pray, Colonel, you must pardon me. This was a private conversation, and I named no names."

"I must know. Do you know where Wickham can be found?"

She glanced at Sir Anthony, who appeared at least as startled as she felt. "I know where he is stationed," she said cautiously.

Colonel Fitzwilliam snorted. "Wickham, risking his precious life in the Army? I do not believe it."

Sir Anthony stepped in front of the colonel. "My friend, you are frightening Miss Bennet."

The colonel drew in a ragged breath and closed his eyes briefly. Reopening them, he spoke more calmly. "Pardon me for allowing my anger at that blackguard to get the better of me. But I would very much like to know his whereabouts."

"He is in the militia, not the Army, and – " She halted when a hand clasped her shoulder, and she looked back to see who had dared accost her. Mr. Darcy, of course. Warmth flooded through her at the sight of him, and her shoulder seemed to come to life under his touch.

"Say no more, I pray you," Mr. Darcy rasped.

The chill in his voice shocked her. "Kindly unhand me, sir!" she snapped, and almost immediately wished she had not. So much for her resolution to be kind to him!

Darcy released her instantly. "Forgive me, Miss Bennet. There are reasons, important reasons, why it is better for my cousin to be unaware of Wickham's whereabouts."

Colonel Fitzwilliam scowled. "You do not trust me to beat him in a fair fight?"

Darcy crossed his arms. "I am certain you would prevail in a fair fight. I do not trust *him* to fight fair."

Sir Anthony nodded. "If this is the George Wickham I knew at Cambridge, I am with Darcy on this."

Elizabeth said firmly, "I cannot believe we are speaking of the same Mr. Wickham. The one I am acquainted with is everything that is amiable."

"Oh, yes," said Lady Frederica, who had come to stand as a barrier between her brother and her cousin. "He is everything that is amiable and charming, and also everything that is dishonest, reprehensible, and selfish. He tried to seduce me once, and when I did not fall for his wiles, he attempted to compromise me."

Colonel Fitzwilliam rounded on his sister. "You as well? Why did you say nothing?"

"Because, my dear outraged brother, I took care of it myself. Miss Elizabeth, should you ever be so unfortunate as to find yourself in a similar position, I recommend appearing to succumb, and then applying your knee with all your force between his legs. It produces most satisfactory results."

"Enough is enough," growled Colonel Fitzwilliam. "His life is forfeit. Where is he?"

"Wait!" Lady Frederica's brows drew together. "You said, 'Not you as well.' Who else?"

Colonel Fitzwilliam exchanged a look with Darcy. "It was a slip of the tongue, nothing more."

"You are lying, I can tell. Who was it?" In the silence that followed, a light of understanding filled her expression. She screwed her face up, her eyes tightly shut. "Oh, no. No, no, no, no. Oh, no."

Darcy cleared his throat. "I beg you to say no more."

She opened her eyes with a sigh. "Of course," she said, her voice flat. "Richard, I take it all back. Pray kill him in the most painful, lingering manner possible."

The crowd of angry Fitzwilliams surrounding Elizabeth did not make for a pleasant atmosphere. "Pray excuse me. I do not belong in this discussion. Colonel Fitzwilliam, if you wish to know Mr. Wickham's whereabouts, you can apply to Mr. Darcy. It is my sincere hope no one will resort to violence over this or anything else." She dropped a perfunctory curtsy and hurried ahead on the path back to the carriage.

Of course it could not be so simple. Her shoulders tightened at the sound of footfalls behind her.

Darcy came up beside her. "Miss Elizabeth, you need not be alarmed by my presence. I only wish to tell you that I am sorry you were caught in that discussion. It must seem odd to you that Richard and I feel so strongly about Wickham."

"A little." A shock ran down her arms as her eyes met his. He no longer appeared angry, just serious.

"You heard what Frederica said about him. The other young lady involved was my sister. Last summer Wickham sought her out, told her he loved her, and convinced her to elope with him. It was only a chance discovery that allowed me to put a stop it. Georgiana was but fifteen at the time. His motive was, of course, her dowry of thirty thousand pounds."

Miss Darcy had seemed little more than a child when Elizabeth had met her at the circulating library in London. It would have been a simple matter for a man with Wickham's charm to take advantage of her. Wickham's sudden interest in Mary King now seemed more sinister than it had. To think she had been fond of the man! Nausea roiled her stomach, but she had to make some sort of reply. "I am sorry to hear she was deceived by him."

"Richard shares her guardianship with me, but I do not wish to see him in trouble with the law for attempting to fight Wickham. That is why I have kept his whereabouts to myself."

"I see," she said shakily.

"Forgive me for disturbing you." Darcy bowed stiffly and turned back towards the cascade.

Elizabeth watched his retreating back for a moment. Would she ever understand that man? It was evident how much he had suffered on his sister's behalf. Now she bitterly regretted snapping at him earlier, but there was nothing to do about it now. With a sigh, she started walking again.

Sir Anthony caught up with her a few minutes later. He took one look at her face and said, "I am sorry if Darcy said something to upset you."

She shook her head. "No. He was simply explaining himself, and it was a sad story."

"I can imagine."

Elizabeth bit her lip. "May I ask you a question about Mr. Darcy?"

"Of course."

"I am puzzled by his beliefs," she said slowly. "Clearly he is comfortable with you holding Radical beliefs, but he does not seem to share them – at least he does not seem to think everyone is equal. Yet he shows concern for the loom breakers. It is confusing." She could not imagine Sir Anthony feeling any person was a degradation to his name.

"Darcy? He is in a different position. He has Pemberley, with its many tenants and servants. For us, the only way to make changes is to change British laws. Darcy makes the laws for Pemberley himself. He is a very involved landlord. When there is suffering, he alleviates it. With the bad harvests, he purchased food from his own pocket so his tenants would not go hungry. His mother started a school for the children of tenants and servants. Darcy has not only continued it, but has made it known that he expects every child to attend it. He sets an example, proving it is possible to be a generous and fair landlord and still have a good income. You may be correct that he is not comfortable with the position of everyone having equal rights, but he does believe everyone should be treated well. If the entire country was run as Pemberley is, we might have no need to change the laws."

"I see. So his beliefs are different from yours, but many of your goals are similar."

"That is a good way to put it. I am glad you are not upset with him. I feared he might have angered you again."

"Not this time." Somehow she mustered her usual cheerfulness. "You may not believe this, but I am usually quite calm!"

"Oddly enough, I do believe you, having first met you in the absence of the Fighting Fitzwilliams. They can be enough to try anyone's patience."

"Yet you manage to remain calm, no matter how much provocation they give you."

"You would not have thought so had you met me a few years ago! But in the work I do as Mr. Hopewell, I cannot afford to be temperamental. It is too dangerous, both for me and for those I work with, so I have learned to appear calm no matter the circumstances. And most of what passes for bad behavior among the *ton* now seems unimportant to me."

Elizabeth hesitated, but her curiosity got the best of her. "But sometimes it does trouble you. I saw your face that day at Rosings when Lady Frederica slapped you."

He gave a sad smile. "You have caught me out. Yes, it hurt that the woman I loved was so angry with me, but it was just that. Anger is something we can talk about, and it is temporary. There are men who love their wives as much as I do who are forced to watch them die in childbed because they are malnourished. I have held a young girl, the apple of her father's eye, as she died of starvation while stout merchants paraded through the streets with money clinking in their pockets. Unlike anger, those things cannot be fixed." He shook his head. "Forgive me; I am preaching again. It is a bad habit of mine."

On impulse Elizabeth slipped her hand into his arm. "You are right about one thing, though. Anger is a problem that can be fixed. I need to remember that."

Chapter Ten

That night Elizabeth seemed subdued during dinner, but not angry. Still, Darcy was relieved when Duxbury asked to speak to him privately after the meal. It would spare him the pain of watching Elizabeth flirt with Jasper, knowing she would never be his.

He followed Duxbury upstairs to his bedroom. Duxbury motioned him to a wooden chair in the corner, seating himself on the only other option, the bed.

"What is the matter?" Darcy asked abruptly. He had been glad to escape, but he had no desire for a long discussion.

"You are in as ill a humor as my wife, I see."

"You knew what she was like, and you agreed to marry her."

"I just wish I had some idea why she decided we should marry. Has she said anything to you?"

"Frederica? No. And before you ask, I have no theories, either. Women's minds are a mystery to me." At least Elizabeth's was.

"I cannot decide if it was to punish me or to preserve her reputation. It certainly does not seem to have anything to do with wishing to be married to me."

"Yet you agreed to it."

Duxbury shrugged. "Of course. She was within her rights to demand it of me, and she already knew the worst about me. I hoped it meant she had retained some sort of affection for me, but I have seen the error of that."

"She will not remain angry forever." At least Darcy hoped not. "Is this what you wished to discuss? If so, I have very little to offer you."

"No." Duxbury untied his cravat and threw it carelessly over the bedstead. "I am worried about Sheffield."

"Why? It seems unlikely Lord Matlock will decline to intervene on behalf of our friends now you are married to his daughter."

"That is not what worries me, or at least not at the moment. I was not jesting when I said the situation in Sheffield is dangerous. According to the landlord here, it is worse now. There was a riot a few days ago. Sheffield is not a place I would choose to stay when accompanied by ladies. I will be safe enough in my role as Hopewell, and I can most likely extend my protection to Frederica as my wife, and hopefully to her mother as well." He scowled. "But I wish we were not riding in a gilded carriage with liveried servants. It makes us a target."

"Would they truly dare to attack the Countess of Matlock? I find that difficult to believe."

"These are the men who are ready to risk their lives facing the soldiers. They are watching their wives and children starve. Desperate men with nothing to lose will not respect rank, and they blame the wealthy for their troubles."

Darcy's stomach plummeted. Elizabeth would be in danger as well. "What should we do?"

Duxbury rose and began to pace the length of the small room, his hands folded behind his back. "It would be safer if we pretended to be a merchant family and drove a rented carriage, or better yet arrived on the stage, but Lady Matlock absolutely refuses to consider it. She can be even more stubborn than her daughter!"

Darcy allowed himself a dry chuckle. "In truth, I find it impossible to imagine any circumstances she could not talk her way out of."

"Darcy, have you ever been in the midst of an angry mob? I assure you, the rules are different from any you know."

"Enough lecturing! What is that you wish me to do?"

Duxbury stopped pacing and eyed him curiously. Odd, the Duxbury he had known of old would have snapped right back at him. This one said calmly, "I would like you to take responsibility for ensuring Miss Bennet's safety."

It felt like a slap to the face. "Miss Bennet may not be willing to accept my protection."

"I have noticed she seems to quarrel with you at the drop of a hat, but surely it would be different if she were in danger."

"I doubt it. She holds even more against me than Frederica does against you." It hurt even to say it.

Duxbury grimaced. "At least you are not tied to Miss Bennet, and she will disappear from your life soon enough." But something in his face must have betrayed him, for Duxbury's eyes opened wide. "You *are*, though!" he exclaimed. "Do not tell me she is the one!"

He should resent Duxbury for knowing his secret, but there was a certain comfort in having a fellow sufferer. "The very same."

"I am sorry. But at least she seems the sort who will understand and forgive."

"That might have been true, if the lady Bingley left behind had not been her beloved sister."

Duxbury whistled. "Oh, bad luck for you!"

"I could kill Richard for telling her," Darcy grumbled. Why had his cousin chosen that particular time not to honor his confidence?

"Before or after he kills me?"

Darcy could not even manage a smile. "You should be safe enough now that you are part of the family."

"I hope so, but the question before us tonight is how to keep Miss Bennet safe. I have a few suggestions."

The following day's travels were to be the shortest of their journey. To Elizabeth's surprise, Darcy joined them in the carriage once more. A few times when she glanced in his direction, he was watching her, but more often his eyes were directed downward. Elizabeth told herself she was grateful for that, but when their eyes met, she felt a shock go down her arms and a coil of heat developing deep inside her.

"We will be lodging at the Royal Oak tonight," said Lady Matlock as the carriage rolled into Sheffield. "I have never been there, but it comes well recommended. Do you know it, Sir Anthony?"

The corners of Sir Anthony's mouth turned down. "Not I, or rather Mr. Hopewell does not. Usually I stay with sympathizers."

Hopewell. That was what had been niggling at Elizabeth's mind all day. Sir Anthony was dressed as he had been the first time she had met him, or rather met Mr. Hopewell. A well-cut, sturdy but plain topcoat and an understated brown waistcoat, his cravat tied in a simple knot rather than the complex one he sported as Sir Anthony Duxbury.

As if he had read her thoughts, he tugged at his cravat. Was he deliberately attempting to wrinkle the fine linen? And his hands — his signet ring was nowhere to be seen. He leaned towards the window with keen interest. Elizabeth could make out nothing beyond the sort of houses one would expect at the periphery of a busy market town.

"Is something the matter?" she asked him quietly.

He jerked his head towards the window. "Do you hear that?"

Elizabeth strained her ears. The shouting she had taken as merchants peddling their wares was angry, and there were too many voices.

Sir Anthony turned to Lady Matlock. In an urgent voice he said, "My lady, I strongly urge you to direct the coachman to avoid the market square."

She gave him a piercing look, then seemed to reach some sort of conclusion and nodded to Colonel Fitzwilliam. He rapped on the roof of the carriage with his stick, but the pace of the carriage did not slow. Perhaps the coachman could not hear it over the clutter of hoofbeats on the cobblestones.

The shouts grew louder and angrier. Sir Anthony cursed under his breath. Elizabeth was abruptly thrown against Lady Frederica as the carriage lurched and suddenly jolted to a halt. The crack of a shot made her flinch.

Outside the coachman's voice bellowed, "The next one won't be over your head, but in the head of the next person who touches this carriage, and I have more pistols ready. Now make way!"

"You can't shoot all of us!" shouted one man.

"That's right!"

Sir Anthony stood, bending to avoid hitting the carriage roof. He pushed his way past Colonel Fitzwilliam. "Let me through, dammit!"

He threw the door open and kicked down the steps, halting on the top one. In a loud, commanding voice he said, "Put those pistols away! These are not our enemies, but our fellow Englishmen, hard-working souls who have been driven to extremity by their circumstances. Put the guns away I say! Immediately!"

Elizabeth's hand flew to her mouth. Were they truly in danger?

"Get on with you! We need none of your sort here," yelled one man, shaking a staff at Sir Anthony.

Sir Anthony held his hands out. "Friends, my name is Hopewell, and I doubt not some of you have heard me speak before. Is that not my friend Stratton over yonder? I worked with you in Doncaster, did I not?"

The shouting was replaced by muttering. Darcy's hand shot out and grabbed Colonel Fitzwilliam's arm. He had produced a pistol and was in the process of cocking it. "No, not yet," said Darcy urgently.

The colonel glared as he lowered the pistol. Sir Anthony's voice rang out again. "I have been in London meeting with members of Parliament, seeking a remedy to your situation. I have returned to meet with Lord

Matlock on behalf of the prisoners. Pray permit us to pass!"

"Mighty fancy coach you have there, Hopewell!" came a sneering voice. "You been trying to play us for fools? The price of it could feed the entire town. Who are your rich friends?" There was more muttering.

"The coach is not mine. I have been given the use of it since I am traveling with my wife and her family."

"You don't got no wife, Hopewell!"

"I did not," said Sir Anthony, sounding amused. "I have just been married today, and now you know why I am very anxious to reach the inn!"

The crowd roared with laughter, but one angry voice rang out, "If your story is true, let's see this wife of yours."

"Oh, stubble it, Milford!"

"He's right! Show us your wife!"

Sir Anthony spoke calmly. "After all you have suffered, I cannot blame you for doubting my word, but fortunately this is simple enough to prove." He turned back into the carriage and held out his hand. "Frederica, my dear?"

Lady Frederica showed no hesitation, shaking off the hand her mother laid on her arm to stand beside Sir Anthony. She waved to the crowd as Sir Anthony kissed her hand.

"My friends, allow me to present my wife!"

Catcalls, whistles, and shockingly ribald comments followed. Elizabeth lowered her head to hide her blushes.

Lady Matlock was across the carriage in an instant, her hand over her son's mouth. "If you make so much as a move, I will make certain you regret it for the rest of your life!" she hissed.

Elizabeth looked up in astonishment. Had the calm Lady Matlock transformed into a Valkyrie? Even more astonishingly, Colonel Fitzwilliam subsided.

One deep voice came through the clamor. "So that's why you hid her away! Afraid she'd leave you for a real man? I'd be happy to show you a good time, missus!"

Frederica laughed, and boldly said, "I will keep that in mind if he should disappoint me!"

Sir Anthony made a shooing motion behind his back. What could he mean? There was no place to hide in the carriage.

Mr. Darcy shifted from the bench, his hand closing over Elizabeth's wrist. Shocked by the unexpected touch, she instinctively drew back, but there was nowhere to go.

"Miss Elizabeth, you must come with me." He sounded more annoyed than pleased by the prospect.

"Out into the mob? No, thank you!"

"If we stay in the carriage, we are trapped. I pray you, for once in your life, just do as I say!" he snapped.

Elizabeth wavered. A new howl of anger from the mob made her hesitate, but despite Mr. Darcy's faults, he had never shown irresponsibility. If Sir Anthony and Mr. Darcy both deemed wisest for them to leave, perhaps she should listen. "But what of Lady Matlock and Frederica?"

"Richard will protect them. Come." He opened the door on the side of the coach facing away from the square. Dispensing with the steps altogether, he jumped to the pavement and turned to face Elizabeth.

Surely he did not expect her to jump as well? But before she could say a word, his hands gripped her waist and lowered her to the ground. Had all the air been somehow sucked out of her lungs?

Thank heavens the mob was on the other side of the carriage where Sir Anthony held their attention! The narrow pavement behind the coach was empty, but a short distance away a handful of men jostled each other, pointing at them.

Darcy tried the latch of a milliner's shop, then pushed his shoulder against the door. Cursing under his breath, he attempted the same at the butcher shop next door. "Barred," he said. "No doubt to keep their wares safe. We will have to get away from the square."

The idea of going anywhere near the mob was terrifying, but they could not hide behind the carriage forever. "I suppose so."

"Take off your bonnet and gloves. They will make you stand out." He stripped off his own kid gloves and dropped them on the ground. A frightened looking urchin darted out of nowhere and snatched them.

With trembling fingers, Elizabeth followed suit. Why had she not listened when Sir Anthony said

Sheffield was dangerous? Her sole reliance now was on Mr. Darcy.

He studied her intently for a moment. "Forgive me." He grasped the lace on her neckline and ripped it away.

Horrorstruck, she could only stare at him. Who was this new and disturbing Mr. Darcy?

He grabbed her bare hand in his. "Do not let go of me. We must not be separated." Without another word, he plunged into the crowd, pulling her behind him.

Rank odor surrounded her as bodies pressed against her. They had almost reached the edge of the square when a large man blocked her way. Darcy's hand was torn from hers.

The man leered at her and grabbed her by the shoulders. "I'll do you better than he can, dearie. Now give us a kiss."

She attempted to pull away, but his face came closer, drowning her in the stench of onions. "No," she pleaded.

He grinned, showing gaps in his blackened teeth. "Nice! I like a woman what fights."

She ducked down quickly, causing him to lose his grip. A fist appeared out of nowhere and connected with his jaw, sending him staggering back.

"Find your own bit of muslin. This one's mine," snarled Darcy in a northern accent far from his usual cultured tones.

Instinctively, Elizabeth pressed herself against Darcy as the man spat blood in their direction. "No need to get..." She missed whatever else he said as Darcy dragged her away in the circle of his arm.

Suddenly there was air to breathe again and they could move forward freely. Darcy had found an alley off the square. He did not release her until they had passed half a dozen houses, and even then she thought he did so reluctantly. "Are you hurt?" he asked.

Missing the weight of his arm around her, she shook her head. "I am quite well, just a bit out of breath. I have never been in a riot before."

"This is not a riot. No one is throwing rocks or burning buildings."

She gave a breathy laugh. "Indeed? I shall be grateful for the lack of rocks and torches, then. I thank you for your most timely assistance."

Darcy shuffled his feet. "Duxbury warned me this might happen and told me what to do, but I do not believe he anticipated how quickly it would occur."

Why was he so uncomfortable with her thanks? She looked closely at him, something she had avoided in the carriage. "You have modeled your wardrobe after his today. I do not recall seeing you so simply dressed before."

The corners of his mouth turned up. "Duxbury suggested it would be wiser to appear to be an ordinary citizen. I had to borrow the coat from my valet."

Oddly enough, it suited him. He seemed more approachable in everyday clothes, with no gloves, hat or cane to mark his status. She had to look away; she did not wish to find him attractive.

"I suppose I should dress the part as well." With a good humored smile, she tugged down the sleeves of her dress to expose her shoulders. "There, do I make a presentable doxy?"

"Very." His voice was rough, and he looked away. "You are brave, Miss Elizabeth."

She wrinkled her nose at him. "My courage always rises with every attempt to intimidate me."

Just then angry voices sounded a short distance behind them. "Trouble," Darcy muttered, taking her hand again. "Come; we must get out of here." He set off down the alley at a brisk stride.

Elizabeth had to half-run to keep up with him, but she did not complain. The faster they escaped, the happier she would be. The alley twisted, then went off to one side. Now that they were farther from the shouting crowd, she could hear the pounding footsteps hurrying after them.

"Devil take it!" Darcy hissed. The alley ended abruptly, a high stone wall blocking their way. He glanced behind them. "Too many to fight, damn their eyes!"

"What shall we do?" Elizabeth's mouth was dry.

His eyes darted from side to side. "We give them what they want, I suppose."

Her eyes widened as he led her roughly to a doorway, then stripped off his coat and dropped it on the filthy cobblestones. "I hope you are prepared to play that part, for I know of no other way to convince them you are not a gentlewoman and therefore not worth taking for ransom. We must pray they take the bait."

Ransom? Her fear overwhelmed the utter shock of seeing Mr. Darcy in his shirtsleeves, but that was nothing to what followed. Mr. Darcy put his arms around her, gently pushing her back into the recessed doorway.

"Place your arms around my neck," he said in her ear, leaning against her in a most inappropriate manner. "Yes, just like that. And try to forgive me."

Was it fear making her heart pound so, or was it the warm pressure of Mr. Darcy's body against hers? She had seen couples engaged this way often enough on her visits to London, though her aunt always tried to hurry her past, men holding light women like this against the wall for quick coupling. And now it was her. She trusted Mr. Darcy not to take this too far, but in truth he had already done enough to ruin her. And that was before his warm lips brushed against hers.

A chasm seemed to open in the pit of her stomach. Without conscious thought she lifted her face to meet his lips halfway, and the sweet pleasure of it shocked her to her core.

Good God, what was wrong with her? She was in a dark alleyway, fleeing from men who wanted to hurt her, with a man she did not even like — and being thrilled by his kisses! Every inch of her felt alive, her senses sharpened. Fear no longer tightened her chest; although she should be afraid, somehow she could not feel anything but safe in Mr. Darcy's arms. But there was nothing the least bit safe about his kisses.

Were those his teeth teasing her lip? She had never before recognized how sensitive her lips could be. As his tongue traced the seam of her lips, instinct took over and suddenly all she cared about was finding a way to be even closer to him. A current of desire washed through her as she met his kiss freely.

Her response summoned a harsh noise from Darcy's throat. His arms tightened around her, his kisses growing more passionate. As Elizabeth tasted his mouth, an odd intoxication took hold of her, demanding something more of her – more, always more.

But she had to remember this was nothing but play acting meant to deceive the men who followed them, with Mr. Darcy exposing his back to them to make her less of a target. She must do her best to keep up a convincing illusion.

What had those women in London done? Experimentally she ran her fingers up into his thick hair, her fingertips tingling at the intimate sensation. She felt tension rising in Darcy as he deepened his kiss. Her tongue met his in a hidden fencing match. Were men's kisses usually like this?

Oh, she had never known she had such wanton instincts! But the scuffling footsteps were coming closer.

What else had those light women done? They had bunched their skirts around their waists, but she was certainly not doing that! Had there not been one who ran her foot up the back of the man's calf? She could manage that. Leaning back against the wall for balance, she hooked her foot around Darcy's boot and began to stroke upward towards his knee.

She had not realized how this would expose her until his hips pressed against her, a hardness rolling against her core, sending spurts of fire deep into her center. Instinctively she returned the pressure, seeking more of the astonishing sensations, even as her sanity tried to remind her this was beyond wanton. What would he think of her? And those men — what were they doing? She could no longer hear footsteps. Had they gone? Was she safe?

Mr. Darcy was still kissing her as if he could never have enough, sending shivers of desire rolling down her spine. Who would have thought such passion lay under his controlled surface? His tongue elicited such pleasure and excitement that it did not matter they were in an alley where anyone could see them. There was something so right about it – and nothing could ever be the same again.

But something was changing. His hands and lips were growing gentler, less insistent. Then, after one last, almost chaste kiss, he twisted his head to look back at the street behind him. He breathed a sigh, but instead of releasing Elizabeth, he leaned his forehead to rest on hers. The warm pressure was comforting, since her head was still spinning from his kisses, but as the silence continued, she remembered where they were. "Are they gone?" The husky voice did not sound like her own.

"Yes." He still did not move.

First she allowed her hands to slide down to his shoulders, but they felt empty when she lowered them to her sides. She must keep this wantonness under control! How could she have permitted herself to be seduced by his kisses?

He took the hint and stepped away from her. "You are a remarkably quick learner."

She flushed. Was he accusing her of being experienced? "I have never done anything of the sort before."

The sternness in his eyes seem to lighten. "I know. That was quite apparent. I am only sorry..."

She did not want to hear about his regrets. He had made it clear enough in the last day that his sentiments towards her had changed. Would he feel obliged to offer for her again now? More urgently, would she feel obliged to accept him? Briskly she said, "There is no need to apologize. We did what we had to."

He studied her. "Perhaps, but still — that is not how a lady's first kiss should happen. I am sorry for that."

She swallowed hard. Talking about kissing was dangerous; it made her wish to do it again. "Do you think it is safe now?"

He straightened his shoulders and looked away from her. "I do not hear anything now. Perhaps the mob has dispersed."

She must act as if nothing extraordinary had occurred. "Shall we go back then? Oh — your coat is gone."

"I expected that. I dropped it there in the hope they would take the easy pickings and leave."

"I see. I hope you did not lose anything valuable."

"You need not concern yourself. I had nothing of value in it."

But something about the way he stared at her made her nervous. She folded her hands behind her back. That would avoid the uncomfortable situation of having to take his arm and walk closely beside him – even if she was longing to do just that.

They found the square empty except for a dozen militia officers lounging with their rifles. Darcy approached the nearest one.

The man caressed the stock of his rifle. "No one is allowed to gather here now."

"I have no intention of remaining. I am a stranger here and wish only for directions to the Royal Oak."

The officer raked an insolent gaze down Darcy, no doubt taking in his lack of coat and general dishevelment, and smirked. "The Royal Oak caters to a select clientele." His tone indicated he thought Darcy did not fit that description.

Darcy gritted his teeth. He was accustomed to deference, not insolence of this sort, and this was poor timing, when his anger and desire warred with self-hatred. "I am well aware of that. Could you tell me how to get there?"

"What's in it for me?" The man had started leering at Elizabeth, and Darcy's best Master of Pemberley glare was making no headway. Was his appearance the only reason he was usually treated with respect? Impotent fury choked him.

He snatched Elizabeth's hand none too gently. "Come. The coach was headed that way. No doubt we will be able to find the inn on our own." He strode away, Elizabeth hurrying to match his pace.

"Wait!" the officer called, sounding worried. "Do you mean the Matlock coach?"

Darcy swung around. "Yes," he said savagely. "It belongs to my uncle." He had the satisfaction of watching the man blanch.

"Turn right at the end of the square, sir. The Royal Oak is two blocks further along, on the left."

Darcy nodded curtly, not trusting himself enough to speak, and set off with Elizabeth in tow.

As they reached the street, Elizabeth tugged her hand away. "Pray pardon me," she said.

"Of course. My apologies. I was not thinking." Expecting to see anger, he discovered her eyebrows were arched in amusement.

She quoted his earlier words back to him. "I know. That was quite apparent, at least as apparent as my lack of experience. I may not know you well, but I am absolutely certain that if you *were* thinking, you would not choose to walk hand in hand with me in public, especially without our gloves!"

He might not be able to resist her sparkling eyes, but he would not make matters worse by telling her he wished they could always walk hand in hand. She did not want to hear it, and he had already taken advantage of her. "I thank you for your faith that my manners may be better than they appear today."

She moved closer to his side. "I think – I think *you* should be in charge of keeping us safe, and *I* will be in charge of attempting to recall we are not savages." But she said it with such arch sweetness that he could not be offended.

They found the Royal Oak without difficulty. Once inside, Darcy looked for the landlord, but instead found his cousins sprawled in chairs by the fire. Richard, holding a poultice to his eye, sported a bruised jaw and a split lip. Jasper was nursing a glass of brandy in his left hand while a barmaid bandaged his limp right arm.

"Good God! What happened to you?" Darcy exclaimed.

Jasper looked him up and down. "The question is what happened to you! I cannot believe you were out in public dressed like that!" His eyes flickered to Elizabeth, then he immediately looked away.

Suddenly Darcy realized the picture she presented, her hair disheveled, no gloves or bonnet, her shoulders exposed, threads dangling from her dress where he had ripped off the lace. Worst of all, her lips were rosy and swollen from his kisses. Good God, what sort of cad was he to bring her in here looking like that?

Elizabeth stepped forward. "Before we exchange stories, I pray you to direct me to my room. I feel in definite need of refreshing myself."

The barmaid tied off the bandage on Jasper's arm with a flourish and tore off the end with her teeth. "Are you Lady Matlock's maid? I can take you up."

Darcy stiffened. "This is Miss Bennet, a traveler in our party."

The maid looked unimpressed. "I hope your party does not always arrive in such a state." But Elizabeth followed her without a word as she marched off.

Darcy eyed Richard and Jasper. "You first."

Richard raised the poultice, winced and put it back in place. "After you and Miss Bennet exited the carriage, some rude fellow started insulting Frederica and saying she was not really Duxbury's wife, so he kissed her in front of them — and kissed her again, in a very improper manner, saying the crowd was keeping him from his wedding night. Bit of a bouncer, that, but the crowd decided to bring them here."

"On their shoulders," added Jasper. "I would have loved to see the look on Mother's face."

"So I thought the danger had passed, but as soon as they were away, other ruffians decided the carriage would be easy pickings. They started pulling off anything they could reach, from the luggage to the lanterns, and two blackguards tried to force their way inside. I shot them, of course. But there was no time to reload, so I pushed my way out and started in on the thieves with my fists."

"That was when I rode into town," said Jasper, "only to discover my brother fighting like a madman, single-handedly holding off a dozen ruffians. I could not see why I should let him have all the fun, so I joined in."

Richard lifted the poultice again. "Rather unfair odds for them, don't you think? A mere dozen of them against two Fitzwilliams."

Jasper laughed, then winced and clutched his side. "I for one did not mind seeing the militia roll in!"

"That made the crowd scatter," Richard said with a regretful air.

"And Mother, showing no sympathy for our wounds obtained in her defense, made us walk here, saying she did not want us to bleed on the upholstery," said Jasper.

Darcy frowned. "I hope Lady Matlock came to no harm."

"Not a bit of it, although she would say her ears are still ringing from the pistol blast so nearby. Can you believe she instructed the grooms to clean the inside of the coach to remove the smell of gunpowder?"

Darcy slumped down in the nearest chair. "So I accomplished nothing by taking Elizabeth out of the coach. She would have been perfectly safe there."

Richard and Jasper exchanged a look, then with unwonted seriousness, Richard said, "As long as both Jasper and the militia made their appearances exactly when they did, yes, she would have been safe. Otherwise... I begin to see why Duxbury did not want the ladies here."

But Darcy had not saved Elizabeth; he put her into danger and taken advantage of her trust. He would never forgive himself for that.

Chapter Eleven

It was only Frederica's continued gaiety and exchanges with their escort that had allowed Duxbury to maintain a superficial air of good cheer as they arrived at the inn. No doubt her laughing and joking was as much of an act as his, but she was somehow managing to continue it.

Of course, she might not have been aware just how dangerous the situation had been, and kissing him had been nothing but an act for her, not the torture it had been for him, the promise of heaven denied him. He should count his blessings; at least now she did not seem angry with him.

Somehow they had to escape this boisterous crowd. "Landlord, a drink for all my friends, and one for yourself." He tossed a pouch of money over the bar as the men cheered.

A giggling barmaid led Frederica up the stairs with Duxbury following close behind. From the bar came uproarious laughter and shouts of "Go to it, lad!"

Little did they know.

Finally they were in a bedroom and the door shut behind them. If only he could sag back against that door, but now he had a new role to play. He had hoped to make some progress with Frederica during the day's journey as they argued about *The Rights of Man*. By God, she would be able hold her own in a meeting of longtime revolutionaries! But now he had to protect that progress, and that meant not frightening her.

There was a bottle of wine beside the bed. He poured two glasses and took one to Frederica, being careful not to let his fingertips touch hers. "I am duly impressed," he said mildly. "You handled that scene very well indeed." If only she did not look so appealing with her cheeks flushed and her eyes sparkling! It was all he could do not to take her in his arms.

She took a cautious sip of the wine and made a face as if she found it sour. "It was most interesting to see you in action. I found it exhilarating."

Exhilarating. Well, there were much worse ways she could have taken it, and she had not slapped him. But those rosy lips, swollen by his kisses, called to him all too powerfully.

Wrenching his eyes away from her, he strode to the window and yanked the curtains closed with more force than was necessary. He took several deep breaths before he could turn back to her with a calm expression. "They will be watching us otherwise. Country manners can be a bit shocking."

"I have already discovered that. I may have three brothers, but my ears may never recover from some of the things I heard today!" Her tone was pleasant and conversational, a far cry from the anger she'd shown him since Rosings.

He would have to play this very carefully. "It would likely not be wise for you to leave this room tonight, as anything which calls our marriage into question could create a dangerous situation. But you need not worry; I will sleep on the floor and you may ignore my presence completely if you choose."

"You are not an easy man to ignore."

He could not look at her. Instead he made a show of hunting through his pockets until he found his small sheathed knife. Pulling back the counterpane on the bed to expose the sheet, he said, "I beg your apology for being crass, but they will be displaying the sheet tomorrow. So..." He unsheathed the knife and dug the point into the base of his left palm. The pain was actually a relief as he held his hand over the sheet until several drops of blood stained the white fabric. "To prove we consummated the wedding and that you were a virgin." He fished out his handkerchief and pressed it against the cut to staunch the bleeding.

Frederica moved a step closer, insisting on holding the handkerchief against his flesh herself. Her hand supported his as she lifted the square fabric to examine his cut. Could she tell how his heart was pounding just from the touch of her hand?

She replaced the handkerchief but did not release his hand. "I had thought perhaps we might prove that in the traditional manner."

His mouth grew dry. Was it possible she meant it? "I thought you did not wish it."

She tilted her head to one side. "When you were kissing me, I could not help but notice that, even if your heart was not engaged, the rest of your body seemed quite happy to participate."

"Freddie." Why was he so hoarse? "My heart was most definitely engaged."

"Yet now you seem oddly reluctant."

He swallowed hard. "Only reluctant to impose upon you. If you are to come to me, I want it to be of your own volition and desire, not because I have forced you into submission or seduced you. It is your right to make the decision."

Her lips curved into a smile. "Mr. Paine would be proud of you."

"I hope so, but I care rather more about what you think of me." Somehow he managed the superhuman feat of remaining perfectly still.

She reached up and began to untie his cravat. "I think we should save this discussion until later."

There was only so much restraint a man could be expected to have. He tugged her close to him and claimed her lips.

It was almost dusk when Duxbury and Frederica came tripping down the stairs, both looking exceedingly well pleased with themselves. Apparently they were no longer at odds. But wait, why was Frederica wearing one of Elizabeth's bonnets? It was plainer than her usual style. Darcy would rather see Elizabeth's smiling face beneath it.

"Going out, Duxbury?" Richard raised his glass to the couple.

"Very observant," said Duxbury dryly. "We are going to meet with some of my friends, and I think it would be wise for me to be Hopewell while I am here. I do not need one more thing to explain to the locals."

"Am I to call you that as well?" asked Frederica coyly.

Duxbury smiled down at her. "You may call me anything you please, my dear. What is your preference? Would you rather be Mrs. Hopewell or Lady Frederica tonight?"

"Mrs. Hopewell, if you please." Their gazes caught and held.

Jasper groaned. "After listening to the two of you arguing for days, pray spare us this touching scene!"

"Hear, hear." Richard's speech was beginning to slur.

Frederica leaned closer to Duxbury. "Ignore my brothers. They are under the mistaken assumption that they possess a sense of humor."

Darcy said nothing. The churning of his stomach brought bile up into his throat. If Elizabeth was not with Frederica, she must be avoiding him — and with good cause.

Elizabeth dipped the cloth in the basin of cold water again and pressed it to her lips. She did not dare join the others until the swelling had gone down, at least not until it was dark enough that she could keep her face in shadows. Of course, it was too late to fool the Fitzwilliam brothers. Would Darcy be able to persuade them to say nothing of her earlier indecent appearance?

Not to mention her indecent behavior! Was it worse to have allowed Darcy to kiss her, or that she had enjoyed it? All those years of proper behavior only to discover she was as wanton as Lydia! And even worse, she had enjoyed kissing a man she disliked. Hot shame burned in her cheeks.

Two days ago Darcy had claimed to love her, but he must have put those feelings behind him thoroughly. Otherwise why would he be so angry to be forced to kiss her? If he found her attractive, he should have enjoyed it, but afterwards he was curt, practically rude, and dragged her along like a disobedient child. But he had told her months ago that his good opinion, once lost, was lost forever. He was most likely thanking his lucky stars she had refused him and hoping he would not now be obliged to marry her for the sake of her reputation.

Eventually someone knocked on the door to tell her dinner was about to be served. Would Lady Matlock be cross with her for being tardy? At least it was dark enough now to hide the worst of her swollen lips.

To her surprise, when she reached the small parlor, only Lady Matlock was present, and the table was set for two. Had Lady Matlock discovered her shame and arranged to speak to her privately?

"It is just you and I tonight, my dear. The others have all deserted us for one reason or another," said the Countess.

"I hope nothing is the matter." If only she could ask directly why the others were not there!

"Apart from the two ruffians who claim to be my sons, everyone is well. They are both in their rooms, having treated their injuries with an excess of port and brandy. My daughter and her husband are visiting some of his Radical friends."

Elizabeth asked, "What of Mr. Darcy?"

Lady Matlock waved a hand. "After discovering my husband was delayed and will not arrive for several days, he rode off to take care of some business. He plans to return in a day or two. So you see, we are quite abandoned!"

She smiled mechanically at Lady Matlock. Mr. Darcy had left without a word to her? He must be powerfully angry with her indeed. Why did it hurt so much?

Although Elizabeth could find no appetite for the food before her, Lady Matlock went out of her way to make her comfortable, asking questions about her family and her life in Hertfordshire. Eventually she relaxed her guard and found herself telling the Countess rather more than she had intended. At least her stories seemed to amuse her ladyship.

Shortly after the last cover was taken away, a caller arrived asking for Lady Matlock. With the bow so deep he almost lost his balance, the portly gentleman introduced himself as the Lord Mayor of Sheffield, although his identity was obvious owing to the chain of office he wore for the grand occasion of meeting such an elevated lady as the Countess of Matlock.

He wrung his hands. "I pray your ladyship will have the very great condescension of hearing my *deepest* apologies for calling on you at such an hour. When I heard of the unfortunate reception your ladyship received on your arrival in our humble town and of the great injuries those *dreadful* ruffians inflicted upon your most *noble* sons, I told myself I should, and in fact I *must*, call on your ladyship immediately to express my most *profound* regrets and to assure you the guilty parties will be brought to justice." He was breathing heavily after this obviously prepared speech. Sweat beaded on his forehead.

To her credit, Lady Matlock replied in the same courteous manner she used with everyone else. "It is very kind of you to show such concern, but I assure you I am not in the slightest bit distressed by today's events. I was already aware of the unrest in the North, and I never felt a moment's fear since my sons were there to protect me."

The mayor mopped his forehead with his handkerchief. "Your ladyship is *most* gracious, most gracious indeed! I will *forever* regret that your first sight of our town was a distressing one which did not reflect the good-hearted, hard-working and law-abiding citizens of Sheffield. But it is true that there has been unrest, mostly caused by some ill-behaved newcomers who became unruly when they discovered there was no work for them."

"How unfortunate! I find people to have a regrettable habit of becoming unruly when they do not have enough food to eat."

He was stammering a reply when Frederica sailed into the room. She paused to kiss her mother's cheek, then said breezily, "Oh, you must be the Lord Mayor! What a handsome chain of office that is! You must be very proud of it. I am Lady Frederica Fitzwilliam. I hope you do not mind that I introduced myself."

This flirtatious behavior was so unlike Frederica that Elizabeth could only stare. The mayor appeared equally stunned.

Frederica said, "Mother, have you asked him yet? Please tell me you have, and that he has agreed."

Lady Matlock's eyebrows rose a fraction of an inch. "I have not had the opportunity, but now that you are here, perhaps you can ask him yourself. I am certain he will be happy to oblige you."

This seemed to set the nervous man on solid ground. "I would be *most* happy to be of service to you in *any* possible way, Lady Frederica."

"Oh, thank you! I knew the moment I saw you that I could depend upon you. You are so very kind! I cannot thank you enough!"

Lady Matlock said dryly, "My dear, perhaps you should be so kind as to inform him what he has just agreed to do."

Frederica clapped her hand to her chest. "Did I not say? How very foolish of me! It is just a tiny thing, in truth. I pray you, may I tour the gaol tomorrow? Please, please do say I can!"

The mayor's jaw dropped. "I... I am of course your servant in every way, but the gaol is no place for a gently bred lady like yourself. It is... it is full of ruffians, and... odorous and crowded."

"Oh, I know! That is why I wish to see it. You see, I belong to the Ladies' Society for the Relief of Prisoners, and I have been to *all* the gaols in London. I promised the other ladies I would visit the gaol here and report back to them. So you see, I truly must go there, for otherwise I would have to face their disappointment in me, and that would be most distressing." She batted her eyelashes at him.

"Well," he said weakly. "If you truly wish it, I will attempt to make arrangements. Perhaps in a few days' time..."

Frederica clasped her hands together in apparent delight. "I knew you would understand! But I am afraid it must be tomorrow, for I must leave for Matlock the following day. Please *do* say it will be tomorrow!"

His eyes started moving from side to side. "Tomorrow? Well, if it must be, I pray you then to excuse me so I can make the arrangements right away."

"Of course! You are so very kind. I will be certain to mention to my father what a great help you have been to me, and he will want to thank you as well."

The mayor trembled as he bowed and took his leave of them.

As soon as he was gone, Frederica flopped into the chair nearest the fire. "Lord, that was exhausting!"

Lady Matlock tilted her head to one side. "Pray, tell me why is it so urgent for you to not only visit the gaol, but to do so tomorrow?"

Sir Anthony appeared in the doorway, his face drawn. "An unexpected situation has arisen. The executions were supposed to take place in a sennight, but they have been moved up to the day after tomorrow owing to the protests. That is why those men were in the square today — to demand their release. Without Lord Matlock here, we must find another way to stop the hanging or to rescue them if we can. I have little hope, but we must try. If we can talk to the two of them, we may be able to make plans." He turned to Frederica. "Well done, my dear." They shared a smile.

So Sir Anthony and Lady Frederica had come to some sort of agreement! It was about time.

Lady Matlock folded her hands in her lap. Thoughtfully she said, "Perhaps I might be able to be of some assistance."

Despite the seriousness of their endeavor, Elizabeth could not but smile at their motley appearance arriving at the gaol — the portly and breathless mayor, a grey-haired magistrate, the delicate and fashionably dressed Lady Matlock, Lady Frederica, and bringing up the rear, Colonel Fitzwilliam in full uniform, sporting two black eyes and a very swollen lip. Elizabeth in her plain clothing most likely looked like Lady Matlock's maid.

As they followed the mayor into the gaol's cold, dark passageway, Frederica whispered to Elizabeth, "At least the odor is not as bad as I anticipated."

Elizabeth laughed. "See how clean the floor is? Most likely they had half the servants in town working all night in order that your ladylike sensibilities should not be offended."

The mayor gestured to a heavy barred door on the right. "This is where we keep miscreants who have not yet been judged by the magistrates – petty thieves and disturbing the peace for the most part. Now and then we have a poacher, but usually landowners will deal with them on their own. Do you wish to speak to the prisoners?"

"Naturally," said Lady Frederica. "How else am I to make a report?"

A guard came forward and bellowed through the bars, "Stand up, you big lugs! The lady has some questions for you."

Elizabeth watched Frederica question the prisoners about the length of their stay in gaol and the conditions there. She shook her head at the responses. The men were clean and dressed in warm clothes, and despite their hollow cheeks and emaciated hands, they assured their visitor they were well fed indeed, never went hungry, and it was tasty grub as well, with plenty of small beer to drink. She wondered what punishment they had been threatened with, should any of them make a complaint.

The occupants of the next cell, men and women awaiting transportation to Australia, were equally voluble about their excellent treatment. The mayor began to look more at ease and even held forth on the importance of treating prisoners well.

At the final door, the mayor said, "In this cell we have the hardened criminals who are awaiting the hangman. Loom breakers and Luddites for the most part."

Lady Matlock said, "Loom breakers are hardened criminals?"

"Indeed, and that is why Parliament has made it a hanging offense."

"Over my husband's objections, I fear."

Colonel Fitzwilliam looked through the bars as the mayor hemmed and hawed. Suddenly the colonel cried, "By God, is that you, Latimer? What in God's name are you doing here?"

"Richard, I will thank you not to take the Lord's name in vain," said Lady Matlock primly.

A slight man, barely taller than Elizabeth, peered out of the cell. "Fitzwilliam," he said flatly.

"See, mother, it *is* Latimer!"

Lady Matlock looked in the direction her son was pointing and pressed a ladylike hand against her chest. "So it is! My dear boy, whatever has happened to you?" Without waiting for an answer, she turned to the mayor and said, "Open this door at once! At once, I say!"

The mayor glanced nervously at the magistrate. "Your ladyship, these are dangerous men. I cannot allow it."

Richard turned smoothly on his heel, his appearance suddenly menacing. "Did you fail to hear my mother's request?"

The mayor shrank back, shaking his head helplessly. "If you think it best..." He gestured to the guard, who hefted a large set of keys, examined each one carefully, and then ponderously inserted one into the lock. The hinges squealed as he opened the door.

Lady Matlock floated into the cell as if it were the finest ballroom, her hands outstretched to Latimer. With a bewildered glance at Colonel Fitzwilliam, Latimer took her hands and allowed her to kiss his cheek.

"My *dear* boy, whatever are you doing in such a place? But never mind that; are you *well*? How is your dear mother and that sister of yours? It has been so long since I have had the pleasure of seeing you at Matlock House! Why, just the other day I was mentioning you to that charming Sir Anthony Duxbury! But I *never* expected to find you here!"

Latimer's eyes widened at Duxbury's name. "Your ladyship, I most profoundly regret that you must see me in such sad circumstances. I would not have wished this to be your last memory of me."

"My last memory? Why should this be my last memory of you? I expect to see you at my Christmas ball, young man, and will not take no for an answer!"

"Your ladyship, I fear I will not be attending any festivities in the future."

The magistrate cleared his throat. "Mr. Latimer is sentenced to be hanged."

Lady Matlock rounded on him. "To be hanged? What nonsense is this? He has done nothing to deserve such a fate!"

"My lady, I regret to tell you he is guilty of loom breaking."

"Loom breaking? Why on earth would that poor boy want to break a loom? He has a fine career ahead of him as a barrister, and nothing at all to do with looms! You did not break any looms, did you, dear boy?"

"No, your ladyship, I did not. I was attempting to stop some of these gentlemen from doing so."

She placed her hands on her hips. "Then why in heaven's name did you not tell the judge so, you foolish boy?"

"I did. Unfortunately, he did not believe me."

"Not believe you? What sort of nonsense is this?" She turned towards the other prisoners, every inch the Countess. "Is this true?"

A tall, gaunt man bowed his head. "It is, yer ladyship, and we told the judge the very same thing."

Lady Matlock pointed to the magistrate. "There, you see? He did not break any looms."

The magistrate's throat bobbed. "He was tried before a jury of his peers and found guilty, your ladyship. The law is the law."

"Not when there is such a miscarriage of justice as this, sir! I have known this dear boy since he was in short pants, and he spent many of his school holidays with us. Oh, I remember it well! All my boys together — you, and Richard, and little Tom Beaumont — whatever has happened to him?"

A tall man stepped forward from the shadows and made a bow which would not have been out of place in St. James' Court. "Your ladyship, I am, as always completely at your service — unless such service involves stepping out of the cell, in which case I fear I would be prevented from obliging you."

Lady Matlock cried, "Not you as well! Richard, pray give me your arm. I begin to feel quite faint."

Colonel Fitzwilliam was by her side instantly with Latimer supporting her other arm. "A chair for her ladyship!"

The guard huffed as he carried in a rickety wooden chair. He wiped the seat with a cloth only slightly less dirty than the chair itself.

As soon as Lady Matlock was seated, the mayor drew the magistrate aside and began whispering earnestly to him. The magistrate shook his head repeatedly. Elizabeth hurried to her ladyship's side and began to fan her. From this new vantage point, she could see Frederica counting coins into the guard's hand. Bribing an officer of the law?

After a few minutes, Lady Matlock appeared to have recovered from her half swoon rather decisively. Had she used the time to concoct a plan?

She beckoned the mayor and the magistrate to her. "I know you must be as disturbed as I am by these discoveries," she said ignoring the magistrate's profoundly dubious expression. "I am but a mere woman, but my son has reminded me what Lord Matlock would say in such a circumstance."

The mayor bowed deeply. "I pray you to enlighten us, my lady."

"Obviously there is need of a new trial, one before a competent judge in possession of all the facts. In the meantime, my two dear boys shall be released to my custody, and will give you their word of honor as gentlemen not to depart the vicinity. As for their friends here," she waved her hand at the other men, "I am certain you can have no objection to delaying their punishment until my husband arrives. I shall personally fund the costs of their food and keep during this time."

The magistrate crossed his arms. "I find this a remarkable series of coincidences."

"So do I," announced Lady Frederica, "but as it happens, it serves my purposes." She marched over to stand in front of Beaumont, her hands on her hips. "Whether you are guilty of loom breaking I cannot say, though I would not be the least bit surprised if you were. As far as I am concerned, gaol is the proper place for you.

242

On your last trip to Matlock House, you hid my very favorite doll, and teased me about it for days. I never found her, either. Is there anything you wish to confess to me in order to convince these gentlemen your word of honor actually means something?"

Colonel Fitzwilliam groaned. "Oh, leave be, Freddie! That was almost twenty years ago. I doubt he even remembers."

"On the contrary; I remember quite well," said Beaumont. "I wrapped her in an old shirt and put her in a trunk in the attic along with her cradle. May I offer my deepest apologies for my crass behavior as a youth?"

A wicked smile crossed Frederica's face. "I told you I would get my revenge someday," she said with great satisfaction.

Lady Matlock stood, leaning on Colonel Fitzwilliam's arm. "Frederica, how many times must I tell you that revenge is not a ladylike sentiment? Now come, I am quite fatigued by all this nonsense and wish to return to the inn. With my boys," she added pointedly.

The mayor tugged at the magistrate's sleeve with a pleading look. "I would be very happy to accept the gentlemen's parole."

The magistrate's eyes narrowed, but he shrugged.

In less time than Elizabeth would have imagined possible, they were all back in the coach, this time with the addition of the two condemned, malodorous men. Latimer began to babble his gratitude to Lady Matlock, but Beaumont cut him off. "I have only one question. Have I the honor to be addressing the Countess of Matlock or Mrs. Sarah Siddons of Drury Lane? That was a masterpiece of acting, my lady."

"Not at all," Lady Matlock said graciously. "It was Frederica who convinced them by bickering with you. That part about the doll's cradle was an excellent touch."

"Misdirection is always most convincing in the details," he replied with a smile. "I hope Matlock House does have attics, though."

On his return, Darcy was in no mood for company. Richard, of course, was off to see his beloved, and Darcy had hoped to escape a long evening with Jasper, but to no avail.

"Darcy." Jasper wore an unusually serious expression. "What happened between you and Miss Bennet yesterday?"

Darcy's gut tightened. "What do you mean?"

"When you brought her here, her dress was torn and she looked as if she had been thoroughly kissed. I'm not a fool."

Thoroughly kissed? That was an appropriate description. "I kept her safe from the mob."

"But was she safe from you?"

Darcy hissed through his teeth. "Why the inquisition? I have never seen you care what happened to any woman outside the family before."

Jasper shrugged. "True, but it is different when the woman in question is my future wife."

Darcy had to force out the words, his throat turned to ice. "You have offered for her?" Was that why she had refused him?

"Not yet, but I imagine I will. Mother wants the match, and Miss Bennet is as pretty and pleasant a girl as I can hope for."

"Your mother wishes it? She has said so?"

"Of course not. Can you imagine her being so direct? But when she invites a girl with no connections to us on a long journey which has a chance of being dangerous, insists I come as well, and then makes certain I am seated next to her every night at dinner, even I can see the pattern."

His Elizabeth married to Jasper? No. Intolerable. He must put a stop to it. "I did not want her to look like a target, so I tore the lace from her dress, then I pretended she was just another bit of muslin and kissed her." Into the silence he added savagely, "Thoroughly."

Jasper pursed his lips. "Well, since it was you, I suppose I can overlook it."

"How very generous of you, but since I am the one who compromised her, I should be the one marrying her."

His cousin waved his hand. "No reason why you should. I do not mind."

Darcy turned his back, pretending to examine the clock on the mantle. Through gritted teeth he said, "You will so easily accept your mother's choice for your bride?"

"Why should I not? Mother is almost always correct, and she understands the female mind better than I ever shall. She picked well, you must admit. Miss Bennet has a sense of humor, is not prone to taking fright or swooning, has not complained or nagged -- at least not in my presence -- and does not seem fascinated by fripperies. I would not enjoy a marriage to any of the fashionable misses at Almack's."

Jasper would not enjoy marriage to Elizabeth, either, not if Darcy had anything to say about it. Perhaps he should tell Jasper that Elizabeth had nagged every man in Hertfordshire mercilessly. But if Jasper was correct, Lady Matlock favored the match, and his aunt always achieved what she set out to do. She was the one he had to convince, and quickly.

Chapter Twelve

Darcy had no doubts he could ride into battle against Bonaparte himself without a second thought, so why did he find his courage deserting him at the prospect of talking to his aunt? A foolish question — anyone acquainted with both would consider Lady Matlock a more wily and dangerous opponent than Napoleon. Reluctantly he raised his hand to knock on the door of her private sitting room.

The room was normally another bedroom, but the innkeeper had converted it to a sitting room for his aristocratic guest. Lady Matlock sat at a small desk writing a letter, while her maid squinted over her sewing in the corner by the window.

Lady Matlock studied his face for a minute. "You look grim, my dear. What is the matter?"

Darcy glanced at the maid, then back at his aunt. "I need your help."

The maid was already packing up her sewing when Lady Matlock gestured to her to leave them. "Well, it is about time, I must say. I was starting to think I would never smoke you out."

Darcy sank into an upholstered chair. He should have known she would be two steps ahead of him. As soon as the door closed behind the maid he covered his face with his hands. "I have made such a mull of it that even you may not be able to save me."

"That remains to be seen," she said kindly. "Who is she?"

He dropped his hands and stared. "You do not know?"

"I do not, although it is not for lack of trying. Even when I made you go to every society event in the hope you would give yourself away when you saw her."

A pained chuckle rose in his chest. "Is that why you made me escort Frederica everywhere?"

"It was true she needed your support, but I did not wish to watch you continue to mope forever, so I stepped in. You have played your cards close to your chest, though. I never was able to spot you behaving differently to any young woman."

"That is because she was not there." How many of those dreadful balls had he endured for nothing?

"And that brings us back to my question: who is she?"

He could not bear sitting still, but there was not even room to pace. His restlessness pushed him to his feet, though, and he stood directly in front of the spot where his aunt sat. "You have seen me with her many times now. Elizabeth Bennet."

Lady Matlock leaned back in her chair. "Miss Bennet? Good heavens, you truly have made a mull of it. She does not even seem to like you. Do not loom over me, Darcy; you are far too tall."

"What does my height have to do with it?"

"Not a thing, but do sit down. Take a deep breath, and tell me all about this mull you have made."

Lady Matlock sipped her tea at breakfast the next morning. "After raising three sons, I thought I was beyond being surprised at how much one person could eat at one meal, but you put them to shame, Mr. Latimer. At the gaol, we were reassured that all the prisoners were well-fed. I assume that must have been a slight exaggeration."

Latimer swallowed hurriedly and set down his fork for the first time since he had begun to tear into his food. "My apologies, your ladyship. I fear I must have misplaced my manners during my imprisonment. I will try to do better."

"You mistake my meaning," said Lady Matlock. "Pray, eat as much as you like. I daresay any of us would do the same in your circumstances. My concern is for your fellow prisoners. I said I would provide for them while they awaited a new trial, and I am considering how best to do so. I could simply send money for their keep, but I suspect it might end up lining other people's pockets rather than the stomachs of the prisoners. No, I think we shall pay another visit to the gaol today and deliver food to them ourselves." She glanced at Latimer's plate. "A great deal of food, apparently."

"That is very generous of you. After spending a fortnight in a cell with those men, I feel as if I know them better than some of my oldest friends, and they have suffered enough." Latimer's hand strayed towards his fork again.

"You and Mr. Beaumont will come with us as proof you have not absconded."

Frederica stopped buttering her toast and looked up. "Would it look suspicious if I come? I did tell the mayor I had to visit the gaol yesterday because I would be leaving today."

Sir Anthony laid his hand on hers. "You should not go in any case, for the same reason I cannot. Too many people have met you now as Mrs. Hopewell, so it would be better if you did not appear in public as Lady Frederica."

"How annoying!" said Frederica. "But I suppose you are correct. I do enjoy being Mrs. Hopewell." She gazed warmly at her husband.

Elizabeth was starting to miss Frederica's quarrels with Sir Anthony now that they had been replaced with a constant diet of sweetness and meaningful gazes. "I would be happy to accompany your ladyship if you wish." The gaol sounded more pleasant than spending the time watching the newlyweds cooing like turtledoves.

"Thank you," said Lady Matlock. "Richard and Jasper, I hope you will join us. Given the unrest two days ago, I prefer to have a larger party."

Finally, an opening for the question Elizabeth had been longing to ask all morning. "A maid said Mr. Darcy returned here last night. Will he be going with us as well?"

Lady Matlock gave her a significant look. "He was here, but he went out again this morning to pay a call. I do not expect him back until dinnertime."

Jasper speared a sausage and held it up. "A call? Darcy did not mention knowing anyone here."

"Either put that sausage down or eat it," his mother said repressively. "Darcy does not tell you everything. He is calling on the daughter of an old friend. I always expected them to make a match of it, and perhaps this time they will."

Bile rose in Elizabeth's throat. There was her answer, but it was not the one she had hoped for. Despite that passionate kiss, Darcy had no intention of resuming his courtship of her. She was his past, and his previous good opinion of her had been lost forever. A fortnight ago she would not have cared. Now her chest ached from her sense of loss. "If you will excuse me, Lady Matlock, I owe

Mrs. Collins a letter to tell her we have arrived safely. Perhaps I can get part of it written before we go to the gaol." She spoke as steadily as she could, but something in Lady Matlock's expression suggested she had not missed Elizabeth's distress.

It was the same expression a cat who had stolen the cream might wear. "Of course, my dear. Do give Mrs. Collins my regards."

Elizabeth fled with as much dignity as she could muster.

"Next time," said Lady Matlock as they prepared to depart from the gaol, "we should bring a cart." As it was, all the food they had carried from the inn had disappeared remarkably quickly.

As the two footmen who had accompanied them were attempting to manage all the empty baskets, Colonel Fitzwilliam opened the door for his mother, but before she could step through, he closed it again. "There is trouble out there. Another mob."

"Richard, open that door. The townspeople know we are here to help them, not to add to their oppression."

"Mother..."

"I am not going to remain in this gaol in fear of a crowd of people," said Lady Matlock. "Open the door, or I will open it myself."

With an exaggerated sigh, the colonel opened the door again. Lady Matlock led the way, but Elizabeth was careful to stay between Beaumont and Latimer. The idea of plunging into another crowd of shouting, angry people was terrifying.

Beaumont leaned towards her. "There is no need to worry. They are angry at the potato farmers. The square is half empty when it should be full of food sellers for market day. The bad harvest come home to roost."

"Why are they angry at the potato farmers?" she asked. Craning her neck, she could see women and men snatching potatoes

"Most likely they are charging an outrageous price, since there is so little food available." Beaumont shook his head. "Taking a profit at the cost of people's lives."

The shouting grew louder. Something flew through the air – a potato? – near the carts, and then the air was full of projectiles. Potatoes, rocks, cobblestones, and some things she could not recognize, and the sound of breaking glass. None of it came near Lady Matlock's party, but suddenly a surge of people ran in their direction.

Out of the confused shouts, Elizabeth could make out Beaumont's name, and then Latimer's as well. Beaumont took her shoulders and moved her towards Colonel Fitzwilliam just before he was surrounded by several men speaking urgently to him all at once. As Elizabeth shrank closer to the colonel, a new voice cried out, "Matlock! Lady Matlock!"

As if nothing untoward was happening, Lady Matlock stopped and turned to the crowd. She held up her hand and said clearly, "What is the matter?"

A dozen men in red coats poured into the opposite side of the square, formed a line, and pointed their muskets at the crowd. "Thank God," breathed the colonel. "The militia."

Screams sounded as the rioters closest to the militia fled, but the majority of the crowd pressed forward towards Lady Matlock. One ragged woman threw herself at Lady Matlock's feet and clutched her skirt. "Don't let them take me, m'lady! I never stole a thing in my life, but my little boy is so hungry, and the baby died a fortnight ago. If they take me, my children will die!"

"We need potatoes!" shouted a man. "Those thieves are charging twice last week's prices!"

Showing no sign of distaste, Lady Matlock helped the woman to her feet. "Your children are going hungry? We cannot permit that. I will help you."

Latimer said quietly, "Your ladyship, half of the children in the town are starving because their parents cannot find work. Many have died already."

"Could this possibly be true? Children starving in our own country?" Lady Matlock asked loudly of no one in particular.

There was a mutter of agreement from the crowd, now quieter but watching closely. "Ever since the looms came," said one woman.

Lady Matlock's brows drew together. "How can this be? We give to charities to help the starving orphans in Portugal, and let our own children go hungry. This is not acceptable. Richard!"

The colonel stepped up smartly. "Yes, madam?"

"Did you hear that? There are babies dying of hunger and their parents cannot afford the price of potatoes. You will buy all that farmer's potatoes and distribute them to these good people!"

"*All* his potatoes?" The colonel eyed the heaping wagons, the leveled muskets, and the rock throwers.

"*All* of them," she said firmly. "Jasper, you will oblige me by finding a baker and doing the same. The children will need bread as well."

"I'll show him the way," said one woman, tears running down her face. "Bless you, madam."

Lady Matlock said firmly, "My husband will be horrified to discover what is happening here. Sheffield may lie outside Matlock lands, but we are all Northerners together."

A ragged cheer answered her. Lady Matlock nodded graciously and waved to the crowd before resuming her journey to the inn. Elizabeth clutched at her skirt to hide the shaking of her hands.

Inside the inn, it was as if nothing had happened. Sir Anthony, sitting with Lady Frederica by the hearth, rose to his feet and raised an eyebrow. "Have you saved the day, your ladyship?"

"Of course," she said with satisfaction. "If saving the day means stopping a riot, calming the populace, preventing children from starvation, and causing the Fitzwilliam name to be honored in Sheffield for generations to come, all for less than the cost of a formal dinner party at Matlock house — why, if that is what you mean, I daresay I was quite successful."

Her new son-in-law laughed. "To think that I once believed an alliance with your *husband* would be a benefit of marrying Frederica! I had no idea what a valuable ally her *mother* would prove to be."

Elizabeth spent the remainder of the afternoon vainly attempting to write a letter to Jane. How could she explain that she had arrived safely, apart from being in two riots, during one of which Mr. Darcy ripped her dress and kissed her passionately in an alley in order to protect her from thieves? That she had visited the Sheffield gaol twice, but the gardens at Bolton House had been lovely, and she had learned how little Wickham had deserved her trust and how important the price of potatoes could be? Not to mention that Mr. Darcy had made her an offer which she had refused and now wondered if she had made the right decision! It had only been five days since they had left London, but it seemed like months ago that she and Frederica had called at Gracechurch Street.

It had to get easier from here.

There was no point in trying to write to Jane, not when her mind was full of images of the hungry men in the gaol and the desperate people outside. Heavens, if she had to see much more of this, she might become a Radical herself! And then there was Mr. Darcy and her confused feelings about him.

On a whim, she picked up the pen she had just set aside, crossed out the salutation in the otherwise blank letter to Jane, and began to write.

Dear Mr. Darcy,

Do you suppose it is fair to kiss a lady as if your future depended upon it, and then to avoid her company by running off, not just once, but twice? I cannot say I do. It is just one more way in which you confuse me. I was so convinced of your disdain for me that your offer came as a complete shock. Of course, you did not hesitate to express that disdain for my family and my position in life, even as you were telling me how ardently you admired and loved me! How am I to make sense of you? On Monday you told me you loved me; on Wednesday you rescued me from the mob and taught me how to kiss, and now on Friday you are pursuing another woman. Is it too much to ask for a little civil conversation in between these events?

When I first saw you at the Assembly, I thought you handsome but unlikely to be interested in anyone in Meryton. Your set-down showed me your manners were not as handsome as your face, and I had seen enough bad manners in my own family. I might have found you interesting during those days at Netherfield, but for everything I saw to admire in you, there was a reminder of how far beneath you I was. You were the only man in Meryton who ever suggested reading books was a virtue for a woman or who could match me in a game of wits. But what woman wants to like a man who does not find her handsome enough to tempt him and considers her unworthy of his interest? Yes, your fortune is far superior to any I might have, but it is not at all pleasant to know someone thinks you beneath their notice. It was much easier to take a pointed dislike to you and to fall into the hands of the one man who did show real interest in me.

I still do not understand your proposal to me. How can you wish to marry someone who you feel is a degradation to you? That my family is not your equal I do not contest, but how can you simultaneously wish to spend your life with me and think so little of me? Instead of refusing you immediately, I wish I had asked you that. Without that answer, I know nothing of you, but your kisses told me you are not indifferent to me.

Her pen flew over the paper so quickly the words were half-illegible and blotted, but as her hand began to tire, she could see the pattern. She had always seen things to admire in Mr. Darcy as well as the proud and disdainful air she disliked, but she had been determined to think ill of him in return for the ill she had thought he believed of her. And she *still* did not know what he thought of her now.

Somehow she had to find a way to have a private conversation with Mr. Darcy. This icy silence between them had tied her stomach in knots. All day she had felt his absence like an open wound.

Even if she had lost his good opinion, even if he had no respect for her, she could not allow matters to be left as they stood. She owed him thanks for protecting her and an apology for the bitterness of her refusal. If he still wanted nothing to do with her then, at least she would have a clear conscience.

His kisses had nothing to do with it. Nothing at all.

Elizabeth went down for dinner early in hopes of finding Mr. Darcy alone, but he was not there. She would have to try to catch him after dinner. She could not stand the idea of having these thoughts hanging over her head overnight.

But he did not appear in time for dinner, nor during the meal. Lady Matlock glanced at the door more than once with a worried expression. After the final remove was taken away, Elizabeth overheard her telling a servant to go out and make inquiries about him.

She could not forget his absence for even a minute, not least because their party was diminished. Sir Anthony and Lady Frederica had once again gone out as Mr. and Mrs. Hopewell, and Colonel Fitzwilliam had disappeared. Frederica had said something about him visiting his lady-love, but this might have been just a guess. Even though Lady Matlock had remarked on his frequent absences, it seemed not to cause her any concern. Darcy's disappearance, though, clearly fit in a different category.

Her mind conjured up all too many possibilities. He might have been thrown from his horse or attacked by footpads, but most of her worries came back to the riot in the square. Had he been caught in it and injured or even killed for his purse? Her stomach seemed to be filled with gravel.

Lady Matlock's servant returned just as the curfew bell rang. Elizabeth could not make out his soft conversation with her ladyship, but the frequent shaking of his head attested to his lack of success in locating Mr. Darcy. And Darcy would not be out on the streets after curfew. Either he had decided to spend the night elsewhere and chosen not to send them word, or something had gone very wrong.

Chapter Thirteen

Why was someone shaking her shoulder when she had finally fallen asleep? Worry and regret had kept sleep away for too long. Elizabeth attempted to roll away from the disturbance. "Go away."

"I am sorry, Miss Bennet, but her ladyship requests your immediate presence."

Elizabeth squinted up at the mob-capped head of Lady Matlock's maid, lit by a single candle. "What time is it?" It looked to be still full dark outside.

"Lady Matlock thinks it is time for her to see you. Do you require assistance to dress?"

"Not unless this is a formal occasion. I do not suppose you can tell me what the matter is?"

"That is her ladyship's business." She lit the candle beside Elizabeth's bed from her own.

The counterpane fell back as Elizabeth pushed herself to a sitting position. "Very well. You may tell her ladyship to expect me."

"Yes, miss." The maid gave a pointed sniff as she turned to leave.

Elizabeth stretched, and then chose a dress from the wardrobe. Not that there was much choice at this point in the journey! But the blue muslin with the buttons in front would be the easiest to put on, even if it had a stain on the hem. No one was likely to notice that at this time of night.

What could Lady Matlock possibly want of her? Could something have happened to Mr. Darcy? A stab of pain stopped her from breathing for a moment.

No, of course not. She was the last person Lady Matlock would send for if Mr. Darcy were hurt. Every other member of their party had a close relationship with him and would be more suitable for such a summons. More likely Frederica had quarreled with her husband once again and Lady Matlock wanted her to soothe her daughter, or perhaps it was for some reason of her own. Lady Matlock always seemed to have a reason for what she did, even if no one else could comprehend it.

She decided to forgo her stays and wound her hair into the simplest of styles. Then it was time to brave the dragon.

The lady's maid was still fastening the tiny buttons on the back of Lady Matlock's dress when Elizabeth arrived. Her ladyship's toilette was much more complicated than her own, but in the middle of the night? She had expected Lady Matlock to be in a dressing gown. But something looked different about her. Perhaps it was the pallor of her cheeks and the worried line of her mouth.

"Ah, Miss Bennet. Thank you for coming so promptly."

"Of course, your ladyship. How may I be of assistance to you?"

"Darcy has been found. He is injured."

Elizabeth gasped. "Injured? Is it serious?"

"He is not conscious. Apart from that, I can make out nothing from the messenger's babblings."

Unconscious? Had he been thrown from his horse? Head injuries were terribly dangerous. What if he did not wake up? Her hands were suddenly clammy.

Lady Matlock said, "I must go to him, of course. Richard has disappeared yet again – and I do not wish to know where he is spending his nights! – and Jasper will have to stay here to guard Latimer and Beaumont. Not that they need it, but I did give my word to keep them in custody. The newlyweds are busy being newlyweds, so I fear you are elected as my companion by default. My apologies for disturbing your rest."

"Of course. I will be happy to accompany you." Her throat was so tight it was painful to swallow. Darcy might not love her any longer, but she could not bear to lose him completely.

Half in a daze she followed Lady Matlock's instructions. Two yawning footmen, apparently their escort, snapped to attention at the sight of the Countess.

A disheveled boy served as their guide. His voice kept breaking as he apologized to Lady Matlock again and again, first for disturbing her and continuing to beg her forgiveness that her nephew should have been wounded in Sheffield. It might have been amusing had Elizabeth not been so terrified.

The town was under curfew, so the streets were empty apart from a pair of militia officers in the square. A quick word from one of the footmen not only assured their party's passage, but led to the officers accompanying them the remainder of the way.

They stopped at a small terraced house on a humble street. The door was opened immediately by a plump woman who bore a distinct resemblance to the boy. She took over the stream of apologies he had begun.

"I am so sorry to disturb your ladyship, terribly sorry. We did not know who he was at first, just some poor gent who was hurt in the riot and we brought home with us out of charity. We found his card case, but none of us can read. It wasn't until I sent my boy to the apothecary for some medicine for the poor man, and he showed the apothecary the card, that we knew. Then we sent word to you straight away."

Lady Matlock held out her hand to her maid, who placed several coins in it. "This is for your kindness and good sense in sending for me and for realizing my nephew was more valuable than his silver card case. Now if you will be so kind as to take me to him?"

"Of course, your ladyship," she stammered. "Just this way. It is very humble, but it is our best bed." She picked up a rush light and led up a set of narrow, none too clean stairs and through a low doorway.

Lady Matlock entered the room but then halted, leaving Elizabeth unable either to proceed or to see what was inside. Oh, how could she wait another minute when Mr. Darcy was injured? Was he still alive? She stood on tiptoe and craned her neck, but could make out nothing in the shadow filled room.

Finally, finally Lady Matlock stepped forward. Now Elizabeth could see Darcy's bandaged head. He was covered with a worn sheet as pale as his face. Lady Matlock placed her hand on his shoulder. "Darcy? Can you hear me?" But his eyes remained shut, and after a minute her ladyship turned her face away so no one could see it.

Elizabeth swallowed hard. If only she had the right to reach out to him! But he had offered her that right, and she had thrown it back in his face. Now it was all too late.

"Aye, this is how he has been. Opened his eyes once or twice, but didn't seem to see nothing."

Lady Matlock said quietly, "I sent for a doctor who will be along shortly. He will tell us whether Darcy can be moved from here. Elizabeth?"

The sound of her name startled Elizabeth. Lady Matlock had never called her anything but Miss Bennet.

But if it allowed her to be closer to Mr. Darcy, her ladyship could call her whatever she liked. "Yes, madam?"

"Elizabeth, perhaps he might respond to you."

She was already moving forward. "I cannot imagine he would respond to my voice if he did not to yours, but I will try." She took his hand between hers. "Mr. Darcy, it is I, Elizabeth Bennet. If you can hear me, I beg of you, squeeze my hand."

To her shock and even more profound relief, his eyes fluttered open. "Elizabeth." His voice was cracked and low. "So tired..." His eyelids dropped down again, but as they did, his hand tightened fractionally on hers.

Hot tears pricked her eyes. He was alive, and knew her. That was enough for now. But she could not bring herself to release his hand.

"Thank heavens!" said Lady Matlock. "That was well done, Elizabeth. Clearly you must be the one to remain with him, so I will return to the inn to make arrangements. Send the doctor to meet me as soon as he has examined Darcy."

"I? Of course, if you wish," Elizabeth stammered.

Lady Matlock turned to the woman of the house. "Pray leave us."

The plump woman made an attempt at curtseying while backing out of the door. "Anything your ladyship wants."

Lady Matlock shut the door firmly behind her. "One of the footmen will remain here with you, so you need have no worries, even if this *is* a den of thieves. One more thing." She removed a gold ring from her hand and, taking Elizabeth's left hand in hers, pushed it onto her fourth finger. "It will be safer if they believe you are married."

Elizabeth stared down at her hand. "Married? But..."

"I will take care of everything, and I thank you for your willingness to stay with my nephew. I feel much safer knowing he is in your hands."

"But what if he worsens?" She must have sounded as desperate as she felt.

"Send me word. The doctor may not arrive until morning, but as soon as it can be arranged, you will have Darcy's valet here with food and other comforts for you. If the doctor says he should not be moved, he can assist you in any other way you need."

And with no further ado, Lady Matlock opened the door and left. Elizabeth stared after her in bewilderment, then looked down at the heavy gold ring adorning her hand.

She sank down in a rickety stool beside Darcy's bed, her chest aching at the sight of his still body. None of this made any sense. Was it all a dream? Lady Matlock's odd, arbitrary behavior, her desire to leave her nephew's bedside so precipitously, and above all her decision to leave Elizabeth alone with Darcy, seemed so like the irrationality of a dream, but this was far too vivid to be anything but reality. Perhaps it was just that she wished Mr. Darcy's injuries were nothing but a bad dream.

She leaned over to examine him more closely. His breathing was slow and even, and his pallor was more pronounced than she had thought at first. The bandage on his head revealed dried blood on the edge. Was that his only injury? She should have thought to ask.

His hand moved to pluck restlessly at his cravat.

"Mr. Darcy?" she asked.

No answer this time, but his desire was clear enough. She moved the lantern closer and saw his stickpin was inserted at an odd angle. Had it been removed to be sold as well and then hurriedly replaced? She pulled it out and set it aside, and then attempted to loosen the knot. Why did men always have to tie their cravat in such complicated ways? It should not be harder than untangling embroidery thread, but she had never been forced to do that while only a few inches from Mr. Darcy, his breath warm on her cheek, his now familiar scent of spice and bergamot taking her back to memories of their kiss. How could his mere scent make her whole being respond to him?

Forcing herself to focus on his cravat, she tugged and twisted until the knot came free. Unwinding it was easier, except when she had to reach under the nape of his neck, an action so intimate her breath caught in her throat. His skin was so much softer than she would have expected.

His head turned towards her. "Elizabeth?" he muttered.

"I am here." She would not tell him how her heart raced at the sound of her Christian name on his lips. Oh, those lips! He *must* recover; he simply must. She could not bear it otherwise.

His lips twitched. "Good." He reached out his hand.

It was so natural to take it in her own, and so comforting.

With a sigh, he settled their linked hands on his chest. "Why is it so dark?"

She did not even attempt to hide her smile of relief. "It is the middle of the night." Her heart swelled simply hearing his voice.

"Oh." His eyelids drifted down.

The weight of the world seemed to have been lifted from her. Her feet itched to dance around the room, but she did not wish to release his hand, not when the contact felt like a deep tie between them. Even if it was not.

But with relief, she began to think of what might happen next. What would Darcy think when he awoke fully and discovered she had spent the night alone with him? Would he understand how her sentiments had altered, or would he believe she was attempting to entrap him? She could not bear it if he withdrew from her again; and like it or not, she was truly compromised now.

If it were not so serious, it might almost be amusing. Which would be considered more compromising —

kissing Mr. Darcy on the street, or this? It did not matter; either one was enough to ruin her completely if word got out. She might have managed to escape notice for the kiss, but now she was well and truly beyond redemption. Lady Matlock could hardly have put her in a worse position had she tried.

She straightened so abruptly the stool wobbled under her. Lady Matlock *had* planned it! Between her inexplicable choice to bring Elizabeth rather than someone more suitable, her odd behavior here, and above all her insistence that she should claim to be married. There could be no other explanation.

But *why*? Her mind was too muddled with worry and lack of sleep to find an answer. She could do nothing about it now in any case. Yawning, she put her free arm on the edge of the bed and rested her forehead on her arm. That was better. If she could just rest for a few minutes, everything was bound to be clearer.

It was still dark when muffled voices woke Darcy from a troubled slumber. His head ached abominably and something poked him in the back.

He turned his head from side to side, still unable to make out anything in the dark, but someone was holding his hand, someone with a scent of lavender. Could it be? "Elizabeth?" he croaked.

"Oh, you are awake! Is there anything I can get for you? A little wine, perhaps? Lady Matlock sent it, so I assume it is tolerable." She made an attempt to extricate her hand, but he held firm to the one solid thing in his universe. He smiled with the realization she did not struggle.

Another woman's voice, her accent betraying low origins, said, "The doctor is here, Mrs. Darcy."

Mrs. Darcy? Elizabeth was going to have a few words to say about *that* misapprehension! Too bad it would likely be the end of her willingness to hold his hand.

But she did not pull away. Instead, she said, "Thank you for coming. Mr. Darcy has suffered a blow to his head. He was unconscious for some hours apart from very brief moments, but he has just awakened." She sounded as groggy as he felt.

The doctor's gravelly voice said, "Mr. Darcy, can you tell me what happened?"

"I... No. The last thing I recall is riding away from the inn." His lips were cracked and dry.

"Not unusual, to forget a bit after a blow to the head. Mrs. Darcy, when was it that your husband rode away from the inn?"

"Just yesterday morning."

Mrs. Darcy again! Could it be? He rubbed his fingers against hers surreptitiously. Good God, there was a band on her fourth finger – and she was staying with him at night. Could he possibly have married her and then

272

forgotten? How could it have happened so quickly? It made no sense. But thinking made his head hurt even more, so he stopped.

He could test it, though. "Mrs. Darcy?" he asked tentatively.

"Yes?" Elizabeth sounded amused, but she squeezed his hand.

Well! He was not about to admit to forgetting their marriage. "Is there not a light which can be brought?"

"A light?" She sounded puzzled. "If you wish."

"Thank you. I do not enjoy conversing with strangers in the dark." His head ached abominably.

The only response was a prolonged silence. Finally Elizabeth said, her voice strained, "It is morning, and it is not dark."

"Not dark? Of course it is dark. I cannot see a thing." The words seemed to resound.

Someone moved towards him. It must be the doctor, since Elizabeth's hand was still in his.

The doctor said soothingly, "No matter, no matter. It is no doubt merely something passing. Please hold your eyes steady, Mr. Darcy, as if you were looking straight ahead."

Blind? He could not be blind! A wave of panic threatened to engulf him, but he obeyed. The air seemed to stir above his face.

"Hmm. I will need to examine you further. Mrs. Darcy, would you be kind enough to leave us?"

"No!" The word seemed to have risen involuntarily from his throat. "She stays."

Another pause. "Very well." The doctor sounded as if he were speaking to an unruly child. "Mrs. Darcy, you may wish to look away."

Fingers moved his head to the side and began to probe at the back of it. Darcy gritted his teeth against the sudden pain of what felt like an anvil dropped into his wound.

"Hmm, it appears you were hit twice. You have a lump the size of a goose egg over your occipital bone, and a laceration above it. I suspect you lost some blood before it clotted. That might explain your loss of vision."

"Then it will return as soon as I recover?"

Another pause. "Perhaps. Head injuries are difficult to predict."

His throat tightened. "Does that also means perhaps not?"

"Perhaps not. I am sorry." Again as if he were speaking to a child. "I will give you some laudanum. Relieving the pain and sleeping will be the best medicine."

He heard a stopper pop out of a bottle followed by the sound of pouring liquid. Normally he detested laudanum and the loss of control it caused, but if it might help his eyes, he would do anything. Anything.

"Mr. Darcy, can you sit up?"

Of course he could sit up. It was only his eyes which were not working.

A voice as familiar as his own said, "I will assist Mr. Darcy with that."

Wilkins! When had he arrived? It did not matter. He could trust Wilkins to keep him safe.

Wilkins took his free hand and placed a glass in it. "I presume you can hold it yourself, sir."

"Of course." At least Wilkins knew better than to assume he was helpless. Darcy carefully brought the glass to his lips and took a sip. The sweetness of the wine warred with the bitter, astringent taste of laudanum underneath it. He finished it and made a face. When he held out the glass, it disappeared from his grip. God, how he hated this!

"Very good. The best thing you can do, Mr. Darcy, is to lie still and be calm and quiet. I will go to Lady Matlock and report these developments."

"No. Do not tell her about my... my vision difficulty. Not under any circumstances, do you hear?"

"But, sir, Lady Matlock called for my services and she has a right to be told."

"Absolutely not!" He tried to signal to Wilkins, but it was difficult when he had no idea where the valet stood.

Elizabeth's warm voice washed over him. "Doctor, I would personally be most grateful if you could respect Mr. Darcy's wishes in this regard. Lady Matlock may need to know eventually, but we should not worry her until matters are more settled. Perhaps you could tell her that his vision is a little blurry, and it may take some time for that to resolve."

The scuffling of feet was followed by the clinking of coins. The doctor said, "I suppose I could present it to her ladyship in that manner, if that is your preference."

Elizabeth's hand squeezed his, giving the message that his response was expected. "That would be satisfactory," Darcy said. "No word to anyone else, either."

"Of course, sir. Your privacy is paramount."

Elizabeth must have bribed him very generously.

Had she truly just bribed a doctor? Well, technically she supposed Wilkins had done it, but only after she handed him the pouch of money from Mr. Darcy's pocket. It was just one more sin to add to her growing list. First kissing Mr. Darcy, then pretending to be his wife, and now bribery. Of course, having the pretense of marriage might be just as well, since it appeared Darcy was determined to hold her hand indefinitely.

Not that she minded.

How horrible this must be for him! "Mr. Darcy, is there anything that would ease your discomfort?"

"Is there any wine without laudanum?"

"I believe so." She looked up, but Wilkins was already pouring it. He hesitated at the bedside, and after a moment he offered the glass to her, rather than directly to Darcy. Did he think Darcy would prefer to take it from her?

She accepted it and raised Darcy's hand to the glass. As he sat up to drink, Wilkins slipped two pillows behind his back. Where had those appeared from? Surely they had not been here before. She surreptitiously poked at one of the pillows. Down, wrapped in fine linen. No, those certainly had *not* been there earlier!

He sipped carefully, not spilling a drop, though Wilkins hovered close with a small towel in his hand. Darcy held the empty glass out. "Thank you." His words were slow. "I think I would like to sleep now."

"Of course, sir." Wilkins straightened the bedclothes around him, frowning, no doubt at the poor quality of the cloth.

"Elizabeth?" Darcy sounded worried.

"Right here," she said soothingly and raised his hand to her cheek as proof.

He cupped her face tenderly. "Elizabeth?"

"Yes?"

He fell silent for a moment. "Elizabeth?"

"That is my name, though you may say it as often as it pleases you," she teased.

"I am glad we are married."

Elizabeth froze, not even breathing. How could *he* possibly think they were actually married? She raised her eyes to Wilkins, asking silently for assistance. He looked as stunned as she felt, and lifted empty hands.

Should she correct him? The doctor had said he must remain calm, and he was only just beginning to relax. But would he be angered at her later for her deception? Lady Matlock's instructions surely had not been meant to go as far as deceiving her nephew!

She blew out a breath between her lips. "I... I am glad to hear it." There — she had neither agreed nor disagreed.

Wilkins must have observed her tension. "Mr. Darcy, shall I remain with you while Mrs. Darcy takes a few moments to refresh herself?"

Darcy frowned. "Elizabeth, you will return soon?"

"Of course." As an afterthought, she added, "My dear."

That seemed to soothe him. She tiptoed out of the room before he could change his mind, only to discover the disconcerting sight of two liveried footmen standing at attention in the ramshackle passageway, looking as out of place as tropical birds in an English winter.

One of them indicated to her the room where she might refresh herself. Not that there was much she could do for her appearance without a mirror, but it was a relief to be alone. Even if all she could do was let her mind spin around the impossible situation she found herself in.

She tried to gauge how long it would take Wilkins to assist Mr. Darcy in taking care of necessities, but her anxiety rose the longer she stayed away. Was he looking for her?

Finally she asked one of the footmen to check if it was appropriate for her to return to Mr. Darcy's bedside. When he held the door open for her, she took a deep breath and entered.

Unsurprisingly, Mr. Darcy seemed oblivious to her entry, continuing to speak to Wilkins in some annoyance. "I know I cannot remain here," he said. "But if anyone sees me returning, they will know something is amiss, so we must go to the inn during the night when no one is about."

"Respectfully, sir, there is always someone about, and sneaking in during the middle of the night is likely to draw the wrong sort of attention. And if you do not return at all, they will wonder what you are hiding."

Darcy's frown turned into a long yawn. The laudanum must be taking effect. "There must be some way I can reach the inn without exposing my difficulties. I will think of something. Later."

Elizabeth said, "What if we said the doctor told you your eyes must not be exposed to light until the blurriness improves? Then you could wear a bandage over your eyes, and no one would think anything of your inability to see."

"Elizabeth." He held his hand out to her. "That is a most sensible idea."

Biting her lip, she took his hand, glancing apologetically at Wilkins. He seemed undisturbed by it, and went so far as to mouth the words, "Thank you."

Elizabeth returned to the familiar stool beside his bed as Darcy's eyelids drooped down. Even so, he turned his head towards her with a slight smile. "Would you sing to me?"

The laudanum must be slowing his thinking more than she had realized. But singing to him was no less odd than anything else she had done since coming to his bedside. "If you wish. Is there something you would like me to sing?"

"Whatever pleases you."

The first song that came to mind was one she had learned recently, a translation of an aria by Mozart.

> *You, who have tasted love's mystic spell,*
> *What is this sorrow naught can dispel?*
> *Fair dame or maiden, none else may know*
> *My heart o'erladen, why is this so?*
> *What is this yearning, these trembling fears?*
> *Rapturous burning, melting in tears?*

Her heart suddenly caught in her throat. *What is this yearning, these trembling fears? Rapturous burning, melting in tears?* This was what she had been feeling since he kissed her! Could it be that she, like the singer of the aria, had fallen not into a sort of liking but into *love* with him?

"Is something the matter?" Darcy's speech was beginning to slur.

"No, not at all. I simply forgot the next line, but now I recall it. Do you like this song?

A smile spread across his face. "Very much." His intimate tone suggested he, too, was considering the words.

"Well, then." Willing her pulses to slow, she began to sing again.

> *While thus I languish, wild beats my heart,*
> *Yet from my anguish I would not part,*
> *I seek a treasure Fate still denies,*
> *Naught else will pleasure, naught else I prize*
> *I'm ever sighing, I know not why,*
> *Near unto dying, when none are by,*
> *My heart is riven night, morn and eve,*
> *But ah, 'tis heaven, thus, thus to grieve!*
> *You, who have tasted love's mystic spell,*
> *What is this sorrow naught can dispel?*
> *What is this sorrow naught can dispel?*

As she continued to sing, Darcy shifted his hand to entwine his fingers with hers. This startlingly intimate gesture sent a shock of awareness through her and made her lose a beat in the song, but she forced herself to continue to the end.

Darcy's eyes were closed, but he whispered, "Again?"

Something warm seemed to invade her chest. "Of course." As she began to sing again, feeling unusually out of breath, the lyrics echoed in her head.

When had this happened to her? Certainly her poor opinion of him had softened as she had seen him among his family and heard their unsolicited praise of him, but when had it moved beyond that? Naturally she was grateful he had told Mr. Bingley about Jane and for his efforts to keep her safe on their arrival in Sheffield, and his kisses had made her think of him in a new way, but...

No, with the sudden certainty she knew the moment her heart had begun to change. It had been when Sir Anthony arrived at Rosings and in the process overturned every belief she had about Mr. Darcy. That was when he showed himself to be more than a proud, ill-mannered man; a thoughtful man who was politically astute, who would listen to the views of others; a generous landlord who was loyal enough to friends he had not seen for years that he would drop everything and travel halfway across England on their behalf; and who did not demean Frederica for her Radical tendencies. He tried to settle differences with discussion, rather than with argument or violence as his cousins did, yet he clearly cared for them deeply.

She had seen all that, yet denied it to herself and held onto her anger towards him. Why? Because she could not admit she had misjudged him. She had twisted everything she had seen to support her impression of him. She had been a blind fool, and continued in her foolishness in the face of all evidence, only for the sake of her pride in her ability to judge his character. Her misplaced pride and her poor judgment — she was as much of a fool as Lydia or Kitty who determined a man's worth by the color of his coat! Till this moment, she had not known herself.

Darcy's chest was moving with even breaths before she finished the song. She hoped he would not wake quickly; she needed time to take in this new knowledge and store it within herself.

Chapter Fourteen

Still nothing but darkness. The knot in Darcy's stomach pulled even tighter. He was on the same lumpy mattress with straws poking at him, the same smell of tallow, sweat and smoke surrounding him. At least he could think more clearly since the pulsing pain in his skull had died down a little. He reached up to explore the back of his head. A goose egg indeed! Even touching it lightly caused a stabbing pain.

Elizabeth's voice floated over him. "Are you awake, Mr. Darcy?"

"It appears so, but I still see nothing."

"The doctor said it might take time."

"I know what the doctor said," he said with an edge in his voice.

"I am sorry; of course you do. It is hard for me to know what you remember and what you do not."

"I believe it is only the time just before my injury that I cannot recall." That, and their marriage. But wait — how could he have forgotten something as important as marrying Elizabeth? And they had not even been on good terms before he left. His earlier thinking had been muzzy and the idea of being married to Elizabeth comforting, but now it made no sense.

"Perhaps that memory will return as well, though I myself would be just as happy not to remember being injured." It was a laughing tone of voice that usually accompanied her arch look.

Abruptly he said, "We are not married, are we?"

A sigh. "No, sir, we are not. That was a fiction perpetuated by your aunt to account for my presence here. I was uncomfortable with the pretense, but she was insistent. It did not occur to me that your memory would be impaired enough that you might believe it or I would never have agreed."

How mortifying, to have exposed his feelings so when she had made it clear she wanted none of them. "I was merely confused, and I could not imagine why anyone would call you Mrs. Darcy if it were not true." If only he could get up and leave! He hated being so vulnerable. Elizabeth must think him both a weakling and a fool.

"Mr. Darcy, you must not trouble yourself over it. It was a natural result of the blow to your head. I am glad your thinking is clearer now."

No doubt she was glad not to have to pretend to care about him any longer. "Is Wilkins there?"

"No. He left a few minutes ago to make arrangements for your removal to the inn. Under the circumstances, we thought you would prefer the closed coach."

A closed coach was only the beginning of what he wanted. He would do anything to keep his infirmity and his shame private. Too bad he could not hide from the world forever.

"He is supposed to keep his eyes covered so they can heal fully," Elizabeth explained to the assembled Fitzwilliam clan.

Jasper guffawed. "He looks as if he is playing blind man's buff!"

Colonel Fitzwilliam elbowed him. "The astonishing thing is that he is cooperating. I would have expected him to rip that bandage off the moment the doctor left the room."

No doubt he was correct. Elizabeth thought quickly. "The ability to read is very important to him. He did not wish to take any chances."

Lady Matlock said, "No doubt that is it. Or perhaps he yielded to the gentle persuasion of his companion." She smiled graciously at Elizabeth.

The front door of the inn slammed. "Where the devil is my wife?" a man bellowed.

With amused alacrity, Lady Matlock opened the sitting room door. "Welcome, my dear. How did you know I was here?"

A broad shouldered man with a beaked nose much like Jasper's strode in, slapping his gloves against his riding leathers. Two weary-looking footmen trailed behind him.

"How did I know? Let me see — I rode into Sheffield, thinking no one knew I was coming but the Master Cutler, and no sooner do I arrive than crowds of people pour into the street, cheering and shouting 'God save your lordship,' even holding up their babies to see me. There were only two possible explanations: either they had mistaken me for the Prince Regent, or my wife had been up to some sort of mischief. I hope I am not stout enough to be mistaken for Prinny, so that meant you must have ignored my express instructions to remain at Rosings. My repeated express instructions." He glared at Lady Matlock. "I await your explanation."

Lady Matlock seemed completely unperturbed. "Of course, my dear. They were cheering for you because I bought them potatoes."

"And bread," added Jasper brightly. "I bought the bread. With your money, of course."

His father ignored him. "I had my reasons for telling you to remain in the South."

Lady Matlock clasped her hands in front of her. "I know. Sir Anthony Duxbury kindly explained to me about the troubles. Where did that boy go? Oh, there he is."

"None of this answers the question of why you decided to disobey me."

"Why, to prevent two of Richard and Darcy's dear friends from being hanged," Lady Matlock said as if that explained everything. "And to stop the rebellion, of course."

Lord Matlock heaved himself into a large armchair and covered his face with his hands. "To stop the rebellion? I do *not* want to know this."

Lady Matlock said, "We have been doing a good job of it so far. In your name, naturally."

Elizabeth decided this was the appropriate time for her to step out of the room and away from this embarrassing scene. Apparently Lady Matlock had eyes in the back of her head, for no sooner had she edged her way to the door than her ladyship said, "Elizabeth, pray do not leave. You are part of the family now."

Lord Matlock's head swung towards her. "What? Who is she?"

"My dear, may I present Elizabeth Bennet, the daughter of Thomas Bennet, a gentleman in Hertfordshire. Elizabeth, my dear, pray forgive my husband's lack of manners. He is under great stress."

Elizabeth took a deep breath. "It is an honor to meet you, your lordship, although I cannot and do not claim to be part of your family."

"Of course you are, my dear," said Lady Matlock soothingly. Turning back to her husband, she added, "Elizabeth is Darcy's... well, I am not quite certain what she is."

"His acquaintance, my lord," said Elizabeth firmly. "I am Mr. Darcy's acquaintance."

"She is *my* friend," said Frederica, with an odd look at Elizabeth. "She traveled with us from Kent at my request."

Her mother said, "In any case, Sir Anthony is in full agreement with you that Sheffield is not a safe place for ladies at the moment. He and Darcy wanted to come here by themselves, but I insisted we should all stay together. By the by, our Frederica has married him. Sir Anthony, that is, not Darcy, of course."

Lord Matlock suddenly seemed to swell to twice his size. "Married him?" he roared. "Without my permission or knowledge?"

Frederica stood stock still. "Yes. I insisted. I am of age, after all."

"My dear, it seems our daughter has developed Radical tendencies, as has dear Sir Anthony. I am beginning to worry they will infect Darcy as well. Not Richard, though – he has his own opinions – and Jasper does not seem to care, but no matter. Both Sir Anthony and Frederica believe in the Rights of Man, and the rights of women, too."

Lord Matlock rounded on Sir Anthony. "You could not even manage to pen a letter to me?"

Sir Anthony met his gaze steadily. "Your wife advised me against it, my lord. You have done an admirable job of encouraging your wife and daughter to think for themselves; I would by no means deny their wisdom."

"Spare me your philosophies!" Lord Matlock's face grew redder by the minute. "By God, I do not know what any of you were thinking. Dammit, was there even a reason why you could not have waited a few days? Duxbury, you are welcome to her, for I want no more to do with her!"

Frederica blanched. "Papa, I did not mean to –"

"Did I ask your opinion?" snarled her father.

Lady Matlock started forward. "Perhaps I can explain--

"You could have stopped it, and you did not. I will not listen to your excuses!"

Colonel Fitzwilliam's voice drowned out both his parents. "While we are on the subject of marrying without your consent, I have something to say."

Both Lord and Lady Matlock turned towards him, their expressions ominous.

The colonel stood with his feet apart, his arms crossed. "I was married four months ago. I have no intention of introducing you to my wife in the near future. She has no fortune and no connections, and I do not give a damn what you think of it."

Lord Matlock's eyes narrowed. "You are making this up, trying to distract me."

"I fear I cannot oblige. It is true."

"Then why are you telling me this now?"

The colonel's cold smile showed his teeth. "I thought if you were going to disown Frederica, you might as well disown both of us and get it all done at once."

Fists clenched, Lord Matlock strode towards his son until they stood almost toe to toe. "Who is she?" he demanded.

"Her name is unimportant."

"Why did you keep her a secret?"

"To avoid such a scene as we have just witnessed, not on my own behalf, but that of my wife's. I do not wish to subject her to your disapproval, especially while she is in a delicate condition."

Lady Matlock sat down with a thump, her face white. "Do I know her?" she asked.

"No. None of you have met her, with the exception of Miss Bennet." The colonel nodded towards Elizabeth.

Elizabeth had been doing her very best to pretend she was both invisible and deaf, but now her head snapped towards him. "I?" she said disbelievingly. Who could his mysterious wife be, and when had she met her? Someone in London, perhaps?

Lord Matlock placed his hands on his hips and loomed over her. "Well, Miss Bennet? Who is this wife of his?"

"I have not the least idea, sir. Until this moment, I was completely unaware he was married." She cast a sidelong glance at the colonel.

"You met her at Rosings," the colonel said. "You were distressed about something, and she brewed a tisane for you."

Elizabeth's mouth opened, but no words emerged. Finally she said, "I did not know who she was."

"I am aware of that. But perhaps you, as a disinterested party, would like to tell my father about her."

There was very little she would like to say to Lord Matlock when he was just a few feet away and primed to explode, but she refused to be intimidated. "I cannot tell you much. I did not speak to her for long. She seemed to be a kind young woman with good manners. The only other thing I know about her is..." Elizabeth glanced at Colonel Fitzwilliam before continuing. "She is French."

"*French*!" spat Lord Matlock. "Dammit, Richard, we are at *war* with France!"

Colonel Fitzwilliam actually smiled. "As I have ridden into battle against Napoleon's troops, you may be assured I am well aware of that particular fact."

Lord Matlock closed his eyes and massaged his temples. "French," he said plaintively. "No doubt a Papist as well."

"Yes," said the colonel. "We were married by a priest."

"French," repeated his father. "Did she have to be French?"

The colonel cast an amused glance at his mother. "Given that she was born in France, I believe she had little choice in the matter."

Seeing Lady Matlock's distraction, Elizabeth decided this was a fine moment to slip out of the room.

A knock came at Elizabeth's bedroom door as she was preparing to dress for dinner. Assuming it was the maid come to assist her, she called for her to enter. Instead it was Lady Frederica and Sir Anthony, and when they had entered, Sir Anthony closed the door behind him. Another strict rule of propriety broken – a gentleman in her bedchamber with the door shut. At least there was a chaperone for a tiny bit of respectability. Not that it mattered to her; of all the gentlemen in their party, Sir Anthony was the only one she would feel safe having in her room.

Frederica appeared pale but composed, though her eyes showed traces of redness. "Elizabeth, we have decided it is best for us to leave the inn and stay with some of Mr. Hopewell's acquaintances in town. I do not wish to abandon you here after having invited you to join us on this journey, so I hope you will consent to come with us. Of course, if you prefer to stay here, my mother would be happy to take you under her wing."

It was hardly a surprise they were departing after her father's rejection of her, but for her to go with them? She would be perfectly happy never to lay eyes on Lord Matlock again, but how could she leave Mr. Darcy behind? True, he had his male cousins, but she was the only one apart from his valet who knew of his blindness. No, she could not do it. "That is very thoughtful of you," she said slowly. "While I would like to come with you, I am not certain my family would approve."

Sir Anthony said, "As your honorary brother, I am perhaps the closest thing you have to family here, and while I would not go so far as to say I would disapprove of your leaving, I do think you would be wiser to remain here. No, do not worry; Frederica is aware of my sentiments and agreed you had the right to hear them as well."

Frederica eyed her husband. "You have the right to say them, and I have the right to say you are *wrong*."

Sir Anthony's eyes twinkled. "Precisely so, my dear. My concerns are two-fold; first, your lodgings would likely be less comfortable than these, and second and more importantly, where we are going is not completely safe. I would not consider it precisely dangerous, but consorting with Radicals has been known to lead to trouble. I am not happy about Frederica being there, but it is her right to make that decision for herself."

"I see. Under those circumstances, I will take your advice and remain here." She smiled at Sir Anthony. She would miss him; he was the one in their group she trusted most. If only she could tell him the truth about Darcy's vision! "But I hope I will still have the chance to see you, Frederica. I will miss you."

"Oh, yes," said Frederica airily, no doubt annoyed by Elizabeth's decision. She would be even more unhappy some day when she found out about the secrets she was keeping.

Sir Anthony took a paper from his pocket and handed it to her. "This is where we will be staying. Any servant can take a message there. I would appreciate it, though, if you did not share that information with any of the Fitzwilliams – or the authorities."

"Of course not," she said. But it felt wrong to let them go without a word about Darcy. How would she feel if it were one of her sisters who was blind, and she had been allowed to leave knowing nothing about it? She would be furious. With sudden resolution, she added, "Sir Anthony, might I speak to you privately for just a moment?"

Frederica crossed her arms, now clearly offended. "There is something I cannot hear?"

Elizabeth willed herself to be patient, and held up the piece of paper. "It is like keeping this secret; this is something I have been asked not to tell any member of your family, much as I wish I could tell you. Of course, if Sir Anthony should choose to share it with you later, I would have no control over that. If you are leaving, it is something I think you ought to be aware of, and it explains why I cannot join you."

"Oh, very well." Frederica flounced out of the room.

Elizabeth watched after her. "I hope she will not be angry long."

"Is something the matter? Something I can help you with?" Sir Anthony sounded concerned.

"It is not about me, but Mr. Darcy. As you know, his injury has affected his ability to see, but it goes beyond blurred vision. He is blind. The doctor is unsure if it is temporary or permanent, but Mr. Darcy does not wish his family to know in case his vision returns in the next few days. He does not want anyone's pity."

"No!" His response was a protest against the reality, not an argument. "God in heaven. Poor Darcy."

"That is the other reason I cannot leave. Apart from his valet, I am the only one who knows the truth."

"Of course you must remain here under these circumstances. Darcy will need you." He paced back and forth. "What a terrible thing. I will tell Frederica, but not until we have left, so she will not be tempted to try to speak to him or her parents."

"I would appreciate that."

"Good God, Darcy blind. I cannot take it in. Will you send me a message if anything changes?"

"Of course."

Frowning in thought, he put his hand on the door, then turned his head back. "Thank you for telling me."

Elizabeth smiled, mostly to disguise a desire to cry. "I am becoming quite attached to this idea of having an honorary brother."

He swept her a bow. "The honor, my dear, is all mine."

Dinner was a cold, mostly silent affair. Colonel Fitzwilliam had gone elsewhere to dine, while Mr. Darcy had a tray sent up to his room, leaving only Jasper Fitzwilliam, his parents, and Elizabeth. Beaumont and Latimer were absent as well. Perhaps Lady Matlock felt it would be better not to introduce those particular complications to her husband at this point.

Lord Matlock scowled at his food. Lady Matlock kept up a stream of light pleasantries to Jasper and Elizabeth, avoiding any mention that over half their party was missing. Only Jasper seemed unaffected by his father's mood, teasing and flirting as he always did.

Elizabeth was glad to retire early after having spent so much of the previous night awake. She drifted off to sleep wishing she had the opportunity to check on Mr. Darcy first. Going from being in his constant company to the complete separation demanded by propriety left her feeling somehow incomplete.

She was aroused by a maid shaking her shoulder. Not again! Was this a conspiracy to rob her of sleep every night?

"What is the matter?" Elizabeth asked.

It was one of the maids. "Sorry to surprise you, miss, but you didn't answer when I knocked. Mr. Wilkins wants me to tell you he would be most obliged to you if you were able to come to speak to him for a moment."

"Mr. Wilkins? Oh, yes, Wilkins." She rubbed her eyes. Why would Darcy's valet want to speak to her in the middle of the night? "Yes, of course I will. Tell him I will be there directly."

"Very good, miss. He is in Mr. Darcy's room. Do you know which that is?"

"Yes. Yes, I do." It was the next room down across the passageway. She swung her feet out of bed as the maid left.

Groggily she poured water from the ewer into the basin and splashed her face. Now she was awake, or at least mostly so. Should she dress herself? She had for Lady Matlock, of course, but it would be silly to do so simply to answer a question for Wilkins. And she was so very tired. She found her dressing gown and wrapped it around herself, and then slid her feet into her slippers. That should be good enough.

She padded down the passageway to Darcy's room. Even if she had not known it to be his, it would have been easy to tell. His raised voice could be easily heard through the door. Why was *he* awake?

The door opened almost immediately when she tapped lightly on it. Wilkins, looking even more tired than she felt, said in a quiet, urgent voice, "Thank you for coming. Mr. Darcy is very agitated and keeps asking for you, and I thought perhaps if you spoke to him for few minutes, it might calm him. Since the doctor said he should stay calm and quiet..."

There was no help for it; she stepped into Darcy's room and closed the door behind her. She must be becoming inured to completely inappropriate behavior!

Darcy, dressed only in a nightshirt, sat up in bed, his arm reaching out blindly. "Wilkins? Where are you?"

Wilkins hurried to his side and placed his hand on his master's arm. "Here, sir, and Miss Bennet has come as well." He motioned to her with his head. More quietly he added, "I have given him two doses of laudanum already. He has been fighting it."

Nervously she approached Mr. Darcy from the other side of the bed and sat in the upholstered chair. "Yes, I am here."

He might be unable to see, but he seemed to have an unerring instinct for where her hand was. As he clasped it in his, he said, "I did not mean to do it, you know."

Elizabeth raised her eyebrows at Wilkins in case he might have some idea what it was Mr. Darcy had not meant to do, but he looked puzzled as well. "I know you did not," she said reassuringly.

"Good. I do not know...now I cannot recall what it was."

She patted his hand with her free one. "We can speak more in the morning when you are better rested."

"That is...that is a good idea. Is it late, then?"

She adopted a teasing tone. "It is the middle of the night. I pray you, try to rest."

He lay back on his pillow and closed his eyes. "You will not go?"

Elizabeth rolled her eyes. "I will stay for now, and if I have to leave, I will tell Wilkins how to find me. He can send for me at any time, and I will come."

The corners of his mouth turned down, his lips on the verge of pouting. "Very well."

She rubbed her free hand over her eyes. "Shall I sing to you?" It had worked the previous night, after all.

"I would...like that."

Tonight she would choose her song with a little more care, something more innocent.

She sang 'Under the Greenwood Tree' twice, and then added 'Greensleeves' for good measure until she thought he was asleep. Unsurprisingly, he stirred as soon as she tried to withdraw her hand. It did not matter; she could stay there a little longer without doing any harm. And truth to tell, she was glad to be with him again, even if nothing he said made any sense.

A light rap on the door startled her awake, and for a moment she could not remember where she was or how she had come there. The dim, grey light of dawn showed outside the window, but it was not her window.

Horror struck her. She could not be found in Darcy's room in her dressing gown!

The latch rattled. "Unlock this door!" It was Colonel Fitzwilliam's voice, pitched low and quietly.

Wilkins rubbed his eyes. "Just one moment, sir," he said. Panic in his eyes, he darted over to Elizabeth, took her hand, and led her to a recessed area by the window. It did not hide her completely, but if no one looked in that direction, she might well be missed. "Coming, sir." He paused to hand Darcy the bandage to place over his eyes before unlocking the door. Elizabeth held her breath.

The colonel tiptoed into the room. "I am sorry to disturb you so early, Darcy, but I wanted to take my leave of you. I am leaving for London in a few minutes."

"Leaving? Why?" Darcy sounded sleepy.

"You must not have heard, then. There was quite a scene last night, worthy of Drury Lane. My father did not take the news of Freddie's marriage well and was about to disown her when I decided to distract him by confessing my own marital sins. So now I have been ordered out of his sight, and I think it wisest to return to London where I can protect Sylvie from anyone he sends to find her. Truth be told, I am relieved to have the secrecy over and done."

"You would not have been able to hide it much longer in any case, unless you were willing to stay away from her completely. But is Sylvie able to manage yet another long journey in her condition? Perhaps you should take her to Pemberley instead. It is a much easier distance, and your father is less likely to look for her there."

"I will accept that offer with gratitude. In truth, I hoped you would suggest it. Sylvie deserves better than my London bachelor's quarters. And then we need to decide on our next step."

Darcy said, "My offer of the stewardship of Pemberley still stands."

"I dislike imposing to that extent."

"You would not be imposing. I will need a new steward once old Sutton retires, and..." He hesitated, then continued. "If my vision does not clear enough to allow me to read, I will need someone I can trust implicitly. You would be doing me a great favor."

"Is that a possibility, then? God, Darcy, I am sorry."

"I prefer not to think about it more than I must."

"Will you be returning to London yourself after everything is settled here?"

Darcy hesitated. "That depends on a number of things. I may prefer Pemberley as well. I will have Wilkins send word to you when I know more."

"I hope your vision will be improved enough to write me yourself."

"As do I. Good travels, cousin."

Elizabeth relaxed slightly. If the colonel left now, while the light was still dim, he would be less likely to spot her.

The colonel came into her line of sight then and had his hand on the latch when he turned to say something to Darcy. He froze partway, looking straight at her.

Her heart skipped a beat. What should she do? She could not look more guilty, standing there in her dressing gown.

"Darcy," said the colonel with a hard edge to his voice, "would you care to explain to me what Miss Bennet is doing in your room?"

Darcy's harsh, indrawn breath was audible even from across the room. "She is still here?"

Such short, simple, damning words! She would have to brazen it out. Stepping out into the open, she said, "It is not what you think, Colonel. My room is just across the passageway, and when I heard Mr. Darcy calling out in the night, I came to ask Wilkins what was wrong. When he told me Mr. Darcy had grown agitated and confused after a dose of laudanum, I offered to see if a woman's voice would be more calming, so I sat by Mr. Darcy's bed and talked to him until he fell asleep. His eyes were bandaged the entire time, and I assure you the most compromising thing that happened was he wanted me to sing to him. It was so dull I must have fallen asleep in the chair. Wilkins has been here the entire time and can tell you the same thing." She tried to sound businesslike.

Colonel Fitzwilliam's eyes narrowed. "Darcy, did you compromise Miss Bennet?"

There was a telltale silence from the bed, and then Darcy said, "I do not believe I compromised her last night, but my recollection of it is imperfect."

How neatly he had turned the question into what had happened last night, not whether he had compromised her at all! But his delay in responding apparently had not passed Colonel Fitzwilliam's notice, since he did not look at all reassured.

"I would have you remember she is traveling under the protection of my family. Of our family."

"I am well aware of that, thank you, and I am willing to protect her reputation, should she wish it. Will that satisfy you, cousin?" Darcy said testily.

So there was her answer – he would marry her if she wished, but it was not his wish any longer. She could hardly blame him. Keeping her voice steady, she said, "There, Colonel, you see you have nothing to worry about. Pray give my regards to your wife."

With another of his mercurial shifts, he grinned and winked at her. "I will do that. Darcy, I will see you soon, either in London or at Pemberley." He bowed and left.

A yawning silence filled the room. Wilkins industriously polished one of Darcy's boots in one corner, pretending to see nothing. Darcy ripped off the bandages and lay stiffly back on the bed, his expression grim. What could Elizabeth possibly say which would not give offense? Despite her aching heart, surely there must be something amusing she could find in this mess. She said archly, "Mr. Darcy, have I happened to mention that at times I find your family just the slightest bit trying?"

Darcy seemed to relax a little. "No, you have not, but I cannot claim to be surprised."

"If I could not so clearly see the resemblance in your faces, I might wonder if you were a changeling. Otherwise, how could such a quiet and grave gentleman spring from the same family tree? I will have to give this matter some thought, preferably after I have made myself presentable again. Mr. Wilkins, might I impose on you to check if the corridor is clear for me to get to my room before the rest of the Fitzwilliam clan decides to put in an appearance here?"

"Of course, Miss Bennet."

With his help, she was able to reach her room with no one else the wiser. Without even bothering to remove her robe or slippers, she crawled into bed and pulled her pillow over her head. To think that the worst of her fears about this journey had been that she might quarrel with Mr. Darcy! But if she allowed herself to think about Mr. Darcy right now, she would probably not be able to stop crying, so instead she recited poetry in her head until she fell asleep.

Chapter Fifteen

When Elizabeth finally went downstairs to the private parlor reserved for the Matlock party, Jasper Fitzwilliam was the only occupant.

"Good morning, Miss Bennet. My family has apparently scattered to the winds, so my mother appointed me to entertain you today. It is a duty I am happy to undertake, although it may prove challenging as we are also forbidden to leave the inn, and I am also responsible for our friends from the gaol."

She was not supposed to know about either the colonel or Frederica leaving. "Where has your family gone?"

"Now that is a mystery to me as well! My father is meeting with the mayor and other officials. Darcy is upstairs in bed. Richard has vanished again, but this time he left instructions for his things to be sent on to him. Frederica and Duxbury have simply vanished. My mother is most likely either with my father or trying to find Frederica."

She helped herself to a roll and butter from the sideboard. "You do not sound particularly worried."

"Worried? Why should I be? Richard can take care of himself, Freddie has Duxbury to watch over her, and I have faith that somehow my mother will miraculously fix everything. She usually does." He held out a chair at the table for her.

"I hope she can. It seemed as if she did not expect Lord Matlock to be so angry about Lady Frederica's marriage."

"Oh, he was probably not angry about that."

Elizabeth raised her eyebrows. "It certainly looked that way to me, and apparently to your sister as well."

Jasper shook his head. "He was furious already because we disobeyed his orders and came North, or more especially because Mother did. He cannot bear to have her in danger or Frederica either. Freddie's marriage was just the match which set it off. He would have taken it differently in other circumstances."

"Does Frederica know that? She seemed very distressed."

"If she does not, she ought to; and besides, she knows his anger never lasts long. You saw him at his worst last night, but he is not a bad fellow, at least not when he does not think his family is at risk. He trusts my mother and has always allowed Frederica an unusual amount of latitude, so I will be surprised if he does not accept the marriage eventually."

"I hope he does."

Latimer came into the parlor and bowed to Elizabeth. "Good morning, Miss Bennet, Mr. Jasper."

Jasper said, "I beg you, just Jasper. Mr. Jasper was the name of a tutor whom I despised, so I avoid it at all costs. I have even managed to convince Miss Bennet to drop the 'mister.'"

"As you wish," said Latimer, already loading a plate of food from the sideboard. "We might as well be informal, since I cannot pretend to present a gentlemanly appearance while wearing clothes that look as if they must belong to my elder brother. Duxbury may be closest to my size, but he still has several inches on me." He gestured to his tailcoat, the hem hanging well below his knees. "Beaumont is doing much better in his borrowed finery with all of you tall Fitzwilliams available to provide for him."

"You are quite right, Latimer," drawled Jasper. "I cannot even see your hands within those sleeves, but I assume they must be there in order to carry that immense load of food. How can you still be hungry after all you have eaten these last two days?"

Latimer set his heaping plate on the table. "When you have spent a fortnight in gaol with nothing more than a bit of maggoty bread hard enough to break a tooth on, you may laugh. It may be months before I feel full again!"

Elizabeth signaled to a maid to replenish the now almost bare sideboard. "Mr. Latimer, I hope this is not something you have experienced often."

"Being imprisoned, you mean? This was the first time, and likely the last, at least until I run afoul of Parliament in London. I will continue to work here for a time, but I will not be trusted in the same way after being exposed as an intimate of Lady Matlock. But I make no complaints – I was beyond happy to get out of that cell. I just wish we could help the others."

Elizabeth spread jam on her roll. "They will be re-tried now, will they not?"

"That is what Lord Matlock is hoping to settle today. He has been surprisingly sympathetic to our cause. Good morning, Beaumont."

Beaumont bowed, and his face fell as he noticed the empty sideboard.

"More food is coming," said Elizabeth with a smile.

Latimer gestured to his own plate. "You may share mine until it does."

After breakfast, the three gentlemen decided to while away the time with a game of cards, but Elizabeth begged to be excused. "I did not sleep well last night and would like to rest."

Jasper said, "I am sorry to hear it. Your room faces the street, does it not? I hope the noise outside is not keeping you from sleeping. We could ask for your room to be changed."

"I thank you, but I have not been troubled by the street noise." It was amusing, especially since she had been deprived of her sleep by Mr. Darcy, whose room faced the opposite direction. "I hope you enjoy your game."

She breathed a sigh of relief as she left the parlor. A game of cards sounded like slow torture at the moment, not as much from fatigue than from the unanswerable questions which her mind kept presenting to her. She was by now tolerably acquainted with her own feelings on the subject of Mr. Darcy, but *his* were a mystery. When struck over the head or drugged with laudanum, his affection for her seemed undimmed. But when he was alert, he became dismissive. He had seemed angry after kissing her, and she would not soon forget his words this morning about marrying her if she insisted.

But could she have misinterpreted him? Perhaps he had been angry with his cousin's interference rather than the possibility of marrying her. After all, his attachment to her was long-standing and had survived several harsh quarrels; there was no reason to assume it could not endure her rejection of his proposal as well. No reason except her deep fear that she might have, out of her own stubbornness, lost the one man who would suit her best in the entire world. Her throat felt painfully tight even contemplating the idea.

How long must she live with this uncertainty? She did not even know what his plans were. Did he plan to continue to travel with them, or would he leave their group now that his sight was impaired? He did not seem to want to spend time with his family now, and with Colonel Fitzwilliam gone, he might prefer to go to Pemberley as soon as possible. She might not even see him again for more than a few minutes. Oh, bother – now she had tears in her eyes!

Or she could take matters into her own hands. Had not Charlotte always said that a woman must show her affection to a man in order to catch his interest? After her earlier refusal, it might be more true than ever in this case.

With sudden determination, she headed for his room. It was improper, and she knew better than to go to a gentleman's rooms, but she did not care. Besides, what was one more impropriety on top of all the others? Squaring her shoulders, she rapped on his door.

Wilkins opened it. "May I be of assistance to you, Miss Bennet?"

"Yes. That is, I am unoccupied at present, and I wondered if Mr. Darcy might like me to read to him." It was the best explanation she could think of, and in truth she would be happy to read a new book even if he were not involved.

"One moment, miss. I will enquire." He bowed before closing the door between them.

That was not promising.

It was impossible to keep from wondering what was being said and, when wondering, to listen for it. Through the door she could hear Wilkins say something which included her name and a short response from Mr. Darcy. He did not sound pleased. Wilkins spoke again, and this time the answer was a definite, harsh 'no.' She closed her eyes as a great weight seemed to settle in her stomach.

Wilkins opened the door again. "Mr. Darcy thanks you for the kind offer, but at present he is too fatigued for such an endeavor." His eyes did not meet hers.

Darcy had not said that many words, of that much she was certain. Wilkins was giving her the gentle version, but it was still rejection. He did not wish to see her and would not even take the trouble to tell her so himself.

She had tried, and now it was time to admit failure. "Pray tell Mr. Darcy I hope he is better soon." She could barely force the words out past the lump in her throat.

"I will tell him, Miss Bennet." Wilkins' usual formal tone was gentler than usual.

His unvoiced sympathy was her undoing. She turned away before he could see the tears in her eyes and hurried to her room where she could throw herself on her bed and cry.

Elizabeth straightened her skirt before entering Lady Matlock's private sitting room. Not that much could be done to make it more presentable after lying on it in bed all day, but she did what she could.

"You sent for me, your ladyship?"

"Do sit down, my dear. I hope your headache is better."

"It is beginning to improve, I thank you." A very real headache brought on by hours of tears had kept her from joining the party for dinner.

"I am sorry you were confined to the inn today. I hope it was not too wearying."

"Not at all," said Elizabeth. After all, there was nothing like crying one's eyes out to pass the time.

"I am glad of it. Now, I need to send a message to my daughter, asking her to meet privately with me to see if we cannot resolve all this nonsense with her father." She looked at Elizabeth expectantly.

"I hope you will be successful."

"That depends upon you, my dear, as you are the only one who knows where she is. Pray do not deny it. I know my daughter well, and since she invited you to travel with us, she would not have left without a word to you. Nor would you have appeared so unconcerned by her absence had you no knowledge of her plans."

Elizabeth did not have the energy left to dissemble. "I do know she is safe and in Sir Anthony's company."

Lady Matlock sighed delicately. "And no doubt you gave your word not to reveal her whereabouts. I will not press you on that point, if you will agree to pass on my message to her."

Agreeing to send the message was tantamount to admitting she knew their location, but no doubt Lady

Matlock had further tricks up her sleeve if Elizabeth refused. "If I can find a way to contact her, I will. I can promise no more than that."

By the following morning everything had changed.

Lady Matlock's battle-axe of a lady's maid crossed her arms. "It is not time for Lady Matlock to rise, and she is not to be awakened early. Ever."

Tapping her foot, Elizabeth said, "I beg of you, I must speak to her immediately. It is of the utmost urgency."

"A matter of life and death, no doubt. Everyone says as much."

"It is terribly urgent!" Elizabeth glanced down the passageway where a chambermaid was clearly listening to every word. "If I could only explain this to you privately, you would understand."

The maid sniffed. "I understand that you will return after 10 o'clock to speak to her ladyship. Good day." She shut the door in Elizabeth's face.

It had been years since she had wished to stamp her foot. There must be a way to reach Lady Matlock. There was no one else she could go to; Frederica, Sir Anthony, and Colonel Fitzwilliam were all gone, Mr. Darcy did not wish to speak to her, and she could not possibly ask for Lord Matlock to be awakened. Trying to reach Lady

Matlock was shocking enough. There was nothing she could do but wait and hope for an opportunity.

She dawdled in the passageway until a maid came with Lady Matlock's morning hot chocolate. Taking possession of the tray from the startled servant, Elizabeth said, "No need to trouble yourself. If you will but knock on her ladyship's door and announce yourself, I will take it in for you."

"That's very kind of you, miss." The maid rapped lightly on the door, calling, "Chocolate tray for her ladyship."

This time when the battle-axe opened the door, Elizabeth did not wait, but strode straight past her at a pace which almost endangered the chocolate pot. She reached Lady Matlock's bedside before her maid realized what had occurred. Thankfully, Lady Matlock was already sitting up, if still in her bedclothes.

Elizabeth said quickly, "I beg you to forgive this rude intrusion, but I have news that cannot wait."

Naturally Lady Matlock did not show the slightest surprise. "Of course, my dear. Would you like some chocolate as well? I assume you have heard from my errant daughter."

"No, I have not." Elizabeth took a deep breath. "I sent her your message last evening. This morning I asked the boy who had taken it whether there had been any reply. It turned out he had never delivered it, as the house was surrounded by soldiers. He found a hiding place to wait, but then the soldiers arrested all the occupants of the house and marched them off."

Lady Matlock's calm finally slipped. "Good God! Frederica as well?"

"It was dark enough by then that the boy could not see well, but he says there was a young woman among those arrested. He tried the house after everyone was gone, but no one remained there, not even a servant."

Her face pale, Lady Matlock turned to her maid. "Pray inform his lordship that I must speak to him at his earliest possible convenience. And fetch Beaumont and Latimer but not a word to Jasper. Miss Bennet, where is the boy?"

"He works in the kitchen. His name is Jamie. Shall I fetch him?"

"Not yet. I wish to hear everything you know of where Frederica went."

The maid bustled out after sparing a moment for a poisonous look at Elizabeth.

Lord Matlock ambled into the sitting room, unshaven and wearing his dressing gown. He did not appear to be in a good humor. "What is all this nonsense about urgent business?" he grumbled.

Lady Matlock was now fully in control of herself again. "It appears our Frederica may have been arrested."

"Arrested? My daughter? Nonsense."

"I'm afraid not."

Beaumont appeared in the doorway, followed by Latimer. At least they had bothered to dress, though the kindest thing that could be said about Latimer's cravat was it was askew.

"My lord, my lady," murmured Beaumont, bowing. "How may I be of service to you?"

Lady Matlock gestured to Elizabeth. "Miss Bennet, if you would be so kind as to tell us what you know?"

Elizabeth took a deep breath. "Two evenings ago, Lady Frederica and Sir Anthony told me they were leaving the inn and would be staying with friends of Sir Anthony's, or rather Mr. Hopewell's. They gave me an address where I could reach them if needed. Last night I sent a boy with a message, and he found the household being placed under arrest."

Latimer whistled softly, while Lord Matlock's frown deepened. Beaumont asked, "Where were they staying?"

Elizabeth handed him the note Sir Anthony had given her.

Beaumont cast his eyes over it. "Duckles," he said to Latimer.

Latimer glanced nervously at Lord Matlock. "Not ideal."

"What are you speaking of?" demanded Lord Matlock.

"Duckles is a local doctor and a known supporter of the Luddites, and he has sheltered fugitives in the past," said Beaumont.

Lady Matlock's maid came in, holding the visibly trembling boy Jamie by his ear. "Here is the boy." She released him with some distaste.

Lord Matlock rumbled, "You are the one who saw the arrests?"

With a terrified glance in Elizabeth's direction, the boy nodded.

"Tell me what you saw, every detail," said Lord Matlock.

Jamie's mouth worked back and forth, but he seemed unable to say a word. No doubt he was utterly terrified to be in the presence of an actual Earl, much less an angry one. The boy dashed tears away with a grubby hand.

Beaumont said calmly, "Latimer, perhaps he would find it easier to speak to you alone."

Latimer smiled at the boy and put an arm around his thin shoulders. "Come with me. You look like you could use some breakfast." He led him from the room.

Beaumont closed the door behind them. "People find Latimer easy to talk to."

As Lord Matlock appeared dissatisfied with this outcome, Elizabeth related to them everything Jamie had told her. Beaumont nodded several times as she spoke.

Lord Matlock drummed his fingers on the arm of his chair. "Send for the mayor and the colonel of the militia. They will answer for this."

"No!" Beaumont stepped forward. "With all due respect, my lord, the mayor has no sympathy with those he views as troublemakers, and he may well be ignorant of the entire matter. We need to discover who has taken them and where they have gone. Latimer and I can ask questions unobtrusively. Once we know their destination, we can make plans."

Lady Matlock asked, "Will they not be in the gaol where we found you?"

"It depends on the charge. Loom breakers are sent there, but if the charge is sedition or treason, they would be taken to York Castle or Newcastle. Unless you wish the entirety of Britain to know your daughter has been arrested, we must proceed with discretion." The ghost of a smile crossed his face. "It is a situation we are familiar with."

The door opened and Latimer stuck his head in. "It was Army, not militia. They were loaded in wagons headed north." He disappeared again.

Beaumont rubbed his hand over his forehead. "It is sedition or treason then, or more likely both."

Lady Matlock turned pale. "My daughter is unaccustomed to rough treatment."

"Then the best thing we can do is to attempt to ascertain her whereabouts as quickly as possible."

Beaumont's voice was not without sympathy. "By your leave, I will start looking into this at once."

"But you are supposed to be in my custody."

"Needs must, madam, needs must. I give you my promise I will return."

"Wait one minute," said Lord Matlock. "I am not going to sit here doing nothing while my daughter is in jeopardy."

Beaumont looked upwards as if hoping for an answer on the ceiling. "My lord, your influence will be critical in obtaining your daughter's release, and if we discover her location, I believe it is likely you will be able to do so. Duxbury is, unfortunately, a more difficult proposition. Those of us who work here are accustomed to operating independently, regardless of rank. I pray you, permit us to do what we do best, and save your influence for when it is needed most."

Lord Matlock scowled. "Very well, but be quick about it."

Beaumont bowed. "Latimer and I will send word as soon as we know anything." He left the room.

Lord Matlock lumbered to his feet. Looking hard at his wife, he said, "Have your trunks packed. I wish to be ready to depart on a moment's notice." The sound of the door closing behind him echoed in the nearly empty room.

Lady Matlock sat so quiet and still that it was a moment before Elizabeth noticed the glistening streaks of tears on her cheeks. Quickly she knelt beside the Countess. "Lady Frederica will be back with us soon, I am certain of it. Sir Anthony will do his best to protect her, as will the others who were arrested with them, and she will be released before she has anything worse to complain of than unpleasant conditions and bad food. Mr. Beaumont seems to know what he is about, and he thinks Lord Matlock would be able to get her released."

Lady Matlock nodded jerkily. "Of course. It is simply unexpected and it is hard not to know whether she will be released as a wife or a soon-to-be widow. Frederica is not always as strong as she appears."

"It may not help, but she did know the risk when she married him. She is not a fool."

"No." Lady Matlock straightened. "Would you be so kind as to inform Darcy of what has occurred?"

"Of course." This was not the moment to explain that Darcy was refusing to see her. If nothing else, she could send him a message through Wilkins.

"Make certain he knows not to tell Jasper anything about this. The last thing we need is for him to charge off looking for someone to fight."

"Indeed not! Is there anything I could bring you for your present relief?"

"Thank you, no." Her tone was a polite dismissal.

Darcy could not bear another day lying in bed in the darkness. It was pointless to get up and dress, as he had no plan to leave his room or to speak to anyone except Wilkins, but it gave him something to do. What an accomplishment — he had managed to allow his valet to dress and shave him.

The long hours of boredom were slowly driving him mad. If there was no improvement in his vision by tomorrow, he would tell Wilkins to make arrangements for him to go to Pemberley. It was not as if he could do any good by being here, apart from occasionally entertaining Latimer or Beaumont with conversation, but all the things he would usually do with a friend were beyond him now — writing, playing cards, billiards, fencing, hunting. And how much could he actually enjoy speaking to his friends when he could not tell them either of the two things that haunted him — his blindness and Elizabeth Bennet?

Elizabeth. She was the true reason he had not yet left Sheffield. What a hopeless position! She had changed towards him after his accident, and he even suspected that if he offered her his hand again, she would accept this time — out of pity. How could he bear such a humiliation? If he had thought connection to her family was a degradation, this was the true degradation — wanting her so badly he was tempted to accept the devil's bargain of her pity. The only thing it would cost him was his self-respect.

Leaving for Pemberley meant giving up all hope of Elizabeth's love. This time might not be a final parting. Now that she and Frederica were friends, his path would be more likely to cross hers. Or if she married Jasper... No, he would not think about that, or he would run screaming mad into the street.

A knock on the door was a blessed relief from his thoughts, even if it was likely just a chambermaid. The rustle of clothing and footsteps told him Wilkins was responding, and then he heard the valet say apologetically, "Mr. Darcy is not receiving visitors at present."

"Yes, I understand he has no desire to see me, but he will have to force himself to tolerate me this one time. Lady Matlock has tasked me with informing him of certain recent events." It was Elizabeth!

The skin on his arms prickled at the sound of her voice, brightening the dreariness within him. But why did she think he would not wish to see her? "Wilkins, Miss Elizabeth is welcome to join me if she so wishes." At least he was dressed and presentable today.

"Very well, sir."

He could not hear her footsteps, only the slight swishing of her skirts. Which of her dresses was she wearing today? The brown muslin that fitted so tightly around her waist, or the blue one with the enticingly low neckline and translucent skirt that had tormented him with glimpses of the shape of her tempting legs? Not that it mattered now; she could be dressed in sackcloth and it would make no difference to him. At least he could still catch the scent of lavender she favored.

"Come in, Miss Elizabeth," he said. "Wilkins, a chair for my visitor."

"There is no need for that," said Elizabeth briskly. "This will not take long, and I have no wish to impose myself on you." Her tone was oddly flat.

"As you wish, although your presence is by no means an imposition."

She ignored this civility. "As you are no doubt aware, your cousin Lady Frederica and Sir Anthony have been staying with friends since Lord Matlock's arrival."

"No, I was not aware of that." Sharpness crept into his voice. Must he be kept in ignorance as well as darkness?

She hesitated. "My apologies. I assumed someone would have told you." She sounded more like herself now.

"It is no matter." And it explained why Frederica had not come to see him.

"I am sorry to report it appears they were arrested last night along with other sympathizers. Beaumont and Latimer are attempting to discover where they have been taken."

He sat up straighter. "Arrested? Freddie?" His little cousin in the indifferent hands of guards, where her spitfire ways would only lead to vicious punishment of the sort she had never imagined! She would never tell them who she was, but Lord Matlock would feel no such compunction. "What else?"

"That is all I know. Lady Matlock also requests that you not mention this matter to your cousin Jasper. She worries he might go off half-cocked when diplomacy is more likely to succeed."

"I cannot argue the point. Will you inform me if anything further is discovered?"

"I will make certain you are informed. Good day, sir." That cool tone was back.

Why was she upset with him? And more importantly, why was she not laughing off whatever it was? "Miss Elizabeth, have I offended you?"

His question was met by silence. Had she left so quickly? She would have had to run out of the room. Damn his inability to see! A fine fool he would look, speaking to someone who was no longer there.

"Offended?" she asked finally. "I have no reason to be offended, but having been turned away from your door before, I know I am unwelcome. I will bring you news as you requested, but I am not in the habit of remaining where I am unwanted."

Before he could come up with a response, he heard her soft footfalls and the sound of the door closing.

Chapter Sixteen

Lady Matlock frowned. "Jasper, my love, would you kindly stop pacing? You are making me dizzy. If you are bored, perhaps you could take Miss Bennet on an outing. She must be pining for the outdoors."

"As am I!" Jasper responded with an abrupt return of his usual good cheer. "Miss Bennet, would you care to take a jaunt into the countryside?"

"That would be delightful, but I do not wish to put you to any trouble." She strongly suspected Lady Matlock's real goal was to remove Jasper from the immediate vicinity, but she needed the distraction as well. It seemed all her mind was good for was worrying about Lady Frederica and brooding over Mr. Darcy, and she was tired of it.

Lady Matlock said, "Nonsense. You will be doing him a kindness. Can you not see the poor boy is chafing at the bit? The ruins of Sheffield Manor would be an easy journey. Mary, Queen of Scots, was imprisoned in the Turret Tower there, so it is quite interesting."

Half an hour later, Elizabeth and Jasper set forth in a light gig borrowed from the inn, a maidservant crouched on the back for propriety's sake. At Lady Matlock's insistence, two armed grooms on horseback followed them. The precautions proved unnecessary, as there was no sign of unrest. Perhaps that was due to the population being well fed on Lady Matlock's potatoes and bread.

But the scenery was interesting and time passed quickly as Jasper flirted lightly with her. She would have described it as a most pleasant day had it not been for the worries she could not forget.

They returned to the inn close to sunset. Elizabeth was not surprised when the innkeeper met them with sealed letters from Lady Matlock.

Jasper frowned as he ripped his open. "Off to York! What business could be so urgent they could not even wait for us? Beaumont and Latimer went with them, but they left the two of us behind!"

Perusing her own note, Elizabeth said soothingly, "Your mother does say they will return in the next few days. Most likely she does not wish to leave Mr. Darcy alone here. She has arranged for a maid to be with me at all times."

"I do not understand why everyone keeps disappearing without explanation! First Freddie and Duxbury, then Richard, and now my parents! I cannot imagine what you must think of our family, Miss Bennet."

Seeing he was in great need of teasing, she said, "I like your family. No one will ever accuse you of being dull and predictable!"

He gave a shout of laughter. "You take everything in stride, do you not? It is an excellent skill to have when dealing with Fitzwilliams."

Darcy found dinner the following night to be a mixture of mortification and stolen pleasure. Eating in front of the others was the most unpleasant part. Wilkins had done his best at breakfast to make it tolerable by serving the food so he could tell Darcy what each dish was, but to be forced to have his valet cut his meat for him like a child made him want to sink into the ground, and having to find the food on his plate by stabbing his fork in every direction was even worse. This morning he had eaten only a few bites, and later Wilkins brought a plate to his room.

But he would tolerate far worse to prevent Elizabeth from eating alone with Jasper. What in God's name had Lady Matlock been thinking when she left Elizabeth behind while she went to York? It was unsuitable at best, a young lady staying with two unmarried men, regardless of whether Elizabeth had a maid beside her at every moment of the day. He would be livid with anyone who put Georgiana in such a position. It did not seem to bother Jasper, who insisted on flirting with Elizabeth despite the situation. At least Elizabeth had refused to go on another outing with Jasper today. Listening to Jasper go on at breakfast about their excursion of the previous day had been a nightmare. Unless his sight returned, he would not be taking Elizabeth or anyone else on an outing again.

Tonight Jasper was late, so Darcy was the one dining alone with Elizabeth. Alone but for her maid, Wilkins, and probably half a dozen servitors he could not see coming in and out. He tried to make conversation, but what could he talk about? The experience of sitting in his room in the dark? So he left the burden to Elizabeth and responded as best he could.

"I hope you do not mind ragout," she said. "I have been longing for a good ragout for days, so this morning I asked for it to be served tonight."

Ragout? An odd choice for a coaching inn, where the fare tended more towards sliced roasts. "Ragout will be a pleasant change."

Wilkins placed something in front of him. "Your ragout, sir," he said, then added in a near whisper, "Spoon on the right."

By moving his hand carefully just above the table, he managed to locate both the bowl and the spoon without embarrassing himself or sticking his fingers in the ragout. With his hand on one side of the bowl, he took a spoonful and raised it to his mouth.

330

Ragout. Of course. She had requested it because she thought it would be easier for him to eat.

"Perfect!" said Elizabeth. "This is just what I was hoping for. I hope you like it as well. I wonder what is keeping Jasper?"

"Most likely he found something that caught his interest and lost track of time." Probably something along the lines of a horse race, cock-fighting, or a brothel, but he could not tell Elizabeth that.

"I hope he is enjoying it. He has seemed restless here."

"Jasper has never been able to sit still for long." A little censure slipped into his voice. Elizabeth deserved to know what she could expect if she accepted a proposal from Jasper. Before he allowed that to happen, Darcy would go down to the public square and announce in front of the world that *he* had compromised Elizabeth. Whether she liked him or not, he would make her a better husband than Jasper.

Laughter was in her voice as she said, "Your family has many virtues, but I would not describe them as restful. This has been an interesting experience for me. At home I often read the newspapers, and they describe Lord Matlock as a great statesman, leader of the opposition, a potential Prime Minister, and a generous supporter of charitable giving. I had envisioned him as somehow greater than other mortals. It has been a lesson to me to discover just how human he can be."

Wilkins announced, presumably for his benefit, "Mr. Jasper Fitzwilliam."

Elizabeth said, "I am glad you are here. I was beginning to worry."

"You might have had reason! There is another ugly scene brewing in the square. So far it is just grumblings, but I would not want to be one of the magistrates tonight. The crowd is threatening to burn their houses."

"Has something happened, apart from the usual complaints?" Darcy asked.

"Oh, ragout," Jasper's disappointment was evident. "Is there no roast? Ah, thank you, Wilkins. There were some unannounced hangings. Loom-breakers, I gather. Apparently my father requested a new trial for them, and the town officials wanted to make an example of them instead. As soon as they heard he had left town, they marched the lot of them out to the gallows."

Elizabeth's gasp was loud enough for Darcy to hear. Silently he cursed Jasper's insensitivity. "Shocking," he said, mostly to give Elizabeth an opportunity to recover herself. "Those must be Beaumont and Latimer's friends. It will be quite a blow to them."

"Not to mention how Father is going to react," said Jasper cheerfully. "He will be furious they went behind his back."

A rustling came from Elizabeth's direction. "I met them. Not formally, of course, but they were in the same cell when we went to the gaol. Poor souls!" That was his Elizabeth!

Darcy could show Jasper how a gentleman should react to news like this. "Wilkins, I would like you to make some inquiries tomorrow regarding the families of those men. With no income and no one to care for them, they will need support."

"Generous of you, Darcy, but they are not your tenants," said Jasper dubiously.

Elizabeth cut in before Darcy could answer. "That does not mean they are undeserving of Christian charity! Pray excuse me, gentlemen; I find I have lost my appetite."

Darcy stood and bowed. "Of course, Miss Elizabeth."

Wilkins said in his ear, "With your permission, I will escort Miss Bennet and her maid upstairs. The taproom also seems somewhat unruly tonight."

Darcy gave a quick nod. He did not like having to consign the duty to his valet rather than doing it himself, but he could be of no use in defending Elizabeth.

In the sudden silence, Jasper said, "I always forget that not all women are as imperturbable as Mother and Frederica. Should I apologize to Miss Bennet tomorrow?"

"Hangings are hardly dinnertime conversation." Darcy hoped Wilkins would return quickly. There was no further reason for him to dine with Jasper, but he was trapped until Wilkins could assist him. Damn this infirmity!

"I suppose not. How much longer must you wear that foolish-looking bandage over your eyes, Darcy?"

"Until the doctor tells me otherwise," snapped Darcy.

"Well, you are certainly out of sorts tonight!"

It was true he was usually more tolerant of Jasper's frivolity. Without a word he turned his attention back to the ragout, each taste reminding him that Elizabeth had been thinking of his needs when she requested it.

It was almost a quarter hour before Wilkins returned. "I am sorry to have been delayed," he said in a subdued voice. "There was ill news in the taproom. The mob has attacked and taken the arms depot. The soldiers guarding it have fled."

"Good God!" cried Jasper. "Where is the militia?"

"I cannot say, sir. They are preparing to close the taproom. Mr. Darcy, may I escort you upstairs? The host has requested my assistance with shutters and shifting the furniture to block the door. Since most of his employees ran off at the first word of the attack, I took the liberty of agreeing."

"Quite right," said Darcy, putting down his spoon.

"How exciting!" said Jasper. "I will help as well."

Darcy heard a scratch at the door. Was it someone trying to get in?

"Who is it?" Wilkins asked softly.

"Elizabeth Bennet."

Darcy heard the bolt slide and the door open, a swish of fabric, and then the click of the bolt again. Wilkins must have shown her in, then locked the door behind her. "Is something the matter, Miss Bennet?" asked Wilkins.

"Nothing except that I am a terrible coward!" Elizabeth gave a breathy laugh. "Someone threw a rock at my window. It broke several panes of glass and then I could hear all the shouting more clearly and smell the smoke. At least the fire does not seem to have moved any closer. I presume I was in no actual danger, but I did not wish to be there alone."

Darcy took hold of the bedpost to orient himself and followed her voice. "What happened to your maid?" he asked.

"She left some time ago, saying she had to go to her family and help keep the shop safe. I cannot blame her, and it did not trouble me until the rock hit the window. I will be fine as long as I am not alone. I know you are not supposed to have visitors, but I will sit in the corner quiet as a mouse and be no trouble at all. This room does not face the street, so it should be safer, should it not?" It was unlike Elizabeth to babble. She must be unsettled to the extreme.

Wilkins said, "Come sit by the fire, Miss Bennet. I have banked it, but it is still warm."

"Thank you. I am sorry to intrude upon you, but my only other choice was to seek out Mr. Jasper, and this seemed the better choice since you are already accustomed to having me intrude in the middle of the night."

Thank God she had chosen him! "You were right to come here," he said. "Wilkins, a glass of wine for Miss Elizabeth."

He could hear the shuffling of slippered footsteps, the clink of a glass stopper, and the sound of pouring liquid. Elizabeth murmured her thanks.

Wilkins asked quietly, "Miss Bennet, might I extinguish your candle? The curtains do not cover the windows fully, and it might be better not to have light showing at the window."

"Of course. I had not thought of that."

A moment later, Wilkins bumped into Darcy's side. "Sorry, sir," he muttered.

Of course. Now everyone was as much in the dark as he was.

"I am not usually so miss-ish," said Elizabeth. "You would think I would be accustomed to riots by now!"

The sound of gunfire penetrated the room. "This is rather worse than that," Darcy said. "It started with a riot, and then the rioters stormed the armory and took the weapons from it. But you need not worry; the doors

336

downstairs are barricaded, and the fire will not spread to this part of town since the buildings here are made of stone."

He could hear her indrawn breath. What he would not give for the right to comfort her! Or at least the ability to protect her, but what use could he be to her when he was blind?

Wilkins said quietly, "If you please, Mr. Darcy, I wonder if it might be wise to move the wardrobe in front of the door in case anyone manages to enter downstairs. The bolts on this door might not hold up to a sustained assault. Not that I expect one, but an extremity of caution seems wise in this situation."

"A good idea. It will take both of us to move it, I believe."

"Yes, sir. If you will come this way. That is good; stand right there. I will pull on the other side and if you could push, sir."

It took several minutes to move the heavy wardrobe. When it was finally in place, Darcy wiped his brow and muttered under his breath, "The next time Duxbury tells me a place is dangerous, I plan to ride in the opposite direction."

"I do not think even *he* anticipated this," said Elizabeth.

A volley of shots rang out, followed by screams of fear and agony. Darcy said, "The militia must have arrived." A second volley confirmed his words.

"Those poor people," she murmured, a catch in her voice.

"Elizabeth." Darcy felt his way to the loveseat by the fire and stood behind it. "It will all be over soon. Tomorrow, as soon as Wilkins can find us a carriage, we will leave this place. Pemberley is but twenty miles from here, and it is free of Luddite troubles. We will be safe there."

Wilkins said, "I will do my best, but you may have to settle for a farm wagon. The innkeeper said all the carriages had been taken, even the donkey cart. I imagine anyone who could find transport has fled."

"I would *walk* twenty miles to leave this place!" said Elizabeth.

"Hopefully it will not come to that." He reached forward, feeling the empty air until his fingers found the warmth of her arm. He hoped she would not be able to see his fumblings in the dark room. "You are trembling." How dare the rioters frighten his Elizabeth so?

"Only a little."

He could not bear standing by impotently while she suffered. With sudden resolution, he stepped around the loveseat and sat, setting his arm around her shoulder as easily as if he could see what he was doing. To the devil with impropriety! "The worst is over, I believe. The militia will clear the streets, and then we will be perfectly safe."

"*We* will be, but what of the poor wretches out there? They are already half starved, and now some will be wounded as well. And those poor men who were hanged.... I begin to think I have lived a very sheltered life."

"That is true of many of us." He tried to sound confident for her sake. "I knew there were troubles here, but I did not understand the extent of them until now. Once matters are settled, I plan to speak to my uncle about what we can do to relieve the suffering here. I can offer a few of them places at Pemberley, but the rest must have food and employment of some sort."

"I hope Frederica is not suffering." Elizabeth shifted, and he could feel the pressure of her head upon his shoulder.

His voice suddenly did not want to work. "I hope so as well," he said huskily. Tentatively he reached out with his free hand until his fingertips discovered the silkiness of her hair. He stroked it gently, glorying in the intimacy of feeling the curls around her face flatten under his hand and then spring back, almost as if alive. Even the scent of her hair somehow soothed him. She must have washed it in lavender water. Oh, for the right to do this every day, not just during a crisis! But it seemed the natural thing to do now, despite the shouts in the street and the occasional burst of gunfire. And she did not pull away.

"Why are you being kind to me?" Her voice was muffled.

His hand halted in mid-stroke. "Why would I not be kind?"

"Because you have wanted nothing to do with me. You would not even let me read to you when you must have needed the distraction."

The shock seemed to steal the breath from his lungs. "I had imposed upon your time enough after my accident." It sounded ridiculous, even to his own ears, so he told her the truth. "I did not want your pity."

"My *pity*? Why would I pity you?"

His voice was taut. "Because I cannot see, of course."

She took a deep breath and blew it out again. He could feel every movement of her chest. "I am sorry for that and I hope your sight returns, but *pity*? I pity the poor half-starved people of this town who would tear their own eyes out without a second thought if it meant they could trade places with you. I pity those men who are hanged and their families who will be in even worse straits than before. But pity *you*? You have every advantage in the world — fortune, a beautiful home, fine food put before you every day, a sister who loves you and family who care for you. If your sight does not return, that will be a great loss for you, but you will still be one of the most fortunate men in Britain. If you think I pity you, you very much mistake me, Mr. Darcy!"

"Do I?" He tensed, her answer seeming somehow of great significance.

"Yes, you *do*!" Her voice was louder now. Lowering it, she added, "I offered to read to you because I had nothing else to do and I thought it might help you pass the time while you were injured. That is a long way from pity!"

Relief flooded him. "I see."

"Besides, I had read my own book at least three times already, and I hoped you might have something different to read."

Nothing she said could have made him happier. Suddenly free from the shadow over him, he said, "Now we reach your true motivations. So you would tolerate even my presence for a new book to read?"

"I believe it was *you* who described *me* as tolerable the first time you saw me! Yet now you seem to *tolerate* me passing well."

Another shot resounded, louder than the others and coming from a new direction, making her bury her face in his shoulder again.

He was only human. He put his other arm around her, enclosing her in an embrace.

Into his shoulder she said, "I will have you know that under normal circumstances very little frightens me."

"As I well know! There is a word for people who are not frightened by rocks thrown at their windows and riots in the street. We call them fools. If I felt there were nothing to worry about, there would not be a wardrobe in front of the door."

"I suppose not." Her tense body seemed to relax a little.

Darcy said, "At least there is one good thing to come out of all this."

She hesitated, then said softly, almost tentatively, "What is that?"

"I had not expected to have the pleasure of showing you Pemberley."

Shifting a little, she said, "I look forward to seeing it. What is it like?"

"Pemberley? The front of the house is modern, in the Palladian style, but parts of the interior are from the Jacobean era. There have been Darcys at Pemberley since the time of Henry I, but the house has been rebuilt several times since then. It stands on rising ground, with a small lake in front which connects to a fine trout stream. The grounds were landscaped by Capability Brown. I think you will enjoy walking through them. Beyond the park it is surrounded by peaks on three sides. The view from the top of them is spectacular."

"It sounds lovely." She seemed more peaceful now.

If telling her about Pemberley was comforting, he would tell her every detail of every room.

He did not stop speaking until he felt Elizabeth's breathing change to a slow steady rhythm. She must be exhausted after all those interrupted nights. A wave of tenderness washed over him.

Could this truly be real? What a contrast – the armed uprising outside and Elizabeth Bennet sleeping peacefully in his arms! Even if he could not see her, he could feel her warm curves and let the scent of lavender wash over him. It was sheer pleasure. She had been right to say he was one of the most fortunate men in Britain.

He ought to wake her so she could sleep in the bed. The loveseat was small and not particularly comfortable, but he would tolerate a great deal more discomfort for the privilege of holding Elizabeth in his arms. Despite the violence outside, this was the first time in days he had felt content rather than ripped asunder, and he would treasure it as long as he could. Soon he would have her at Pemberley, but even there they were unlikely to have the privacy for a moment like this. But perhaps they did have a future together after all.

Perhaps. He would not make assumptions, not this time.

Chapter Seventeen

Elizabeth awoke slowly from a confusing dream of rolling hills and gunshots, conscious of sore muscles and something digging into her side. She opened her eyes and then immediately squeezed them closed again.

How had this happened? Could she truly have slept like this, half on Darcy's lap? His warmth was all around her, and his arm provided a pillow for her head. Someone had placed another blanket across the two of them — Wilkins, no doubt.

Wilkins! Had he been there to see this? She raised her head and looked across the room. Yes, there he was, industriously looking in the opposite direction.

She smothered a giggle. Of course he was still in the room. There was a wardrobe in front of the door, after all.

The sun was shining, and no one was shouting or shooting outside. A definite improvement on last night! Except that it was acutely embarrassing to find herself entwined with Darcy.

Darcy stirred. Her slight movement must have disturbed him. Quickly she pushed off the blanket and sat up.

He blinked at her. "Elizabeth." His voice was groggy.

"Pray pardon me, sir. I must have fallen asleep." Her hair was halfway out of its plait.

"Elizabeth!" Now he sounded excited. He put his hand on her cheek and turned her head so she looked straight at him. "*I can see you.*"

She caught her breath. "Truly? That is wonderful news!"

"I can *see* you." He kept staring at her as if he expected her to disappear at any moment — or perhaps it was simply shock at her current state of dishevelment.

Wilkins asked, "Is your vision back to normal then, sir?"

Darcy swung his head around as if he had forgotten Wilkins's existence. "Some things are blurry, but still, I can *see*."

"That is excellent news, sir. Might I impose upon you to help me shift the wardrobe again so I can look into transportation?"

Darcy rubbed his chin. "Yes, of course." Then he looked at Elizabeth and smiled.

Darcy was in altogether too good a mood for a day following tragedy and civil unrest. His vision was still blurry for anything more than a few feet away, but he could see, and that was the important thing. He could not bring himself to sit still in his room while Wilkins was searching for a carriage. He had been doing that for days. He went downstairs for the sheer pleasure of being able to do so without someone to guide him.

He stopped short at the entrance to the main room of the inn. It looked rather more like a hospital than a taproom, and a badly organized hospital at that. Blurry figures sprawled in different places, one asleep with his head on the dining table, while a barmaid scrubbed the floor. Removing bloodstains? The innkeeper might have battened down the hatches during the riot, but the aftermath had come home to roost.

So much for any hope of breakfast.

He nearly stumbled over Jasper, who was lying on a bench. "Good God! What happened to you? Brawling again?" He leaned closer to examine the bruises on his cousin's face.

"I had no choice. There were four militiamen beating some poor soul right in the street outside. I had to even up the odds."

"Of course you did." Darcy's voice dripped sarcasm. "Did you even know who it was or what he had done?"

"No, but I knew it was an unfair fight," Jasper said promptly. "If only they had not brought their pistols, it would not have been a problem. Cowards."

"Pistols? Jasper, do not tell me you were shot!"

"Only a little." Jasper gestured down to his thigh, which had a dark cloth wrapped around it.

"You cannot be shot *only a little*," said Darcy severely. "You are either shot or not shot."

"Killjoy."

"Has a surgeon looked at it yet?"

"Of course not. If there is a surgeon left in this town, it will take him days to treat everyone." Jasper winced as he shifted his weight. "I do not suppose you could find me some brandy? Wine would do. Hell, I would take gin if that is the only thing available."

"I will try."

Wilkins hurried in from the street as Darcy was attempting to oblige his cousin. "There you are, sir." He sounded breathless. "There are no carriages of any sort available for hire, but there is one place available on the stage to Hathersage. I put Miss Bennet's name down for it. You and Mr. Jasper can ride alongside, and I will follow as soon as I am able. But the stage leaves in a quarter hour from the inn next to Cutlers Hall, so there is no time to lose."

"Jasper is not going anywhere," Darcy said somberly. "He has a bullet in his thigh. I do not see how we can leave after all. He would not even be able to tolerate sitting on the stage, and he certainly cannot ride."

Wilkins hesitated. "I will stay with him, sir. You must take Miss Bennet away from here while you can."

Darcy nodded. "If it were not for the question of Miss Bennet's safety, I would remain as well, but if you are willing to do so, I thank you for it. This goes above the bounds of duty. I will send a carriage for you as soon as we reach Pemberley."

"That would serve admirably, sir. But there is no time to lose. You must find Miss Bennet and go. I will explain to Mr. Jasper."

Elizabeth looked up at the battered stagecoach and shook her head with a smile. "Only a few months ago I swore I would never ride a stagecoach alone again!"

"I promise you, I will not let the coach out of my sight, and all you need to do is to call to me," said Darcy. "It is the only way out of Sheffield apart from horseback."

"I would rather *walk* than attempt to ride for twenty miles! I would not make it as far as the outskirts of town. Do not fret; the stage will be perfectly suitable."

"I will check on you at each stop." He did not like this separation, even if they would only be a matter of yards apart.

"Mr. Darcy, do you always worry this much?" She said it with an arch smile, so there was no sting to it. "The driver is scowling at me, so I must board."

He could not resist. He kissed her hand as he helped her into the stage.

It was a relief to see Elizabeth descending from the stage in Hathersage, not because he truly thought anything might happen to her, but simply because he did not like having her out of his sight. Not after the events of last night.

She held her bonnet as she tipped her head up and turned in a slow circle, taking in the hilly terrain. "It is beautiful here."

Her words warmed him, as if he were personally responsible for the scenery. "I am glad it pleases you. Would you like some refreshment before we continue on?"

"I certainly would not object to it!"

"The George sets a good table. I hope you do not mind eating in the main room," he said quietly. "I do not wish to draw attention to our presence, given our lack of chaperones."

"I suppose that is wise. How much farther is it to Pemberley?"

"It depends. It is almost ten miles by winding lanes. I imagine they will have a gig I can hire, but we might not reach Pemberley before dark. Alternatively, if you feel so inclined, going across country is less than half the distance. If you rode before me in the saddle, we would be there sooner. It is up to you."

"Why, that is an easy distance! I could walk that. It was three miles from Longbourn to Netherfield, and that did not tire me."

He smiled. "It was three *flat* miles to Netherfield. I assure you, it is much more exercise when half of it is uphill."

She seemed to consider this. "Hiring a gig would draw attention, would it not?"

Inclining his head, he said, "I would have to tell them who I am, rather than being an anonymous traveler."

"Then let us go across country."

"It will not make you nervous to ride double?"

She looked up at him through her lashes. "Compared to what we faced in Sheffield, I daresay it will trouble me not at all."

After a quick meal of bread and cold meats, they returned to the courtyard. A stableboy went to fetch Hercules. As Darcy waited, he overheard a familiar voice from a gilded carriage say, "Fresh horses, and quickly. We are hoping to reach Sheffield tonight."

Darcy turned. "Howard, is that you?"

"Darcy! This is a surprise. You remember my wife, do you not?"

"Of course. It is a pleasure to see you again, Mrs. Howard. I cannot tarry at present, but if you are headed for Sheffield, I urge you to reconsider. I have just come from there, having fled the unrest. There have been riots and protests, and last night the arms depot was seized and many people were wounded."

Mr. Howard exchanged a concerned glance with his wife. "We left Tarkington Lodge to escape the violence. Riots and loom-breaking to the north of us in Stockport convinced us to go to London, but there was worse to the south in Macclesfield – the mob broke into the gaol to free prisoners, then gutted shops and attacked an alderman – so our only choice was to go east through the Peak to Sheffield and then south. We will have to reconsider. We have the children with us, asleep in the coach."

Darcy said, "Perhaps you could head south to Matlock and meet the London road at Derby. It would be slower but safer."

Howard sighed. "A good thought. I thank you for the advice. Who would have thought we would ever see such violence in England?"

Darcy bowed his head. "It is a tragedy. I hope your journey is safe and successful."

Elizabeth had gone to stand by the road. Had she been hoping the Howards would not notice her? Darcy led Hercules towards her. "Shall we walk to the edge of town, and ride from there?"

She smiled up at him. "I imagine that would draw less attention."

Once they were past the last houses, he lifted Elizabeth to the saddle, trying not to allow his hands to linger on her waist, and vaulted up behind her. It was not comfortable to share a saddle designed for one, but it was all too comfortable to have Elizabeth sitting in front of him, his arms on either side of her. As he turned the horse down a track off the main road, her feet bumped against his leg with each step. No doubt it would leave bruises, but that would be a small price to pay.

He was grateful it was familiar ground; his vision was still less clear than he would have wished. It had been easy enough to keep pace with the coach, but watching the track ahead was more of a challenge. Fortunately Hercules was surefooted enough he need not worry about failing to see small obstacles. "Are you comfortable enough?" he asked.

"So far, although I imagine I may feel it tomorrow. I am enjoying the scenery."

As they crested the first hill, a cool, damp breeze licked against Darcy's face. Were those dark clouds forming to the west? It was all a blur. A rumble of distant thunder answered his question. He touched his heels to the horse's sides to urge him to a brisker pace. Trotting was out of the question when riding double, but he would make what speed he could.

It was not enough; a few minutes later the first drops began to fall and quickly turned into cold, driving rain that slapped against his cheeks. Elizabeth turned her face into his chest.

It would not take long at this pace for them to be soaked to the skin, but there was no easy shelter nearby. Pemberley was still two miles ahead. A gust of wind took him by surprise, and he grabbed for his hat a moment too late. It flew off behind him, allowing icy rain to run down the back of his neck.

This was a poor rescue; saving Elizabeth from the mobs in Sheffield only to allow her to be drenched and no doubt catch a chill. "We must make better speed," he told her. "If you will hold onto me, we can canter the rest of the way."

He could not see her face under her bonnet, but she wrapped her arms around his waist. "Like so?"

"Yes." With the reins in one hand, he pulled her tight against him with his free arm. "Hold on."

Hercules broke into a canter. Carrying both of them, he would not be able to keep it up long, but it should get them to Pemberley. He would miss the opportunity to show Elizabeth the view of Pemberley from the drive, but at least he could hold her and attempt to protect her from the rain.

Finally he reined in Hercules in front of Pemberley's portico. A groom dashed out from the stable block before he had even dismounted. Odd, since they were not expected, but it made matters easier. He swung off the horse's back and reached up to lift down Elizabeth. This time he had no urge to let his hands linger, not when he needed to get her inside as quickly as possible.

His butler Hobbes had the door open before they even reached it, ushering them in, and then looking past them. He said, "Mr. Darcy, sir. Is Lady Matlock with you?"

What an odd question! Darcy reached for his hat, only to remember he had lost it. "No. We are traveling alone."

"Sir." Hobbes bowed.

Mrs. Reynolds appeared in the back of the entrance hall. "Mr. Darcy!" She sounded surprised. "Welcome home."

"Thank you. Miss Elizabeth, may I present my housekeeper? Mrs. Reynolds, Miss Bennet will be staying with us."

Mrs. Reynolds bustled directly to Elizabeth and helped her remove her sodden bonnet. "Poor dear! You must be soaked through and half-frozen. If you will come with me, we will get you dry and comfortable."

"I thank you," said Elizabeth, "but my luggage is still in Sheffield; I have nothing beyond the clothing I am wearing."

"Mrs. Reynolds, I believe she is about the same height as my sister," said Darcy.

"Yes, indeed. We will find something of Miss Georgiana's for you. Right this way, Miss Bennet." She gestured to the grand staircase, and Elizabeth followed her.

Richard strode into the entry hall and stopped short. "Darcy, what brings you here? You are soaked! Is my mother with you?"

"Your mother is in York. Miss Bennet and I fled the riots in Sheffield."

"York? Not that it matters, as she is apparently arriving here soon. She sent a message to the staff telling them to prepare rooms and to have a doctor available for her arrival. When I heard the door open, I assumed she was the one arriving."

"That sounds ominous. She gave no reason?" Darcy asked.

"None."

"It could be anything, I suppose. I hope no one is seriously hurt," Darcy said heavily. "Duxbury was right, you know. The rebellion is spreading – Sheffield, Stockport, Macclesfield. They seized the armory in Sheffield. Your brother took a musket ball in his thigh. Since he could not travel, I left Wilkins with him."

"Good God! I suppose I should not be surprised he was in the thick of it. That must be why my mother wanted the doctor."

"No, it must be something else. She left Sheffield before he was injured."

"Hmm. Did you tell my mother I was here?"

Darcy shook his head. "No. I thought you did not want your parents to know."

"Then she may not expect me when she arrives. This will be interesting."

"Interesting in the way riding into battle is interesting? But if you wish to keep discussing this, I would prefer to do it in dry clothes."

Richard waved towards the stairs. "Make yourself at home. After all, it *is* your home."

Elizabeth followed Mrs. Reynolds up the stairs and through a long gallery with portraits along one wall. Her primary concern was to move carefully to avoid dripping on the beautiful floors, but she noted with admiration that nothing at Pemberley was either gaudy or uselessly fine. The furniture had less of splendor, and more real elegance, than that of Rosings.

The housekeeper held open the door to an attractive bedroom with painted Chinese wallpaper on one wall. A four-poster bed with embroidered hangings in pale green silk was set to one side. "You will be here in Miss Darcy's room. I hope you will be pleased by it." She opened the wardrobe and produced an elegant dressing gown.

"Perhaps you would like to wear this while your bath is prepared."

"I thank you, but there is no need to put your staff to the trouble of making a bath." Although a bath sounded heavenly, it would likely take an hour to get enough water heated and carried up to her room.

"After a ride in that nasty, cold rain? A hot bath is just the thing for you, Miss Bennet. We do not wish you to take a chill. Come, your dressing room is through this door." The housekeeper opened the door to reveal a small chamber. A maid entered through the opposite door with an ewer of hot water which she poured into the bath and then disappeared.

Elizabeth raised her eyebrows. "I am impressed. I have only just arrived and I did not hear you give an order for a bath."

The housekeeper drew herself up to her full height, but her proud smile took away any sense of outrage. "When a wet, cold young lady arrives at Pemberley, the staff does not need orders to start preparing a bath. Shall I assist you in undressing?"

Why would the housekeeper lower herself to act as a lady's maid? She did not wish to offend Mrs. Reynolds, especially if...she would not think about that possibility, she would not! "I do not wish to impose..." Suddenly she longed for nothing more than the ability to sit down without ruining one of the lovely embroidered chairs. She rubbed one cold hand over her brow.

Apparently taking this as an affirmative, Mrs. Reynolds moved behind her and began to undo the tiny buttons down the back of her dress.

It would not do to have Mrs. Reynolds think her the shy, miss-ish sort either. "Thank you. It has been a very long few days." Elizabeth stepped out of the dress. "That reminds me. Would you be able to make certain that someone checks the wound on Mr. Darcy's head? Wilkins was taking care of it, but he is still in Sheffield, and I fear Mr. Darcy would be happy just to ignore it."

Mrs. Reynolds's hands on the ties of Elizabeth's stays stopped for a moment, then resumed. "You may rely on me, Miss Bennet. If I might be so bold, may I ask how he came to be injured?"

"We do not know. It was during one of the riots, and he does not remember being hit, but he was unconscious all through that night and lost a great deal of blood. It was only a few days ago, and he has not left his room except for meals until today, and of course he had to insist on riding all the way from Sheffield which was no doubt far more than he should have, and in the rain, too."

"Mr. Darcy was in a *riot*?"

"Yes, and last night the rioters seized the arms depot. That is why we left in such a hurry without our trunks."

"As well you should have!" The housekeeper held out the blessedly dry dressing gown for Elizabeth to slip her arms into.

"But we had to leave Wilkins behind to care for Jasper Fitzwilliam, who was shot in the leg, and he is the one who knows best about Mr. Darcy's injuries." Elizabeth sank down into the nearest chair. Heaven! "Forgive me, Mrs. Reynolds, I am babbling; it is the result of too much worry and too many nights with too little sleep. Under usual circumstances I am a reasonable and sensible person, I assure you!"

"And I assure *you*, Miss Bennet, that *no one* here will think ill of you for worrying about Mr. Darcy! Has he other injuries?"

Elizabeth hesitated. "His vision is still not clear, especially more than a few feet away."

Mrs. Reynolds made a disapproving sound. "And he rode all that way when he could not see clearly? Ah, well, I suppose he had no choice. But he has always been like that. He was the sweetest-tempered, most generous-hearted boy in the world, but he always refused to change his behavior when he was ill or to let anyone fuss over him."

Warmed by the housekeeper's obvious affection for her master, Elizabeth said, "Colonel Fitzwilliam said something about how unusual it was that Mr. Darcy was following the doctor's instructions. I see this is a well-known quality of his!"

The maid came in from the dressing room. "Your bath is ready, miss."

"There you go," said Mrs. Reynolds briskly. "Now, if you will excuse me, I will go attend to this question of Mr. Darcy's injury."

Feeling a little self-conscious in Georgiana Darcy's elegant dinner dress, Elizabeth made her way downstairs to find Darcy, Colonel Fitzwilliam and Sylvie in the sitting room. Sylvie greeted her like an old friend and kissed her on both cheeks in the French manner. She looked even further along in her pregnancy now than when they met in Kent – had it really been less than fortnight ago? It felt like another lifetime.

Sylvie asked Colonel Fitzwilliam, "Do you think your mother will still come tonight? It is full dark."

"She might," he replied. "Her carriage has lanterns, and now that the rain has stopped, there is enough of a moon to see by. But she might also decide to stop somewhere else for the night."

"Perhaps we should dine now, in that case."

How odd it was to sit down to dinner in this intimate grouping! Or perhaps it was merely odd because it made them seem like two couples, and Darcy's intent gaze on her only reinforced that sensation – and several other sensations which were better not to think about at present.

The servants had just taken up the first remove when a clatter of hoofbeats and wheels on gravel indicated the arrival of a new party. Colonel Fitzwilliam pushed himself up from his chair with a groan. "To think it was only yesterday I was saying how peaceful I find Pemberley!"

Darcy said, "You need not come to meet them. That is my task, after all."

"I have never shirked a battle, and I have no intention of starting now. Sylvie, will you remain here with Miss Bennet? I would rather let them get past the first shock of finding me here before introducing you."

As Darcy and the colonel left the dining room, there was an unusual amount of shouting from outside, or perhaps it only seemed that way because of the darkness and the late hour. Elizabeth smiled gently at Sylvie "Courage. Lady Matlock at least will not be unkind." Or so she hoped.

Sylvie gave a Gallic shrug. "It does not matter. Nothing they say will stop Richard from loving me, and that is the only matter of importance to me."

"True. They may be preoccupied with other matters in any case." Presumably the Matlocks would not have left York if Frederica or Sir Anthony were still imprisoned, but would the young couple have agreed to come with them?

Lady Matlock's crisp voice came from the hall. "We need a litter, as quickly as you can manage it."

"Good God! What is the matter?" Colonel Fitzwilliam's voice was loud enough to echo.

"Richard, what are you doing here? And Darcy as well? Never mind; it can wait. Pray help Frederica inside."

Why would Frederica need assistance? Elizabeth rose to her feet. Something was very wrong.

Darcy said, "Lord Matlock is not with you?"

"Not now, Darcy!" Lady Matlock snapped. "If you wish to be useful, find the doctor!"

Was Frederica hurt? Elizabeth hurried towards the hall. She had never heard Lady Matlock speak so sharply before. She almost collided with Darcy in the doorway.

He said, "I was coming for you, Elizabeth. Can you assist Frederica?"

"Of course." To her astonishment she found Lady Frederica kneeling on the floor, her face covered with her hands, keening softly and rocking. Colonel Fitzwilliam stood over her looking as helpless as only a large, powerful man can.

Elizabeth crouched down beside Frederica and put her arm around her. "Is there anything I can get for your present relief? Some wine, perhaps?"

Frederica dropped her hands long enough to look at her with reddened eyes. "Oh, I cannot bear it. I just cannot *bear* it!"

"What has happened? Are you hurt?"

But there was no need for an answer. An agonized moaning filled the room. Two servants carried a makeshift litter holding Sir Anthony, his face all but unrecognizable from swelling and bruises.

His voice taut, Darcy said, "Put him in my room. It is the closest."

Colonel Fitzwilliam cursed under his breath. "Someone will pay for this."

"I cannot *bear* it," Frederica repeated hopelessly.

It seemed there was little Elizabeth could do apart from holding Frederica and murmuring calming words that seemed to have little effect. Poor Frederica, having to spend hours in the coach watching her husband suffer and unable to do anything for him! It was enough to break anyone's spirit.

After a time Sylvie joined them, a cup in her hand. "Here, I have a nice tisane for you. Take a sip." She offered it to Frederica.

Frederica pushed it away. "I do not want it."

"Just a sip," coaxed Sylvie. "Just a sip, I pray you."

Frederica barely touched her lips to the cup, then pushed it away again. "It tastes horrid."

Sylvie's voice became hard as a sword. "Your husband, he is in terrible pain, and you will not even drink a bitter posset for his sake?"

Elizabeth tensed, expecting Frederica to throw the tisane at Sylvie at the very least. Instead she grabbed the cup, drained it, and dropped it on the floor.

"Good girl," said Sylvie. "Now come, we must take you into the sitting room."

Frederica shook her head and began sobbing brokenly. Sylvie gestured to Elizabeth, and together they raised her to her feet by main force. Sylvie looped Frederica's arm over her shoulder as Elizabeth took her other side. Slowly they half dragged her into the sitting room and onto a fainting couch.

Sylvie produced a blanket and wrapped it around Frederica's shaking shoulders. "There, now. You have a good cry, that is the best thing. We will be right here with you, and soon your husband will be feeling so much better, you will see."

A distant agonized scream was followed by sudden silence. Frederica covered her ears and curled up into a tight ball. Elizabeth took a pillow from a nearby chair and tucked it under her head.

It seemed an eternity before Frederica's trembling disappeared and she began to relax, but it was probably no more than half an hour. Sylvie wrapped the blanket more tightly around her, then whispered to Elizabeth, "Chamomile, lemon balm, and sweet woodruff to ease the nerves; and enough laudanum to make a horse sleep through the night."

Chapter Eighteen

After speaking to the doctor, Darcy and Richard returned to the sitting room to find Lady Matlock seated silently beside her sleeping daughter. Elizabeth half dozed on one side of the settee. Sylvie was nowhere to be seen.

"Well?" asked Lady Matlock.

"He will live," said Darcy, "though he may wish otherwise over the next few days. His arm, his nose, and most likely his ribs are broken, and he has bruises everywhere. What could he have done to deserve such ill-treatment?"

"I do not know," said Lady Matlock. "At first they refused to let us see him at all, and when they finally released him to us, he was like this. The few times he has tried to speak he has done no more than to babble apologies. I wanted to get a doctor for him immediately, but my husband said we should come here directly."

"He did?" asked Richard disbelievingly.

"It was most curious. He said, 'Go. Go to Darcy's house. Go now, without stopping for anything.' But why would he say Darcy's house instead of Pemberley? Still, it was clear he wished us to leave immediately, so we did, but poor Sir Anthony has suffered greatly for it."

"He did not want anyone to find you," growled Richard. "But what is *he* doing in York still? Darcy explained to me about the arrests, but why did he stay after they were released?"

Lady Matlock dropped her head, seeming somehow smaller than usual. "I have no idea."

"Where are Beaumont and Latimer?"

"Still with your father. He said he needed them, and I did not ask why."

Elizabeth roused herself and joined them. With a significant look at Richard, she said, "I gave Frederica a tisane with some laudanum in it, so I suspect she will sleep through the night."

Richard nodded, apparently understanding her message. "I will carry her to her room, then. Do you know which it is?"

Darcy said, "I do not believe Duxbury will be moving from my room any time in the near future, and she would likely prefer to be with him."

"Very well." Richard crouched down beside Lady Matlock. "Mother, is there anything I can do to help you?" he asked gently.

Lady Matlock straightened her shoulders. "I do not need anything, but I thank you. You should go to bed.

Everyone should go to bed, and perhaps things will look brighter in the morning."

When Elizabeth came down to breakfast the following morning, it was as if none of the previous night's excitement had occurred. Lady Matlock, the only person in the breakfast room, asked, "Did you sleep well, my dear?"

"Very well indeed," said Elizabeth. The comfort of Miss Darcy's bed and her recent sleepless nights had made for a much needed long, sound sleep. At this late hour, she was surprised Lady Matlock would be the only one at breakfast. "Have you heard anything of Sir Anthony's condition this morning?

"He is slightly improved. He has been in less pain since his broken arm was set and splinted and he is able to converse. Frederica is taking her breakfast at his bedside."

Elizabeth looked up at the sound of footsteps to see the colonel entering with Sylvie on his arm. Had they waited for Elizabeth to arrive to avoid being alone with Lady Matlock for this formidable introduction?

"Good morning, Mother, Miss Bennet," said Colonel Fitzwilliam. "Mother, may I present my wife? Sylvie, this is the Countess of Matlock."

Lady Matlock raised an eyebrow. "How very formal you are today, Richard. If you are anticipating an ill-bred reaction from me, I am sorry to disappoint you. Mrs. Fitzwilliam, it is a pleasure to meet you. Do sit down and allow Richard to serve you; I cannot imagine it is comfortable for you to stand for long."

"It is an honor, Lady Matlock. Richard has told me so much about you."

"I cannot say he has done the same for me, but I hope we will have a chance to become better acquainted. Richard, the fruit pastry is particularly good this morning. I recommend it highly."

Colonel Fitzwilliam looked over his shoulder at his mother. "I will try it, thank you."

Lady Matlock pounced. "Were you ever planning to tell me about your marriage?"

Colonel Fitzwilliam did not answer right away; he waited until he had brought a plate of food for Sylvie and filled one for himself. As he carried it to the table, he said, "I had hoped to do so after my brother's baby was born since no one would care who I married then. After the stillbirth it seemed better to wait, at least until Sylvie was past her confinement. She has been through a great deal already, and I did not want that added stress on her."

"Yet Darcy has been acquainted with the matter for some time."

Hoping to avoid notice, Elizabeth busied herself with spreading blackberry preserve onto a slice of bread with more attention than the task deserved. How soon could she justify leaving the room?

"I introduced them in Kent. Darcy and I had a quarrel about whether to marry for love, and I wanted to show him why I had changed my mind on the question. And if you have nothing civil to say to Sylvie, we will take our breakfast elsewhere."

"I have said nothing at all uncivil to your wife." Lady Matlock's voice dripped ice, but her eyes were suspiciously shiny.

"It is true, Richard," said Sylvie hurriedly. "It was very kind of Lady Matlock to consider my condition and ask me to be seated right away, especially when my presence was a surprise to her. Your ladyship, I meant no discourtesy in failing to meet you last night. It seemed as if you had enough concerns at the time."

Colonel Fitzwilliam continued to glare at his mother, who remained in stony silence. Suspecting she might be too upset to speak, Elizabeth decided to stall for time. "To be fair, Sylvie was also quite busy helping me with Frederica at the beginning. She made her a calming tisane. It was very effective. Was it a French recipe?"

Sylvie's eyes darted back and forth between her husband and his mother. "It was of my own devising."

"I imagine things must be very different in France," Elizabeth continued reflectively. "I have often wondered whether it is a peculiarity of English gentlemen that they respond with their fists when another man injures their pride. Do men in France behave in the same way, Sylvie?"

"Oh, yes," said Sylvie, sounding bewildered. "With their fists or more likely with their sword."

"Sometimes I wish it were as simple for women. We have only our words to express ourselves when someone hurts us, and words are so much more prone to misunderstanding than a simple blow to the jaw."

"Touché, Miss Bennet," said the colonel dryly. "I see you have been taking lessons from my mother."

Elizabeth tilted her head. "Thank you. Hers is an example I would be proud to follow," she said gravely.

The colonel bowed to Lady Matlock. "Mother, I apologize for my testiness."

Sylvie leaned forward as far as her swollen belly would permit. "Lady Matlock, Richard has been very concerned about protecting me, but it has never been *you* he was worried about, just the other — how do you say? — untempered members of your family."

"I believe you mean intemperate," said Elizabeth with a smile.

"Intemperate. I will have to remember that. Intemperate, yes."

Lady Matlock said, "It is kind of you to say so. I must say that your English is excellent. How did you learn it?"

Sylvie's relief was obvious. "I was still a child when my family came to England fleeing the Terror, and I learned English then. We left for India after a few years, but I still had an English governess."

"India?" asked Elizabeth. "How exotic!"

370

Colonel Fitzwilliam's eyes were on his mother. "Sylvie's father is on Lord Wellington's staff, so she is well-traveled."

Carefully folding her napkin, Lady Matlock asked, "So you must be accustomed to following the drum. Do you plan to continue to do so?"

"I think...it is difficult to do so with an infant." Sylvie looked desperately at her husband.

"Sylvie is attempting to avoid being the one to tell you I have sold my commission," said the colonel. "I had already been inclining towards doing so, and when you suggested at Rosings that I should consider selling out, I decided to proceed with it. I am being considered for a position at the War Office, and if that should not work out, Darcy has offered me the stewardship here. You need not worry that I will have insufficient funds for my family."

"Your father may be able to assist you in locating a position," said Lady Matlock.

Colonel Fitzwilliam flashed a wry smile. "Thank you for the suggestion, Mother, but if you recall, he disowned me a few days ago."

"Oh, Richard," she said reproachfully. "You know your father better than that. He disowned Frederica as well, but the minute she was in difficulties he rode to her rescue."

The housekeeper entered and curtsied.

"Yes, Mrs. Reynolds?" said Lady Matlock.

"Your ladyship, Mr. Darcy left me instructions concerning Miss Bennet. Since he is unable to give her the tour of the house he promised, he suggested I could do so in his place. If that is of interest to Miss Bennet, I would be at her disposal whenever it is convenient."

Darcy was unable to do it? Was he again avoiding her presence? "That is very kind of you, Mrs. Reynolds," Elizabeth said. "I would be happy to do that after breakfast. I have been admiring the parts of Pemberley I have seen on my own and would enjoy learning more about it. I hope nothing untoward has happened to Mr. Darcy."

Mrs. Reynolds looked surprised. "Mr. Darcy left for Sheffield at first light. I assumed he had informed you."

Lady Matlock delicately patted her lips with a napkin. "Sheffield? Why would he wish to return there?"

"I cannot say, madam. He took the carriage, but no one went with him apart from the footmen."

"I can venture a guess," said Elizabeth. "When we left Sheffield, Mr. Darcy told Mr. Jasper he would send the carriage for him. Perhaps he decided to accompany it."

Lady Matlock's brows drew together. "But why? Jasper is perfectly capable of traveling here on his own, and if he did not wish to go with you yesterday, I fail to see why he would agree to it now. Does Darcy think he will be more inclined to leave Sheffield when he hears I am at Pemberley as well?"

Oh, dear. Apparently Darcy had not told his aunt about Jasper's wound. Now she was trapped into delivering the bad news, and when Lady Matlock was already upset. She wet her lips. "Mr. Jasper was unable to travel with us because of his wounded leg. There were no carriages available for hire and he could not ride. But we did not leave him alone; Mr. Darcy's valet stayed to care for him."

Lady Matlock's lips tightened. "How did he come to be wounded?"

Elizabeth swallowed hard. "I thought Mr. Darcy would have told you. He was shot in the thigh. As I understood it, the wound was not a serious one."

"My son was *shot* and no one saw fit to inform me?"

Elizabeth lowered her eyes. "Had I known you were unaware of it, I would have said something last night." Not that there had been any opportunity in the chaos of the previous night for her to tell Lady Matlock anything, but it seemed wiser not to point that out.

"And how, pray tell, did he *happen* to get shot?" Lady Matlock's hand trembled as she raised her teacup.

"I am not certain, but Mr. Darcy would know the details. It happened on the night of the riots. I saw him only for a quick farewell since we had to leave quickly to catch the stage, but he seemed in good spirits."

Colonel Fitzwilliam said calmly, "Darcy did mention it to me before you arrived, and it sounded as if Jasper was merely grazed by the bullet. I have seen wounds like that many times, and while they may be painful, they are not dangerous. Except, perhaps, to the person caring for Jasper, who is no doubt the recipient of his ill temper. You know what Jasper is like when he is forced to remain still!"

Lady Matlock gave her son a serious look, and then smiled. "Do you remember when he broke his leg and his nursemaid tendered her resignation, saying she would as soon care for an imp of hell? But I thank you, Richard, for the reassurance."

The tour with Mrs. Reynolds was illuminating, not least for the stories she told of Darcy's childhood. She seemed to be of the opinion that there was more of an understanding between Elizabeth and Darcy than existed in reality, but Elizabeth chose to ignore those hints. She could not help falling in love with the house, though, especially since the housekeeper simultaneously showed her the lovely rooms while praising her master.

Afterwards, she was pleased to discover Sir Anthony in the sitting room, reclining on the same fainting couch his wife had occupied the previous evening. Apparently walking downstairs had exhausted what little strength he had, but he was talking to the others with more good than Elizabeth thought she could manage under the same circumstances.

But not everyone shared his good cheer. Lady Matlock was tapping her foot impatiently. "Since no one else seems so inclined, I will ask the obvious question. What happened? *Why* were you arrested?"

Sir Anthony grimaced. "I was not the target of the raid. They planned to arrest the friend with whom we were staying on suspicion of sedition. We were just taken up with the rest."

"Tell them the truth," Frederica said in a low voice. "It was my fault. They had no intention of arresting us at the beginning. I tried to argue with the officer about... Well, it does not matter. Sir Anthony tried to stop me, but I would not listen, so they arrested us as well."

Reaching his hand out to her, Sir Anthony said, "I do not blame you. I did something much the same before I learned the hard way that Mr. Hopewell did not have the same rights as Sir Anthony Duxbury or Lady Frederica Fitzwilliam do. You were trying to help."

Lady Matlock shook her head. "It does not make sense. I saw the other prisoners in York, and you are the only one who appeared to have been pummeled within an inch of your life. Why you?"

Sir Anthony looked down at his hands. "That was *my* fault. I was worried Frederica would be mistreated, especially as she had already angered the officer. I did not know how to protect her except by revealing her identity. At first they would not listen when I told them she was the Earl's daughter, and they hit me then for making a nuisance of myself. Then, for some reason, they decided I was telling the truth, and the real trouble started."

Frederica said, "They sent someone to my cell to call out my name — Lady Frederica, that is, not Mrs. Hopewell — and without thinking, I responded. Ten minutes later I was released, and the captain of the guard was on his knees begging my forgiveness for the terrible error of his men." Her lip curled.

Sir Anthony nodded. "*That* is why they beat me. The guards realized they were going to be punished, and they took their anger out on me." His shrug turned into a wince. "I would have had more sympathy for their position if they had not kicked me quite so hard."

A tear slipped down Frederica's cheek. "They *deserve* to be punished."

Lord Matlock's deep voice came from the doorway. "And so they shall be. Discharged or broken in rank, most of them. The ringleader will most likely be transported."

"Father!" Frederica threw herself into his arms. "Thank you, thank you for saving him!"

Lord Matlock put his arm around his daughter, using the other to point at Sir Anthony, who was attempting to rise from the fainting couch. "Lie down, you young idiot!"

Sir Anthony slumped back, looking as if the small effort had exhausted him. "My lord, I also thank you for your timely intervention in York."

"As well you ought. And now I have a few things to say to you." Lord Matlock glowered at his son-in-law.

"I understand you have every reason to be angry because I endangered your daughter. I assure you, her well-being is of great importance to me."

"*Angry*? That does not begin to describe it. This idiocy you have been involved in must end."

Sir Anthony managed to retain a calm demeanor, but it was clearly a struggle. "Sir, I understand your sentiments, but I must act in accordance with my beliefs."

"I am not talking about changing your precious beliefs, but your ridiculous way of acting on them. Writing petitions, speaking at meetings — it will accomplish nothing beyond making you feel virtuous. Parliament will continue to ignore every petition you send. *You* have the ability to make a real difference, and you are wasting it. If you wish to waste your own time, that is your business, but I will not have you hurting my daughter by playing the martyr to your precious cause!"

"Sir – "

"Did I ask your opinion?" Lord Matlock roared. "I cannot control what you choose to do, but by God, you will first *listen* to what I have to say!"

Sir Anthony's lips were now in a tight line. "I will listen, but it will change nothing."

"Fool! Nothing will change in this country, *nothing*, until Parliament decides it will. I am given to understand you are an eloquent speaker and you are a baronet.

Instead of wasting your time writing useless petitions, you should be in the House of Commons using your skills of persuasion on the men who can actually make a difference."

"And have them ignore me as they ignored Lord Byron and anyone else who has stood up for the common people?"

Lord Matlock loomed over the fainting couch where Sir Anthony lay, but his voice became suddenly quiet. "*They* tried to change men's minds by shaming them and making them feel selfish. That will never work and and only makes Parliament resist their cause more than ever. The way to accomplish change is to start by agreeing with the other members of Parliament, and then, when they conclude you are a reasonable person, you can mention one little new idea — perhaps that it is a shame to have such little children working with dangerous machinery. You keep mentioning it until it stops sounding radical. Meanwhile, you make it fashionable to buy fabric from mills that do not employ young children. Then fashionable people can feel proud of themselves for protecting those children at very little cost to themselves, and you let them prance around town preening themselves for being so noble. Then you suggest a new tiny idea, and start all over again. It will not make you feel as noble as when you demand votes for every man and woman, but it will create actual change, and in twenty years, when you bring up universal suffrage, you will get a hearing."

"It is not as simple as that. One man cannot change the fashions."

"Ha! Tell Beau Brummel that! Perhaps the average member of Parliament might have trouble changing the fashions, but *you* have something he does not — a wife who has been trained all her life for a future as a fashionable political hostess. She can convince the finest ladies of the *ton* to form societies for the relief of those poor children injured in mills, and she can plant ideas, too, in the ladies who influence their husbands."

Sir Anthony's eyes narrowed. "Lovely. You are suggesting we spend our entire lives play-acting, pretending to hold beliefs we abhor! All on the mere chance of accomplishing some small change."

Lord Matlock placed his knuckles on each side of Sir Anthony's shoulders. Very quietly and coldly, he said, "What the devil do you think *I* have been doing these last thirty years? Do you think the reform of abuses in public offices happened by itself? The Whig support for the rights of American colonists? Catholic emancipation? All of those were *unthinkable* when I first took my seat."

Sir Anthony's mouth dropped open, but no words came out.

Lord Matlock straightened and paced across the room. "But if you still must do something straightaway, you can invest in a model mill, one that is safe, where men and women do not work until they drop from exhaustion and are paid fairly for their labor. Have your political hostess wife introduce their products in a way that everyone simply must have one. Force them to see how things can be different without risking anything. It can be done. I tried it with coal mines and showed a safe mine could still be profitable, but coal cannot be made fashionable and one lump is much like another. Fabric, though..." He trailed off, apparently deep in thought.

"A pattern," announced Lady Matlock. "A unique pattern in the fabric which is instantly recognizable. It could work very well in shawls."

Lady Frederica moved back to Sir Anthony's side and took his hand. Her eyes shining, she asked, "Where could we build such a mill? We would need to have housing for the workers as well, and a school for the children."

Lord Matlock said, "It might not be suitable, but I have an estate on the Derwent which is well-suited to powering a mill. I bought it to keep it out of the hands of a greedy mill-owner. I did not want him preying on my tenants for laborers."

Beaumont took a step forward. "Building the mill is only half of it. You would need to find merchants sympathetic to your cause to bring your products to market."

Elizabeth sat up, suddenly alert. "My uncle is a fabric merchant. Some mill owners blacklisted him after he complained about working conditions in one mill, so he is looking for new suppliers. Lady Frederica has met him. I think he would be very interested in your project."

"I liked him," said Frederica. "He was very gentleman-like. I was surprised to discover he was in trade."

Lady Matlock held up her hand. "Before our family actually begins to build this mill, perhaps someone ought to ask Sir Anthony if he has any interest in pursuing this course. He may have other plans."

A small smile played on Sir Anthony's lips as all faces turned towards him. "It is an intriguing concept which could be beneficial to many, but I cannot say my skills are suited to it. My gift is in swaying people's minds, not in organizing their lives. On the other hand..." He turned his head towards Frederica, whose crestfallen look told its own story. "On the other hand, it might be admirably suited to my wife, if she is so inclined. That is, when it does not interfere with being a political hostess."

Richard said disbelievingly, "Freddie? Building a mill and a village? That is not women's work."

Frederica's eyes flashed. "Women are every bit as capable as men."

"Why, yes," said Sylvie in her light French accent. "If Lady Frederica would like my assistance in her project, I would be honored to help."

Lord Matlock turned on Sylvie. "Who, pray tell, are you?" His voice was ominous.

Richard put his arm around her protectively. "Father, allow me to present my wife, the former Sylvie de Rostand."

Sylvie curtsied. "It is an honor, sir."

Lord Matlock's brows drew together. "Are you related to the Comte de Rostand?"

"He is my uncle."

Lord Matlock gave his son a withering look. "You said she had no connections."

"I lied," said Richard without the slightest hint of shame. "She is, however, indubitably French."

"*Mais oui,*" said Sylvie demurely.

His lordship gestured to Sylvie's swollen belly. "When?"

Richard took this impropriety in stride. "A month, or perhaps a little longer."

Lady Matlock said sharply, "I will thank you to choose a more appropriate topic of conversation when ladies are present."

Her husband did not acknowledge her words, but he waved Sylvie away. "We will speak of this later, Richard." His tone seemed to imply it would not be a pleasant discussion. "In the meantime, where was I?"

Latimer, who had been conferring quietly with Beaumont, now said, "Lady Frederica, if I could be of any use to your project, you need only ask."

"Not you," Lord Matlock said. "I want you as my representative in Sheffield. You will go there once a fortnight and hear the complaints of anyone who feels treated unfairly, and then you will report your findings to the mayor and to me. If he knows I am watching him, he will not be able to ignore the problems."

Sir Anthony said mildly, "Does Latimer have a choice in the matter?"

Lord Matlock snorted. "If he truly wishes to help the common man, he would be a fool to refuse. If he does not want the position, I will find someone else, but having someone the people there already trust would be valuable."

"If he does not wish to do it I would be happy to," said Beaumont.

"No, you will not." Lord Matlock sounded exasperated. "Latimer listens to people. You are good at organizing things. I have a different project for you, setting up a respectable workhouse where those in need can receive adequate food and shelter in exchange for reasonable labor. As for you..." Lord Matlock pointed at Sir Anthony, "you are the orator. You convince people with your speeches. That is why *you* belong in Parliament."

Sir Anthony looked quizzically at Frederica. "Does he always do that?"

"Do what?" she asked.

"Categorize people and put them in position like chessmen on a chessboard?"

"Always, and he is usually right," said Frederica. "He always wins at chess, too."

Richard added, "It is very annoying but not as annoying as our mother, who magically makes you do things whether you wish to or not."

"That is enough disrespect towards your father," said Lady Matlock severely. "You are setting a bad example."

"Fine, fine. Then let us speak of this mill," Frederica said.

Elizabeth, deciding she was better off staying out of the family bickering, retreated to a loveseat in the corner where Sylvie had gone after her dismissal by Lord Matlock. "May I join you in hiding?" she whispered to Sylvie.

Sylvie was embroidering what appeared to be a gown for a baby. "Of course. It is much calmer here."

"Is that for the christening? I would have thought there would be a Fitzwilliam christening gown," said Elizabeth in a hushed voice.

"There is," replied Sylvie. "But there is no guarantee they will recognize the baby as a Fitzwilliam. I prefer to be prepared."

"That is terrible!" Elizabeth had to fight to keep her voice low.

Holding her needle still, Sylvie was silent for long enough for Elizabeth to worry whether she had offended her. Then, her good humor suddenly restored, she said, "I can see why he did not wish for me to meet his family!

But I do like Darcy. He is a kind man. Richard thinks you will be marrying him."

Taken off-guard, Elizabeth could only attempt to stay calm. "That remains to be seen."

"Well, I hope you do. You will be good for him and teach him to laugh more. Oh! *Mon Dieu*!" Her face grew suddenly pale.

Could Lord Matlock have said something to the others that distressed her? Elizabeth had not been listening to him. "Are you well? Would you like a vinaigrette or perhaps glass of wine?"

Sylvie shook her head with uncharacteristic fierceness. Was she offended? But then the Frenchwoman reached towards Elizabeth and dug her fingers painfully into her wrist.

Shocked, Elizabeth stifled a gasp of pain. It seemed completely out of character for Sylvie, who was now blinking rapidly with a patently false smile on her face.

What was wrong with the woman? Then Sylvie glanced down, frowning, at her swollen abdomen.

Oh.

"Not a month from now after all?" Elizabeth said.

As the fingers trapping her wrist relaxed, Sylvie said quietly, "Will you be so kind as to give me your arm, Miss Bennet? There is... something I must attend to."

"Of course!" Elizabeth stood and held out her arm.

"On the other side, I pray you."

Mystified, Elizabeth rose and stepped to her right. Of course — this way she stood between Sylvie and the others.

Sylvie took her arm, but did not lean on it; whatever had troubled her a minute ago seemed to be gone, and she walked at her usual pace. Once they had safely reached the hall and were out of sight of the sitting room, Sylvie dropped her arm and halted. Reaching down, she tugged at her skirt to show the back of it. "Of course I can see nothing beyond this belly of mine!" she exclaimed. "Elizabeth, does it show?"

Elizabeth took a step back to see. "It is wet, but colorless." At least it was not blood.

"Of all the possible moments! Will you accompany me to my room? Richard will be cross if he hears I tried to go alone."

"And rightly so! Of course I will go with you." As they passed the footman at the bottom of the stairs, Elizabeth said to him, "Fetch Mrs. Reynolds to Mrs. Fitzwilliam's room instantly." She did not wait to see if he obeyed.

"There is no need," said Sylvie. "Childbirth is a perfectly natural thing."

"Yes, but if I did not seek assistance for you, your husband would be cross with *me!*"

"Ah, so true."

Sylvie's bedroom was at the far end of the north wing, not a great distance, but it felt long, especially when the Frenchwoman stopped suddenly and leaned against the wall, breathing erratically. "I have been having pains all day, but not like this!" she panted.

Elizabeth stared at her. "And you said nothing until now?"

"Richard has enough to worry about without me, and there was nothing he could do to help. Men are useless at these times! There – that is my room."

Once inside, Sylvie accepted Elizabeth's assistance in removing her stained clothes. Mrs. Reynolds arrived halfway through the process, breathing heavily, with a maid behind her. "What is the matter?" the housekeeper asked without preamble. "Is it your time, madam?"

"Aieee!" Sylvie squeaked before sitting down hard, clutching her stomach.

Presumably that was answer enough, but Elizabeth added, "Her waters just broke."

"All over the damask loveseat, I am sorry to say!" Sylvie spoke through gritted teeth.

"Do not fret about that!" Elizabeth exclaimed.

Sylvie let out a breath, and then looked down and shook her finger at her abdomen. "Are you planning to be a wicked one like your papa? Such a moment to make your appearance! He will blame his lordship for causing it, which he did not!"

Mrs. Reynolds turned to the maid. "You must fetch the midwife immediately."

Sylvie reached out her hand. "And pray take that blue sack of herbs by the mirror and brew it into a tisane for me. I mixed it last night, even though I did not expect to need it for another month."

Elizabeth could not help smiling. "Of course you did! A tisane for every ill."

Mrs. Reynolds cleared her throat. "Miss Bennet, there is no tisane in the world that will soothe Lady Matlock if she discovers this was kept from her."

Elizabeth looked at Sylvie who gave her a resigned shrug. "Very well. I will try to extricate her from the others."

She hurried back to the sitting room where the others were still deep in conversation about their mill. How was she to gain Lady Matlock's attention without the gentleman noticing? She had no desire to be the one to break news of this sort to the Fitzwilliam men. In the end, she simply stared at her ladyship from the doorway and waited for her to notice.

Naturally, it was no more than a minute before Lady Matlock appeared to feel the weight of her gaze and looked in her direction with a delicately raised brow. Elizabeth tilted her head towards the hall.

Lady Matlock managed to make a far more natural and graceful exit than Elizabeth and Sylvie had earlier. But once in the hall, she did not waste time with her usual social niceties. "What is it?"

Not even a 'my dear'? Lady Matlock was indeed not herself! "Madam, Mrs. Fitzwilliam has reached her time. I thought you would wish to know."

Lady Matlock closed her eyes for a moment. "And to think I had such hopes of a few calm hours! Ah, well. Where is she?"

"In her room. The housekeeper is with her and the midwife has been sent for."

"Show me the way, my dear."

Chapter Nineteen

Every bone in Darcy's body seemed to ache with fatigue. After all those days in bed, bringing Elizabeth to Pemberley yesterday had been tiring, and rising today at dawn to travel to Sheffield and back left him feeling as if he had depleted his last reserves.

Unfortunately, he suspected the worst part of the day was yet to come.

He handed his hat and gloves to Hobbes. "Where is Lady Matlock?"

"In the sitting room, sir, with Lord Matlock and your other guests."

"His lordship is here now, too?" Now he was truly dreading the upcoming scene.

"Yes, sir."

The proper thing would be to freshen his appearance first, but if he sat down long enough to change his boots, he might not find the wherewithal to move again. No, it was best to get past the difficult part first.

The sitting room seemed overcrowded with his uncle, Frederica, Duxbury, Richard, Beaumont and Latimer all talking excitedly. Where was Elizabeth? Hers was the only face he truly wanted to see right now.

Frederica was the first to notice him. "Darcy, you are back! Where is Jasper? Is he well?"

Trust Frederica to come directly to the difficult part! "Jasper is still in Sheffield, despite my best efforts to extract him, and he is physically as well as anyone who recently had a bullet removed from his leg can be."

Lord Matlock narrowed his eyes. "But?"

Darcy pulled up a chair beside Richard. "But he will not leave. After the riots, half the town was arrested, and the other half descended on the inn to beg assistance of you. Since you were not available, they turned to your miscreant of a son instead."

Lord Matlock rubbed his hand over his eyes. "What has he done?" he asked heavily.

"Apparently he heard them out, then led them en masse to the Town Hall where he met with the mayor and accused him of tyranny and abuse of power, not to mention maligning your family's honor."

"Jasper?" asked Frederica disbelievingly. "Jasper has never taken anything seriously in his life."

Lord Matlock frowned. "How does the family honor come into it?"

Darcy said, "He saw the hangings as a personal insult to you, sir."

Duxbury said sharply, "Hangings? What hangings?"

Duxbury did not know? Of course not. Only Elizabeth knew the full story, and she was unlikely to have wanted to discuss it. He had mentioned it to Richard, but only in passing.

"I thought you knew. Beaumont, Latimer, I am truly sorry. The men who were arrested with you were hung, quite without warning, once my uncle left Sheffield. That is what provoked the fires and the storming of the armory."

Lord Matlock frowned ferociously. Beaumont turned away, his fist pressed over his mouth while Latimer, his face ashen, hurried out of the room.

Duxbury said softly, "Damn them."

"They violated their agreement with me," Lord Matlock said harshly. "They will pay."

Darcy nodded. "That is what Jasper has been saying as well, albeit rather more colorfully. It surprised me, as he did not seem particularly concerned with the hangings until the townspeople pleaded with him for help."

"No doubt he is only making matters worse," muttered Lord Matlock.

"He seemed to be doing reasonably well. My valet has been there with him throughout and does not seem overly concerned about Jasper's behavior. Well, except inasmuch as he should be resting his leg, not tearing all over town."

Beaumont said harshly, "I must return to Sheffield tomorrow."

Lord Matlock snapped, "You will return to Sheffield when I do and not one moment sooner. Do you want them to hang you on sight?"

"His lordship is correct," said Duxbury. "Going now would be an unnecessary risk, and it sounds as if Jasper is handling matters adequately. Perhaps he will thrive with the responsibility."

"I will not have you encouraging my son to become a Radical agitator!" growled Lord Matlock.

"Why not?" asked Duxbury mildly. "Someone will need to take my place, and who knows? Perhaps after a year or two of seasoning, he will have settled enough that you could put him into Parliament."

Lord Matlock frowned. "You think yourself very clever, do you?"

"In general, I..."

"What?" Richard cried, staring at a note and half-rising from his chair.

The footman beside him said, "Sir, I was only charged with delivering it. I know nothing of the contents."

"I must..." Richard stopped speaking and sank down again in his chair.

Lord Matlock eyed him suspiciously. "What is it?"

Richard rubbed his hand over his lips and then opened his mouth as if to speak, stared down at the note, and closed his mouth again. Shaking his head, he handed the note to Darcy.

Darcy's eyebrows flew up as he perused the short message. "Do you want me to tell them?"

His cousin nodded, looking dazed.

How could he phrase it in a way that would not offend Lord Matlock, who had not yet given his blessing to Richard's marriage? Carefully, Darcy said, "It seems my new godchild will be making an appearance in the immediate future. The very immediate future."

Frederica clasped her hands together. "Truly? That is wonderful, Richard! I cannot..." Her voice trailed off under a quelling glare from her father.

As if Richard's news had never existed, Lord Matlock said, "Darcy, your valet who is with Jasper, is he a sensible man?"

"Very much so, and he will not hesitate to send word if he has concerns. I left a footman there today as well." Darcy cast a sideways glance at Richard, hoping he was not too disturbed by his father's snub.

"Then there is no particular reason to worry," said Lord Matlock. "After all, they would never dare to lay hands on my son."

Duxbury whispered something to Frederica, who nodded and crossed to the sideboard. She poured a generous glass of port and brought it to Richard.

So much for Darcy's planned quick escape and rest.

"I thought the first child was not supposed to be in such a rush!" muttered Sylvie a moment before grabbing the leather strap and biting down on it again.

Lady Matlock smiled. "Too true, but this is a Fitzwilliam baby. Fitzwilliams are always in a hurry. You had best accustom yourself to it." She patted Sylvie's clenched hand. "At least it should be over quickly at this rate."

When the spasm eased and Sylvie spat out the leather strap again, Elizabeth said, "It has grown to be quite a crush in here. Perhaps I should leave to give you more space to move." She felt half suffocated herself. The midwife, her assistant, a maid, Mrs. Reynolds, and Lady Matlock were all crowded into a room that was not large to start with.

Sylvie's eyes were closed, but she nodded.

Lady Matlock shook her head. "I need you here, Elizabeth."

Elizabeth frowned. What could Lady Matlock's desires matter compared to Sylvie's comfort at such a time? "I am only in the way here, and it might ease matters for Sylvie."

Lady Matlock sat back, lines of fatigue showing in her face. "When you marry the second son of an earl, you lose certain rights, such as privacy at moments like this. Until such a time as my eldest son produces a living heir, this child, if a boy, will be an heir to Matlock. We need witnesses to the birth. You are gently born and not yet a relative and thus an impartial witness."

Elizabeth closed her mouth. Had Sylvie realized the importance of this event? No wonder the question of Colonel Fitzwilliam's marriage was such a weighty one. She dipped a washcloth in a basin of cool water, wrung it out, and wiped Sylvie's forehead with it. "You are being very brave."

The midwife touched Sylvie's arm. "Mrs. Fitzwilliam, it is time. With your next contraction, you must push as hard as you can."

"Thank God!" groaned Sylvie.

Outside the sitting room, Elizabeth asked Lady Matlock, "Would you prefer to hold him?"

Lady Matlock looked longingly at the swaddled newborn in Elizabeth's arms. "I cannot acknowledge him until my husband has done so. Remember, you must present him to Lord Matlock even before Richard. This is usually a formality, but..."

"I remember," Elizabeth said firmly. Despite being completely enchanted by the infant, she was not pleased with these instructions. Well, both Richard and Frederica seemed to disobey their parents, so why should she hesitate to do so?

"Come, then." Lady Matlock led Elizabeth into the sitting room.

Silence fell as the others spotted them. Elizabeth chose a path which took her directly past Colonel Fitzwilliam and paused at his side. "You have a son, Colonel," she said softly.

"Sylvie?" he asked, his voice catching. Were his eyes actually misting?

"Asleep and doing well."

The colonel let out a long breath. But apparently he understood the rules in this little drama, since after briefly gazing into the baby's sleeping face, he took a step backwards. Darcy, looking paler than usual, sat beside him.

This must be how actresses on Drury Lane felt as they made their entrances. Elizabeth came to a stop in front of Lord Matlock and delivered the line as she had been instructed. "My lord, Mrs. Fitzwilliam has been delivered of a son."

The Earl made no move to take him. "He is very quiet," he said suspiciously.

"He is *asleep*," she said with a hint of asperity. "A quarter hour ago I thought I would be permanently deafened."

He studied the newborn as if attempting to read something in his red, wizened face, and then he took the baby from her arms. There was an almost audible sense of relief in the room, but no one said a word. As the earl shifted from one foot to the other, the infant woke and emitted an earsplitting wail. Elizabeth winced, ready to take him back from his grandfather.

With surprising dexterity, his lordship tickled the baby's lip with the tip of his little finger until he abruptly stopped howling and settled to suck on it. A smile crept over Lord Matlock's ruddy face. "Now *those* are Fitzwilliam lungs," he pronounced.

Colonel Fitzwilliam, looking relieved, hurried forward to his father's side and stroked his son's cheek tentatively with his forefinger.

Elizabeth found herself blinking back tears as Lady Matlock and Frederica also gathered around the baby. Her part was apparently done. As she turned away with relief, she saw Darcy was watching her intently. Since everyone else was distracted, there was no reason she had to keep her distance, so she crossed to his side.

A smile warmed his face, even through the evidence of fatigue. "Well done."

"Thank you. If I should happen to fall asleep standing up, pray wake me before I fall over."

His smile broadened. "It will be my pleasure."

Now that she was closer to him, the pallor of his face was even more noticeable. "I have been wondering about you. These must have been long days for you, with your wound not yet healed."

"It gives me no difficulty, apart from a headache now and then. I understand I have you to blame for setting

Mrs. Reynolds on my trail." But he said it with a warmth that belied his words.

She lowered her voice in mock conspiracy. "I knew Wilkins would never forgive me if I did not."

"A very frightening man, my valet," Darcy agreed teasingly.

"Terrifying, I assure you! If I angered him, he might do anything – even give you unstarched cravats!"

"A dreadful prospect." But despite his humor, there was tension in his forehead.

Now actually concerned, she said, "Headaches now and then? Does this qualify as *now* or *then*?"

"It is nothing to worry about. Things at a distance are still blurry, and the harder I try to make them out, the more my head aches."

Elizabeth nodded sagely. "Then I will assume 'now and then' means most of the time. Fortunately, there is one thing to your advantage."

He seemed to relax a little. "Why do I think this thing will in fact be trouble for me?"

"Not at all." Elizabeth tilted her head to one side, pretending to examine his face. "I was referring to my own pleasure. I think you would look quite distinguished in spectacles."

"In that case, I shall..." He paused. "I shall admit I was hoping to say something clever to the effect that anything which pleases you gives me pleasure, but I find I am more weary than witty tonight."

"You simply require more practice at teasing, I think. But I must go deliver the news to Sylvie that Lord Matlock is pleased with his grandson, or more precisely, I will deliver it to whoever remains with her, as she is no doubt still catching up on much needed sleep."

"As you and I should do as well." He looked into her eyes. "Elizabeth?"

"Yes?"

"I will see you in the morning." It was more a question than a statement.

She pretended to consider this. "At this point, I may sleep until afternoon!"

"We may all do that." He nodded towards the four Fitzwilliams who were squabbling over who would hold the baby next. "It does not appear they plan to go to bed any time in the next fortnight!"

When she finally did reach her bed, Elizabeth held the memory of his smile close.

Chapter Twenty

Elizabeth awoke in cheerful spirits despite the grey skies outside. She stretched luxuriantly as she recalled her conversation with Darcy the previous night. Would today be the day he finally made her an offer again?

Why did women always have to wait? It had not worked for Frederica; she had tried waiting for Sir Anthony, but the only reason they were together now was that Frederica had overcome his doubts by insisting that he marry her. If she had simply waited instead, they would still be distant strangers.

Waiting had not served Jane well either. She had pined away waiting for Mr. Bingley to return to her, and it would never have happened if it were not for a series of coincidences. If Elizabeth had not encountered Darcy in Kent, she would not have traveled with him long enough to discover his role in separating Bingley from Jane. Even then, had she not confronted him about his actions, nothing would have changed. Bingley had come back to

Jane not because of her patience, but because Elizabeth had taken action.

Now it was her own turn to wait for a gentleman to make up his mind. But why should she wait when it had not worked for either Jane or Frederica? Did she have any other choice?

She could confront Darcy about those compromising events and make him feel honor bound to marry her. If he still loved her but could not bring himself to propose again, he might even be glad of it. But what if he had decided against her? If he felt forced into a marriage he no longer wanted, would he resent her forever? Such a marriage could not be happy.

Or could it? Could enough of his affection for her remain that they would be able to move past this, even if he might be reluctant at first? He might not forgive easily, but he had shown her warmth during the riots and again last night, and he was not an unreasonable man. The question was whether she was willing to take a chance to win him.

Yes. If Darcy did not take the initiative to propose to her today, he was going to be in for a surprise.

Darcy's first thought on opening his eyes was that Elizabeth was at Pemberley, and there was nothing stopping him from seeking her out, gazing into her fine eyes, and taking her into his arms and kissing her until she agreed to marry him. Nothing except the knowledge that he would be taking advantage of her if he did.

She had already refused him once, and despite the evidence suggesting she might have changed her mind about him, he could not be certain she would not reject him again. If she did refuse him, it would put her in an untenable position until such time as she had the ability to leave Pemberley. Given the arrival of Richard's son and the extent of Duxbury's injuries, it was unlikely Lord and Lady Matlock would offer Elizabeth an escape by leaving Pemberley anytime soon.

And the most damnable part was that he could not trust himself to keep his hands off her.

Elizabeth had always been a temptation he had to fight, but it was ten times worse now. He had held her while she slept in the riot and again as they rode to Pemberley. Instead of sating his need for her, it had only made him crave more. Now seeing her in his home, the place he had imagined her so often, dreaming of her touch, her silky hair spread across the pillow as she lay beside him in his bed...

He had no idea what Wilkins had just said to him.

In his eagerness to see Elizabeth, he was the first at the breakfast table, and was soon joined by his aunt and uncle, Latimer and Beaumont. He managed to keep a seat next to him empty in the hope Elizabeth might choose to sit by him. And then she herself stood in the doorway, a bewitching smile on her face.

He had to keep his gaze on her face. Georgiana's day dress was revealingly tight on Elizabeth's curves.

He waited impatiently while greeting were exchanged and she filled her plate. And then she sat beside him, and he could breathe in her lavender scent. The dark curls around her face danced as she turned to speak to Lady Matlock.

It was a good thing that asking after the baby, Sylvie, and Duxbury took several minutes. It gave him time to gather his wits again.

And then she turned that arch look on him. "Mr. Darcy, I hoped to seek some advice from you. I have not yet had the opportunity to explore the grounds which you spoke so highly of, so I plan to walk out after breakfast."

He tore his eyes away from her long enough to glance at the window. "In the rain?"

She seemed taken aback. "Ah, yes. In the rain. It can be quite refreshing. I hoped you might be able to recommend a particular walk to me."

"I..." It would be the height of rudeness to refuse to escort her. It would also be sheer insanity to be alone with her, even in the rain. Especially in the rain. It had not passed his notice two days ago when the rain had made Elizabeth's clothes cling to her. He opened his mouth to suggest they invite Frederica to join them, but that was not what came out. "Might I have the honor of accompanying you? That way I can show you the best walks." Perhaps he could do it while wearing a blindfold and with his hands tied behind his back.

"That would be delightful," she said demurely.

He attempted to rally his thoughts. "I fear Pemberley's grounds may not show at their best in the rain. Would you like to see the formal gardens? The customary circuit around the lake is considered the highlight of the grounds, but it may be a long walk in the rain."

"Oh, let us do the circuit! The trees will keep the rain off us." She gave him a sly look. "Unless, of course, it is too far for you."

"Miss Elizabeth, I believe you are teasing me." And that was a particularly poor idea since he always longed to kiss that amused look away. "I will manage to keep up with you somehow."

Lady Matlock said, "Actually, Darcy, I had hoped to speak to you privately after breakfast. Perhaps Miss Bennet would be willing to delay your walk for a short time."

Darcy wanted to strangle his aunt. It was beginning to feel as if he were under some sort of curse which made it impossible for him to talk to Elizabeth for more than a few minutes a day. "Or we could speak after the walk."

"I think not," said Lady Matlock. "This should come first."

This was not going to be pleasant, whatever it was.

Breakfast now seemed to last forever, even with Elizabeth beside him. But eventually everyone had finished eating.

"Shall we retire to the library, Darcy?" Lady Matlock said. "Perhaps you would like to join us as well, Miss Bennet." It was more of a command than a suggestion.

Apparently Lord Matlock would be joining them as well. Now he was truly dreading this. He would need to be prepared to step in if his uncle became harsh towards Elizabeth. If worst came to worst, he could take her out of the room, but as a precaution, when they reached the library, he took the seat beside his uncle. At least that would give her a little distance from him.

Lady Matlock folded her hands primly on her lap. "I realized today I have overlooked how quickly time has been passing, and as a result, there is a delicate situation we must deal with now."

Even Lord Matlock looked surprised at this admission of fault from his usually faultless wife. "Well, what is it?"

"Darcy, I hope you and Miss Bennet will forgive me for relating history you already know, but this is new to his lordship." Lady Matlock turned her head to address herself directly to her husband. "You will recall that when you arrived in Sheffield, I told you Darcy had received a blow to his head the previous day. We were preoccupied with our own troublesome offspring at the time, so I never divulged the entire story. After his injury, Darcy was unconscious and was taken into a private home. When I received word in the middle of the night, I asked Miss Bennet to go to see him with me, suspecting he might respond better to her than to me."

Elizabeth's mouth dropped open. Apparently this was news to her as well.

"In fact, she was the only person he responded to at all, and she was kind enough to honor my request for her to remain with him. Since it was still night-time, I told everyone there she was his wife."

Lord Matlock gave a disapproving grunt. "What were you possibly thinking? You backed Darcy into a corner by compromising her!"

His wife shook her head. "Since I expected them to be engaged in a matter of days, I did not think it mattered much. Be quiet, Darcy, and let me finish. I did not foresee one major difficulty, though. When Darcy awakened, he was blind."

Elizabeth gasped. "You knew?"

"Of course I knew. You are not the only one who can bribe a doctor, my dear, and my pockets are deeper than yours. It was obvious he was hiding something about Darcy, and I wanted to know what it was."

"But you said nothing!"

"I preferred to wait for him to tell me of his own volition. He has his pride, you know."

"Yes," said Elizabeth, now sounding amused. "I do know."

Darcy let out a breath of relief. If she was not angry, there might still be hope.

"The doctor felt his blindness was likely to be permanent. You can see now he was incorrect, but I had to make a decision based on that information." She gave Darcy an apologetic look. "So I wrote to the London newspapers with an announcement of their engagement, and dated it the previous day."

"What?" Darcy could not believe his ears. "How dare you!"

"Darcy, pray do not say "what" in that coarse manner! It was the obvious thing to do. I also wrote a letter to Miss Bennet's father, explaining that Darcy was unable to write him as he had been injured shortly after Elizabeth had accepted him, but he planned to ask her father's permission as soon as possible."

Elizabeth dropped her face into her hands.

Lord Matlock nodded. "Quite the correct thing to do, my dear. Do not glare at me like that, Darcy. You had compromised the girl, even if you were unconscious, and for the sake of your reputation and the Darcy family name, it must be believed you offered for her prior to your injury, rather than that you had settled for her because you were blind."

Darcy rubbed his forehead. There was no point in getting angry with them now; what was done was done. "I wish you had spoken to me first."

"You were not in your right mind at the time," his aunt retorted. "I planned to wait a day or two before telling you what I had done. Unfortunately, events overtook us – learning of Richard's marriage, Frederica's flight and arrest, Sir Anthony's injuries, and all the rest. I meant to speak to you yesterday, but you had already left for Sheffield, and by the time you returned, we were all thinking about the baby. I am afraid I rather lost track of how much time had passed."

Darcy nodded curtly. He did not trust himself to speak, or even to look at Elizabeth. If she blamed him for this, he might never forgive his aunt.

Lady Matlock picked up a stack of letters from the table beside her. "This morning, when my maid gave me the letters you collected from the inn yesterday, I realized that either Miss Bennet had very active correspondents or I had left it too late."

He could not bear not knowing, so he looked at Elizabeth and his heart sank. Her hands still covered her face, but now her shoulders were shaking. Damn his aunt and her officiousness! But there was no time for that. He knelt beside Elizabeth's chair and said softly, "I am so sorry, Elizabeth. I never meant to force you into marrying me, but I will do my utmost to make you happy."

Elizabeth slowly lowered her hands, and he realized she had not been crying. She was laughing. "Well, I will have to agree to the same, then, since I planned to use our walk to force *you* to marry *me*."

Could he believe his ears? "Truly?" His breath caught in his throat.

"Truly. Your aunt has saved me from some embarrassingly improper behavior." She reached out and took his hand. "I hope *you* are not disappointed to be forced into this."

He shook his head. "Not in the slightest."

Lady Matlock said with satisfaction, "See, as I told you, it was simply a matter of time."

"I suppose I should be grateful that *this* time I was told about a marriage before it happened," grumbled Lord Matlock.

"Darcy has never been as troublesome as our own children, my dear," said Lady Matlock reassuringly.

"In any case, Elizabeth, here are your letters."

Without looking away from Elizabeth's face, Darcy said, "If you do not object, I would like some time alone with my newly betrothed." Just saying the words filled him with a rush of happiness.

"Precisely what I was about to suggest. Come, my dear." Lady Matlock led her husband out of the library, and Darcy heard the latch click behind them.

There were definite advantages to being an engaged man.

He took her hand in both of his and pressed his lips against it, then raised it to his cheek. "I cannot think why you would see a need to try to make me marry you, but it makes me happy that you did."

Elizabeth tentatively reached out and touched the disobedient curl of his hair that always fell across his forehead no matter how hard he tried to keep it in place. "Perhaps because I have barely seen you since we arrived here."

A smile grew on his face. "I was not avoiding you. Well, perhaps I was avoiding being *alone* with you, but that was only because of my own ungentlemanly impulses. What would you think of a gentleman who pressed his attentions on a lady who was a guest in his house, and one who had refused him previously?"

She gave him an arch look. "I would not generally recommend such a course of action, but in this particular case, I had been wishing you would!"

Darcy swallowed hard. "It is probably just as well I did not know that, especially – " He bit his tongue just in time.

"Especially?"

His cheeks grew hot, and he said in a low voice, "Especially after seeing you holding Richard's baby. Do not ask me more, I beg you!" He had barely restrained himself from throwing her over his shoulder, carrying her to his bed, and doing his utmost to make sure she would be holding *his* baby next time.

She leaned forward to kiss his forehead. "I will indulge you just this once. But do you not wish to know what I planned to say to you on that walk?"

He nodded vigorously. After her soft lips had brushed his forehead, his ability to speak was severely limited.

Her hand cupped his cheek. "I planned to embarrass you by bringing up the first day we were in Sheffield, assuming you would try to avoid talking about kissing me, and then I was going to tell you my only regret about it was that you had not done it again. Would that have worked?" Her last word came out as a squeak as Darcy stood and pulled her into his arms.

Enough with self-restraint. Enough with gentlemanly behavior. He was dying of thirst in the desert and she was the only thing that could save him. Just one brush of her tender lips, one taste of the sweetness of her mouth, and he would stop. If he could.

Apparently he could not, at least not when her arms slipped around his neck and she met his lips halfway, nibbling and cajoling until he surrendered the last vestige of civilized behavior and took possession of her mouth. Good God, but she was intoxicating!

As she pressed herself against him, he lost the last of his ability to think.

Some time later, the sound of the latch barely penetrated Darcy's desire-filled thoughts, but Elizabeth at least had the presence of mind to stop kissing him. He did not remove his arm from around her shoulders, though. After all, this was *his* library in *his* home and *his* lovely, passionate betrothed, and anyone who did not like what they saw could go elsewhere.

It was Frederica, of course, the one person who would not be in the least intimidated by interrupting an intimate moment. He turned his best glare on her, and as usual, it had no effect whatsoever.

"Elizabeth! I have questions for your uncle that cannot wait. Will you write to him about the project so I can send him my questions? Or better yet, convince him to come here?"

Elizabeth's look of amusement was delightfully enhanced by her rosy, slightly swollen lips, at least in Darcy's eyes. "I would be happy to be of assistance, but it might have to wait until tomorrow. I already have a great deal of urgent correspondence I must deal with today." She gestured towards the stack of letters beside her.

"Tomorrow! Well, I suppose if you must. Or perhaps *I* could write to him today. Do you think he would mind, or would he find it too forward of me?"

"I am certain he would be delighted to hear from you." Elizabeth's voice was full of laughter.

"I will try that, then." Her tone changed to wheedling. "And perhaps you could write a very short note to him to include with my letter?"

"I suppose I could manage that. I might need to do so, if he is responsible for one of these letters." Elizabeth picked up the letters and began to sort through them. "Let me see. Jane, my mother, Charlotte, good heavens! Even one from my father, who *never* writes. Here we go – this one is from my aunt, so there may be something from my uncle in it. This one I do not recognize." She broke the seal, glanced inside, and tossed it aside. "Mr. Collins," she said darkly.

Darcy held out his free hand. "May I see that one?"

Elizabeth eyed him askance but gave it to him. "If you wish to be preached at."

"No, but if it is anything like I suspect, I am looking forward to responding to it on your behalf."

"If it is anything like I suspect, I am perfectly happy not to even read it! And this one I do not recognize either." She opened the last letter.

Frederica snatched it from her hand before she could look at it. "That is Lady Catherine's hand. Let me see. Oh, yes. She is in fine form. *Are you lost to every feeling of propriety and delicacy? Are the shades of Pemberley to be so polluted?* This one definitely goes to Darcy to answer."

Elizabeth seemed to sober. "In fact, I would prefer to answer that one myself."

Darcy tightened his arm around her shoulders. "Elizabeth, she can be very unkind, and there is no need for you to answer it."

"I know, but it... oh, there is no way around it. There is a subject I must ask you about, a rather delicate one." Elizabeth glanced at Frederica, then back at Darcy. She took a deep breath, and then the words tumbled out. "Do you still believe marriage to me will be a degradation?"

"No," Darcy said instantly. "I would never have proposed to you if I had believed it."

"Then why did you say it?" Her lip was trembling.

"I cannot recall precisely what I said, but it was not about my beliefs. I think it likely the *ton* will say it is and will mock me because of your connections, but I do not care."

Elizabeth closed her eyes for a moment. "Thank you. It has been my greatest fear, and I could not tolerate having my own children learn from their father to be ashamed of my connections."

"That will never happen. I confess there was a time when I considered the opinions of the *ton* to be more important than my feelings for you, but now having the honor of marrying you far outweighs that, and the struggle has made me a better man. The *ton* can go hang for all I care."

"Well, no," Frederica said. "You cannot ignore the *ton*. You have Georgiana to launch into society soon, but that does not mean their opinions should rule you. In any case, they will be more interested in spreading rumors about Richard's marriage when his marriage is made known. And my mother has already given the *ton* notice that she will not tolerate criticism of your marriage."

"She has?" Elizabeth looked puzzled.

"In the announcement. 'The Earl and Countess of Matlock are pleased to announce the engagement of their nephew, Mr. Fitzwilliam Darcy, to Miss Elizabeth Bennet,' and so forth? And I must say I am a bit cross you did not tell me about your engagement sooner!" Frederica gave them both a reproachful look.

Elizabeth shook her head with a mischievous smile. "We could not. We may have been engaged for days, but even *we* were not told about it until today."

"How could you be engaged without knowing it?" Frederica demanded.

Darcy laughed. "Do you need to ask?"

Frederica's eyes opened wide. "Mother? Oh, dear. She did not say a word to us about that."

"Of course she did not," said Darcy. "After all, she must keep up her reputation for working miracles."

Elizabeth was opening another letter. "Oh, my. From my aunt –

My dear Lizzy, was it only seven days ago that you told me you did not wish to travel with that proud Mr. Darcy because all you would do was quarrel? And today I hear from the newspaper – not from you! – that you are engaged to that very same quarrelsome, disdainful Mr. Darcy? You must have had a most impressive quarrel with him!

I fear there will be a great deal of teasing in my future."

Frederica was staring absently into space. "And I will write to your uncle. Oh, I forgot – Mother says you have been behind a closed door quite long enough, and if you do not go to the sitting room now, she will come here and march you out herself."

"Damned interfering woman," Darcy muttered.

Elizabeth kissed his cheek softly. "At least it will give me the opportunity to write my letters. And perhaps later we could take that walk together, just the two of us."

Darcy said in her ear, "So we shall – even if it is pouring rain outside. I know a few places where we can stay dry."

Four days later, after one of their very long walks, Darcy and Elizabeth returned to the house hand in hand, entering through the garden doorway rather than the front entrance to avoid unnecessary attention. But someone on the staff must have alerted Hobbes, since he appeared before them at the bottom of the cantilevered stairs. With a bow, he said, "There are visitors for Miss Bennet. Mr. and Mrs. Gardiner arrived half an hour ago. Lady Frederica took them into the sitting room. I took the liberty of asking Mrs. Reynolds to prepare a room for them."

"Here already?" exclaimed Elizabeth. "And my aunt as well? They must have traveled by post to arrive so quickly."

Darcy, more attuned to his butler's expressions, said, "What is the matter, Hobbes?"

Hobbes hesitated. "Lady Frederica was most eager to speak to them."

"Let me guess – did the Gardiners have a chance to refresh themselves when they arrived?"

The butler bowed. "No, sir. I attempted to suggest it, but Lady Frederica had other plans."

"I will go and see what I can do." Reaching up, Elizabeth removed a twig from Darcy's hair and smiled at him. "Perhaps you should change your coat first. It is rather...leafy."

Despite the butler's presence, Darcy kissed her lightly. "Very well. I will join you shortly, minx."

Elizabeth stopped at a mirror to check her hair. A few stray curls needed to be tucked back under her hairpins, but it could be much worse, especially after a walk alone with Darcy. It had been a lovely walk, though, even if they did not do much walking. After touching her warm cheeks, she headed towards the sitting room.

She paused just inside the door and found a lively conversation taking place.

"They must be seen to be exclusive and highly fashionable," said Frederica, leaning forward.

Mr. Gardiner nodded. "In that case, they should only be sold to the finest milliners and mantua makers, a very limited clientele."

"Precisely!"

"So it must be a new channel of sales. Usually all fabric goes into a warehouse, and anyone who can pay the price may buy it. These would need to be directly sold to the shops without being sent through warehouses, so you would need to have a salesman who presents them directly. Someone elegant, I would say. That will require some consideration. Lady Frederica, will your name be attached to the enterprise, or is the mill to be owned anonymously to avoid the taint of trade?"

Frederica paused, glancing at Sir Anthony as if in search of an answer.

"A charity," pronounced Lady Matlock. "It must be attached to a charity which Frederica runs, with proceeds to go towards some good cause."

"In that case, selling them to the shops will not be difficult if we can say that we represent Lady Frederica's charitable endeavor. Her name will encourage them to buy. I would suggest offering very limited quantities at first in order to create a demand. If only certain customers are able to obtain them and others are turned away at first, then everyone will feel they simply must have one. Of course, your mill will be producing much more fabric than would be sold that way, so you will need someone at the mill managing sales and making certain the fashionable name only goes on certain products and is only sold directly to the appropriate buyers."

Lord Matlock had appeared not to be listening, but he said gruffly, "You will need a separate company to handle it, Gardiner."

Mr. Gardiner did not bat an eyelash at this attention or his lordship's demanding tone. "You are correct, my lord. I did not wish to assume Lady Frederica would choose me as her seller, although naturally I would be honored if she did so. I am happy to offer her my advice regardless."

Lady Matlock looked approving of this gentlemanly response. "That is very kind of you, Mr. Gardiner. You will discover my daughter makes her decisions quickly and firmly, and would not have asked you here had she not already made a decision."

With a bow, Mr. Gardiner said, "You honor me greatly, Lady Frederica. May I ask what fabrics you are planning to manufacture at the mill?"

Frederica laughed. "Fabrics? I fear we have completely neglected that important detail, though we did plan the worker housing and the school. Do you have a recommendation?"

"That is a complex question. If you are aiming for the luxury market, silk is a likely prospect. Now that silk thread is being spun in this country, the fabric is simpler to make than when it had to be imported from China.

But if you are hoping for some of the fabric to be used for clothes for the common people..."

Elizabeth could see it was unlikely there would be a break in the conversation in the near future, so she approached Mrs. Gardiner. "Welcome to Pemberley," she said quietly. "I am sorry I was not here when you arrived."

"Lizzy!" Her aunt rose and hugged her, but Mr. Gardiner was so deep in the discussion he did not even notice her presence.

Elizabeth led her aunt back to the Great Hall. "We can speak more freely here. I had not expected you to come with my uncle, but I am delighted you did!"

"How could I resist the opportunity to visit Pemberley? With all the unrest, I did not expect we will be able to take our Northern tour this summer after all, and I have been so longing to see Derbyshire again. Since Jane is still at our house with Mr. Bingley calling every day, I could feel comfortable leaving the children with their nursemaid. Has Jane told you her news yet?"

"Yes, she wrote to tell me I was not the only engaged Bennet daughter, but that her dear Bingley was being torn from her to go north to see to his mills. It is a good thing, too; some of our guests here are very perturbed about the state of his mills."

"I can see mills are becoming a fashionable topic! But I had another reason to come here. I have a few pointed questions to put to you, Lizzy!"

Elizabeth laughed. "I can imagine you do! But should I rescue my uncle from the business discussion first?"

"No, indeed! I cannot tell you how delighted he is by this opportunity. It has distressed him for years that his warehouse was full of products made by people in miserable circumstances, but there has been no other choice before. Why, he is so engaged in the discussion now he will not even notice time is passing! It is good to see him so excited about something again. Had I known it would take you less than a fortnight to solve all our problems, I would have told you about them much sooner!"

"It was pure luck, I assure you!" Elizabeth spotted Sir Anthony moving towards them. "Aunt, I assume you have been introduced to my honorary brother, Sir Anthony Duxbury?"

"Indeed she was," said Sir Anthony with a bow. "And I took my honorary brother duties seriously and did my best to protect your poor uncle from being badgered with dozens of questions from all directions during his first few minutes here, but he seems to be holding his own. I might add, Mrs. Gardiner, that it is quite an accomplishment for anyone to hold their own with my wife and her parents."

"I have observed that already!" Mrs. Gardiner tilted her head to one side. "But I had not realized Lizzy had a brother, honorary or otherwise. Inobservant of me, I must say."

Elizabeth laughed. "I did tell you about him once. He is the gentleman who protected me by saying I was his sister when I took the stagecoach to London alone."

"Indeed? You told me he was an elderly gentleman!"

"I did not think you would be happy if I told you a handsome young gentleman was my protector! And he *is* handsome when his face is not all shades of purple and yellow as it is now. That is the result of one of the many shocking events since we left London. All is well now, but I fear you will not be pleased when I tell you everything that has happened!"

Mrs. Gardiner paled. "I have been imagining terrible fates for you since reading in the newspaper about the riots in Sheffield. To think I encouraged you to go there!"

Elizabeth said archly, "It was not so very bad, was it, Sir Anthony? After all, the only people in our party who were seriously injured were Mr. Darcy, Colonel Fitzwilliam, Mr. Jasper Fitzwilliam – twice, in his case! – and, as you can see, Sir Anthony. There was, of course, the night Lady Frederica spent in gaol, and poor Latimer and Beaumont were half-starved and are still sentenced to be hung. I thought myself quite fortunate to have no more difficulties than being compromised three or four times! So you can see, Aunt, it was a providential thing I had an honorary brother to rely upon."

Her aunt's look of dismay was almost humorous. "I do hope you are exaggerating."

Elizabeth exchanged a glance with Sir Anthony, and they both laughed. "I did leave out a few tiny details, like the three riots, having to escape from Sheffield with nothing more than my bonnet and gloves, and Lord Matlock disowning two of his children. Oh! And here is Mr. Darcy come to greet you." She held out her hand to him. "You remember my aunt, I believe. I would introduce you to my uncle, but Frederica is holding him hostage in the sitting room."

"I am not surprised, at least about Frederica. She has been most anxious to speak to him," said Darcy. "It is a pleasure to see you again, Mrs. Gardiner, and I hope to have the chance to prove to you I am not as proud and disdainful as you may have been led to believe."

"I never thought you were," said Mrs. Gardiner. "You seemed perfectly amiable to me that day at the circulating library, and I even told Elizabeth I thought you liked her. There, now I have said, 'I told you so,' and we can forget the matter." She smiled warmly at Elizabeth.

"Yes, Aunt, you were right and I was wrong! And it would have saved us both a great deal of trouble if I had believed you."

"It all ended well, and that is what matters," said Darcy, shifting closer to Elizabeth's side. "On the subject of ending well, Elizabeth, do you know anything about this paper I just found on my desk?"

Elizabeth examined the paper he held out and laughed. It was a marriage license in both their names, dated a sennight past. "I can guess where it comes from, or rather who it comes from, and I am starting to wonder whether she might have said our vows for us at the same time!"

"Of course not." Lady Matlock advanced on them from the sitting room door. "One can only bribe a clergyman so far."

Darcy held up the license. "Is this supposed to be a hint?"

"Of course not. My preference, especially after two of my own children married clandestinely, would be to have your wedding at the beginning of the Season at St. George's Hanover Square."

"No," said Darcy instantly. "We are not waiting until next winter."

"Oh, be quiet, Darcy. As I said, that would be *my* preference. However..." Lady Matlock turned to Mrs. Gardiner. "You seem like a sensible woman, so I hope you will not be shocked by the very practical thing I am about to say."

Mrs. Gardiner raised her eyebrows. "I hope I am sensible, and I am not easy to shock."

"My first grandchild was born a few days ago, barely five months after his parents were married. I do not want to see that happen to you, Darcy. From what I have observed in the past few days, I believe the clock is ticking, and if you hope to have *your* first child born at least nine months into your marriage, I do not think you should waste any time in setting a date."

Scandalized, Elizabeth protested, "Your ladyship!"

"I did not ask *you*, Elizabeth! Now, I am not saying anything has happened that should not have – "

Darcy interrupted in an ominous voice, "No, it most certainly has not!"

"As of *yet*," continued Lady Matlock. "But, Mrs. Gardiner, unless you can assure me that Elizabeth's patience and self-control when faced by extreme temptation are far better than my nephew's, I think even a three month engagement would be over-optimistic." Mrs. Gardiner's eyes were dancing with amusement. "Sadly, I do not believe I can make such an assurance on Lizzy's behalf – at least not if the temptation is extreme."

"I knew you were a sensible woman!" said Lady Matlock.

Elizabeth put her hands on her hips. "And I cannot believe you are having this discussion at all, much less when you have just met, and my poor aunt has not even had a chance to refresh herself after her long journey!"

Sir Anthony cleared his throat. "I do believe Elizabeth may have a point," he said apologetically.

"Nonsense. Darcy was the one who raised the subject, waving that marriage license around."

Darcy spluttered. "The one you put where I was certain to discover it?"

Elizabeth put her hand on Mrs. Gardiner's arm. "Now you can see why I needed an honorary brother! If the rest of you will excuse us, I will take my aunt to her room."

Lady Matlock said cordially, "Of course, my dear. An excellent notion."

"Your room is this way." As they reached the door, Elizabeth gave a mischievous look back over her shoulder. "And I have a great deal to tell you about, Aunt!"

Epilogue

"We are going dragon hunting," Annie Duxbury bounced up and down on her heels. "Do you want to come?"

"I will be a viscount someday, and I do not play with little girls." Six year old Francis Cathcart looked down his not insignificant nose at the younger girl.

"Then you are a fool, for I daresay I can climb a tree better than you can!" she retorted. "I dare you to climb to the top of that pine tree!"

Francis shook his head with a fine imitation of adult disdain. "If you wish to be childish, go play with your dolls."

Will Fitzwilliam put his fists on his hips. "Why not take the dare? Are you afraid? I may be an earl someday, and I play with anybody who is brave and clever. I am not sure you are either."

"Are you calling me a coward?"

Will considered the matter for at least two seconds. "Yes, I am."

The viscount-to-be put up his fists. "You need to be taught a lesson."

George Darcy elbowed his way between the two boys. "Stop it, both of you! Lady Matlock told us specifically not to make a mess of ourselves today."

"What, are you afraid of an old lady like her?" taunted Francis.

"Yes," said George calmly. "I am not stupid, unlike some people I could mention. Oh, look! Here comes Freddie."

A little boy charged up, a wooden sword in his hand. "Where's the dragon?"

"Who are you?" Francis sneered.

"I am Frederick Gardiner, and I do not care who you are because you have no manners." Freddie slashed at an enemy sapling with his sword.

"Gardiner? Who is your father?"

"My father is a purveyor of fine fabrics," said Freddie proudly. "And a supporter of the Rights of Man."

"First a girl and now a Cit?" Then a heavy weight fell from the tree above him, knocking Francis to the ground, and a small fist sank into his stomach.

"Don't you dare call my friend names!" Little Annie Duxbury sat on top of him. "Freddie's father is smart and has helped a lot of people. What has your father ever done?"

Francis pushed her off. "My father is a viscount. He does not need to do things."

"Well, there you are. He is just a useless aristo," said Annie with perfect logic. "You had better run home to your mama before the dragon comes and eats you. Come on, who needs *him*?"

"Let's go!" cried Freddie. "Last one to the cave is the dragon's dinner!"

"Wait!" cried Francis. "There's a cave?"

The other four children were already racing out of sight as Francis picked himself up off the ground and dusted his trousers. Then, without a second glance, he stalked back towards the house.

Behind the window overlooking this little scene, Elizabeth and Sylvie were helpless with mirth. "She is her mother all over again!" said Elizabeth. "He was almost twice her size."

"A useless *aristo*?" Sylvie echoed. "Perhaps they are teaching their children a bit too much egalitarianism."

A small hand tugged on Elizabeth's skirt. She looked down to find Annie's flaxen-haired twin, Henry, struggling to carry a squirming puppy.

"He is the runt," said Henry pleadingly. "The other puppies were being mean to him so the kennel master was going to drown him, but he said I could have him if I wished. Do you think I can keep him, Aunt Elizabeth?"

It was hard to tell which pair of imploring brown eyes looking up at her was more pathetic. Elizabeth crouched down to pet the little ball of fur. "I suggest you ask your father," she said in a conspiratorial tone. "He can never resist the story of someone in need. But you must ask the kennel master for a collar and rope for him first, and be careful not to step on Jane on your way out."

"Oh," he said, looking around the room until his eyes lighted on two-year-old Jane Darcy who had fallen asleep on the hearth rug, a white cat draped over her chubby legs. "I will not step on the kitty, either."

"I am certain the kitty appreciates that," said Elizabeth solemnly as he tiptoed out of the room.

"Now there is a match made in heaven!" exclaimed Sylvie.

"Henry and Jane, or the puppy and the cat?" asked Elizabeth with a laugh.

"Do not even think it!" Darcy's voice came from behind them. "There will be no more planning marriages between cousins in this family." He slipped his arms around Elizabeth's waist.

She leaned her head back against his shoulder. "Oh, very well, if you insist!"

"Darcy, I will thank you to behave yourself in my house!" Lady Matlock stood in the doorway. "You are setting a bad example for the children."

Elizabeth said, "I think it more likely we are setting a bad example for Sylvie! Jane is asleep, Henry is searching for a lead for his new puppy, and the others are off hunting a dragon."

"That is what I wished to speak to you about," said Lady Matlock, neatly sidestepping the sleeping child and cat. "Lady Cathcart said her son came to her covered with dust and claiming that Freddie, Will, and George had attacked him."

Sylvie giggled. "I am not surprised he did not wish to tell her the truth!"

Elizabeth said, "We saw it all from this window, and the villain in question was Annie. She dropped down on him from a tree and punched him. It cannot be pleasant to admit to being bested by a little girl he had told to go play with her dolls!"

Lady Matlock did not seem inclined to question Annie's role, but she said, "And the boys did nothing to him?"

Elizabeth shook her head. "They did not touch him, although Will called him a coward, George suggested he was stupid, and Freddie said he had no manners. But nobody touched him until he called Freddie a Cit. That was too much for Annie."

Darcy chuckled. "She should have saved her energy for the dragon. Lord Matlock told them not to come back until they could bring him the head of the dragon."

"He said that to *Will*?" Sylvie asked disbelievingly. "I had best call out the infantry, or we will never see him again. That boy cannot resist a challenge, even when it is to bring back the head of a mythical creature."

"Consider yourself fortunate," Lady Matlock said. "I had three boys who were like that. I am amazed they all survived to adulthood. For that matter, I am amazed I survived the experience."

"I do not understand it at all," Elizabeth said. "George is much less trouble than Will, but even he is exhausting!"

"This morning Will told me it was kind of Uncle Jasper to get married because this way he could play with George and Freddie." Sylvie crinkled her nose. "I am sure that was one of Jasper's key motivations!"

"His father's threat to send him to India if he did not marry was no doubt secondary to that," agreed Elizabeth solemnly.

Lady Matlock said, "Will should thank his aunt and uncle Duxbury, not Jasper! If Sir Anthony had not come to Rosings seeking Darcy's help and dragged us all to Sheffield, there would be no George Darcy or Annie Duxbury for him to play with. I suppose Freddie Gardiner would still have been born, but his parents would not have moved to Derbyshire to help with Frederica's mill."

Elizabeth shook her head. "The mill simply gave them the excuse to leave London. My aunt Gardiner had always wished she could live in Derbyshire again."

"On the other hand," continued Lady Matlock, "Jasper would not have developed his taste for heroics on behalf of the downtrodden common people, and my husband would not have had to pay a fortune in bribes to keep him out of prison."

Elizabeth laughed. "When the rest of us are dead and forgotten, Jasper will be remembered in the North as a legend along with Robin Hood."

Lady Matlock said tartly, "My husband says Sir Anthony will be remembered, most likely as a fine prime minister. They call him the rising star of the Whigs."

"As long as I have Elizabeth, I am perfectly happy being forgotten," said Darcy. "Why would anyone in the future wish to remember Fitzwilliam Darcy or Elizabeth Bennet?"

"Or Richard Fitzwilliam," Sylvie chimed in.

Outside the room a maid wailed, "Oh, no, Master Henry! You must not!"

A moment later Henry's puppy appeared, dragging Henry behind him, and made a beeline towards the cat. A flurry of yaps, hisses, and extended claws erupted, followed closely by howls from little Jane Darcy. Elizabeth scooped her daughter up in her arms.

"*My* kitty," wailed Jane.

"The puppy just wants to be friends with her," Darcy told her. "See how he has lowered his front half to the ground? That is how dogs say they want to play."

The cat did not appear to share the sentiment. She growled, her back arched and her tail fluffed out, and swiped at the puppy's nose with her front paw. The puppy whimpered, but held his ground.

"Want my *kitty*! Now!"

Henry crouched down and spoke to the animals. "You must not fight, you know. It is very bad manners, and you will be in trouble with Grandmama."

"Now there is a potent threat!" said Elizabeth as the cat gave one more hiss, turned her back on the invader, and began to wash her face.

Darcy spoke in Elizabeth's ear. "I like that cat. She reminds me a little of you when I first tried to win you."

"That is nonsense," Elizabeth said. "*I* never tried to scratch your nose."

I hope you enjoyed your visit with Elizabeth, Mr. Darcy and their friends! If you liked this, please consider trying one of my other books like *Alone with Mr. Darcy*, *Mr. Darcy's Noble Connections*, *The Darcys of Derbyshire*, or any of my other books. You can find out more about my books, as well as some free stories, at my website, www. pemberley variations.com. Thanks for reading *Mr. Darcy's Journey*!

Yours, &c.
Abigail

Historical Note

The events in this book were historically accurate to the extent I could make them so, although by inserting Lady Matlock's intervention during the Sheffield food riot of April 14, 1812, I split the events of that day into two different days. The hangings did not occur in Sheffield, but later in York. Details of the Sheffield riots can be found on the excellent Luddite Bicentenary website www.ludditebicentenary.blogspot.com/. The riots and attacks in Stockport and Macclesfield mentioned by Mr. Howard did occur during the same time frame as the Sheffield riots.

My Earl of Matlock is based loosely on the real-life William Fitzwilliam, 4th Earl Fitzwilliam, a prominent Whig politician with extensive holdings in the West Riding of Yorkshire. Given his political prominence, Jane Austen would certainly have heard of him, and a surprising number of character names from her novels turn up in association with him. His main estate was Wentworth Woodhouse, and his mother was a Watson-Wentworth. His family structure is purely my invention, but the real Earl

Fitzwilliam's generosity was legendary, as can be seen in this poem written about him by Lord Carlisle:

Say, will Fitzwilliam ever want a heart,
Cheerful his ready blessings to impart?
Will not another's woe his bosom share,
The widow's sorrow and the orphan's prayer?
Who aids the old, who soothes the mother's cry,
Who feeds the hungry, who assists the lame?
All, all re-echo with Fitzwilliam's name.
Thou know'st I hate to flatter, yet in thee
No fault, my friend, no single speck I see.

Sir Anthony Duxbury was loosely based on Sir John Hobhouse, Baronet, later 1st Baron Broughton. Hobhouse attended Trinity College, Cambridge with Lord Byron and later joined him on his travels in Greece, Turkey and the Peninsula. On his return from his travels, he became an active Radical. He was imprisoned at Newgate in 1819 for a Radical pamphlet he had written. I recommend Wikipedia's article on Radicalism for a brief summary of the Radical movement. Sadly, the Parliamentary reforms Sir Anthony sought did not come to pass until the Reform Act of 1867.

The Luddite rebellion was a storm with many causes beyond machinery. You can find a good summary of it at The Luddites at 200 website.

Astute readers of Pride & Prejudice may find it odd that Jane Austen had the Gardiners and Elizabeth taking a pleasure tour of Derbyshire in August, 1812, a time when no one in their right mind would go into Luddite territory for pleasure. This riddle likely goes beyond Austen's preference to leave almost all politics and war out of her books, and instead may have been related to the publishing dates of the book. Austen had written the first version of Pride & Prejudice in 1796-7 and revised it starting in 1811. At some point, she set the dates in the book to match those of 1811-1812. The book was published in January, 1813. If you subtract time for an editor to go over the book, printers to typeset each page by hand, then bookbinders to cover one book at a time, leaving days for the glue to dry, it seems likely Jane Austen must have turned the book in sometime in mid-1812. The Luddite uprising didn't start until November 1811, and wasn't as violent and widespread until April 1812, right when Darcy is visiting Rosings. But by that time, Austen was already putting the finishing touches on a book she'd been writing on and off for 15 years.

Her position would have been similar to that of writers after 9/11 who had set their novels-in-progress in New York City with references to the World Trade Center. A few novels already in press were pulled from publication and others were delayed for rewriting. In Jane Austen's case, the outcome of the rebellion was less certain, since many people thought it would be put down quickly. As a writer, I can comprehend how frustrating it would be to have to rewrite large parts of a novel that close to publication. She also might have assumed her novel wasn't likely to be pored over by generations of scholars who obsessed on each date and what year she had based it on! We'll never know why, but she went ahead with publishing the book as it stood, with no year stated in the text – and we are all the richer for it.

Acknowledgments

I used a wide variety of research sources for the history in this book, but I have to single out the Luddite Bicentenary website for particular praise for providing original sources and day-by-day information about the Luddite Rebellion. Their April 14, 1812 entry for Sheffield Food Riot and Arms Depot Raid provided specific information for the events in Sheffield:

www.ludditebicentenary.blogspot.com/2012/04/14 th-april-1812-sheffield-food-riot.html.

My critique group provided invaluable feedback and suggestions, companionship, and a great deal of teasing. Susan Meyers, Sara Kass, Susan Shelton, and Terri Kennedy were also infinitely patient in tolerating my Jane Austen obsession.

Maria Grace, Nicola Geiger, Catherine Grant, Dave McKee, MeriLyn Oblad, Colette Saucier, and David Young gave me great feedback on the final version and are responsible for there being far fewer typos than there otherwise might have been. The readers and my fellow writers at Jane Austen Variations provided encouragement and occasional threats throughout the writing of this book.

My family, as always, deserves endless thanks for their patience and support.

About the Author

Abigail Reynolds may be a nationally bestselling author and a physician, but she can't follow a straight line with a ruler. Originally from upstate New York, she studied Russian and theater at Bryn Mawr College and marine biology at the Marine Biological Laboratory in Woods Hole. After a stint in performing arts administration, she decided to attend medical school, and took up writing as a hobby during her years as a physician in private practice.

A life-long lover of Jane Austen's novels, Abigail began writing variations on *Pride & Prejudice* in 2001, then expanded her repertoire to include a series of novels set on her beloved Cape Cod. Her most recent releases are the national bestsellers *Alone with Mr. Darcy* and *Mr. Darcy's Noble Connections*, as well as *The Darcys of Derbyshire*, and *Mr. Darcy's Refuge*. Her books have been translated into seven languages. A lifetime member of JASNA, she lives on Cape Cod with her husband, her son and a menagerie of animals, including Snowdrop the miracle kitten. Her hobbies do not include sleeping or cleaning her house.

http://www.pemberleyvariations.com